'Who are you to talk[...]
you!' This from the [...]
named Stone.

Elinor paled.

'Ah . . .' the sca[...]
named Cloud-Drea[...]
'I ssee that hitss true.'

Elinor felt herself flush hotly. There was clearly
some dreadful misapprehension at work here, but the
fur-man's accusation had struck a tender spot: she had
done too many terrible things with the blade at her
side – necessary or not – to feel altogether innocent of
the accusation. She felt the faint, seductive tingle of
strength through the dragon hilt in her grip. Blessing
and curse, both: it was no simple weapon to carry, this
razor-edged, shining blade.

THE SONGSTER

Adam Nichols

Copyright © Adam Nichols 1999
All rights reserved

The right of Adam Nichols to be identified as the author
of this work has been asserted by him in accordance with
the Copyright, Designs and Patents Act 1988.

First published in Great Britain in 1999 by
Millennium

An imprint of Victor Gollancz
Orion House, 5 Upper St Martin's Lane,
London WC2H 9EA

To receive information on the Millennium list, e-mail us at:
smy@orionbooks.co.uk

A CIP catalogue record for this book
is available from the British Library

ISBN 1 85798 572 9

Typeset at The Spartan Press Ltd,
Lymington, Hants
Printed in Great Britain by Clays Ltd, St Ives plc

This book is for
Mary Jurewicz and Mike Orkish
in thanks for their many kindnesses

Prologue

Scrunch the bear sat dog-like, watching two figures walk away through the woods beyond the Settlement clearing.

One was a young woman, altogether human, dark-haired, slim and strong of limb, dressed in loose forest garb and high-topped walking boots. She had a travelling pack on her back. One hand swung as she walked. The other rested on the bronze hilt of a sword that hung at her side in a crimson leather scabbard.

The other figure was a young man, and human at least in part. He was of a height with the woman at his side, but where she went booted and clothed, he walked barefoot, and, save for a pouch hung from a string belt at his slim waist, he went entirely naked, his body covered only by his own sleek brown fur. He carried a short bow in one hand and, instead of a travelling pack, he had a quiver full of grey-fletched arrows slung over his shoulder.

The two of them strode away through the spring-greened forest, disappearing and re-emerging amongst the trees. They paused for a moment and waved, silhouetted against the faint lightness of the dawning sky, their two hands raised in unison. Scrunch lifted his paw in return.

Then they were striding quickly up across the crest of a wooded hilltop.

Going . . .

Not looking back now.

Going . . .

Hardly visible at all.

Gone.

Scrunch the bear dropped his broad paw to the earth and let

out a long, snuffling, sighing breath. Against the soft grey of the dawn light, the flowing forest that surrounded the Settlement clearing seemed a solid-dark mass. Far off in the distance there was a dim muttering of thunder. The morning-chilled spring air smelled . . . charged. Through his bones he could feel the world *thrum* softly, hugely.

The thunder sounded again, still dim, a thing of the bones as much as the ears – like the deep sound of the world itself. Scrunch felt his guts tight, the hackles along his spine prickling. He wanted, suddenly, to run and fetch them back, the woman and the fur-man. But it was too late for that. They were gone on their journey now. All would be well, they had assured him, and they would return before the summer was out.

But with their departure, something was aborning in the world. Scrunch could sense it, this grey, spring-dawn moment, in his bones and blood. The world was beginning to shift, in the slow, ponderous, subtle way that it could, and he felt, suddenly, as if he were perched upon the edge of some moving precipice, waiting for the downwards slope to open up for him and reveal a long view into . . .

He knew not what.

I

They buried Ziftkin's mother with the dawn.

Ziftkin stood, dry-eyed and stiff, while they lowered her thin, shrouded body into the hole. In her last days, she had withered away to little more than skin and bone, and those putting her in the ground had to strain not at all.

It was a mercy to let her die, Naoma had insisted, to let her have surcease from the pain. A mercy . . . Aye, perhaps.

But what was he to do *now*?

Ziftkin blinked, determined to keep his eyes free of any tears. The whole of the farm was gathered here. He would not give them the pleasure of seeing him break. Never that.

'Rest now,' Harst began, speaking the Death Litany, as was his duty as Master of the farm. Standing beside the yet-unfilled grave, head bowed, he recited, 'Rest from life and strife and pain. Rest and sink and rise again. Departing soul, returning soul. Departing hurt, returning whole.'

Harst held his broad-brimmed hat before him in both hands. Revolving it through his thick fingers absently, he glanced sideways to the fields, where there was work waiting to be done, then down at the grave. He shook his head. 'A wayward woman, my sister. And too prone to frivolity and musicking. But . . .' he sighed. 'But a good soul, despite all. Well . . . she has made her final journey into the Shadowlands now, and she will face what she must face. May her sojourn there be short. And may she make less mistakes and be happier in her next life.'

Across the way, Mechant looked up. There was the trace of a gloating smile on his face as he regarded Ziftkin.

Ziftkin bit his lip. He could feel everybody's eyes on him. He would not allow Mechant, nor any of them, the pleasure of seeing him goaded.

3

'Goodbye, Malinda,' Harst said. 'Journey well.' Then, 'Cover her.'

The first spadeful of dark earth went over her shrouded body with a soft *crumpp*, followed by the next, and the next, and the next after. Ziftkin stepped closer for a last look, but there were only the folds of the pale, anonymous winding sheet and the mounded spadefuls of crumbly dark earth. Another spadeful went on, and another yet, till his mother was gone and only the dark earth showed.

Gone.

It was suddenly hard for him to get breath.

Gone . . .

'Right,' Harst said, setting his hat back on his bald head. 'Finish up quick as you can. We've a full day's work ahead of us still, death or no death.'

Bryan and Gavie, as the morning's assigned grave diggers, threw the earth into place and thumped it down with the backs of their spades. Those gathered about the grave waited, shifting from foot to foot, till it was finished.

'Breakfast,' Harst said. He looked across at Naoma. 'But quickly, wife. Hear? We've work to get done.'

Naoma nodded and turned back towards the house. The rest began to straggle after.

Ziftkin swallowed, wrapped his long arms about himself. He could not move.

'Come on, lad,' old Korrel urged him, once the rest had all trailed off. He reached a hand up gently to Ziftkin's shoulder. 'Life goes on, whether we will it or no.'

Ziftkin shrugged the hand off.

'She was a good woman, your mother,' Korrel said. 'Don't take Harst's talk of mistakes to heart. He always was a too-serious man.'

'She was the finest woman in these parts!' Ziftkin said with quiet anger.

'Aye,' Korrel agreed. 'She was that.'

Ziftkin turned. He could keep the tears back no longer. He felt them soaking his face. 'Oh, Korrel, what am I to do *now*?'

Old Korrel impulsively put an arm about him. But Ziftkin was tall and skinny as a young tree, and Korrel shortish and stout, and the gesture brought them together for an awkward

4

moment only, Ziftkin half bent, Korrel straining up, both off balance.

Korrel stepped back, sighed, patted Ziftkin on the arm. 'What you *do*, lad, is . . . you breathe. You eat and you walk and you work and you sleep and you go on with life. That's all there is *to* do.'

Ziftkin pushed away, rubbed at his wet eyes, wiped his nose, sniffed. 'Easy for *you* to say. I've nobody, now. *Nobody!*'

'You've Harst, and the farm here. You're Harst's sister's son, after all.'

Ziftkin laughed bitterly: 'Harst? He'd as soon see me dead as alive. And as for—'

'Harst will live up to his responsibilities, lad. He'll see you right. If you think otherwise, you don't know Harst.'

'Oh, aye? That's as may be, but if you think Mechant and his brothers will leave me be, you don't know *them*!'

Korrel opened his mouth, closed it, shrugged uncomfortably.

After a long moment's silence, the older man gestured towards the house and asked, 'Feel able to come in for breakfast?'

Ziftkin blew his runny nose through his fingers onto the grass, wiped his face on his sleeve, gathered himself. 'Don't tell any of them you saw me like this.'

Korrel nodded.

Ziftkin took a deep breath, another. 'Right, let's be going, then.'

Seshevrell Farm was no mean place. The farm buildings formed a large quadrangle, with the Big House at the top end, the Smithy at the bottom, the long Barn forming one entire side, the Short Barn and the Granary together forming the other.

Walking into the quadrangle with Korrel from the grave site, Ziftkin could hear the noise of breakfast coming from the Big House. He stopped dead. His feet felt heavy as lead. His heart did. The place seemed to loom over him oppressively, like some huge deadfall. He felt like a man in one of the Sword Tales Mechant was always spouting about, faced with an overwhelming array of foes. But Mechant's heroes were always equipped with magic weapons – swords, axes, gems, staffs, rings – with which to face down their foes. He had none such.

'Come on, lad,' old Korrel urged him. 'You've got to eat.'

Ziftkin sighed, nodded, having long ago learned the consequences of attempting a long day's farm-work on an empty belly. Work would go on this day, just like any other day. The spring hay crop needed making, death or no death. Malinda or no Malinda.

He would never, *ever* see her again . . .

Korrel took him by the elbow and led him up the steps into the Big House.

When he came in, conversation died.

Mechant was seated together with his brothers, Bryan and Gavie, the three of them stuffing their faces with red bacon and thick slices of buttered bread. They looked at him and grinned sly grins at each other. Ziftkin shivered, seeing them like that. They had the sudden look of jackals.

Naoma came and took him from Korrel and sat him down near her end of the table, where she had reserved a seat for him. 'Here,' she said, putting a bowl of honey-sweetened oat gruel before him. 'Start with this. It's your favourite. I made it special. Eat. You look like you need it.'

Ziftkin nodded his thanks, but it was hard to swallow, and harder still to keep the food down. He wanted to curl up in a corner and sink away into a long darkness.

The table ate in continued silence after that, till Harst stood up. 'Right,' he said. 'East field today. Ought to be finished by sunfall if we put our backs into it.'

There was a general scuffling of chairs, a last chewing of food and gulping up of tea, and they trooped out.

Naoma put her hand on Ziftkin's arm as he passed her on his way out. 'Come back here if it's too much for you today, lad,' she said softly. 'I'll make sure Harst lets you be.'

Ziftkin shrugged, nodded, thanked her with a wan smile. He was tall enough so that the top of Naoma's head came barely above his sternum. He remembered when she had been the tall one and he only a little lad. He felt a sudden mist of tears fill him and took her hand in one of his. She had never been hard with him, had always kept the other boys off him when she could.

'You don't *have* to go, you know,' she said. 'You could just stay here with the womenfolk for the day. I'm sure Harst would . . .'

Behind Naoma, Ziftkin could see Harst looking back at him from outside the door. 'Let the boy be, wife,' he called, jamming on his broad-brimmed hat. 'There's work to be done!'

Ziftkin let Naoma's hand go. 'It's all right. I'll go. I'm all right.'

'You certain *sure*?' she said.

There was real concern in her, and it warmed him. But she did not understand. He was not about to give Mechant and his brothers the opportunity to crow over him. Could not give them such an opportunity.

'Come on,' Harst called again impatiently from the doorway. 'There's *work* to be done!'

Outside, as Ziftkin rounded the corner of the Big House, he looked back to where his mother's little mound of earth lay. The sun was well up by now. The long white streaks of mare's-tails filled the sky. The raw grave looked sad and derelict. He bit his lip, remembering her in a thousand ways at once: her shining red hair, the way she danced sometimes when she was gleeful, the melodies she played on her long flute . . . The way her face had changed in the last weeks, growing wrinkled and caved-in and white, like some old and broken doll's . . . buried in the dark earth now and still for ever, food for worms and burrowing grubs and . . .

He turned away, not able to stand more of it, tripped over something and hit the ground, hard, face first.

Behind him, Mechant guffawed.

Ziftkin scrambled to his knees, his face hot. Mechant stood over him, arms crossed over his thick chest, grinning maliciously. He brandished one of his big, booted feet. 'You ought to be more careful, Goose. Clumsy thing that you are.'

Ziftkin felt a wash of impotent fury go through him.

'Clumsy Goose,' Mechant repeated.

'Ziftkin!' Harst shouted back over his shoulder from where

he was striding on ahead. 'What are you doing there on the ground, boy? Come *on*. There's work to be done, and it won't get done with you lolling about like this.'

'Aye, come along, Goose,' Mechant said. 'Quit lolling about.'

Ziftkin got to his feet, shaking with anger. But Mechant had already turned his back and walked away after his father, Gavie and young Bryan at his side, chuckling. Ziftkin rubbed at a smear of dirt on his cheek.

'Come on, lad,' old Korrel said, coming back for him. 'It's a bad day for all of us.'

A bad day, indeed, it was, binding and sheaving and sweating in the sun, with all the time his mother's spirit hovering about him, seeing her in the green hay all around, hearing her voice.

By mid-day Ziftkin was utterly spent.

Naoma herself brought out the noon meal. 'You're welcome to come back with me, lad,' she offered him. 'You look none too well.'

'Let the boy be, wife,' Harst ordered her. 'You mollycoddle him. What do you want? That he hang about the house all afternoon, useless and moping? What's the good of *that*? Nothing's wrong with him that a good solid day's work won't cure.'

'Is that all you ever think of?' Naoma snapped. '*Work?*'

'Work is a man's meat and bread, woman! You ought to know that. Without work, a man's not a man. And without work . . . where would we be on this farm of ours, eh?' He went over to her, hugged her roughly, then shoved her off, giving her a swat on the behind for good measure. 'Now away with you back to the house. Get back to your own work and leave us menfolk to ours.'

Ziftkin watched her go, straightening herself after her husband's swat, a small woman with thick, grey-blonde hair, no longer young, no longer light on her feet. But tough and kind and careful. She had been his mother's only true friend here. And now she was his. He was grateful to have one ally, at least.

He chewed on a cheese and cress sandwich, working on

8

getting the food down. Watching a lone hawk circle in the blue dome of the sky, he felt a pang of bitter envy. The hawk was free and whole and lord of all he surveyed, while he . . .

Ziftkin sighed, not wanting to think on it. He watched the sky instead, the play of the clouds, the way they tumbled and tattered softly. It had always fascinated him, the way the world rolled by. There was a simple beauty in it that filled him with calm. The blue of the sky glowed. The hay burned green-gold all about him. The continuous insect *buzzz* in the hay field was like a kind of music . . .

Which made him think of his mother and her flute playing. Which he did *not* want to think on. Not now. No more memories now. He did not feel able for it.

'Should have let her take him back, Father,' Ziftkin heard somebody say suddenly.

Mechant came sauntering over towards where Ziftkin still sat, the remains of his lunch on the ground at his side. 'The Goose here doesn't do no more work than a girl. He belongs with the girls back at the Big House. It takes *men* to work the fields. Look at him!' Mechant gestured. 'No muscle. No strength.'

It was old ground, this. Ziftkin stared off into the sky, avoiding Mechant's hot gaze, trying to keep himself disengaged as best he could.

'Why don't you go back with the girls in the Big House, then, Goose?' Mechant prodded. 'You can take out your little tootler and play dancing tunes for them. That's about all you're good for.'

Almost, Ziftkin hit him. He felt the sudden rage go through him like a current of scalding water through his guts. What kind of a world was it in which a good soul like his mother died in agony from a wasting sickness, and those like Mechant and his kin throve?

'Leave it be, can't you?' old Korrel said, drifting in. 'It's a bad day for all of us. Poor Ziftkin here especially.'

Mechant snorted. 'It was a bad day when Malinda first came crawling back with *him* making her belly big.'

'Leave him be, son,' Harst said. 'Go sit down. Save your energy for work.'

But Mechant stayed where he was. His brothers sidled up to him till the three of them stood shoulder to shoulder like a pack of hounds.

'I always said he was no good to us.' Reaching down suddenly, Mechant yanked Ziftkin to his feet by one long arm. 'Look! Just look at him, father. How did any sister of yours produce *this*? He's no Seshevrell, that's certain sure.'

'He doesn't look *nothing* like us!' Gavie added.

It was true. Harst and his sons were all from the same stock: thick-limbed, heavy-boned, as if built especially for hard work. Ziftkin was head and shoulders taller than any of them, but skinny as a starved dog. They were dirty-straw-blonde and light-eyed and round-faced, bearded, with hands and teeth like spades, and blunt feet. He was long-fingered and long-toed, sharp-chinned and narrow of face and beardless, with a mass of dark hair and big dark eyes.

'Why did you *ever* take Malinda back in?' Mechant demanded of his father.

'Family is family,' Harst responded. 'This is old ground you're turning up, boy. To no account. Go sit down.'

'*He's* not family,' Bryan said.

'Right!' Mechant agreed with his youngest brother. 'He's no family to *us*. And with Malinda dead and gone now, I say—'

'Sit down!' Harst ordered him. 'I'll have no ruckus from you this day. Any of you. We've work to do.'

Mechant stood his ground, fists and face clenched.

'Did you hear me, boy?' Harst said, his voice hard. 'Go sit *down*.'

Mechant hesitated, then backed off, glaring venomously at Ziftkin.

'Family is family,' Harst said to Ziftkin, who still stood awkwardly where Mechant had dragged him to his feet. 'You're my sister's son. Family is family,' he repeated, as if that explained everything.

Turning, Harst surveyed his small haying group – Korrel, his three sons, young Polli who was on loan from Tolk Farm for the haying and who had taken no part in the squabble – and shook his head. 'Right. Come on, you lot. If you've the energy

10

to squabble, you've the energy to work. Enough of lunch. Let's get back to it.'

Slowly, with considerable muttering and grumbling, they did.

II

That evening, Ziftkin stood alone in his little cubby-hole room above the Long Barn. His heart felt like it was going to choke him. Looking out through the small rectangular window that was the only light in the room, he saw the sky westering towards night. Day was dying.

Death, death, and more death.

'Oh, Malinda,' he moaned softly. 'How*ever* am I going to live without you?'

He wanted to hit something, hard. He felt his mother's passing to be terribly *wrong*. The stars, that were beginning to show faintly now in the sky, they ought to tumble from their places, the world ought to tremble, for it seemed to him that the very Powers themselves – those great live forces that moved the world, animating all – had to be fatally out of kilter.

He yearned for something to appeal to, or to be able to perform some act that would bring back the lost balance between Power and Power and thus bring his mother back.

But there was nothing. Folk might put shape to this Power or that, but the Powers, he knew, were greater, or lesser, than human images of them. The Powers were . . . themselves, like strong currents under smooth water, save that the water was the world entire.

Ziftkin shivered, gazing out through his window at the darkling sky. The Powers might move the world and move him – the same Power that made the rivers run making his own blood pulse; that which drove the thunder clouds to violence feeding his own tempers – but there was nothing in them for him to appeal to. They were simply beyond his need.

His mother had made the long, final voyage to the Shadowlands – whence none returned except to be born into a new life entire. She was gone from him. *Gone*. And there was nothing he could do to change that.

He could not bear to think on it. Tears filled his eyes. He turned weakly away from the window and back into his little room. It seemed like a very coffin to him, darkening with the dusk. And him alone as could be. He wanted to flee, suddenly, to escape everything and fly up into the sky like some magical bird. He laughed, almost. Ridiculous thought. Where was there for him to flee to?

He looked about his room listlessly, at the shelf he had made himself from spare planking, at the two stacked boxes where he kept his clothing, at the little woven rug on the floor that kept his feet warm in the winter. Malinda had hooked it for him when he had first moved up here. He sniffed back more tears – he had had enough of tears.

It had been such an excitement for him, the move up here and out of Malinda's room in the Big House. Him only a little lad and filled with his own importance at having a room of his own in the barn at last. He had been filled with such big dreams.

Ziftkin shivered. The dreams had all come to naught. It had been after the move here, once he was away from Malinda's side, that Mechant and his brothers had really begun on him – as remorselessly as the hen-chicks out in the yard would peck at a defective sibling.

And now . . .

Ziftkin shuffled over to his hard, narrow bed and plonked himself down. An endless stretch of meaningless days – that was what awaited him now. With Mechant and his brothers less kind than ever, if that were possible. And this room a coffin.

With the dying light, it was getting hard to see, but he could not bring himself to light the little oil lamp. It, too, Malinda had given him. Everything . . . *everything* reminded him of her. He could not bear to touch any of it. Could not . . .

Over on the shelf his flute lay, the flute Malinda had bought him for his twelfth birthday. Who knew how much she had had to sacrifice to buy it for him? The thing was a wonder, and must have been outrageously expensive. And certainly not the sort of object to buy a twelve-year-old farm lad – as Harst had never tired of expounding.

He got to his feet and impulsively reached the flute down from the shelf. His hands shook, holding it, and he was memory-stricken, seeing the shining look on his mother's face when first she had handed him the mysterious, carefully wrapped package. He ran his fingers along it, cherishing the perfect smooth length of it. Long as his forearm, it was, ivory and black wood and glowing silver, carved and inlaid.

A thing of utter beauty.

He lifted it to his lips and blew a long, low, soft note.

Too good for him . . . That's what Mechant had said, what he still said. Too fine a possession for a poor, long-faced farm lad to own. Ziftkin shivered. True enough, that. It *was* too fine an instrument in the ordinary way of things. Malinda had sacrificed too much. But . . .

But he knew its value, had learned to make it sing. It had been her joy as much as his. Lifting it to his lips again, he blew a long note, another, slid deftly into the graceful flurry of The Starry Morn, one of his mother's favourite tunes.

He sat down on the edge of the bed when the tune was done, staring at the flute in his hands. Then, softly, he played for his mother, feeling her near him, somehow. The Starry Morn, The Fair Girl's Lament, Dancing Shoes, Lacy Water . . . he played all her favourite melodies, all she had taught him. And then went on, his fingers dancing of their own accord it felt, the soft, dark coolth of the evening air flowing round him, the flute notes rising like marvellous, invisible birds to flock about him.

He paused for a moment, the flute held suspended. There were tears running down his cheeks, but he did not try to stop them, did not wish to. He felt . . . He was not sure how he felt. From his seat on the bed, he could see the stars twinkling in the darkened sky outside his little window. He could feel the blood-pulse in his fingers. It was a moment in which his entire life seemed to coalesce. All the joys and agonies of his days here at Seshevrell Farm, all his hopes and terrors, the awful emptiness Malinda's going had left in him, the great rolling tapestry of the world . . .

He somehow felt very tiny and very huge at the same time,

utterly stricken and yet filled with a strange sort of joy. He felt this moment to be an end and a beginning.

Of what, he could not guess.

He held to it as long as he could, not moving, cherishing the strange poignancy of it.

Till an owl hooted softly outside and the world shifted somehow and he drew a breath. And a voice said, 'Look at him. Staring out the window, slack-jawed like some silly goose.'

Ziftkin turned and saw it was Mechant, looming up on the top of the narrow steps leading up to the doorway to his room, a barn lantern held aloft in his hand. Gavie and Bryan came behind.

Outside, the owl hooted again. Ziftkin blinked, trying to bring his mind into focus.

Mechant pushed into the room, lantern up, staring about him. 'Enjoying yourself, bastard cousin? Perched up here on your little bed with your . . . your stupid instrument that cost the price of five good sheep?'

Perhaps it was the special moment he had just lived through, but Ziftkin did not feel the usual hot rush of impotent anger at Mechant's baiting. Instead, he turned to Mechant and said, as he had never said before, 'Why do you hate me so, cousin? What have I ever done to you? Why do you all *hate* me so?'

The three brothers stared at him for a long moment in silence. Gavie, indeed, looked a little distraught and took a step forwards, his hand out placatingly. But implacable Mechant elbowed him back.

'I don't hate you, cousin,' Mechant said. 'I *despise* you. You, with your silly long face. You, the bastard, who thinks he's so much better than any of the rest of us. And don't try to deny it. We *know* you do!'

Mechant was white-faced and panting now. He hung up the lantern he had been holding on a rafter-hook and turned back to Ziftkin. 'You, who can't do a decent day's work. Who spend half your days staring at the wide world like some stupid sheep. Who brought ruin upon poor Aunt Malinda. Who wrecked the good name of Seshevrell Farm. Sitting up here with *that* . . .'

15

Mechant stabbed a finger accusingly at the lovely flute which Ziftkin still held in his hands. 'You're like some evil vulture, tootling away, driving the rest of us crazy. Tooting and piddling away up here . . . Like some sick night bird crying its song over the rest of us, crying how much better it is, how it will soar over the rest of us, how it will—'

'Mechant,' Bryan said, coming up to his older brother. 'Mechant, you're raving.'

But Mechant brushed him off and stomped unsteadily over towards Ziftkin.

For the first time, Ziftkin became aware of the sick-sweet odour of alcohol in the air. Mechant staggered against the wall, elbowed himself properly upright. 'Your time is coming, bastard cousin,' he threatened, stabbing a finger at Ziftkin. 'You can't hide behind Malinda's skirts any more. Your time is coming, I tell you!'

'Come on,' Bryan said, trying to take Mechant by the arm. 'It was a bad idea to come up here. There's nothing we can accomplish by coming here.'

'There's one thing I can accomplish!' Mechant replied. Shrugging his brother off, he staggered over to the bed and hauled Ziftkin bodily upright by the shirt.

'I'll make you rue the day you ever came to this farm,' he hissed, breathing sour alcohol in Ziftkin's face. Then, with a hard, clumsy thrust, he shoved Ziftkin into the log wall.

The back of Ziftkin's skull smacked hard against the unyielding wood and he staggered, dropping the flute.

Mechant snatched it up triumphantly.

'No!' Ziftkin cried. He lunged for it, but his vision was filled with sparky lights from the thump to his head and he could not move quickly or surely enough.

Mechant skipped back, brandishing his prize. 'Look!' he called. 'I'm Irik Blood-blade, hero of the battle of Shelling Way.' Gripping the flute by one end, he swiped it through the air like a short sword, dancing clumsily about Ziftkin's small room. 'Back! Back, I say, you rabble.' He laughed and whirled the flute above his head theatrically. 'Or face the wrath of the great Irik Blood-blade!'

Ziftkin intercepted him. 'Give it back. You're drunk, Mechant. Give it to me.'

'Give it back, Mechant,' Bryan echoed. 'Before you damage it.'

'Damage it?' Mechant said. 'Damage Ziftkin's precious possession? Well, we wouldn't want *that*, now, would we?' He held the flute out towards Ziftkin. 'Here. Take it, then.'

With a sigh of relief, Ziftkin reached for it.

Mechant rapped him hard across the knuckles with the flute and skipped clumsily away, laughing.

'*Mechant!*' Ziftkin cried angrily, rubbing his bruised fingers.

'What?' Mechant said. 'What? Do you have a *problem*, then, bastard cousin?' He stabbed the flute at Ziftkin as if it were, indeed, a sharp-pointed weapon. 'Think you're so wonderful, do you? Think you're too good to put in a full day's work like the rest of us?'

'No, Mechant,' Ziftkin interrupted. 'No. I—'

But Mechant went on, all unhearing, 'Think you can make the rest of us feel no-account and little because you have *this*, do you?' He held the flute out, stared at it for a long, silent moment, then took it up in both hands. 'Well you won't have this . . . this *thing* to taunt us with any longer!'

Lifting the flute above his head, a hand gripping it at each end, Mechant brought it down over his thigh, splintering it with a *kraack!* like a stick of old wood.

'No!' Gavie called out. 'Mechant, *no!*'

But it was too late. The flute had split open. Mechant lifted it again, brought it down against his thigh, snapping it entirely in two this time. 'Aye!' he cried triumphantly. 'You won't have *this* to torment me with in the night's dark. Not now. Never again, now! Never *again!*'

Mechant flung the two halves of the broken flute at Ziftkin's feet, panting, his face twisted into a leer of triumph. 'How do you like *that*, cousin?' He laughed maliciously. 'Nothing to say? Barn rats got your tongue, then?'

Ziftkin could only stare at the broken remains of the flute. He felt sick. He felt as if it were his own bones that lay there smashed. He felt utterly empty.

'Mechant,' Bryan said. 'Come on! Let's away from here.' He tugged at Mechant. 'You too,' he urged Gavie.

But Gavie only stood staring at the smashed flute.

'Come *on!*' Bryan urged. 'The both of you.'

17

Mechant shook him off, pulling away. 'I want to hear this *cousin* of ours say something. I want—'

There was a sudden pattering of footsteps on the stairs leading up from the barn to Ziftkin's little room, and all turned.

It was Naoma.

She halted uncertainly, faced with the tableau before her. Seeing Ziftkin's shattered flute, she paled. 'What *happened* here?'

Mechant straightened himself. 'We . . . we came up here to . . . to pay our respects, Mother. But Ziftkin here . . . he . . . he spurned us, tried to turn us away like trash. He shoved me, tried to push me down the stairs.' Mechant pointed down at the smashed flute. 'Then he hit me with *that* and broke it.'

Naoma glared at her eldest son, hands on her hips. She sniffed. 'Is that *liquor* I smell?'

Mechant looked around at his brothers: 'Isn't that right? Just as I told it. Isn't that how it happened?'

Gavie nodded. 'It was just how Mechant says, Mother. Ziftkin tried to—'

But Bryan shook his head. 'It was Mechant did the shoving. And it was Mechant who broke the flute.'

'No!' Mechant said. 'Don't listen to him.'

'Mechant shoved Ziftkin against the wall,' Bryan said softly. 'Then he snatched the flute from Ziftkin, and broke it over his knee.'

Naoma paled. 'Just wait till your father hears about this, Mechant. He'll—'

Mechant laughed. 'Father? Father likes Ziftkin no more than we do. Bastard cousin that he is. Malinda brought nothing but shame upon this family when she brought *him* here!'

With that, Mechant stormed unsteadily out the door and down the stairs.

His two brothers looked at each other uncertainly for a moment, then scuttled out after him.

Naoma turned after them, shook her head, turned back. 'Oh, Ziftkin,' she said softly, looking at the shattered flute, 'I'm so *sorry*.'

18

Ziftkin said nothing. He felt empty as a sack.

Naoma went to him. 'I'll see it gets replaced,' she said. 'How *could* Mechant have done such a thing? Where did he get the liquor? He knows better than to drink himself into such a state. Liquor always turns him mean. He's just like his father in that.'

Ziftkin reached for the shards of the flute. 'Mechant hates me.'

'No,' Naoma said hurriedly. 'Don't say that. He was too deep in liquor. He'd have never done any such thing fully sober. Why, he—'

'He hates me,' Ziftkin repeated softly. 'They all hate me, he and Gavie and Bryan.' He turned round, sniffing back tears. 'Why, Naoma? Why do they hate me so? What have I *ever* done to harm them?'

'Nothing, chook,' Naoma replied. 'Nothing at all.'

'Then why? *Why?*'

Naoma sighed. 'People are not simple creatures. You . . . you frighten them, I think.'

Ziftkin blinked. 'What?'

'You frighten them, lad.'

Ziftkin sat down on his bed with a little *thump*, the broken flute cradled in his lap. 'But that's *ridiculous*! How could I ever do anything to frighten them?'

'It's not what you do. It's what you . . . *are*.'

Ziftkin slumped. 'What I *am*, is a too-tall, long-faced bastard cousin who—'

'Shush!' Naoma said. She sat next to him on the bed and put a hand on his arm. 'Shush. What you *are* is more than that.'

'What, then? Tell me. What!'

Naoma sighed again. 'It has to do with your father.'

'*Him*,' Ziftkin spat disgustedly. 'Malinda never talked of him. What sort of a man is it that fathers a child on a woman and then . . . *abandons* her forever. Leaving her to the charity of her relatives, abandoning his . . . his *son* to the ungentle hands of—'

'He was perhaps not,' Naoma said, 'entirely a . . . a *man*.'

Ziftkin stared at her, his eyes wide: 'Meaning . . . what?'

'I . . .' Naoma shifted uncomfortably. She got up from the

19

bed and paced over to the little window. The light of the lamp made deep shadows of her eyes. 'Malinda was a . . . a wild child as a girl. You never knew her like that. You couldn't . . .'

One hand on the window sill, Naoma peered out at the star-dappled night. 'She was always running off, was Malinda. She and I were good friends when I first came here. It was hard, so hard for me when I came here at first as a young bride. Not knowing anyone here save Harst. Finding myself alone in a strange steading. Malinda was kind. Kinder than Harst . . .'

'And my *father*?' Ziftkin said.

Naoma turned back to the room. 'Malinda was always wandering off into the wild lands. She would take that little flute of hers, or the stringed citern if she were in the mood, and spend whole days gone from the farm, playing and singing and wandering the wild.'

Naoma laughed softly. 'Drove old Hagamat wild, it did. You think Harst is a serious-minded man? You should have seen his father! He shouted and raved, locked her away for days on end. But it did no good. She was like . . . like a wild deer. You can't keep such a creature chained to a farm all day. It has to run free. Or go mad.'

'And my mother?'

Naoma sighed. 'A little of both, perhaps. Dour old Hagamat chained her enough to drive her a little mad, I think. Yet she wandered free enough, too, to be able to laugh and live and be a joy to the rest of us with her musicking.'

'And my *father*?' Ziftkin insisted.

Naoma sighed again. 'Malinda came back from one of her wild jaunts changed. It was the longest she had ever been gone, I remember. The whole farm was worried sick. We had been out looking for her in the woods and up the long slopes of the hills for days. Hagamat was simply wild about all the work-time wasted.

'And then she came back to us, skipping through the fields. "Where have you been?" we demanded of her. She pointed behind, I remember. A little casual lifting of her hand. "Just back there," she said. And then, "Why are you all staring at me so?"'

Naoma came back and sat down on the bed again at

20

Ziftkin's side. 'Malinda insisted she had been gone only for the morning, you see. But it had been near a half dozen days.'

Ziftkin ran a hand over his face, shook his head. 'But what does any of this have to do with my *father*?'

Naoma patted him softly on the arm. 'You came into this world nine months after her return from . . . from wherever it was she had been.'

Ziftkin bolted out of the bed, the broken flute spilling from his lap. He stared at Naoma, turned, shook his head, stared back at her. 'What . . . what are you saying?'

Naoma lifted her hands in a gesture of calm. 'Your . . . father was . . . was perhaps, *perhaps*, mind you . . .' She hugged herself. 'It is said that there are Fey still living up in the hills.'

Ziftkin shivered. 'You mean to say that my father is—'

'I don't know for sure, lad. Poor Malinda never could recall any of it. But I heard her call out in her sleep once, just a day or two after her return. I'll never forget it. I rushed to her room when I heard her cry out. She was moving strangely in the bed, as if she were dancing or some such. I held her though the blankets, tried to calm her, to wake her. She shook and shivered and moved about so. And then she cried out one last time, a long wail full of such sad anguish I shall never forget it.' Naoma shivered.

'Then she woke suddenly, in my arms. Her eyes were filled with tears. "He's gone," she said. "Who?" I asked her. In reply, all she said was, "*Him*", as if I must know who she meant. And then, "His eyes were dark as night, Naoma. And he was gentle and so, so, *so* beautiful . . ."'

Naoma sighed. 'With that, she fell into sleep again. In the morning, she remembered none of it. But for weeks she went about with her head hanging, sad as sad could be.'

Naoma reached a hand out to Ziftkin. 'And in her proper time, she gave birth to you.'

Ziftkin sat down on the bed with a soft *thump*. 'But . . . but if this is true, why did she never tell me? She never breathed a word. None of you. *None* has ever, not once, even so much as *hinted* . . .'

Naoma nodded. 'It would have brought no good to the

21

farm, such news. There are those who believe changelings bring bad fortune.'

'*Changeling?*' Ziftkin said. 'Is *that* what you deem me?'

Naoma shrugged. 'I don't know, truly, what you may be, lad. But it's plain as plain you're not from the same stock as my boys. And they see it clear as any of us and cannot forgive you for it.'

Ziftkin stared down at his feet.

'You're open to the world in ways Mechant and his brothers aren't. You see things . . . I've seen you stand stock still for ages, riveted by a sunset. When you were little, you'd spend whole days, almost, peering at the tiny life in the grass. My boys could no more do that than . . . than pigs could fly.'

Naoma sighed softly. 'And you play that flute of yours like you were a very Fey, do you know that? Such music you make . . . Malinda used to boast of you to me, in the quiet hours. She thought you a very special sort of songster indeed.'

Ziftkin stared off into the empty air. 'But why, *why* did she never tell me anything of . . . of my . . . my *father?*' he demanded. The very word felt strange in his mouth.

'Malinda thought it best to keep things secret. She saw the way Mechant and his brothers looked at you. She hoped they would accept you better if—'

'Hah!' Ziftkin spat. 'Them accept me? Never a chance of *that.*'

'It broke her heart,' Naoma said, 'to see the way they treated you.'

'Broke mine, too,' Ziftkin said after a halting moment. He had to stop and breathe before he was able to go on. 'I used to look up to Mechant so, when I was little.'

Naoma reached to him. 'Oh, Ziftkin, lad, I wish things were different. I wish . . . Oh, I don't know what. Just that you and my boys could be reconciled. That—'

'That we could all live happily ever after, like the ending of one of Mechant's Hero Tales?'

Naoma nodded. Her eyes glistened with unshed tears. 'Those tales. You all used to huddle about the evening fire, eyes big as apples, while old Termant recited them to you. They were the last good days, those.'

Ziftkin hugged himself. 'The good days are gone, Naoma.

22

Long, long gone. And Malinda, too, is gone. It's all gone, now. Everything . . . It's not *fair*, Naoma! Why did she have to die? She never did anything to deserve an illness like that. Not that terrible wasting away. What did Malinda ever do to deserve a fate like that? What did *I* ever do?'

'You mustn't think like that, lad. Life's just *hard* sometimes. People die. It hurts and it's terrible, but that's the way of things. But you . . . You're young. You've your whole life ahead of you yet.'

Ziftkin laughed bitterly. 'Some life!'

Naoma took Ziftkin's hand in hers. 'Yours is a *special* life, lad. Malinda always felt it. I always felt it. You are special.'

Ziftkin pulled away. 'I am a bastard child, kept on the grudging charity of my mother's relatives. That's what I am!'

'No!' Naoma said, hurt.

'Oh yes. That's *exactly* what I am. And if you think you can . . .' He stopped abruptly, seeing the hurt on her face. 'I'm . . . I'm sorry, Naoma.' He reached a hand to her. 'You've always been good to me. You don't deserve to have me rail at you.'

'It's all right, lad,' she replied softly, 'I understand.'

The two of them looked at each other for a long moment in silence.

Then, 'Thank you, Naoma,' Ziftkin said, 'for all you did, and tried to do for me today. And for all you have done over the years. I owe you more than I can say.'

Naoma snuffled back a tear. 'You're a good lad, Ziftkin. I only wish—'

'Wife!' a voice called suddenly from the quadrangle outside. 'Wife? Where *are* you?'

'It's Harst,' Naoma said. 'I have to go.'

Ziftkin nodded.

Naoma pushed herself off the bed, dabbed at her wet eyes with her farm wife's shawl. 'Ziftkin, I—'

'*Wife!*'

'Go,' Ziftkin said. Despite himself, he was smiling ruefully. 'Before he works himself into a temper.'

Naoma hesitated for a moment, smiled at him, then hurried off.

*

Ziftkin sat unmoving on the bed for a long time, staring out of his room's little window at the dark, star-flecked rectangle of the night.

Then, 'Father,' he said, slowly, savouring the feel of the word in his mouth. *'Father.'*

For long years he had ached for his vanished father, dreamed with a boy's desperate yearning of a day when a tall stranger would come riding into the farm and ask for him, talk with him, offer him a new life, a new home, take him away to a place where he was needed, where he could belong. Now, perhaps, he had an inkling of why no such man had ever come.

Ziftkin got up slowly. The lantern that Mechant had brought was burnt out. The broken flute lay, a mere half-guessed shadow, on the floor. Padding over to the window, Ziftkin leaned out. The window frame was so narrow he could not get his shoulders properly through it and had to tilt sideways.

The sky was brilliant with stars. Off on the horizon, a new moon glowed, twin-horned, the colour of polished pewter. A soft wind played the trees. He felt its touch upon his face, like cool, invisible hands pulling at him with gentle insistence.

A dog barked softly, sleepily. The farm was abed by now, and all lay silent below him. His whole life had been spent here. It was all the world he knew. All the world entire . . . And, perched up here, leaned out his little window, he felt, suddenly, like a complete stranger. As if he came from, belonged to, another world entirely.

Ziftkin let out a long, sighing breath.

Another world entirely . . .

The words of an old song stole slowly into his mind, a song his mother had used to sing to him:

> *Far and away o'er the slopes of the hill,*
> *Moving like ghosts in the whispering green,*
>
> *The wild Fey abide in the deep places still,*
> *Though seldom by human folk now are they seen.*

Lonely and aging and chary and wild,
Lonely and longing for some human child . . .

The wild Fey.
  His father's folk.

III

In the black drag-end of the night, Ziftkin slipped down the ladder from his room and into the dark interior of the Long Barn.

The cows sidled back away from him, uncertain. But they knew his smell well enough, and they made no noise. Softly, he padded past them, lifted the latch to the barn door, and tried to ease it open.

Kreeek! went the old hinges.

He thought his heart would leap up out of his throat and choke him. He stood frozen, one foot out of the barn, one still in.

The night stayed quiet.

With infinite care, he eased the door open enough to slide through, then shut it behind. Quietly, he padded across the quadrangle, past the corner of the Big House, and out beyond.

The bare mound of his mother's grave stood dark and lonely-looking. It was hard to believe she was really there, buried and still, lying under his feet. Never to rise again. *Never.*

Ziftkin knelt down at the graveside. The naked earth was still a little damp and soft. He dug his fingers in it, trying to feel her presence through the soil. 'It hurts, Malinda,' he said softly. 'It *hurts* your going. I hope . . .' He swallowed, blinked. 'I hope you're . . . happy. Wherever you may be.'

He stayed like that, on his knees, hands buried in the soil above her, for long moments. Then, softly, he said, 'Goodbye, Mother. Fare you well. I . . . I'll miss you like I'd miss the sun.'

Slowly, he stood up. The soil clung to his fingers. He rubbed them, feeling the damp richness of it. Good soil. Made richer, in the years to come, by his mother's mortal remains.

For an instant, anger flashed through him. Even in death, poor Malinda would feed Seshevrell Farm. They who had

26

given her nothing, save grudgingly, who had judged her and judged him and found them both wanting. They who . . .

But it mattered no longer.

Ziftkin took a great breath of the chill night air. It was like inhaling the very stars themselves. The sky was thick with them, and they blazed so. The crescent moon was high now, the new day not terribly far off. Over at the Big House not a light was to be seen. It stood as a solid, dark shape against the flashing brilliance of the star-ridden sky. Ziftkin lifted his fingers in an insulting gesture, at the house, at its occupants, at the whole of his life there. Of them all only Naoma had ever shown him any kindness.

'A curse upon the rest of you,' he hissed. 'By oak and ash and bitter thorn, may you rue the day that you were born.'

Then he turned and strode away.

Ahead of him there lay tilled fields for a little, then only the open, rolling hills. And beyond that, the truly wild land of the mountains eastwards. It was towards these he walked, the smile still on his lips.

The wild mountains, where the Fey still lived.

His father's folk.

Ziftkin had nothing with him save the boots on his feet and the clothes he wore, carried no supplies. He felt like a bird taking flight. He felt light as air.

Striding through the last of the night, he whistled softly the flurried notes of The Starry Morn – his mother's favourite tune – and never looked back.

Not once.

IV

Squatting on the bank of a little burbling forest stream, Elinor shrugged off her travelling pack and splashed cold water on her face. She drank a double handful, ran a dripping hand across the back of her neck, then stood up, settling the hang of the sword at her waist more comfortably. With a soft sigh, she massaged her scarred leg, which ached from all the rough walking they had been doing these past days.

It was cool and dim here in amongst the trees. Too large, most of them, for her to be able to get her arms around, they reared up, all wide torsos and great-thewed but intricate limbs of wood. Whispering leaves formed a moving roof high overhead, which dimmed but did not entirely hide the blue-bright afternoon sky. The ground was ankle-deep with a carpet of moist dead leaves, soft as damp fur. It was hushed in here, save for the small gurgles of the stream at her feet and the faint leaf-rustle above.

'It iss my people'ss foresst, thiss,' Gyver said, coming back, padding silently through the trees. His eyes were shining with joy, and he patted the knobbed bole of one of the trees as if it were a large, well-beloved friend. 'Iss it not wonderful to be here, you and I? With the wild world all about uss like a great cradle for our happinesss?'

Elinor nodded and smiled, but the smile felt brittle on her face. It did indeed feel good to be with him here. But her belly was tight somehow with a constant, niggling tightness that had been nagging at her for days now and that ruined all her joy.

Gyver gazed at her, his furred face wrinkling in a little frown of concern. 'We might sstill go back to the Ssettlement, uss,' he said softly. 'If you feel to do sso.'

'No,' Elinor replied. She shivered and reached her hand to

the hilt of the sword at her waist. The bronze dragon's head of the pommel was most realistic, with tiny rubies for eyes, glinting in the soft forest light almost as if they were alive.

'What iss wrong, my Elinor?' Gyver asked.

Elinor shrugged: 'Nothing. Everything. It's just . . . I've had this knot in my belly for days now. I was hoping it would go away . . .' She sighed a long, weary breath and gestured at the sword. 'It's *this*. Ever since this blade came to me, my life has been so . . . complicated.'

In the bones of her hand, where she gripped the bronze hilt, Elinor felt the faint, uncanny tingle of the sword's power and shivered. Made long, long ago by a master smith out of a lump of molten star-matter, fallen from the sky, the sword was no ordinary weapon. Its perfect, razor-edged blade shone mirror bright, and it moved in her hand, when she wielded it, like a live thing almost. She had done wonderful and terrible things with this blade, brought about a great, bloody upheaval, and led folk to a new life out of the chaos and blood and destruction.

'It's as if something won't let me go, Gyver,' she complained softly. 'As if I'm being . . . *pulled*. My belly's twisted tight in knots.'

Gyver reached out a slim, furred hand to her. 'The world, it iss . . . tight, my Elinor. Ass you ssay. And my belly, too, it iss tight.'

'It *is*?' Elinor said.

Gyver nodded.

'But you never said . . .' Elinor bit her lip and went silent for a moment. She shook herself. 'I won't let it happen again, Gyver. I won't be a . . . a *utensil* again!'

Gyver laid the back of one of his softly furred hands gently against her cheek. 'You are ass you are. The world iss what the world iss. The bird doess not tell the wind which way to blow.'

Elinor shook her head. 'I don't . . .'

Gyver's finger went to her lips, shushing her gently. 'The world iss ass it iss, my Elinor, and movess uss ass it movess uss.'

Elinor shook her head and laughed softly. 'Sounds like the sort of thing you tell me your mother would say.'

Gyver laughed too, a soft, hissing chuckle. 'My mother, sshe would ssay, "The waterss, they flow ass they flow. And sso with uss, too, if we are to—"'

29

Elinor snorted: 'All very nice to *say* something like that. Very wise-sounding indeed. But the world is not always an especially friendly place to . . . "flow" through, Gyver. Or have you forgot? My twisted-up belly hasn't forgot, at any rate. Nor my scarred leg, when it aches.'

Gyver lifted his sinewy arms and gestured to the forest about them. '*Thiss* place, it iss a friendly place.'

'So it seems,' Elinor agreed. She sighed. 'I *want* to be on this voyage with you, Gyver, to visit your land, see your people. And most of the Settlement folk were glad to see the back of me, I'm sure.' She gestured at the sword in its crimson leather scabbard at her waist. '*This* makes me uncomfortable company for most folk. But though they may not like me much, they still *depend* on me, Gyver. On me and my blade. What if something happens to them while we're away?'

'We can sstill—' Gyver began.

Elinor shushed him with a gesture. 'I know. We can still return. But we've come all this way, now. It's just . . .' She ran a hand over her face. 'Sometimes I just don't know what I ought to do. I don't even know how to know what I ought to do . . .' She gestured about her. 'There's no threat, no danger, nothing special happening. And yet I feel as if every move I make is crucial to . . . to I don't know what.'

'My mother, sshe would ssay you sspend too little time in the world, you, and too much time wound up insside yoursself, like a ssnake in a hole.'

Elinor snorted.

'The waterss,' Gyver said softly, 'never worry about where they will flow. And they flow *perfectly*, them.'

'Easy for . . . for blind *water* to flow perfectly. What other choice does it have?'

Gyver looked at her. 'What other choice do you or I have, then? The waterss, they flow in their own way. Uss, we musst flow in ourss.'

Elinor opened her mouth, closed it, took a breath. 'So would say your mother,' she said, half mockingly. 'Your mother, the wise soul.'

'My mother the wisse ssoul,' Gyver agreed. He smiled, flashing his sharp white teeth at her. His eyes, dark brown and glistening, lit up with sudden anticipation. 'Me, I am mosst happy that you will meet her, my mother. Sshe iss very sspecial.'

Elinor looked at him and felt herself filled with warmth. He was such an amazing being, was Gyver: shaped like a man, slim and sinewy-strong, yet furred like an otter, feeling himself a part of the world in ways that she did not – and perhaps could not. 'Your mother has a special son,' she said to him, grinning.

He grinned back, a glimpse of white teeth in his darkly furred face. 'Sshall we flow like a river through thesse treess then, uss?'

Elinor took a breath, smiled, nodded. She reached up her travel pack from where she had left it next to the stream and settled it on her back. Aside from the clothing she had on and the sword at her waist, it was all she owned in the world: a sleeping roll, a change of clothes, a few dry journey cakes. Gyver carried no such luggage at all. He had an arrow-filled quiver and a short bow slung over one shoulder, and a pouch on a string belt at his waist. Otherwise, he walked barefoot and free, clothed only in his fur.

'Let's be off then,' Elinor said, gazing ahead through the quiet, dim maze of the trees, 'before I have a chance to complicate everything all over again.'

Gyver turned and beckoned her along happily, walking backwards. The day was fading now, the shadows amongst the trees growing thick. Elinor's scarred leg throbbed. She felt achy-tired.

Gyver, however, seemed buoyant with energy. 'The old tree folk,' he was saying, 'they have grown here forever. They and the wild folk and the Green Fey.'

'The Fey?' Elinor said. 'Here, in these woods?' She looked around a little uneasily. 'I thought the Fey were . . . well, only figures out of children's tales.'

Elinor remembered being a girl-child back in the city of Long Harbour, hearing stories from her mother of the wild Fey who would come and steal naughty little girls from out of their beds at night.

'What manner of creature are they, the Fey?' she asked Gyver.

The fur-man lifted his slim, furred shoulders in a shrug. 'They are what they are, them.'

'Very helpful, that,' Elinor responded.

Again, Gyver shrugged. 'The Fey, they are . . . *sspecial*. Like sspirit creaturess, they are. And yet not. Like uss. And yet not. More . . . pure than uss.'

'More *pure* . . .' Elinor repeated. She was not quite sure what to make of such a description. Sometimes, Gyver seemed so completely understandable, as if he were like any ordinary man, save for the fur pelt that clothed him. At other times, she was forcibly reminded of just how different – and how strangely different – he really was. All this talk of the Fey . . .

Standing before her now, Gyver seemed barely a creature of flesh and blood himself. In the dimming forest light, his dark fur made him almost invisible. Only his eyes showed clear; they appeared to glow with a soft radiance. Elinor shivered pleasantly.

'Come,' Gyver said, reaching a hand out to her. 'There iss ssomething I wissh you to ssee.'

Elinor looked about uncertainly. With the day dwindling fast now, the forest was growing dark and thick. 'How far are we going?' she asked. 'Night's coming on.'

Gyver smiled. 'Grandmother Moon, sshe will light our path for uss. Her face will be full thiss night. Come, now.'

'Come *where*?'

But Gyver only grinned, his teeth flashing. 'It iss a ssurprisse.' He tugged gently at her. 'Come!'

Gyver led her by the hand over root-laced ground, their feet *kerwishing* softly through the leaf carpet where it lay deep in the occasional hollow. How the fur-man kept any sense of direction, Elinor did not know. There was nothing but thickening dark all about, and trees every which way.

As they went on, and night drew in, a soft glow of light began to appear ahead. Elinor squinted, wondering what the glow might mean. Could it be some manner of habitation Gyver was leading her towards? Were his folk that close? She had thought them a good ways ahead yet. 'Gyver,' she said uncertainly, pulling him to a halt. 'Who are we—'

He put a furred finger to her lips, gently shushing her. 'We musst move ssilent, uss.' His eyes glowed with suppressed excitement. 'Sshussh,' he said softly, then led her on again.

The glow increased, and soon Elinor realized it could not be coming from any ordinary sort of habitation. It was a radiance of palest white gold, soft and cool. Through the dark, intricate webbery of the trees, it seemed to float like airy lace. She blinked, trying to fathom what it could be.

And then, unexpectedly, they were out of the tree-shadow and into the open once again – or at least partially in the open. The ground dropped away abruptly, leaving them on the lip of a jagged stone bluff. Below them lay a narrow cleft, with more trees thick on the rising, steep slopes of the further side. And above those further trees . . . the moon.

It was full-faced, as Gyver had said, and glowing palest gold. As Elinor watched, it lifted gradually, softly from behind the dark teeth of the trees and floated free into the sky.

'Grandmother Moon,' Gyver said softly. 'We greet you. I, Gyver, and Elinor, we greet you.' He nudged Elinor gently with his elbow.

'Grandmother Moon,' she said, feeling a little foolish. 'We . . . we greet you.'

Gyver had once explained his sense of the moon to her: 'Long and long ago, the moon wass a woman,' he had said. 'A very wisse woman, with many children. But when her children were grown, and it came time for her to leave thiss world, sshe could not, would not do it. Sshe wisshed to remain and watch over them forever. Sso sshe wove a great magic, with the sstrength of her will. And when her time came, sshe did not die away, her. Insstead, her sspirit rosse up into the ssky where sshe could watch over all her children, and her children'ss children, and theirss, forever.

'Me, I am one of her children'ss children'ss children, I think. I musst let her ssee me sso that sshe may know I am well, sso that sshe may be content, sso that no terrible thing will happen to the world.'

'Grandmother Moon,' Gyver said softly now at Elinor's side. 'I am well. We are well. Watch over uss, if it pleassess you.'

'Watch over us,' Elinor repeated.

She could not, truly, bring herself to believe that the moon had once been a woman, nor that Gyver was one of the moon's many-times-grandsons. It was all story, surely, and one of Gyver's strangenesses. But standing here, the world huge and dark all about, the moon ghosting into the star-flecked sky, she felt a shiver run along her spine. It was such a strange place at times, the world. Strange and wondrous . . .

Suddenly, from somewhere in the dark forest, she heard a long, softly wailing cry.

It made the short hairs on the back of her neck prickle. 'What is *that*?' she demanded of Gyver. Her hand had gone to the sword's hilt and she stood, staring, trying to make out form or movement in the dark about them.

But Gyver only grinned. '*That*,' he said, 'it iss the ssurprisse.'

V

In the thick woods it was difficult to see what might lie ahead.
The moonlight that filtered through the trees helped not at all,
for it wove a myriad of confusing shadows. Elinor had to
follow Gyver's lead slowly, awkwardly. He seemed to see in
the dark as well as any cat, and moved with an uncanny, silent
grace that she envied most profoundly. She felt foolish,
stumbling along in his wake like this.

Ahead, she heard that same soft wailing.

'What *is* it?' she hissed at Gyver for the dozenth time.

But he obstinately refused to answer her, merely putting his
finger to his lips, grinning.

'Hmmph!' she said, but let him lead her on.

Again came the wail, an eerie, ululating sound unlike anything Elinor had ever heard. It began low, almost like a great
hum, and then wavered up into a long, drawn-out cry. Not quite
comfortable on the ear, but not truly disturbing, either. A cry of
pleasure or pain? She could not tell. She tried to think what
manner of creature might make such a cry, but could not.

And then, suddenly, it came to her. She yanked Gyver to a
halt. 'Is it . . . is it to the Fey that you're bringing me?'

'The Fey?' Gyver said. 'Not unless we are mosst fortunate,
uss. It iss to the Old Oness that I bring you.'

'The . . . Old Ones?'

'The Old Oness,' Gyver repeated. 'But let uss hurry, or we
may be too late.'

'Too late for what?'

Gyver tugged her on. 'You will ssee, you.'

They were drawing closer now, for she was beginning to
hear soft sounds of movement from ahead that could only be
coming from Gyver's 'Old Ones' – whatever manner of
creature they might be.

Gyver drew her close and hissed very softly in her ear, 'They are jusst the other sside of thesse treess, them. Uss, we musst be *ssilent, ssilent,* yess?'

Elinor squeezed his hand by way of acknowledgement. She rubbed her ear, where his furred lips had tickled, and peered ahead, her heart beginning to thump. There was a little night-breeze, blowing into their faces. She could detect, faintly, a kind of musky scent, like a mix of wet black black mud and roses.

Gyver led her by the hand, slowly, bent low and stalking through the tree-thick darkness. She did her best to emulate his silent, fluid passage.

And then, ahead, she heard a crackle of branches, caught movement.

Through the screen of the trees it was impossible to properly see what manner of creatures were ahead of them, but it was clear enough that they were . . . *huge.* Fully twice the height of a tall man at the shoulder, Elinor reckoned, catching a clear glimpse of one for a moment in a splash of moonlight.

She halted, pulling Gyver back. She could feel her heart banging under her ribs. These creatures could squash her and Gyver with one good stomp of their feet – of one foot – if they were of a mind to. 'Why did you . . .' she began in a whisper.

Gyver shushed her quickly, putting a hand over her lips. Elinor stood frozen, trying to breathe as quietly as possible.

One of the great creatures came gliding round a tree, swinging its head slowly from side to side. To Elinor's astonishment, she saw that it had a flexible, astoundingly long snout. It snuffled the air suspiciously. Elinor stared. She had never heard of such creatures as this, never in her wildest dreamings even imagined such. The snout was like a long, impossibly flexible arm, quivering this way and that.

The creature seemed to be peering about in the night. It had large, very bright eyes, set wide apart in its broad head, and little flapping upright ears. As Elinor watched, another such creature appeared, slightly smaller than the first but still huge enough, moving with incredible quiet for something of that bulk. The first one made a kind of uncertain rumbling sound deep in its chest, so low that Elinor felt it in her bones as much as heard it through her ears. The second patted the first with its snout – a gesture that seemed to Elinor to be one of reassurance – then raised it high in the air and gave vent to the strange, wailing cry she and Gyver had heard earlier.

It was answered from the forest by another, similar cry in the near distance, and then another again.

Slowly the two great creatures began to move off through the trees in the direction of the cry.

Elinor let go a long breath of relief.

Gyver laughed softly, so softly it was barely audible. 'They are sso wonderful, yess?' he murmured.

Elinor did not know what to think. 'What *are* they?' she whispered into his furred ear.

'The old wisse oness, them. The Old Oness. Phanta, we call them. They live very old, very long livess.' Gyver pointed to the larger of the two disappearing creatures. 'Ssee? That one is Sstarbrow. Sshe has sseen more than a hundred ssummerss, her.'

Elinor shook her head. 'How could you know that?'

'My grandmother'ss mother wass her friend.'

'Your grandmother's . . .' Elinor ran a hand over her face. 'How do you know what your grandmother's mother . . . How do you know what happened so long ago?'

'We have the sstoriess, Elinor. We have the livess of our ancesstorss going back many, many generationss. We *remember*, uss. Back to when we firsst came into the world.'

Elinor looked at the disappearing forms of the great beasts – mere half-guessed shadow-shapes now – and shook her head wonderingly. 'Your great-grandmother really knew that creature?'

Gyver nodded. 'Oh, yess. Sstarbrow.'

'Why . . . Starbrow?'

'To watch the stars is her joy. In the nightss, we ssee her often, sstanding by the waterss, her head lifted high, gazing at the far-away sspiritss of the sstarss.'

'Are they . . . mindful creatures, then?' Elinor shivered. 'Are they . . .' she was not sure how to phrase the question delicately, given the origin of the fur-man and his folk.

'Are they *made* creaturess?' Gyver finished for her. 'From the old dark Sseerss? Like my ancesstorss were?'

Elinor nodded.

'We do not know, uss. Perhapss. But they have been in thesse woodss a *very* long time, the Old Oness. Sso perhapss not, too.'

Elinor turned from Gyver and gazed at where the two huge creatures had disappeared.

Gyver tugged at her gently, pointing in the direction the pair had gone. 'Come, we will follow them, uss.'

Elinor hung back. 'Are you certain it's . . . *safe*?' She had never imagined that living creatures could grow to such great size.

Gyver nodded, grinning. 'Oh, yess. Quite ssafe. Sso long ass we behave oursselvess.' He set off slowly and quietly, leading her by the hand. 'Come.'

She went along with him, her heart thumping. She could not see anything clearly in the forest's moon-shimmered maze. How on earth did such huge beasts move about here at all? she wondered uneasily. The trees seemed much too close together to give them room.

There was a sudden *crack*, and a tree limb came ripping off in the distance. Elinor saw the moon-gilded leaf canopy shiver with it. She pulled back, tugging at Gyver, peering about uneasily in the darkness.

And then, suddenly, there was a soft grumbling mutter from ahead of them.

Gyver froze.

Elinor saw a great form approach. Despite all its huge bulk, it moved in utter quiet, like some enormous spirit, coming straight at them. She saw the strange, serpentine snout raised, caught a glimmer of moonlight on a large and glistening eye. She turned to Gyver. 'Run!' she hissed.

But Gyver held her fast. 'Don't *move*!'

She wrenched at his hold on her. 'That great beast'll trample us like . . . like we were two bugs.'

Gyver nodded. 'He knowss that.'

Elinor stared at him. 'But how can you . . .'

'Sshussh,' he said. 'Be sstill. It is Ssharp-eye. He knowss we are here, and helplesss before him. He will treat uss gently, only sso long ass we don't sstartle him. The Phanta, they do not ssee so well in the night'ss dark, them. Ssudden movementss from little folk like uss make them nervouss.'

38

'Well, we certainly wouldn't want *that*,' Elinor snapped in response.

But her desperate sarcasm was lost on Gyver. He was staring with rapt attention at the huge creature drawing near them.

For the first time, Elinor got to see one of the Phanta in its entirety. It was covered in short grey fur, barred with lighter stripes across the back and flanks. The shoulders were higher than the hips. It had a short, tasselled tail, and four legs that seemed heavy and solid as tree boles. Its head was large, with two limber, sticking-up ears like a dog's.

But the strangest thing about it was the snout that it had instead of anything like a normal nose. Fluid in movement as a snake, it was fully as long as one of her legs, and as thick around at its base as her thigh.

The huge beast – Ssharp-eye, Gyver had named it – approached to within a few paces of them. The air grew thick with the odour of wet mud and roses that emanated from it. Its snout darted out. Elinor flinched back, but Gyver held on to her.

'Be sstill,' he hissed.

The snout hovered over her. It was furred, like the rest of the beast, and ended in a pair of small glistening lips – or perhaps a kind of flapping nostril. She was not sure. It felt at her and sniffed at her simultaneously, making small *wuffling* sounds.

Elinor's heart was hammering. The Phanta seemed like a veritable flesh-and-blood mountain. She could feel the very warmth of the creature, it was so close to her, could hear the soft, liquid rumble of its guts. It had short, thick teeth, she saw, jutting outwards. It could kill her in half a dozen easy ways. Not even her sword could help; against such a mountainous beast, it would be of hardly more use than a butter knife.

But the touch of the creature's furred snout was gentle and deftly soft. It hovered for long moments over the sword where it hung at her waist, and then the moist tip of it went up along her arm and across her chest, the snuffling breath warm across her face.

The Phanta lifted its snout away then, and made a deep, rumbling grunt.

Gyver grunted back.

The wandering snout went to him, hovering before his face, sniffing delicately. 'Greetingss to you, Ssharp-eye,' the furman said softly. 'I am Gyver, of Waterwissher'ss folk. You know me, you.'

The Phanta grunted again. He bent closer, turned his huge head sideways, peering down at Gyver with one of his large, glistening eyes. Elinor saw that the eye was lashed as luxuriantly as any cow's.

But this was no simple domestic animal. It was a wild creature, capable of . . . anything.

The eye turned on her and their gazes locked. In the Phanta's eye, she saw . . . She was not certain what she saw. Intelligence of a sort – absolutely. A slow, deep sort of consideration. Great age. Something entirely not human, and yet not entirely unhuman. Looking into that eye was like looking down a well and seeing something mysterious and perhaps wonderful reflected at the bottom – but being unable to make out, exactly, what it might be.

Slowly, the Phanta swung its head – and its gaze – away. Gyver reached up a hand and stroked its cheek. The great creature blew a long, soft sigh. Then, with ponderous grace, it turned and moved silently off.

Elinor stared after it. It took her long moments to remember to breathe.

'Are they not entirely *wonderful*, the Phanta?' Gyver said.

Elinor nodded, sighed, staring into the darkness where the creature had disappeared. The skin on her cheek still tingled slightly from the Phanta's warm, moist touch.

From the distance, they heard the wailing cry come floating through the trees.

Gyver tugged at Elinor gently. 'Come, we will follow after them, uss.'

Elinor hung back. 'Why?' One night-meeting with such an enormous, incredible creature seemed enough to her for the moment.

'To ssee them dance,' Gyver said.

'To see them . . . *what*?'

'Dance. It iss very wonderful.' He tugged at her again. 'Come!'

Elinor let herself be pulled along.

40

They worked their way through the moon-dappled, dark maze of the trees, Gyver in the lead, for what seemed to be a very long time. The fur-man took especial pains to move – and have her move – as silently as possible.

Which helped calm Elinor not at all.

She was beginning to have serious misgivings about their sneaking blindly about like this in the vicinity of such huge creatures: she felt like a reckless mouse creeping up upon a herd of great cart horses. The creature that had seemingly accepted them had appeared gentle enough. So too were cart horses gently enough dispositioned; but it was no sensible idea to disturb them overmuch if you were small and vulnerable.

The wavering Phanta cry sounded once more, close now. Gyver crouched against a tree bole, pulling her down with him.

Elinor sank to her knees, shifting the weight of her travel pack. 'Are you sure we should . . .' she began.

From ahead, the wailing cry came again, followed by another, and then others still – till, together, they began to form a kind of eerie almost-music.

Gyver hummed a sort of response, very softly. She could just see the pale flash of his grin in the darkness. 'Look around thiss tree,' he whispered to her. 'But sslow, sslow.'

With thumping heart, Elinor eased herself round the edge of the tree and peered ahead.

She and Gyver were on the crest of a hill, she discovered, with a kind of clearing ahead and below them. Moonlight washed in like a flood. In the clearing, there were . . . It took her long moments to count them, for they were milling about in a slow, strangely graceful, but thoroughly confusing manner.

A dozen, nearly. That was the best count she could manage. A dozen or so of the huge creatures, gliding in and about each other in silence – except when one or more of them would lift a long, flexible snout and wail at the moon.

For that, as far as Elinor could make out, was what they were doing. Great heads rolled back, long snouts lifted . . . the creatures were dancing to the moon.

It was preposterous.

It was, almost, a little ridiculous.

It was entirely wonderful.

Their upright dog-ears flapped, their thick legs lifted in ponderous grace. They nudged each other, intertwined their snouts, wove complex, slow patterns, all the while calling out intermittently, sometimes one alone, sometimes several together in a swelling chorus.

Elinor stared, transfixed.

Then she heard Gyver draw a sharp breath near her ear. He nudged her and pointed.

At first, Elinor could see nothing beyond the massive, dancing shapes of the Phanta. Then, for an instant, she thought she saw a smaller, pale form in amongst them.

There and gone.

Then there again.

One, two . . . several of them.

'We are blesssed, uss,' Gyver breathed.

Elinor could not make out clearly what it was that she saw in amongst the dancing Phanta. They were pale, moving . . . *somethings*, perhaps the height of a tall man. In fact, the more she looked, the more they seemed to resemble human folk.

But what would any human folk be doing down there amongst the great, dancing Phanta?

And such *strange* human folk . . .

Stare and peer and blink and squint as she might, Elinor could not seem to get a good look at them. One moment she would catch a glimpse of a long-fingered, pale hand lifted in an elegant, floating gesture. The next she would be certain she had merely imagined it.

She felt Gyver tugging at her, but was too enthralled by what was before her to pay him proper attention. 'Elinor!' he hissed.

Glancing down, she saw him crouched at her feet . . . and realised that, all unknowing, she had stood up out of her concealment. She must be in full view of the dancers below, should any of them care to look up here in her direction.

The dancers slowed. She saw several sets of glimmering Phanta eyes focus on her.

But then one of them sounded their long, wailing moon-cry. Another answered. The dance picked up its tempo again.

It was the pale man-shapes that filtered towards her.

Elinor stood frozen, staring. Away from the obscuring movement of the Phanta, they were a little easier to make out. She could see that they were, indeed, human-like, but with unhumanly slender, long limbs. They were pale as the moonlight itself, and moved like so many shadows – but shadows composed of light, if such a thing were possible.

They came towards her, their long legs moving high, as if in the steps of some complex dance of their own. Elinor felt Gyver's hand, which still held hers, shiver.

'It iss them,' he whispered. 'The Green Fey.'

'The Fey . . .' Elinor breathed.

They were both terrifying and wonderful. The moonlight made them glow palely, as if they were somehow lit from within. Each movement of arm or leg had a kind of ethereal grace to it, like a stalking heron, yet more . . . delicate somehow. They moved in and amongst each other so that it was impossible for Elinor to make out exactly how many of them there might be.

Towards her they came, in utter silence and in utter grace, until they had formed a gently wavering crescent about her and Gyver. Then, abruptly, they went still.

Elinor shivered. The hairs along her scalp prickled in a shiver of wonder. It was like being surrounded by so many statues carved of ice. She could see clear through them, or so it seemed. But then they again would appear as solid and substantial as she.

'We greet you, people-who-ssing-the-world,' Gyver said softly. He was on one knee now, as if performing some kind of formal obeisance. Glancing up at Elinor, he gestured her down with him.

But Elinor stood as she was, transfixed, staring.

The Fey said not a word, made not a sound.

They were wonderfully beautiful, Elinor felt. Beautiful as new snowfall on the trees, or the first bright heads of the spring flowers. Beautiful as the slow-burning colours of a sunset. She shuddered, feeling herself filled.

One of them stepped slowly towards her.

This close, she could see his features: a long, triangular face, very human and yet not quite so. He gazed at her unblinking, with eyes that were huge and dark and fathomless.

A moon-pale, too-long-fingered hand came out. It opened like a flower, and on the palm Elinor saw . . . She was not certain what it might be: something slim and straight, as long as her little finger, perhaps.

Instinctively, she reached for it.

She heard Gyver gasp.

The Fey lifted a hand. Fingers brushed her face. Cool and dry, they felt, palpable as any human touch, light as the kiss of a butterfly's wings. The dark, unhuman eyes stared at her.

Then, in a sudden and unexpected whirl, she felt the world come apart. The sky seemed to dissolve, the stars whizzing in a dizzy mass. Trees and ground and Fey and Phanta all fell together in a single mingled form – dense and troubled and heavy, and yet also light as air and moving with unmatchable elegance.

Everything shimmered. She felt her insides swirling in rhythm, felt her mind spill out of her in a gush.

The world throbbed.

Elinor throbbed with it.

And then there was a great burst of light within and without her . . .

. . . and she found herself sprawled upon the ground, Gyver bent over her.

'Are you well, my Elinor?' he asked concernedly.

She did not know how to answer.

'Elinor! Sspeak to me.'

She looked up and saw his face close to hers, saw the way his eyes glistened in the moonlight, the way his head was haloed by a dusting of far-away stars. She gasped and smiled, filled with something she did not at all understand.

She felt him, the world entire, to be . . . *painfully* beautiful. She felt . . .

'Elinor?'

She sat up. The world seemed to beat like a great heart, all about her, the pulse of it resonating through the earth and through her, her own small pulse echoing that greater rhythm. She looked up, seeing . . . *feeling* the world so intensely that it hurt her – but it was a joyous pain. Floating moon and stars and the great black vault of the heavens, the old stone bones of the mountains, the whispering leaping-greenly trees . . .

Elinor breathed in the world.

And then she felt a dizzy surge go through her, felt something ebb away.

The world dimmed.

She stared, saw Gyver still bent over her in concern. 'Wha . . . what happened?' she stammered.

'You are blesssed, you,' Gyver responded quietly. He put a hand on her. There was a touch of genuine awe in his manner.

'But what *happened*?' she demanded of him. Looking about, she saw now that she and Gyver were alone by the verge of the trees. No dancing Phanta, no Fey, only the empty clearing below and the dark forest on all sides, with the silent moon gazing down from the sky overhead.

'They are all gone,' Gyver answered. 'You have been . . . unaware for ssome time, you.'

Elinor tried to struggle up to her knees and felt a strange tingling in her left hand. Looking down, she saw she was gripping a slim piece of bone in that hand. Underneath the bone, glowing in the moonlight, the image of a face showed clearly on her palm.

'The Lady . . .' Gyver breathed.

Elinor stared at that image: a female face, pointy-eared, part human, part animal. Her belly felt, suddenly, as if it had been turned upside down. As she had in the past before, she felt herself in the presence of deep, dim currents, as if she were somehow standing upon the surface of some fathomless sea, feeling the echo and surge of movement in the great deepness beneath her.

The Lady . . . The mysterious embodiment of long hope for the humanimals – those beings with the shape of animals and the knowing eyes and spirits of human folk.

Elinor's hand quivered with a body-memory of pain, for the image of the humanimals' mysterious Lady had been branded in some uncanny manner into her flesh back in Long Harbour, in the strange house of Mamma Kieran. A price and a gift, the old Wisewoman had named it.

But the image of that face had been visible only twice before: when it had first been burnt into her palm; and when, through her, the great forces channelled through the humanimal's Lady and the effigy of the Brothers' dark Jara had met in a violent spasm of conflict in the crumbling, walled city of Sofala.

And now, once again, that image was visible, clear and detailed for all its small size on her palm, glowing softly in the moon's light. Dark, knowing eyes in a humanesque face, gazing at her . . .

But even as she and Gyver bent over it, staring, the image of that face slowly dissolved away, leaving only the small shard of bone sitting in her palm.

Elinor took a breath, feeling her whole self shiver.

Uncertainly, she turned the piece of bone with her fingertips. It was straight and slender, with what seemed to be intricate carving running along it. She peered closer, but could make no clear sense of that carving. Like a miniature tanglewood it seemed, all twisting limb and leaf, elbow and crook and shadow of tree.

She looked up, blinking, feeling the hairs along the back of her neck shiver. The world seemed almost painfully . . . *present* to her senses still. 'What can it mean, Gyver?' she asked, thinking of the shard of strange bone in her palm, the appearing/disappearing image of the humanimals' Lady, the dancing Fey, her own lingering strangeness, everything.

Gyver reached a finger towards the bit of bone, pulled back. 'Me, I do not know. But you are gifted, my Elinor.'

Elinor shuddered. 'I have been gifted before,' she said, glancing at her sword. 'It is no easy thing.'

'No,' Gyver agreed solemnly. 'Not eassy.'

They looked at each other.

Elinor felt dizzy, as if she were perched upon the edge of a great, moving precipice, waiting for the downwards slope to open up for her and reveal a long view into . . . She knew not what.

Gyver reached for her, his slim strong hand an anchor. 'Take what iss given you, my Elinor,' he said softly.

'But I don't . . .' Elinor felt a spasm go through her, a blurring mix of uncertainty, anger, fear, exaltation. 'I feel so . . . so *blind*,' she said, shivering. 'So out in deep waters.'

Gyver's hand stayed on her, gentle and strong. 'Accept what hass been given.'

Elinor had a sudden vision of herself as she had been, child of the Long Harbour Streets, so sharp-willed, fighting her mother's nagging worry and her step-father's orders, so utterly sure of what she wanted out of life – with absolutely no sense at all of how big, how strange a world lay outside the confines of her dockside home. And now? How would that former self have reacted if, by some magical contrivance, she could have seen into her own future, seen this moment as she stood here in the moonstruck wilderness beside a man clothed only in fur, the uncanny, white-bladed sword scabbarded at her waist, having witnessed the strange dance of the great Phanta, and been touched by the very Fey themselves?

Elinor shivered. It was no future her former self could ever have imagined – or understood.

She folded her hand uncertainly round the piece of Fey-bone. It seemed to have a strange warmness to it – but she was not certain it was not her imagination. The world seemed to *thrum* about her. Almost, she could hear the huge note of it, a deep bass reverberation that echoed in her flesh and her bones like the after-sound of a great, ringing bell.

'The great world, it *flowss*,' Gyver said.

Elinor nodded. She could sense the moving current of it, however dimly. As Gyver said, the world flowed, or something flowed through the world. 'The Powers . . .' she breathed, putting name to it. She had been hearing of the Powers all her life – the hidden undercurrents that moved the world – but never till this moment had she felt them so clear, like a great, many-streamed, hidden river flowing through all. And she, will she or nill she, was born up and along by the flowing current.

But born along where, to what?

Standing there under the glowing face of the moon, gazing out across the mysterious, rolling hugeness of the wild lands all about, Elinor could sense no clear answer. There was only

47

Gyver's warm, reassuring touch, and the steady beat of her own heart.

That and the absolute knowing in her guts that she *was* being born along towards . . . something.

She did not know whether to weep or laugh, rage or sing, fling herself down upon the earth or dance.

She drew Gyver close to her, cherishing the strength and the furred warmth of him, grateful to have him here with her.

Her life was grown so utterly *strange* . . .

VI

Scrunch the bear ambled down the slope through the trees. He could smell woodsmoke and turned earth, and the good odour of cooked food. In the distance ahead, he made out the sound of human voices.

He had been gone into the deep green of the wilds for long days – how many, he was not sure. It was like coming up out of deep water into thin, dry air, coming back thus into the Settlement once again; his mind, which had been diffused in the deep of the wild, now was returning to focus.

He stopped and sniffed the air carefully. The world still felt . . . tight, and he felt a little stab of groundless anxiety: for the furred and feathered watchers he had passed had seen nothing unsettling, and all things seemed as they ought to here. He let out a long, snuffling breath and padded onwards.

At the edge of the forest, he stopped under the shadow of the trees. It was nearly mid-day, hot and cloudless, and he was loath to leave the pleasant coolth of the tree-shade. So he sat, dog-like, on his big haunches and gazed out into the sun-lit clearing.

The Settlement formed a kind of broad crescent, where the wild trees had been laboriously felled and cleared away, with the log houses in which the human folk lived all clustered together in the middle. The fields fanned out on either side of the clustered buildings, lapping against the verge of the trees in a green wave. Those near Scrunch looked thicker and greener than he remembered them being.

It was always a little magical to him, the way in which human folk managed to coax the green plants to grow for them the way they did. He sat for a little admiring the undulating rows. Out in the field nearest him, a man and three women were working, despite the heat of the sun.

Further out, he could see the stiff-upright form of a scare-crow.

They were so ingenious, human folk. It was their blessing and their curse. They could not help creating things, endlessly creating new things – both good and bad. Scrunch let out a long, sighing breath. They were such tight beings. Like so much twine bound tightly into a complex pattern. And sometimes the tension would get too great and the twine would snap and—

'Scrunch!' a voice called out suddenly.

Scrunch grunted, startled. Peering off to his left, he made out the form of a man coming in his direction. He shook his broad head. He would never have been so easily surprised as this out in the green wild. There, he was *in* the world and aware. Only here, in the Settlement amongst human folk, did he get so immersed in his own mind-tracks like this that he let the world drop away from his awareness.

He squinted at the man approaching in the sunlight and recognized grey-bearded Collart. Scrunch grunted and lifted a broad, stubby-thumbed paw in greeting.

'Back again, I see,' Collart said, drawing near. He had a long hoe balanced across his shoulder and he smelled of sweat and earth. 'All's well in the wilds, then?'

Scrunch nodded, knowing Collart's perennial concern. 'There is no sign of Brothers anywhere abouts.'

'Good,' Collart said. 'Good!' He shook his head, shrugged. 'There's still those who're complaining that Elinor should never have gone away and left us without the protection of that white blade of hers. They claim we'll wake one morn and find ourselves overrun by one of the Brothers' armed troops.' He shrugged. 'Not likely, I reckon. We've been safely here the better part of a year now. And even if the Brothers were to somehow stumble across our steading here, with you humani-mal folk running look-out for us, it's not likely they'd be able to take us by surprise, is it?'

Scrunch nodded: 'Not likely.'

Collart stood silent for a moment. Then he sighed. 'I just wish my guts would believe it, like my head does. They've been tied in knots ever since Elinor left us.'

'The world is tight, Man,' Scrunch said.

'So you've said. And we all blind as bats in a hole.' Collart sighed again, then gestured to the field. 'Well, be all that as it may, there's still work to get on with.' He gazed at the fields, shading his eyes with his hand. 'Good enough beginning to the summer so far, but there's an infestation of hook worm in the cabbages. And Nellit was complaining about the thieving deer again.' He glanced up at the sky. 'And we could do with a tad more rain . . .'

Scrunch lost the thread of Collart's talk. It was all too detailed for him. He did not – and did not especially feel any need to – understand all this about digging and seeding and hoeing, and all the other careful, complex matters involved with keeping the green plants healthy and growing. For friendship's sake, he tried to make out he was listening attentively, but Collart knew him too well.

'I'm boring you,' Collart said with a laugh. 'It's farmer talk, all this. And not anything to interest any of the Free Folk. Best I should direct my energy into my hands rather than my mouth.' He nodded and turned out towards the field. 'Good to have you back. See you about, then. Bye.'

'Bye,' Scrunch echoed, and watched Collart walk off to join the others in the field. He smiled his bear's smile, a little lifting of the lips over his big ivory fangs. He liked Collart very much. Collart was one human who understood Scrunch and his like, who was willing to let them be what they needed to be, and not place unreasonable demands upon them.

Not like some.

Scrunch sighed. Human folk . . . they thought they knew so much.

Even Collart, sometimes, understanding soul though he was.

They were such a peculiar lot, so solid and complete, yet so blind. Difficult, complex creatures. Scrunch shook his head and smiled again. The world was a place of mystery. He liked mystery, did Scrunch. It made him feel larger inside, somehow, to know that the world was not an easily understandable place.

Looking out, he saw Collart join the folk working in the field. The four of them turned and waved at him. Scrunch waved back. It felt good to be back. He had been out long enough, airing his insides to the wild, letting his mindfulness sink low. He felt younger than when he had left. It was time to rub shoulders with folk again now – human and humanimal alike. With a contented sigh, Scrunch pushed himself back onto his feet and ambled out of the tree shade and across the clearing along the edge of the field towards the centre of the crescent and the housing – where there was likely to be both folk and food.

The first person he encountered was Pykla. She came loping across the slope of a hill ahead of him with her tongue hanging out the corner of her long mouth, her eyes wide. 'Better hide yourself,' she warned him. 'They're at it again.'

'Who?' Scrunch asked. 'At what?'

Pykla slowed. She was a slim little thing, all long legs and sinew, part dog, part other things. When she ran, her feet seemed hardly to touch the ground. 'Human folk, of course,' she said, with a shake of her narrow head. 'Arguing.'

She laughed a dog's laugh – a sort of soft, huffling bark – and skipped ahead. 'I'm away,' she called over her shoulder, and disappeared past the curve of the hill.

Scrunch sighed. He did not know why human folk had this tendency to argue. But had it, they did. It amazed and dismayed Scrunch. Argument took such hardness and force of mind. When he found himself embroiled in such human-centred disputes, Scrunch always felt as if he were trying to keep to some complex and confusing dance step in the midst of slippery mud. How human folk managed to do it so often without falling prey to complete exhaustion was a mystery to him.

Normally, he would do what Pykla did in such a situation, what all the humanimals would do when they could – which was to leave well enough alone. At first, arguments amongst this human group had fascinated them. Now, they mostly tried to avoid such things. But Scrunch was feeling especially full of himself this day, after his long sojourn in the wild. He felt, almost, that he would welcome an argument, or, at least, find the hearing of a human argument stimulating. He had been alone in the deep green silences for long enough.

So he headed in the direction Pykla had come from.

It was a little group, he spotted, clustered before one of the barns. There were three barns up now, Scrunch saw. A new one had been added while he had been gone. Several human men and women stood before the new barn, in heated discussion.

There was not a furred or feathered person in sight.

Scrunch padded closer, keeping silent as he could.

'There's too much work, I tell you,' one of the men was saying. 'We'll never be able to get the harvest in once autumn comes. Not without help. And then where will we be?'

Scrunch recognized the speaker as a man named Olundar.

'Well, I say we can harvest whatever we need to,' one of the women said.

Scrunch did not know the woman who had spoken; there were still more than a few human folk in the Settlement whom he did not know.

'It's just a question,' the woman insisted, 'of our putting our backs to it.'

'We haven't enough backs,' Olundar replied irritably. He was a short man, thick in the shoulders, with a round barrel of a belly. 'And there's no more to be found out here in the middle of absolutely nowhere at all.'

'What about the humanimals, then?' asked one of the other men.

'*Them?*' said Olundar. He spat, wiped the back of his hand across his bearded mouth. '*They're* no use. Why, they haven't even the—'

The woman who had spoken put her hand on Olundar's arm and shushed him, gesturing with her chin to where Scrunch had come padding silently over.

Olundar turned, spied Scrunch, and blinked. He took a hasty step back, then stopped himself. 'Him!' he said, pointing at Scrunch. '*He's* a perfect example of what I mean. Just look at him! Great shambling, powerful brute that he is. Does *he* do any field work? Oh, no! Not *him*. He spends his time eating our food, ambling about, sitting in the sun. And when we need him, where is he? Off swanning about out there in the wilds. Keeping watch. Or so he *says*! How are we to know what he really does? How are we to know that he doesn't just lie about gorging himself on fat grubs and fish free from the stream?'

Scrunch sat down, taken aback by the man's vehemence. It felt like rounding the side of a rock to be met by a sudden blast of cold wind.

'Shush, Olundar!' one of the group said hastily. 'You don't want anger to him.'

'What do I care?' Olundar responded. 'Do you think me scared of the likes of *him*? Not likely!' He faced Scrunch. 'Where have you been, then? Wandering the woods?'

Scrunch nodded. 'Out in the wild lands, Man. Yes.'

'See?' Olundar said to his companions. 'As I told you. Out swanning about, never a care for us back here working our fingers to the very bone.'

Scrunch regarded the man. He smelled angry, but a little scared, too. 'I will help, Man,' Scrunch said mildly. 'Any way I can.'

'There!' said the woman. 'See, Olundar. So much for *your* opinion of the Free Folk.'

'Oh, aye,' said Olundar scathingly. 'The bear will help, all right. They all *say* they will. But where are they when we need them? They're no more reliable than little children. Here one day, gone the next. Off wandering about who knows where whenever the fancy takes them.'

Scrunch rose and padded closer to the group. 'You do not understand, Man,' he began patiently. 'We are not like you. We cannot . . . cannot hold the bright light of mindfulness forever as you are able. We need to have silence and green peace, to let our mindfulness lapse, to—'

Olundar *hummphed* impatiently. 'All very fine and nice, that. But what your little philosophy really amounts to is that you and yours are feckless as a spring breeze.'

Scrunch shook his broad head. The man could no more understand Scrunch's need – the need of all humanimal folk – to have respite from the tension of mindfulness than could a clam understand a diving otter's need to come up for air.

'You are blind, Man,' Scrunch said to Olundar. 'There is nothing I can say to open your eyes.' With that, he turned and walked off.

'Hoi, you!' Olundar called after him. 'You can't say something like that to me and then just walk *away*. Come back here!'

But Scrunch just kept on going, moving with a swinging, distance-eating stride that soon left the man's complaints dwindling behind him, till they sounded like little more than the scoldings of a jackdaw.

Scrunch sighed. All his pleasant feelings of a little while ago had faded. Men like that Olundar made him feel old. They were so blindly self-assured in their certainties. And so many of the human folk were like that. They weren't wicked folk; not at all. They simply could not see.

Slipping along quick as he could, Scrunch regained the soothing dimness and coolth of the trees and headed away from the clearing. He would return in a little while, but, for the moment, he had had enough of human folk. They were such exhausting creatures to be around.

Scrunch worked his quiet way through a bramble thicket and thence towards a stream that he knew, letting the deep contours of the land lead him over, through, across the rolling, wooded slopes until he could hear the liquid music of the flowing water just ahead. There were delicious little trout here, if one knew where to look. This time of day, they floated hidden in the shadows under the rocks at the water's verge.

He crept slowly forwards to the stream's edge, then slipped a broad fore-paw with slow care into the chill water. The paw was furred and heavy-boned, with thick sharp claws, but he had fingers and a thumb that, in their own way, were nearly as dexterous as any human hand. Gently, he groped about in the shadow-dark water until he felt a flutter. Then, with a quick snag, he jerked out a trout. It was a beautiful thing, with shining rainbow sides and smelling of cold rock and water and hidden fishy life. He gazed at it for a long moment in gratitude for its beauty. The he popped it into his mouth. It was hardly more than a couple of slow chews, but it was delicately delicious.

Licking his lips, Scrunch thought of trying for another. But this was a little stream, and there were not so very many fish in it. If he were too greedy, he would soon deplete the stream entirely. So he satisfied himself instead with sitting there gazing into the water, and thinking encouraging thoughts at the fish.

After a little, he rolled over on the grassy-leafy hummock of the stream's bank, relishing the spongy softness of the ground under him. Then he reared up and scratched his back, between his shoulder blades, against a tree bole. With a sigh of content, he sat back down, blinking sleepily. It was pleasantly cool here, with the stream murmuring its soft water song, the dim light easy on his eyes.

Life was good.

A bird in a tree nearby sang a few notes, *tee dee tooo, tee dee tooo doo-oo*. It was a pleasant sound. Scrunch looked up but could not spot the bird amongst the complexity of branches. It mattered little. He rolled over and listened to its singing. *Tee dee too toooo, tee dee tooo . . .*

Further off, another bird answered. *Tee deee, dee dee . . .*

Then the near one again. *Tee dee—*

The singing stopped abruptly. With a little shriek and a *kerwupp* of wings, the bird dived away.

Scrunch swivelled his ears, lifted his snout and tested the air. He could hear movement, not too distant. It was no ordinary, belonging-here forest creature, or the bird would not have disappeared in such a flap as it had. Human most like, he reckoned. But human who?

He felt his pulse thump. There was surely no chance of the Brothers ever stumbling across the Settlement here. They had settled too far into the wild lands for that.

Still . . .

Scrunch got quietly to all fours. Moving with all the silent caution he could, he slipped away from the stream and through the trees towards the source of the noise.

He could make out the movement of more than one body, a little splashing as something went through water, then the soft sound of voices. Definitely human.

He paused uncertainly. They – whoever they were – seemed to be heading towards him. If he stayed where he was, and if he had things reckoned aright, they ought to pass right by him.

Scrunch sat down softly.

Peering ahead through the webbery of the trees, he spotted shadowy movement, heard the soft *krukk* of a branch broken underfoot and the murmur of human voices. But there was something particular about those voices . . .

He spied a hand then, a small pale hand against the dark bark of a tree bole. Then more movement, and three small figures appeared from behind the tree.

Human children.

Scrunch was not entirely sure of human children's growth, but these seemed quite young. Whatever was this small threesome doing out in the forest this far from the Settlement?

He heard a little voice say clearly, 'We'll never get home now. We're lost for*ever*!'

Peering closer, Scrunch saw that the threesome was made up of two boys and a girl. It was one of the boys who had just spoken.

'We're not lost,' the girl answered him. 'We're just . . . just uncertain.'

The three of them stopped, then.

'It's *your* fault, Anstil,' one of the boys said petulantly to the girl. 'It's you who made us come out here.'

'That's right!' agreed the other boy. '*You* got us lost! We ought never to have listened to you.'

'We're not lost,' the little girl insisted. 'It's only that . . .'

Scrunch came out of the trees, moving slowly and softly, not wishing to frighten them. But all his good intentions came to naught. So caught up in their argument had the children been, that they did not see him till he was quite close upon them.

The girl, spotting him first, stopped in mid-word and stared. One of the boys let out a shriek and fell to his knees. The other turned and fled, wailing.

Scrunch faltered, startled by this unexpected and dramatic response to his appearance. Then he loped forwards, hoping to catch and calm the fleeing boy before he had got too far.

The girl leaped in front of him, her arms up. She screwed up her little face into a great scowl and screamed at him, loud as could be, baring her tiny white teeth in a ridiculous imitation of a snarl.

Scrunch skidded to a halt. It was that or run her down, for she remained obstinately in his path.

'Raghahrrr! *Raaaghagh*!' she roared in her shrill little voice, jumping up and down and waving her arms and snarling wildly all the while. Behind her, the boy still sobbed on his knees, staring white-faced. The third had disappeared into the trees.

Scrunch sat back, dog-like, not knowing quite what to do.

'Go away!' the girl shouted. 'Go away, you wicked, wicked bear! Run away!' She snatched a stick up from the ground and threw it at him.

Scrunch ducked, and the stick bounced off his furred skull harmlessly. He blinked, shook his head. 'I will not harm you,' he said to her.

She went silent, staring at him. Then she took a long, shaky breath of relief. 'You're one of *them*!' she said. 'Not a wild bear at all.'

'One of *them*,' Scrunch agreed. 'And no threat to you.'

'Come away from him, Anstil!' the boy who had fallen to his knees said. He struggled to his feet, wiped his face with a hand. They're *dangerous*, my daddy says.'

The girl did not move, and he made quick, panicky motions for her to back away from Scrunch. 'Your daddy says they're dangerous, too. I've heard him.' He pointed at Scrunch. 'You never know what they'll do. They're not like . . . like *real* people.'

The girl stayed where she was. 'I know what my daddy says. But . . .' She gazed at Scrunch, 'Aren't you like . . . like *real* people, then?' she asked.

Scrunch had no idea how to answer such a question. Instead, he gestured with one broad paw towards where the other boy had fled into the trees. 'We had better find your small friend.'

The girl looked back into the trees. 'Yes,' she agreed seriously. 'We'd better. Dyll's not very sensible.' She turned again to Scrunch. 'My name's Anstil,' she said. 'What's yours?'

'Scrunch,' Scrunch replied.

'I think I've heard of you,' Anstil said, looking up at him, her head cocked to one side. She was a delicate little thing, with pale hair and skin and thin limbs, dressed in baggy coveralls. Her eyes were big and blue, set wide apart in a triangular face. She reminded Scrunch of a small pale squirrel, for she had a squirrel's alert quickness of movement.

'This is Peager,' she said, pointing to the boy behind her. 'He's afraid of wild animals.'

'I am not!' Peager said quickly. 'I just . . . I just tripped is all.'

Anstil lifted her thin shoulders in a shrug. 'Let's go find Dyll,' she suggested to Scrunch.

Scrunch nodded.

Anstil turned, started out in the direction the boy had fled, then stopped uncertainly. 'How,' she asked, 'are we ever going to find him in all these trees?'

Scrunch touched a paw to his nose. 'I can smell him out.'

'*Really?*' Anstil said. 'What does he smell like?'

'He smells like a boy,' Scrunch answered. 'A particular human boy.'

'Oh,' Anstil said.

'Come,' Scrunch said. 'Let us find him.'

They discovered him, eventually, huddled in the root-hollow at the base of a great beech tree. Anstil had been calling for some time, but he had made no answer. Only Scrunch's nose let them find him.

'Dyll!' Anstil said reprimandingly, when she finally spotted him. 'Why didn't you *answer*?'

But Dyll only stayed as he was, arms wrapped tight about his skinny chest, head tucked low.

'Dyll?' Anstil said. She poked him with her finger. '*Dyll!*'

Dyll glanced up at her, saw Scrunch standing behind, and began to whimper. 'I want to go home. I want to go home! I want to go *home*!'

'We will. We will go home,' Anstil assured him. 'Soon. Scrunch will see us home safe and sound. You'll see.'

'Who's . . . Scrunch?' Dyll asked in a faltering little voice.

'*Him*,' Anstil replied, gesturing at Scrunch.

Dyll shivered. 'He's . . . he's a . . . *bear*!'

59

'Of *course* he is. But he's one of *them*, a humanimal bear. One of the Free Folk. He won't hurt us, silly.'

Dyll peered uneasily at Scrunch, one arm over his face for protection.

'It was him who found you, silly! We'd have never done it, Peager and me. You ran too far.'

'I'm a good runner,' Dyll said.

'Too good,' Peager put in.

'He's got big teeth,' Dyll said then, pointing at Scrunch.

'He's got big *everything*,' Anstil replied. She tugged at Dyll. 'Come on. Stand up!'

Dyll stood, still glancing at Scrunch uncertainly. 'Are you sure he won't eat us?' he asked Anstil in a whisper.

'Of course not!' she replied. 'He's our *friend*.' She turned to Scrunch, reached a small hand out to his big, furred shoulder. 'Isn't that so, Scrunch?'

Scrunch nodded. 'It is so. I would never harm the likes of you.'

'See?' Anstil said triumphantly. 'Told you!'

Scrunch felt her curl her fingers in amongst his fur. 'I will lead you to the Settlement,' he told the children.

But the boys still hung back from him, uncertain.

'Do not be afraid,' he said.

'I'm not,' said Anstil.

Scrunch swung his head to look at her, squinting to make her out she was so close. There was no scent of fear to her. She still had her fingers laced in the fur of his shoulder.

'Your fur's *soft*,' she said.

Scrunch blinked.

'I thought it would be all harsh, like . . . like twigs or something. And it's so long and thick. Don't you get very hot in the summer sun?'

Scrunch laughed, a soft rumble in his chest. 'Don't you get very cold in the winter? You with no fur at all save on the very tip of your head?'

Anstil reached a hand up to her pale hair.

The two boys were staring, standing shoulder to shoulder, backs against a tree.

'I want to go home,' Dyll complained. 'We should never have come out here.' He hugged himself, glancing uneasily around at the trees all about, as if he expected some wild, rough thing to leap out at him at any instant.

'Whatever brought you here so deep into the wood?' Scrunch asked them. He did not like to think on what might have happened if he had not chanced upon them.

Peager pointed accusingly at Anstil. 'It's all her fault!'

Scrunch turned to Anstil.

'I . . . I wanted to see the wild Fey,' Anstil said.

'The Fey?' said Scrunch.

Anstil nodded. She released her grip on his fur and came to stand before him, one foot digging a little hole in the ground. 'They live in the woods. I heard somebody say that. I wanted . . .' Anstil sighed. 'I wanted to . . . to see one. Maybe talk with one.'

'My daddy says there's no such thing as the Fey,' Dyll said. 'My daddy says they're only creatures in tales. My daddy says—'

'Then why did you come?' Anstil demanded.

He glared at her sullenly. 'I wish I hadn't. It's no fun, this. I don't *like* it here.'

'Me either,' added Peager. 'I want to go home now.'

'But we're *lost*!' Dyll wailed softly.

'I'm not lost,' Scrunch said.

'You're not?' Peager demanded. 'There's nothing but trees here, everywhere. How can you know where the fields and everybody are when they're all hidden by the trees?'

Scrunch shrugged. 'The land speaks to me.'

The children stared at him.

'In words?' little Anstil asked, her eyes wide. 'Could *I* hear it, too, if I listen right?'

Scrunch shook his head. 'Not in words, no. But the land has . . . currents. I feel the currents. They lead me.'

The children still stared at him, uncomprehending. He did not know of any way to explain it properly to them, this deepness of the land. They were human folk, and closed to some things by their very natures.

'Come, then,' Scrunch said. 'Follow me and I will lead you home. I feel the way.'

'Really?' Dyll said.

Scrunch nodded: 'Really.'

The two boys pushed away from the tree against which they had been standing, but Anstil stayed as she was. She looked up at Scrunch. 'Can I . . . Would you let me . . . ride you?' she asked hesitantly. 'Please?'

'Ride me?' Scrunch said.

Anstil nodded. 'On your back. Like on a horse. Oh, please may I? It'd be such fun!'

Scrunch hesitated, then nodded. 'Why not?'

Anstil beamed.

Letting himself down, Scrunch waited while she pulled herself up onto his broad shoulders, clutching handfuls of his thick fur coat. He rose up, and she laughed, sitting astride him. She weighed almost nothing, and he was so broad, her thin little legs stuck out straight on either side. It felt strangely enjoyable to have her clinging upon his back. He gave a little shimmy of his shoulders and heard her squeal delightedly.

'Anstil!' Dyll said. 'Come down. It's too dangerous. What'd your daddy say if he saw you?'

Anstil only laughed.

'Anstil!' the boy said, wringing his hands in frustration.

Anstil ignored him. Grabbing little fistfuls of fur, she urged Scrunch onwards. 'Let's go!' she cried, jubilant. 'I'm so high, I can see everything!'

The two boys stared at her, their faces tight.

'Would you like to ride too?' Scrunch asked them. 'I could take you all by turns.'

They only stared.

'Well?' Scrunch urged.

Dyll shook his head, sullen and unhappy. Peager, at his side, looked enviously up at high-riding Anstil, then looked away and hung his head.

Scrunch sighed. He did not know why his presence filled these two with such unease. He would have wished things otherwise.

Slowly, he headed off, following the hidden contours of the land, keeping one eye on the two boys to make sure they stayed close.

He could feel Anstil's joy in the ride, like a warmth radiating from her. But the two boys radiated only miserableness. They trudged along, staring up at Anstil on Scrunch's back when they thought their gaze would not be noticed, envious and angry and afraid – but entirely unable to break out of whatever it was that constricted them.

Scrunch sighed. Human folk were such self-complicated creatures. Even the young ones . . .

They came out of the trees and into the Settlement just as the sun was lowering in the western sky. Dyll and Peager burst ahead, leaping relievedly past the fields and towards the central clearing where the houses stood. But Anstil stayed on Scrunch's back.

'Look,' she said.

Scrunch peered ahead. He could make out an agitated clump of human folk gathered before the houses. He felt Anstil shiver.

'I think my daddy's going to be mad at me,' she said. 'He told me never to go off into the woods.'

The two boys had run on by now. Somebody in the gathering before the houses spotted them and cried out. With a quick surge, the group encompassed the boys. Scrunch saw a woman lift Peager into her arms, laughing and crying.

Scrunch went onwards towards them, Anstil still on his shoulders.

The group of human folk was milling about, everybody speaking at once, laughing and shouting. As Scrunch neared them, he saw one of the men standing over little Dyll. 'Where have you been, boy?' the man demanded.

'You know you aren't supposed to wander off into the wild woods!' a woman added. She bent down to Dyll and shook him, hard, then hugged him and sobbed.

'Let him alone, wife!' the man said. Then, 'Answer me, boy,' he insisted. 'Where have you been? What happened?'

'We . . . we got lost in the . . . the woods,' Dyll answered haltingly, sniffing back tears and peering up at the man over his mother's shoulder. 'He . . .' He turned and gestured at Scrunch, who had come up close to the group by now. 'He led us . . .'

Before Dyll could finish his explanation, the man rounded

on Scrunch. *'You!* How *dare* you lead my child off into the wilds?'

At this moment, another man came pushing his way into the group. He was bearded, thick-shouldered, short. 'What's this?' he demanded wildly. 'Folk are saying the children're back. Where's my Anstil?'

'There!' the man who had rounded on Scrunch said. *'He* led them into the wild. My only son . . . and he leads him astray into . . .'

The newcomer glared furiously at Scrunch. 'Give my daughter over. Now!'

Scrunch could only stare in confusion. He could not quite grasp how things had come to this so all of a sudden.

'Give me my daughter!' the man shouted. It was Olundar, Scrunch realized – the same complaining man he had conversed with this morning by the new barn – though the man's face was so twisted with anger that he was hardly recognizable.

A woman came dashing up, screeching, 'Anstil . . . Anstil!'

Scrunch felt little Anstil cling to him.

The woman ran up, her arms waving wildly, and skidded to a halt before him. 'You . . . you . . . just leave her alone, you . . . you *creature*!' the woman shrieked at him. 'How *dare* you? Spiriting her away off into the wilds like that! I always knew your kind weren't to be trusted! Let her *go*!'

Olundar sprang forwards, reached a hand out, and yanked Anstil off Scrunch, flinging her to the ground in the process.

Scrunch growled. He could not help it. Olundar's actions were so rough, so unnecessary. Little Anstil lay on the ground whimpering, the breath shaken out of her.

The group gathered before him in a menacing crescent.

'Drive him off!' one of them cried.

Somebody threw a rock at him. It thumped against his shoulder with bruising force. He reared up on his hind legs for an instant, a surge of anger going through him. Then he turned and ran. It was either that or fight. And he was not about to spill the blood of these human folk.

Behind him, he heard triumphant shouts and harsh laughter – and Anstil's small voice crying, 'Scrunch . . . Scrunch!'

Then he was away under the cover of the trees and safe.

He went only a little ways into the woods before he slowed, for there was no sign of any pursuit. Scrunch let out a long, growling sigh. How had it happened? Human folk were so disorientingly quick, so desperately *certain* in their judgements sometimes. He could not help but feel a thrill of righteous anger. It had all been so utterly unfair . . .

He felt an impulse to abandon them all altogether, to strike off for the deep green of the wild and never, ever return to them. He had been fooling himself, he thought with a sudden, bleak certainty, he and all his kind. There would be no new life for them here with these human folk in the Settlement. Despite all the promise they had once felt, it was just the same old bitter pattern re-weaving itself again. Perhaps that was why the world was so tight these days. They had tried to push the world into a new shape, but the world was not ready. Or they were not. Or, more likely, the human folk were not.

Perhaps if Elinor were still here . . .

Scrunch shook his head. It was all too complicated. His mind throbbed with it.

He dearly wished for the peace of the deep green, to sink into the soothing wild, to let his mind unfocus. But in his mind he heard Anstil's small, pleading voice calling his name. It was like an invocation.

Somehow, despite everything, he could not bring himself to turn his back upon it.

VII

Ziftkin stood, catching his breath, and gazed back behind. He had come a long ways.

The folds of the hills stretched out below him, a mottled tapestry of forest and meadow, rising, always rising upwards towards the mountains. He stood now upon a rocky promontory, mid-way up a long ridge of stone. The air was thin and cool.

His belly rumbled emptily. He had long ago lost track of how long he had been travelling. Or how many days it had been since last he had seen proper food. His clothing, his very skin, had grown brown and green and grey, like the hills. His vision was laced with a kind of glow. The world seem bigger, brighter than it ought.

Off in the distance, he saw a lone hawk spiralling. It put him in mind of the hawk he had seen on the day of his mother's burial. Alone and free. Well . . . now he was the same. Certainly alone, at any rate.

Slowly, he turned and continued onwards.

The slope was steep, and clambering up it beat the breath out of him. He was grown weary of this constant uphill struggle. His thighs burned. His knees creaked. There were times when he had to go on all fours, so steep was the way.

Upwards, upwards into the wild lands.

The sky seemed bigger here. The mountains reared up like sentinels of some hidden land. The nights were black as black and cold and filled with far-away stars and strange sounds – and recently with the growing moon.

Upwards he struggled.

No sign of his father's folk had he seen. The land was empty and silent. And he had no notion of how to go about finding such beings as his father, save to blunder about and hope – till his strength ran out.

Some days back – he could not recall how many – he had passed the skeleton of some large animal. A mountain elk, perhaps. The bones had been grey-white and dry as old fire-wood. The skull had rolled, or been rolled, a little apart and lay tilted against a rock, the empty eye sockets staring blindly into the sky. Ziftkin shivered, remembering. All too easily, could he end up like that. He was growing weary and weak, and he was no woodsman. He was no longer even sure he could find his way back to settled lands.

But he had no wish, and no intention, to go back. There was nothing for him there. His life lay ahead, with his father's folk . . .

Towards day's end, Ziftkin came to a high-slope forest. The ridge he had been struggling up veered off into a kind of valley, tree-thick and sheltered. Walking in amongst the trees was like coming into a building after long days out-doors.

The air was still and silent and dim, and the trees filled all his vision. They were evergreens of some sort, very big, with gnarled trunks. Their knotty branches did not begin till well up above his own height, leaving a clear space for him to walk in the dim light. There was no undergrowth. The forest floor felt spongy with untold seasons of mulched brown needles.

It was like nothing he had ever experienced. The silence was complete. A runnel of golden, day's-end sunlight lit a tree bole before him, making the flaky bark glow red-brown and gold, turning the needles of a dipping branch emerald. The air was filled with piney tree scent.

He went onwards with an eager heart. This was a special place. He could feel it in his bones. And the day was nearing that special moment of transition between light and dark, when the world hung poised, neither entirely one thing nor the other.

Perhaps now. Perhaps here . . .

Ziftkin wove a way through the big trees, trailing his hands across their raspy-barked trunks. The ground went downwards at first, then up again, but at a gentle slope. He walked on, his breath and pulse loud in his own ears, seeing no sign of life about, hearing nothing, moving through the stillness as softly as he might, till, coming through a last cluster of the big trees, he found himself unexpectedly on the edge of a steep-sloped little bowl of meadow carpeted with blue-green grass.

Small white meadow-flowers bobbled in the light touch of the evening breeze. Ziftkin felt the breeze's unseen fingers upon his face. He sighed. Over the line of the trees, he could see the western sky. It was the pale colour of a river salmon's belly, with the red sun sunk away beneath the horizon. To the east, the moon was lifting, a round, gold-glowing visage.

Ziftkin stood transfixed. The moon seemed fuller, huger than he had ever seen it before, glowing as if it were made, truly, of burnished gold.

Up here in the hugeness of these wild lands, he could feel more clearly the Powers that flowed through the world – informing both the wind and his own breath, the world's stone bones and his own, the rolling sky and his own thoughts.

He felt something stir inside of him. Never before had he felt himself so strongly . . . *other*. His whole life so far, he suddenly felt, was but a preparation. Now was the moment to slough off that old life, to take up his father's heritage – blood and bone and spirit – and begin a new existence . . .

Something howled – a wavering, wailing call.

The hairs along Ziftkin's arms lifted. It was an utterly deserted place, this. His were probably the very first human feet to bruise the grass here. The trees bordering the meadow seemed to loom over him suddenly like a throng of enormous, wrinkle-jointed, uncanny old men, caught in the very midst of some incomprehensible act and frozen immobile.

The creature, whatever it was, howled again.

Ziftkin remembered stories told round the fireplace in the farm's Big House when he had been a lad. The Utang was said to roam these wild hills. Twice the height of a tall man, the Utang was reputed to be, walking upright like a man, yet covered all over its body with long dark hair.

Again the howling.

Was it getting closer?

They were said to tear men's limbs off, the Utang. Ziftkin looked around anxiously. He could duck back into the cover of the trees, perhaps. But that would prove no especially good place to hide for, surely, any Utang would scent his presence here, concealing trees or no. They were said to have better noses than most hounds.

He sidled closer to the trees nevertheless. Perhaps if he clambered high enough . . .

The howling came yet again.

But it was definitely further off now, dimming with distance.

Ziftkin let out a long sigh of relief. He ran a hand over his face, shook himself, trying to get rid of the sudden jitters that had gripped him. There was nothing here in this deserted place to threaten him, surely. It was his father's land this, and, through his father, *his* land, too.

Turning away from the trees, he saw that the moon had risen nearly whole into the sky now. Only the bottom edge was still cupped by the jagged stone roofing of the mountains. As he watched, the golden-pale orb of it lifted entirely free – a movement of utter grace, almost too slow to see, yet not.

He sighed.

And realized, abruptly, that he was not alone.

It was not sound that alerted him. Nor movement. Some instinct made him turn and glance quickly into the dark verge of the trees.

A pair of eyes stared back at him. Big eyes, unblinking, high as his own head, almost.

Ziftkin faltered backwards across the meadow, his heart kicking in his chest.

The creature came out of the trees, moving with a ponderous grace. It was furred, four-legged, uncannily quiet.

At first, Ziftkin thought it one of the great mountain cats that were reputed to hunt the wilds. But it was not like any cat he had ever seen. Its front paws resembled human hands, with big thumbs. It was longer and slimmer than any normal cat, with ears that were far too small and a snout too short.

69

And the eyes . . . The eyes in that furred animal's face somehow seemed entirely human.

The creature came out into the meadow and stood, one thumbed front paw raised, gazing at Ziftkin. Then, with a little grunt, it raised itself suddenly up on its hind legs.

Ziftkin faltered backwards, snagged his heel on some hidden thing in the grass, and sprawled awkwardly on his behind.

The cat-creature stood over him. Upright as it was, it was easily half again as tall as Ziftkin. From his supine position on the ground, it seemed entirely huge.

It took a step towards him, staring down at him with its eerily humanesque eyes. Then it raised its snout and snuffled the air, stared about into the trees this way and that. Apparently satisfying itself about something, it dropped down to all fours and sat on the grass. It cocked its head to one side, gazing at him, and said, 'Why do you come into these high lands alone, Man?'

Ziftkin stared. He scrambled to his knees, open-mouthed with shock.

'I will do you no harm, Man,' the cat-creature said.

Ziftkin could only stare. As a boy, he had heard fireside stories about all manner of wondrous things, amongst which were the humanimals, the talking animal folk. Part animal, part human, they were said to be from the long-ago time of the ancient and once all-powerful southern Seers. Most people these days reckoned the talking animal folk to have died out long ago, or to have been entirely imaginary in the first place.

Ziftkin had never expected to . . . to actually *meet* one in the flesh. He had never known anybody who claimed to have done so.

The creature gazed at him. Its lips drew back a little, revealing long ivory fangs. Its tongue lolled out the side of its mouth, pink-purple and glistening. Its altogether human eyes were wide with wonder. 'You are a *very* strange being, Man.'

Ziftkin did not know what to say. The cat-creature's eyes might be humanish, but its fangs were large and sharp-seeming as so many ivory knives, entirely bestial.

The cat-creature eased to its feet and came towards Ziftkin, who knelt still in the grass, frozen. It sniffed at him, its nose black and glistening, gliding wetly over his arm, his shoulder, snuffling in his face. Ziftkin could smell the creature's hot breath, not exactly sour, but not sweet, either.

One of the great front paws came up, long black talons protruded from the furred fingers and thumb. Ziftkin felt himself plucked, pulled, kneaded. He kept perfectly still, though his heart was thumping hard. He could think of nothing else to do.

Abruptly, the creature let him go. It backed away, stared at him for a long moment. Then it shook its furred head, grunted, turned, and disappeared amongst the trees, moving with startling quickness for its size.

Ziftkin took a long, gulping breath. He felt dizzy and a little sick. His heart was still thumping away madly. One instant it had been there, staring at him; now, he was alone in the little grassy meadow.

He did not know what to make of such a strange encounter. He felt piqued and confused. If only he had talked back to it. It had meant him no harm, clearly: had said exactly that. But he had only knelt there, mute, like a silly farm lout, too shocked and scared to do anything.

Ziftkin shook his head, disappointed, shivering. It was all too strange.

So . . . wonderfully strange.

Suddenly, he was overwhelmed by a sense of the utter mysteriousness of the world. It was a huge, huge place, filled with . . . with who knew what sorts of strangenesses.

He looked over the trees to where the moon sailed softly up into the darkening sky. It was a wondrous sight: red-gold and glowing, floating light as air. Ziftkin felt his heart quicken at the sight of it. Mysterious entity that it was, beautiful as any dream, floating free above the world.

Far off and faint, a bird called *kee-link kee-link*. Once, twice, thrice, as if in greeting to the sailing moon, and then was silent.

Ziftkin felt himself to be balanced *between* things, like a bird holding itself on a current of air. The whole of the great world hovered about him, mysterious as could be. He felt the wonder of it. His old life in Seshevrell Farm had been all too familiar, with the same day-in day-out round of chores and squabbles. Now . . . now he was utterly freed from all that, with nothing to stand between him and the great mystery of the world.

He watched the moon for a long time, till his eyes were full. Till his very self felt full, somehow, with the mystery of the wide world, as if he were a container into which the world was pouring itself entire.

He had never experienced anything quite like this. It was as if a part of him were just now coming awake, a part that had remained dormant all his life back at Seshevrell – his father's heritage, surely, coming alive inside him, quickening his blood till he could hear the pulse of it singing in his ears.

Ziftkin felt his heart jump. He looked to the moon again. Was his father watching this same moon, as he was? Perhaps . . . perhaps he and his father would watch the moon one day, together. He imagined it: his father seated at his side, the two of them leaned shoulder to shoulder companionably, gazing at the moon as it sky-sailed through the stars.

It made his heart beat fast, the very thinking of it.

And then, suddenly, he felt some . . . *presence*.

Whirling, he looked about. Had the cat-creature returned? But the meadow was entirely empty of any physical presence he could make out. The trees stood dark in the failing twilight. He peered and stared and shifted around, looking first this way then that.

Nothing.

But he could not shake the sense of something near, something watching him.

'Father?' he said haltingly, hardly daring to hope, his voice barely a whisper.

And then, a little louder, 'Father?'

Still there was nothing.

He went to the edge of the trees, thinking that his father, or one of his father's folk, might be more comfortable in the shelter of the forest. He took a step in, another, leaving the open meadow behind.

The presence did indeed seem stronger here. The small hairs on the back of his neck prickled.

This was the moment, then, with the moon sailing the darkening sky above, the world poised for the slow plunge into night, the trees whispering ever so softly now all about him. This was the moment when his life would change, when his future would come to him, when . . .

He whirled, thinking he had caught some pale form moving at the edge of his vision. Like a man, it had seemed, but taller, impossibly long of limb.

'Father?' Ziftkin called. *'Father!'*

But there was only silence.

The sense of presence faded, as if a shadow had passed over him and gone.

'Father . . .'

Nothing.

'Father!'

Only the forest, entirely empty now of any sense of presence.

Only himself, alone.

Ziftkin slumped to his knees. He felt, with a strange and utter certainty, that it was over. He felt empty and cold.

He was abandoned.

All his quaint, foolish-boy hopes. It was all too ridiculous and improbable . . . What was *he*, he thought bitterly, that some special dispensation should be made? Even if his father were one of the Fey, why should such a being be concerned with the likes of *him*, a hopeless, dullard lout from a backwater farm?

The moonlight filtered in through the branches of the trees like liquid silver. But it was an empty beauty, an empty forest, an empty world.

Ziftkin felt his heart breaking. There was nothing for him. No hope now, no home, no future. Nothing.

Nothing,

Only the growing dark all around him, and he alone as alone could be.

The world was dark, dark as a pit. He felt that darkness engulf him. The moonlight could not illuminate it. Darkness and cold and anguish without end, that was what truly lay under the bright surface of the world. The sun was an illusion.

The moon more so. The world was all dark at its heart. He was all dark in his heart. There was only darkness and emptiness . . .

VIII

Morning light made Ziftkin squint. His back ached fiercely, and his head. He was terribly thirsty.

For long moments, he could not think where he was. This was not his little cubby-hole room above the Long Barn. There were big trees all about. A shaft of morning sunlight lay across his thighs. It was certainly no bed he had slept upon.

Then it all came to him in a rush and he scrambled to his knees, shaking.

The forest was empty and silent. He was alone.

Alone.

He could have wept, but he had used up all his tears long days past. His eyes were dry. He swallowed, stretched stiff and paining muscles, turned . . . And saw it resting on the ground before him, laid carefully against the elbow of a tree root.

At first, he thought it no more than some manner of stick, the bark peeled away, leaving the exposed wood pale and naked. But it was too straight, too smooth to be a simple stick. He bent closer, reached out a hand.

It was . . .

He could not believe his eyes.

It was a . . .

His fingers touched it, feeling the long, smooth roundness. It was a flute. Carved from bone, by the feel of it. A single, long, slender bone. The colour of it was unlike natural bone, more like the soft amber of new honey, though whether from age or exposure to the elements or treatment with some special substance, he could not tell. It felt smooth and strangely warm under his touch.

Where had it come from? How had it *got* here?

He could not tell what manner of bone it had been carved from. Something very slim and straight. Unlike any bone he had ever seen. Lifting it up from the ground, he cradled it in his hands. It had none of the carefully crafted elegance of his own destroyed flute. No inlay, no intricate melding of metal and wood under a master maker's knowing hands. The lines of it were elegant, true, but this instrument, by contrast to his own lost one, was a primitive-looking thing.

He lifted it to his lips, blew tentatively across the sounding hole.

A long, rich note filled him.

It *sang*, this flute!

He played a slow tune. It was like nothing he had ever experienced before. Always, previously, he had played set pieces, tunes and melodies he had either learned from his mother, or from travelling songsters, or tunes that he had composed himself – but always within the accepted structures and rhythms of things. A tune had a beginning half, an ending half, a bridge between . . .

But what he found himself playing now was no tune as he knew it. The melody seemed almost to come *through* him, long, eerie notes flowing like water, washing through him. Slow, deep notes . . . a green melody of leaf and limb and slow-growing deepness.

He jerked the flute away from his lips, shivering.

No ordinary instrument, this. He had been . . . He had . . .

Staring about him, Ziftkin realized that, in some way he could not yet truly understand, he had been *playing* the trees. Or they him.

He put the flute to his lips again, gingerly, blew a long, soft note. He could 'hear' the trees. It was a little like what he had experienced last evening, the world flowing through him. But this was softer, clearer: like a soft-voiced, many-voiced choir.

He felt the deep green of the song all around him, the slow, sun-hungering growth of the trees. The good hardness of wood. The wonder of water from the sky. He heard it all, *felt* it all somehow with the flute in his hands and upon his lips, and he played it back, catching the rhythm and the sense of it and transforming it into human-made melody, singing the trees' lives to them.

And they, in turn, heard him. Or did whatever it was trees

were able to do. They *responded*, straining with their stiff limbs towards his melody making.

He nearly dropped the flute then, he was shivering so.

Where in the world had an incredible instrument such as this ever *come* from?

But a part of him knew the answer to that. His heart beating fast, he whirled, pivoting about and staring off into the thickness of the soft-singing trees. 'Father!' he called. '*Father!*'

He peered through the trees, searching for a glimpse of movement, of long, pale limbs, a flash of eyes or face . . . anything. Anything at all.

But there was nothing.

'Father!' he called. 'Show yourself. Please come to me. *Please!*'

For an instant, he thought he saw a a figure stepping softly through the trees, moving with the easy grace of the very breeze itself. It was pale as new bone, and seemed almost to glow softly in the dim, tree-filtered morning light. He thought he saw one impossibly long-fingered, slim hand against the dark bark of a tree bole, and a face, dominated by huge eyes, dark, unblinking eyes, such deep, deep eyes . . .

Shivering, Ziftkin found himself standing all alone amongst the trees. 'Father,' he called. And, 'Father!' one last time, his heart aching.

He blinked, shook his head. Had he really seen anything? It felt like a dream . . . save for the bone flute in his hands. He felt the long smoothness of it under his fingers, the strange warmth it emanated. 'Thank you,' he said softly into the air. 'Oh, thank you . . .'

From the forest all about him, there was only unbroken silence.

IX

Elinor and Gyver worked their way down through a long, thickly treed slope.

Gyver was fairly flying, he was so excited. 'Ssoon, *ssoon*, now!' he called back to Elinor. He leaped lightly over a fallen tree that lay across their way and pivoted, beckoning her on. 'Very closse now, my people. Their camp, it will be here-aboutss.'

Elinor clambered over the tree. She could feel herself quivering a little with nerves – far from certain that Gyver's folk would be as eager to embrace her as he claimed. Experience had led her to believe that first meetings with new folk were never easy.

'Thiss way!' Gyver said and was off again.

Elinor shook her head, but she smiled. He was like a little boy, all excited arms and legs and teeth flashing in a perpetual grin.

'Come on!' he called from ahead, beckoning urgently. 'You're sso *sslow*, you.'

Elinor laughed. 'You're so excited, you.'

He nodded and laughed back. 'I'm sso excited, me. Now come *on*!'

So onwards they went, more quickly.

Because of the trees, Elinor did not get a glimpse of the village of Gyver's folk until they were already upon it.

Though 'village' was hardly the right word.

She was not sure what she had expected, but it was not this.

What she saw was a collection of low, leaf-roofed shelters scattered haphazardly about, blending into the surrounding forest so as to be nearly indistinguishable from it. And in the dim forest light, Gyver's folk, too, were not so easy to make out, for their dark fur made them, at times, little more than half-guessed shapes in the leaf-shadow.

They had risen to their feet one by one as Gyver and she had appeared, and the whole band stood now, staring and silent.

'What's wrong?' Elinor asked Gyver in a whisper. She felt her belly twist up. The air was so thick with sudden tension, she could almost taste it.

She felt a sudden pang of unreasoning terror, like a blade of ice thrust through her guts. They seemed demonic, these silent, staring creatures, like figures materialized out of nightmare, different, strange, utterly *other*. Instinctively, she gripped the bronze dragon hilt of her sword, feeling her pulse race, ready to assume a defence posture and draw.

'Let's away from here,' she urged Gyver. 'Quickly! There's something wrong here.'

But Gyver stood staring at his silent folk. He fidgeted from one foot to another uncertainly. 'Thesse are my people. They will not harm uss.' He let go a long, sighing breath. 'But thiss iss not the greeting I looked to ssee, me.'

Elinor stood her ground, unmoving, wary, waiting uneasily for something to happen, one way or another.

There were perhaps two dozen or so fur-folk ranged before them – though it was hard to count them precisely – varying in age from suckling infants to silver-furred elders. Like Gyver, they wore no clothing. Most of the adults, she now realized, male and female both, were armed with barbed javelins or bows and arrows. They gripped their weapons firmly, as if expecting to have to use them at any moment. Two bowmen had their bows half-drawn, arrows nocked and ready.

An elderly fur-woman came a little forward out of the silent band. She was thin and gaunt-cheeked, and limped slowly, leaning on the joint support of a gnarled walking stick and a big-eyed young girl. Elinor saw a long, still-healing scar showing through the fur along the woman's thigh and up across her pelvis. Looking on that puckered scar, Elinor felt a sympathetic twinge in her own leg – where she had been opened up by the blade of one of the grim brethren of the Ancient Brotherhood of the Light.

79

How had this old fur-woman received such a terrible wound? she wondered uneasily.

The fur-woman stared at Elinor. Her dark eyes seemed huge in her gaunt face, and bright and hard as river stones. Fur obscured whatever wrinkles there might be on her face, but that fur was age-silvered, not only on her head and face, but on her breasts and belly, too, and along the backs of her arms and down her thin legs. She moved forwards towards Elinor and Gyver, the young girl at her side helping her, moving with slow dignity despite having to hobble.

'I greet you, Cloud-Dreaming,' Gyver said to her and performed a little formal movement, bending forward from the waist with his arms crossed over his breast.

'I greet you, young Gyver, Flow'ss-sson,' the old fur-woman returned stiffly, speaking with the same soft, hissing voice Elinor had become accustomed to in Gyver. She made no move in response to Gyver's bow.

After a long moment, he straightened up and said, 'Me, I am returned. And I bring with me ass my companion . . .' he gestured at Elinor, 'a fair ssmooth woman unlike any you have ever sseen before.'

'We have sseen the likess of *thiss*, uss,' the elder fur-woman said. She made a quick motion with her hand, as if carving something invisible in the air with her fingers, then spat upon the ground at Elinor's feet.

Elinor felt a queer cold shiver go through her and skipped back away a startled pace. Gyver, she could see, was completely taken aback by the old fur-woman's action.

One of the silent fur-folk came padding up, a middle-aged male, thick about the arms and shoulders with muscle, with just a hint of silver in his dark fur. He held a short javelin in his hand, a slim wooden shaft with a nasty-looking, barbed bone point. 'What are you doing, Flow'ss-sson, in company with one of *them*?'

'Them?' Gyver said. 'Who iss . . . them?'

The fur-man jabbed his javelin towards Elinor. 'The furlesss, naked-sskinned oness,' he said in the hissing accent of the fur-folk. 'Her kind. The killing kind.'

'I do not undersstand.' Gyver stood himself between Elinor and the javelin's barbed point. 'What are you ssaying, you?'

The fur-man before Gyver revolved the javelin's shaft slowly through his fingers. His eyes were hard. 'Why do you bring her here amongsst uss now, Flow'ss-sson? What iss *wrong* with you?'

'There iss nothing wrong with me, Sstone,' Gyver returned. 'I bring her here in joy, becausse . . .' But Gyver's words dwindled away.

The fur-man Gyver had named Stone stood rock still, his eyes hard and unblinking. The rest of the band stood in similar, hard silence.

Gyver looked at the gathered fur-folk and shook his head in unhappy confusion. 'What iss wrong with you all? Me, I return from long journeying, and none here sseemss happy to ssee me? And none of you rememberss your mannerss? What of hosspitality? What of the greetingss? What of—'

Gyver stopped in abrupt mid-word and stared about. 'Where iss my mother? And Wing? And—'

'You assk that, while in the company of one of *them*!' a young fur-man spoke up accusingly from the back of the group.

Gyver's furred face screwed up in utter incomprehension. 'One of *who*?' he demanded exasperatedly. 'Sspeak plain, you!'

The young fur-man who had spoken up came forwards, long, gangly-limbed, moving in an awkward-graceful shuffle. Like Stone, he, too, carried a barbed javelin; he had it balanced lightly in one hand, ready for use. 'It iss *you* who musst sspeak plain,' he told Gyver. 'Did you bring thiss furlesss one here to uss to allow uss revenge, you? Or did you bring her here to taunt uss?'

Gyver only stared.

'Well?' the young fur-man demanded. He swung his javelin round, took a two-handed grip, and gestured menacingly. 'Ansswer me, Gyver.'

Elinor stepped closer to Gyver. He had several of his sharp flint finger-blades in a little pouch on the string belt about his waist, she knew, and his short bow and quiver of arrows on his back. But neither could he reach in time should the fur-man before him decide to use the javelin. And Gyver seemed too stunned to respond effectively.

She renewed her grip upon the hilt of her sword, steadied the scabbard with her other hand, ready to draw if the need arose. She did not know what was happening here, but she would not let these folk harm Gyver – whether they were kin to him or no.

A tense silence held. Gyver still seemed to have found nothing to say. The young fur-man before him stood with his javelin up, tense and angry and expectant.

'This is a fine way for kin to act,' Elinor said into the silence.

It was like a rock flung into a pool. The fur-folk skittered back away from her.

'Who are you to talk of kin and kin-wayss? Murderer, you!' This from the thick-shouldered man Gyver had named Stone.

Elinor paled.

'Ah . . .' the scarred, elder woman Gyver had named Cloud-Dreaming said with some satisfaction. 'I ssee that hitss true.'

Elinor felt herself flush hotly. There was clearly some dreadful misapprehension at work here, but the fur-man's accusation had struck a tender spot: she had done too many terrible things with the blade at her side – necessary or not – to feel altogether innocent of the accusation. She felt the faint, seductive tingle of strength through the dragon hilt in her grip. Blessing and curse, both: it was no simple weapon to carry, this razor-edged, shining blade.

'Where iss my mother?' Gyver demanded, coming abruptly out of his silence.

'Dead,' Stone responded flatly.

'Ass you well musst know,' added the young fur-man.

Gyver sat down – fell down, rather – staring about him, head in his hands, his eyes wide and stricken.

For the first time, Cloud-Dreaming's manner softened a little. She reached a hand out to Gyver, palm flat. For an instant, it seemed to Elinor that the hand glowed softly in the dim forest light.

'Gyver,' Cloud-Dreaming said softly. 'Gyver . . .'

He stared at her, shivering. 'How can sshe be dead, my mother? Sshe wass too wisse to die needlesssly. Wha . . . How could it be that sshe . . . And you all . . . What terrible thing hass *happened* here?'

'He doess not know, poor Gyver. It iss clear to ssee.' A fur-woman slipped past old Cloud-Dreaming and Stone and knelt beside Gyver. She reached a slender, furred arm about him. Though clearly nowhere near Cloud's advanced age, she was no young girl either. 'Ssisster'ss-sson,' she said softly to Gyver. 'I grieve for you, me. Flow wass taken from thiss life by *them*.'

Gyver looked at her. 'By *who*?' he said plaintively.

'*Her* sort!' the younger fur-man said, making a violent, accusing gesture at Elinor with his javelin.

Gyver pushed aside the woman trying to comfort him and surged to his feet. 'No!' he said. 'No, no, and *no!*' He struck down the young man's javelin and scowled at the fur-folk, who were beginning to gather in closer, more threateningly, now. 'You are wrong, you folk. Elinor, sshe iss innocent. People like sshe, they live far, far from here. They could not—'

'Folk like *sshe*, they killed your mother!' the younger fur-man said. 'And Bubbless, and Tar-Baby, and my brother Lark! Sstand asside, Gyver, and we will take our jusst revenge!'

'No!' Gyver returned. He stood himself squarely before Elinor. 'You are misstaken, you. All of you.'

The young fur-man stepped menacingly forwards, his barbed javelin up. Others drew close behind him, weapons raised. Elinor heard the soft *hruspp* of an arrow shaft along a bow-stave as the arrow was drawn fully back. Half-drawing her sword, she looked about her grimly, not relishing at all the prospect of what was to come. It had been a full year, nearly, since she had last drawn the white blade in earnest and spilled men's blood with it. She did not wish to re-wet it now with the blood of Gyver's kin.

'Sstand asside, Gyver!' the young fur-man hissed, showing sharp white teeth in a snarl. 'Or I sshall—'

But old Cloud-Dreaming hobbled forwards and held up her hand commandingly. 'Sswift! You have ssaid enough, you.'

The young fur-man looked at her. Cloud-Dreaming's gaze was implacable. He opened his mouth, closed it, went grudgingly quiet.

Cloud-Dreaming regarded Gyver and Elinor, standing side by side now, protective of each other. She pushed aside the young girl who had quietly helped support her all this while and came forwards stiffly towards Elinor, who still had her

83

sword part-drawn. One hand on her walking stick, Cloud-Dreaming raised the other before Elinor's face in a slow, queerly graceful, beckoning gesture. 'Who are you?' she said softly. 'Who are you?' making of her voice a kind of singsong chant. 'Who are you? Who *are* you who comess into our foresst? Who are you? Who *are* you?'

Elinor felt herself shiver. Her belly lurched, as if she had leaped suddenly from a great height.

'Who are you? Who are you?' Cloud-Dreaming kept on. 'Who *are* you?'

Elinor blinked, feeling her limbs heavy and soft. The sword slid back into its scabbard.

'Who are you? Who *are* you?'

Cloud-Dreaming's eyes were big and glistening, like dark mirrors, like cold wet stones, like holes in that silver-furred face of hers, holes that went deep, deep into some otherwhere place where light and dark were shadows of each other and Elinor found herself somehow naked and exposed and . . .

With a long, cold shiver, she was her ordinary self again, standing in the forest clearing staring at Cloud-Dreaming's silver-furred face. She felt a little sick in the pit of her belly, and it seemed hard to get enough breath into her lungs.

Once before, she had experienced something like this; back in Long Harbour it had been, in old Mamma Kieran's hut – Mamma Kieran the Wise Woman, the far-seeing, who had set her life on a new track entirely.

Elinor remembered this feeling, remembered standing in Mamma Kieran's strange conical hut, shivering sickly – feeling as if invisible fingers had just somehow sorted through her insides.

She looked at the elder fur-woman before her and shuddered.

For a long moment there was complete silence. Then Cloud-Dreaming turned to Gyver, 'Doess far-travelling make you forget your mannerss entirely, Flow'ss-sson?'

Gyver blinked, shook himself, bobbed his head. 'I am ssorry, elder mother. It hass been . . . I did not expect . . .'

Cloud-Dreaming smiled a wan smile. 'Thiss, it iss not the homecoming you expected, iss it?'

'It iss not,' Gyver agreed soberly.

Cloud-Dreaming glanced across at Elinor questioningly.

Gyver cleared his throat. 'Thiss fair, furlesss woman, sshe iss named Elinor.' He pointed at the sword. 'Elinor Whiteblade, for the blade sshe wearss.'

There was silence again for long moments.

'Thiss iss Cloud-Dreaming,' Gyver continued, gesturing to the old fur-woman. 'She iss—'

'A see-er into the hidden ways of the world,' Elinor finished for him.

Cloud-Dreaming looked sharply at Elinor. 'And what would you know of ssuch thingss, far-away woman?'

'I have . . . have known your sort,' Elinor replied.

'My . . . *ssort*?'

'See-ers into the world's hidden patterns.'

'Ahh . . .' Cloud-Dreaming breathed. 'And you, you know of such hidden patternss, then?'

Elinor shook her head. It was hard to read expression on the old woman's furred face, but she thought she saw little yet in the way of any real friendliness there. 'I intend you and yours no harm, Cloud-Dreaming, if that is what concerns you.'

The old fur-woman lifted her shoulders in a noncommittal shrug.

'Cloud-Dreaming,' Gyver started, leaning forwards. 'You do not—'

'Mannerss!' the old fur-woman admonished him sharply. 'Do not interrupt uss, you, while we are talking, Elinor Whiteblade and I.'

Gyver nodded, accepting the chastisement, and went silent. He glanced across at Elinor, his face tight. Elinor felt her belly clench up. 'You . . . you are no ordinary woman,' she said to Cloud-Dreaming.

'Nor you,' the old fur-woman returned. She leaned forwards and reached a furred hand out, taking Elinor's left hand in hers. For a long moment, she stared into Elinor's empty palm, as if there was a message there for her to read, then she let go Elinor's hand and placed her own unerringly over the little hard length of the bone that the Fey had gifted Elinor with – which was attached to a thong, hung hidden underneath Elinor's shirt just above her breasts.

'You have been touched, you. And chossen.'

Elinor felt her heart jump – Cloud-Dreaming must have felt it too, with her furred hand still pressed against her breast as it was.

The two women regarded each other for long moments.

'You have seen into me,' Elinor said. 'You know that, whatever I may be, I mean you and yours no harm. You must know that for truth.'

Cloud-Dreaming stared at her, unblinking. Then, slowly, she nodded. Letting go a long, sighing breath, the old fur-woman pulled her hand back. Turning stiffly, she addressed the clustered, uneasy fur-folk. 'Perhapss,' she said, 'we have been over-hassty, uss . . .'

The children were the first to approach Elinor, sidling up, hesitant yet irresistibly curious. One small girl-child, eyes wide with wonder, lifted up a small furred hand and rubbed it gently along Elinor's bare arm. 'Sso ssmooth . . .' she whispered.

More children were soon clustered close, feeling at Elinor's exposed skin, fingering her clothes, her hair. One of them tried to pull at the sword's hilt, in all innocence. She pushed his hands away, gently but firmly as she could.

Small hands led her into the camp clearing proper, then, tugging her gently down to sit in an open area underneath the canopy of a great, spread-limbed tree. She knelt rather than sat, for the sword at her side made ground-sitting a little awkward.

The grown-ups, meanwhile, watched her from a distance, still not altogether easy. They had laid the javelins to rest, though, and un-nocked the arrows from their bows. By that much, at least, had they accepted her.

Elinor knew the genesis of these fur-folk from Gyver: how they had been created long ago – as the humanimals, too, had been created – by the darksome knowledge of the old Seers. But where the humanimals had been fashioned so as to keep their animal form, the fur-folk had been created in human shape, arms and hands and upright stance.

They had been kept in cruel bondage in the old time, the fur-folk, chattel to the great Lords of the ancient Domains.

Only in the last days of blood and chaos, when the Lords of those aging Domains had torn everything apart in their final struggles against each other, did the fur-folk manage to escape, fleeing into the wild lands to find a new life.

The story of their beginnings was familiar to Elinor. Through Gyver – whom she had been companion to for more than a year now – she had learned something of fur-folk ways, and she knew the fur-folk to be more recognizably human than many of their humanimal cousins. But she still shivered, looking upon them. All were sinewy-slim, as Gyver was, with large dark eyes and moist black-button noses that quivered now and again as they tested the air. Their fur pelts were sleek and dark, and they moved with a kind of quiet, animal grace, like so many gazelles.

So very like human people, they were, and so very not. Standing here, surrounded by such beings, Elinor felt as if she had been suddenly dropped into the midst of a child's wonder tale.

Sober and silent, they padded softly about, or crouched, or sat, or stood leaned against tree boles all around her, looking, waiting. She now saw that several of them showed the scars of not-yet-healed wounds, though none of these seemed as serious as the elder fur-woman's.

'What hass *happened* here?' Gyver demanded of them, setting himself next to Elinor.

Elder Cloud-Dreaming came forwards and let herself down slowly, with the aid of her walking stick and of the girl still at her side, till she was sat in front of Gyver and Elinor, wounded leg splayed out straight before her. She winced, rubbing at her scarred hip, shifted position, sighed. The fur-folk gathered in closer behind her.

'They came upon uss,' she began. 'From none knowss what terrible place. Like *her* they sseem, naked and pale ass any musshroom, them.'

'*Who?*' Gyver demanded.

Elinor felt her heart lurch. Violent men, 'naked-skinned' as she . . . She had a horrible feeling that she knew exactly who had savaged Gyver's folk. From the look on Gyver's face, he, too, felt the same.

It could only be Brothers: the violent, fanatical members of the Ancient Brotherhood of the Light who inhabited the crumbling city of Sofala, long-ago capital of one of the ancient Domains. It was her fault, what had happened here . . . like so much else. The Brothers would have been out hunting her. Gyver's folk had merely got in the way.

'A *bad* folk, them,' the young fur-man named Swift was saying angrily. 'With heartss of rock. They kill ass eassily ass breathe!'

Elinor leaned towards Cloud-Dreaming. 'I am sorry,' she began. 'This is . . .' She sighed, took a breath. She could feel Gyver looking at her. 'It's my fault, what has happened to you.'

The fur-folk stiffened.

'You see,' Elinor went on, 'it will be me they are after. They want me . . . dead. They will have followed me from the west, or come through here blindly in hunt of me.' She looked about at the hurt fur-folk, feeling her guts churn. 'If only . . .'

The broad-shouldered fur-man named Stone strode up and settled on the ground at Cloud's side. 'They came from over-mountain, them,' he said.

Elinor looked at him quizzically.

'From the eassternesss?' Gyver said.

Stone nodded.

Gyver turned to Elinor. 'It cannot be Brotherss. Not if they came from the cassternesss over the far mountainss.'

Elinor blinked, digesting this. 'If not Brothers, who, then?'

Gyver shook his head, as mystified as she, and turned back to Cloud-Dreaming.

'We tried sspeaking with *them*,' Cloud-Dreaming was saying. 'Plume and Sstarwoman and I. When *they* firsst appeared in our foresst. It fell to uss, ass the Elderss, to be the firsst to greet them and learn who they might be . . .' She lapsed into silence for long moments, her gaze blank. Then she shivered and said, 'They cut Plume and Sstarwoman into piecess with their big sshining knivess. Me too, almosst. Only, me, I can make mysself mosst difficult to ssee at timess. And I can sstill run fasst. Or could . . .'

'Green-leaf and Russhing,' Stone said, 'they tried to sstop thesse violent sstrangerss, to talk ssensse into their headss.' Stone clenched his fists and the fur along his shoulders lifted like a dog's hackles. 'But the furlesss oness killed them. Uss, we could not believe it when we firsst knew.'

Stone's solid, dark-furred fists opened and closed spasmodically. 'What manner of creaturess kill thosse who wissh only to talk? They are utterly mad, them! We thought it wass becausse they had been all damaged, sstripped of their proper fur-sskin and left naked. We thought it wass that which had driven them mad. But now . . .' He gestured at Elinor. 'Now I do not know, me.'

'Elinor, sshe comess from the wessternesss,' Gyver said. 'Where I have been.' He paused, put a hand on Elinor's arm. 'We are mated as man and woman, uss two.'

Silence greeted this.

Elinor could see the fur-folk trying to come to terms with what Gyver had brought them. They cast quick, flitting glances at each other, ran their hands over their furred faces uncertainly, shifted about. It was no easy thing Gyver was asking them to accept – Elinor saw that clear enough. To these folk, she represented a bitter enemy.

Cloud-Dreaming gazed at Elinor. 'We did not know, uss, that there could be any other ssuch naked-sskinned folk in the world.'

'There are many ssuch furlesss folk in the wide world,' Gyver said. 'Where I have been, nobody hass ever sseen furred folk ssuch ass uss.'

A general murmur of disbelief greeted this.

'It iss true,' Gyver insisted. 'The world, it iss very wide, and mosst sstrange.' He turned to Elinor momentarily and ran a hand softly along her forearm. 'And mosst beautiful, ssometimess, in itss sstrangenesss.'

Cloud-Dreaming blinked, looked across at Gyver, let out a soft breath. She shifted her injured leg carefully. 'Sshe doess not have the feel about her that *they* have. And all of *them* we have sseen have been men . . .' Cloud-Dreaming leaned forward, her eyes going hard once more. 'But there iss that about her, Gyver, that sstinkss of ssome Power. I can feel it in my old boness, me. Thiss iss no ordinary persson you bring amongsst uss. Do you know, you, what it iss you travel with? There iss the sscent of death about her.'

An unquiet murmur went up from the fur-folk.

Gyver held up his hands: 'Elinor, sshe iss no ordinary persson, ass you ssay, Cloud-Dreaming. But sshe iss no danger to you. Sshe hass told you thiss. And thiss, I sswear to you, iss true. By my mother'ss sspirit, I sswear it.'

Cloud-Dreaming sighed. 'It iss unquiet timess in which we live, young Gyver. The world iss grown mosst sstrange.'

'The world *iss* mosst sstrange, Cloud-Dreaming,' Gyver returned.

Cloud-Dreaming nodded. 'The world, it iss that.'

There was silence between them for a little. Then, 'My mother . . .' Gyver said abruptly, his furred face puckering with upset. 'How did it happen, her . . . dying?'

There was silence.

A fur-woman came up, whom Elinor recognized as the woman who had named Gyver 'Sister's-son' – which made her Gyver's aunt, Elinor reckoned. 'None ssaw the moment of her dying,' the woman told Gyver. 'Sstone and me, we found her and Tar-baby and Ssquintss . . .'

'All dead,' Stone finished for her. 'Not a . . . a clean death. Cut apart by *them*.'

'But *why*?' Gyver demanded. 'My mother, what had sshe done to *them*?'

'That iss their madnesss!' the young fur-man named Swift said bitterly. 'They kill for no reasson. Like a pack of wolvess gone utterly, *utterly* viciouss-mad.'

'How many?' Gyver said. 'How many fur-people have died?'

'Too many,' replied Stone.

Gyver was staring blindly at the ground. Elinor put a hand on his slim, furred arm. She did not know what to say. This was all so completely unexpected. He had looked for a happy homecoming, and had found only bitter tragedy instead.

'They musst be sstopped!' Gyver said, lifting his head.

Thick-shouldered Stone nodded agreement. 'They musst be sstopped. But sstopping *them* iss no eassy matter. Ass we, and otherss, have found to our cosst. They have great sshining bladess that never break. And thick sskinss about their breastss, sso that our javelinss and arrowss, they jusst bounce off.'

'But surely . . .' Elinor said. She looked at Cloud-Dreaming, 'You must be able to do . . . something. A woman such as yourself, a woman of *knowledge*, must surely not be power-less.'

Cloud-Dreaming sighed. 'I, and thosse ssuch ass I, we are not powerlesss, ass you ssay. But they have . . . protection, them.'

'What sort of protection?'

'Ssome persson-of-knowledge hass woven them protection. It iss not like anything I have ever known.' Cloud-Dreaming let out a long breath. 'Neither I nor any of the otherss of my kind have been able to turn them from our landss.'

Gyver looked at Elinor, and she could tell what he was thinking. Whoever these violent invaders from the east might be, Gyver's folk were clearly overmatched. She let out a long breath and nodded to him slowly.

He turned to his folk and said, 'We have ssome experience in sstopping ssuch ass thesse fell sstrangerss sseem to be, Elinor and I. Iss that not sso, Elinor?'

Elinor nodded again. She felt at the hilt of her sword and a little shiver went through her. Cloud-Dreaming was right: the world was indeed grown most strange. That she and Gyver should arrive amongst his people at just this moment . . .

Elinor shivered. She saw herself like a leaf on the swirling surface of a river, swept along by the great current of the world, with no more self-volition than such a leaf, turning and tumbling at the current's whim without end. The thought of it made her a little sick. *Without end . . .*

'Elinor,' Gyver said, 'sshe hass a sspecial blade. I have told you, her full name iss Elinor Whiteblade, from that which sshe carries.' He gestured to the sword at Elinor's belt. 'Sshow them the white blade.'

Elinor paused, feeling her heart beat hard. She *hated* this sense of being driven, like some hapless sheep, by forces too great, too deep for her to properly grasp. She felt at the little length of warm Fey-bone that hung from its thong about her neck. Her life was become full of strange meetings and mysteries and portents.

But it was too late to play at running away now. Her life was her life. She felt the solid weight of the sword at her side. It was hers, it and all that came with it. For good or ill, she was the bearer of this shining blade. Hers the terrible thrill of it. Hers the pain. Hers the responsibility.

Slowly, she rose from her kneeling position and stood. All eyes were upon her. She drew the sword. Its mirror-bright blade shone like a bar of purest light in the dim forest-shadow.

The gathered fur-folk gasped.

As always when the sword was unsheathed, Elinor felt the full shock of the uncanny strength of it flowing through her. And she felt herself *change*.

Once, she had been Kess of the blade; Kess who could remember no life before coming to awareness on the sea strand at Minmi, whose whole short existence had been her blade-training at the hands of Weapons Master Karasyn. A blow to the head, her Elinor-memory gone, and Kess had come into being, with the white-shining blade feeling like it had been made especially for her.

Recollection flooded through Elinor as she stood: the blank purity of the newborn self who recalled nothing and who knew only the sword; the halting, awkward melding of the two parts of her, the old and the new, as her old memories returned.

She was Elinor now, entirely. The Kess side of her had dwindled away into little more than memory. But when she held the blade, there was still an element of Kess there, a ruthless purity of blade and balance and movement. She felt herself to be lithe and strong and indomitable . . .

Only with an effort did she keep from swinging the blade in wide, flashy arcs. Instead, she held it perfectly still, assuming what her blade-teacher, Weapons Master Karasyn, had named the Horse Stance, feet braced wide apart, blade in low-guard position.

'It iss a *sspecial* blade,' Gyver said. 'A terrible blade – to her enemiess. None can sstand againsst her when sshe wieldss thiss ssword. I have sseen thiss with my own eyess, me.'

The white blade was long and straight and completely without blemish. It shone as if it were lit from within. And the edge of it, Elinor knew, was sharp as any razor. Gyver was right in what he had said: she had cut men in two with this blade, near as easy as slicing a melon. None could stand against her.

With a slow flourish, she sheathed it. It was not good to keep the thing naked in hand for too long. And it had been a long time since last she had wielded it. The strength of it was too much of a thrill; unless she were to use the blade, the power of it would bottle up inside her and make her feel ill – or make her do foolish, terrible things.

She could feel the muscles in her forearms and thighs quivering, and she stretched, bent her legs, clenched and unclenched her fingers, till the sword-tension began to loosen.

'They musst be sstopped,' Gyver said softly, 'thesse murdererss of innocent folk. We will help you sstop them, Elinor and I.'

The fur-folk were staring at Elinor.

'It is as Gyver says,' she told them. 'In the land we have come from, there were men such as these you have told us about. There are ways to stop such men.'

Cloud-Dreaming took a long breath. 'You have a sstory to tell uss, I think.'

Gyver nodded. 'We have a sstory, uss.'

'Let uss hear it, then,' Cloud-Dreaming said.

The fur-folk gathered closer, settling themselves in a loose ring round about Gyver and Elinor, and Gyver began: 'They call her Elinor Whiteblade, in the land from which we have come, for with that sshining blade of herss, sshe brought down a cruel enemy and helped resstore the livess of many innocent folk, leading them to a new place of ssettlement.'

It made Elinor a little uncomfortable to hear him put it thus, as if she were the hero of some old-time valour-tale. Almost, she did not recognize herself in the woman he talked of.

Gyver lifted his arms in an orator's gesture. 'The Ancient Brotherhood of the Light, they named themsselvess, thosse whom Elinor faced with her white blade. Grim men and violent, who wisshed to overrun the landss and peopless all around them, who tried to kill all thosse creaturess who were not of their own sshape, who fought to bind the world to their own twissted willss . . .'

93

The fur-folk gathered closer.

'Me, I wass there,' Gyver went on. 'I played a part in what transspired. It came to passs like thiss . . .'

X

Scrunch the bear heard the noise on his back-trail before he had got very far away from the Settlement. He turned and hid himself quickly and quietly, peering back to see what it was that followed him.

A familiar, small human figure came scurrying through the trees, skipping and stumbling in her haste.

Scrunch let out a long, uncertain breath.

Anstil.

He did not know quite what to do.

The trouble between him and the human folk had been cleared up – thanks to the patient perseverance of those like grey-bearded Collart, and to Scrunch's own determination to stay out of everybody's way as much as possible and to take no offence. But despite the settling, there had never been any apologies given to Scrunch for the blind harsh temper or the unfair accusations levelled against him. And Anstil's father, backed by no few of the other human folk, had made it bluntly obvious that they wished neither him nor the other humanimals to have any contact whatsoever with Anstil – or any of the Settlement's human children.

Best just to slip away quietly and avoid any sort of meeting here, then, Scrunch reckoned. He had a longish journey ahead of him in any case. Best to get that journey started and put Anstil and all that went with her behind him.

But, somehow, he could not.

Little Anstil might get herself lost again, traipsing around in the woods like this. She was too strong-willed for her own safety. He remembered the way she had faced him at their first encounter, roaring her small head off, brave as could be. What a solid little soul she was. She sat inside herself like a rock in a field. In his own humanimal way, Scrunch had felt too deeply the hurts that mindfulness brought, and the cold despair that could accompany it; he could not look upon solid little Anstil without admiring her fiercely for her courage.

She was pushing her way through a brambly thicket, thrusting the prickly branches aside determinedly. Scrunch saw her like a rock in a stream – only the current was still and it was the rock that surged forward, sending up white water all about it.

Such was Anstil to him. He was pleased with the image.

He watched her progress. She would come out of the thicket a little ways off from him. All he need do would be to slip away now and head off, and she would never know he was near. And neither her father nor any of the other human folk would have anything to make a fuss about. It was the only sensible path: he reminded himself of that in the full certainty that it was truth. He did not wish to bring on further trouble between his kind and theirs.

He turned, quiet as a ghost for all his bear's bulk, took one step, another . . . and then stopped. There was something in him that would not let him go, as if there were some hidden slope in the world that tipped him inevitably towards her.

He turned back and stayed put, waiting. As she drew near, he called out her name, softly.

'Scrunch!' she cried in delight, and rushed over to where he was sitting, dog-like. She flung herself at him, giving him a huge hug, entwining her little hands in his fur, laughing and wide-eyed, with a smile like a spring morning sunrise.

Scrunch felt his heart beat warmer. 'Hallo, little Anstil,' he said.

'Oh, Scrunch!' she replied. 'I looked *everywhere* for you. I was beginning to think I'd *never* find you. Everybody said you'd gone away. My daddy said you'd gone away *forever* and that I was to forget all about you.'

She pulled at the thick fur along Scrunch's forearm, as if to prove to herself that he was actually here before her. Then she looked up at him sideways, a little uncertainly. 'You're not mad at me, are you? It was so *unfair* what they did. Dyll's so *stupid*. And his father, too! They never even said they were sorry. I don't . . .' She stopped, swallowed. 'You still . . . *like* me, don't you?'

Scrunch nodded. 'I still like you. And I'm glad you didn't forget all about me.'

Anstil's face lit with a great smile. 'Oh, I could never do *that*. You're much too huge to forget!' She laughed.

Scrunch laughed, too, a soft, hooting bark of chest-deep laughter that felt very good to let loose.

Anstil looked up at him. 'Dyll and Peager wouldn't come looking for you. They said their daddies'd get too mad. Dyll's frightened of his daddy. His daddy hits him when he's bad.'

'Won't your father be angry, too, if he finds out?' Scrunch said a little uneasily. He had never truly grasped the relationship between grown-up human folk and their children. Humans seemed so hard on their young ones so much of the time. No humanimal parent would think of using physical violence on their children – a slap of exasperation, perhaps, but never the sort of ritualized brutality humans seemed to use when they wished to show displeasure or disapproval of their children's actions.

'What will your father do if he finds you have been here in the forest with me?' Scrunch asked.

Anstil shrugged, but her face went tight. 'There's nothing he can do to me that I can't take.' She looked at Scrunch defiantly, as if challenging him to dispute what she had just said.

But Scrunch said nothing. There was a wealth of small suffering in her response. And courage, too. Scrunch felt a thrill of admiration for her. He put one broad paw about her and gave her a gentle squeeze.

It was a humanimal gesture. Humans tended to rely far more on words than humanimal folk did – for whom gestures carried as much if not more significance than words. He would not have made such a gesture with most human folk; most would have been too intimidated by his bulk. But little Anstil leaned into him and hugged him tightly back.

'You're so warm, Scrunch,' she said.

Scrunch kept his gentle hold on her. He could feel a tightness that had been in her slowly ebbing away. But for all he tried to radiate calm and comfort for her, he felt uneasy in his belly. By being here with her, he was involving himself in something that could, potentially, endanger the whole of

97

the relationship between his kind and the human folk here in the Settlement.

He ought to send her off back home again at once. Nicely, yes. Gently, of course. But firmly, none the less. It was the only thing to do, given the circumstances.

And he had his voyage to make . . .

'Can I ride on your back again, Scrunch?' Anstil asked. 'Please?' She slid out of his hold and reached up a hand. 'It's almost like riding a horse you're so big, only better, 'cause I can talk with you. Can I ride you? *Please*, Scrunch?'

Scrunch looked into her child's blue eyes, bright and clear and empty of any of the confusing guile that marked so many adult humans. 'All right,' he agreed. Against everything he had just been thinking, against all common sense, he was loath to part company with her. She was like a bright flower. Just the one ride, and then he would send her home.

'Bend down,' she ordered him, 'so I can climb up.'

He did as she bid, hunkering down on his knees and elbows. She hauled herself up by grabbing handfuls of fur and scrabbling with her feet.

'Oomph!' she said, settling herself behind his shoulder blades. 'You can get up, now.'

He levered himself to his feet, feeling her sway a little unsteadily and compensating as best he could so as not to spill her off.

Grabbing little fistfuls of the fur of his neck, she cried, 'Giddee-yapp!' and kicked him in the ribs with her heels, hard.

Scrunch grunted. He turned his big head and looked back at her. 'Why did you kick me?'

'That's how my daddy says you make a horse go,' she answered. 'And you're almost big like a horse, to ride.' She looked at him, blinked, and her face screwed up in thought for a moment. 'Did it . . . *hurt*?' she asked him.

'No,' he said, for she was far too little to do him any hurt. 'But you don't need to kick me to make me go. Just tell me which direction. You can talk to me. Remember?'

She thought about this for a moment, then said, 'All right,' and smiled. Then she pointed off through the trees. 'That way. And fast. Fast as you can!'

'Hold on tight, then,' Scrunch said, and took off with a lumbering bound.

Anstil squealed in glee.

Down a slope Scrunch went, smashing through the tangly branches of a thicket in his way. His big feet thumping the ground, he lolloped along, finding a stride he could keep up, making sure he kept clear of hanging limbs that might sweep little Anstil from his back.

'Faster!' Anstil cried. 'Oh, Scrunch, run *faster*!'

They were coming across a stony ridge now. Scrunch scrambled over it, his blunt claws *krup-kurupping* softly on the rock. For an instant, at the top, Anstil nearly tipped off, letting out a little shriek. But then she re-caught her balance and they were down the other side and out of the trees and into the little stretch of grassy meadowland Scrunch had known was here.

Scrunch let himself out then, running for all he was worth, the downward slant of the slope giving him momentum, Anstil squealing excitedly in his ears, him feeling the rushing exhilaration of it, shreds of sod flying behind them, startled rabbits shooting off in all directions, till they fetched up, finally, at the foot of the slope and he had to stumble to a halt, his breath coming in great gusting pants and his heart thumping.

Anstil slid from his back and landed with a little *hrumph* on her behind on the grass. 'Oh, Scrunch,' she said breathlessly. 'That was . . . *wonderful*!' She sat up, her eyes glowing. 'Can we do it again?'

It was a long moment before Scrunch could get enough breath to speak. He sat with his tongue hanging out of his mouth, gasping for air. Not for years had he run like that. 'Not . . . not to-today,' he managed after a little. 'I don't think I'm able for it.'

She reached up and patted him soothingly on his forehand. 'Are you getting . . . old?' she said.

He shook his head. 'No. Not . . . so old. Though not young any more. Why?'

'Old people can't run fast. I've noticed that.'

Scrunch laughed. 'Look at me. Do I look like I'm made for running fast?'

Anstil cocked her head to one side, regarding his bear's bulk critically. She walked all around him, first one way, then the other. Then she nodded. 'You're made for just walking.' She patted him again. 'You did very well.'

Scrunch smiled.

Anstil looked down at herself. 'What am I made for, do you reckon?'

'Many things,' Scrunch said. 'You human folk can do almost anything.'

'Anything? Like what?' Anstil said.

'Anything like run, or climb trees or rocks, or swim, or . . . or almost anything, except fly.' Scrunch held out his broad, furred fore-paw, with its thick, clawed fingers and thumb. 'And your hands can do such delicate, complicated things.'

Anstil looked down at her own hands. 'They're so . . . *small* compared to yours.' She wriggled the fingers, flexed them. Then she looked around her and said, with a human child's sudden change of thought, 'I'm thirsty.'

'There's a stream further down by the trees, there,' Scrunch said, pointing.

So off they went, Anstil walking through the grass at Scrunch's side now, one hand against his flank.

The meadowland fell away in a short series of hummocks to wash against a rank of trees. Just in amongst them, Scrunch knew, there was a flashing little stream of cold water, with a lovely small falls. Scrunch could just hear the soft music of it. 'Do you hear the water?' he asked Anstil, unsure of how acute the human child's hearing might be.

She nodded.

Without thinking, Scrunch led off towards it, following the inherent contour of the land.

'Why are you going this way?' Anstil asked him. She pointed. 'The water's over there.'

'This is the way to the water,' he replied.

'But it's over *there*,' she insisted. 'Straight *that* way. I can hear it plain. Why do you want to go over *here* to get over *there*?'

Scrunch stopped. Human folk were mostly blind to the land's hidden contours. He remembered the way she and the two boys had stared blankly as he had tried to explain it to them.

For Scrunch, it was so obvious: there were hidden currents in the world, not clearly tangible to the ordinary bodily senses, yet there and feelable nonetheless. The very heart of the land those under-currents were, providing subtle contours that were firmer and simpler and broader than the complex intricacy of upthrust stone and tree limb and green sod. Humanimals followed these subtle contours when they travelled the wild, going with the under-currents.

But human folk, mostly blind and insensitive as they were, stumbled along in ignorance of these deeper contours of the land.

Scrunch, who would no more ignore such a current's prompting than he would ignore the scent of a forest fire on the breeze, had taken the good pathway towards the water instinctively; ignoring or pushing against the land's under-currents only brought on fatigue and confusion and bad fortune.

But how to explain any of this to little human Anstil?

'This is just . . . just the good way to the water,' he said finally.

'But why?' Anstil said.

'It just *is*.'

'You sound like my daddy,' Anstil told him. The way she said it, it was no compliment.

Scrunch sighed. 'The world is a bigger place than you know, little Anstil.'

She pulled back away from him. 'You still sound like my daddy.'

He could not stand the disappointment in her voice. 'The world is like a great . . . river,' he tried to explain. 'And like all rivers, it has currents in it. If you try to swim against the current in a river, you get tired very quickly, and confused. But if you swim with the current, you can swim more surely.'

Anstil regarded the meadow about them. 'I don't see any river. I just hear it. And it's over *there*.'

Scrunch shook his head. 'No. The world is *like* a great river, Anstil. Imagine a great invisible river running through everything, forming a hidden contour to the land.'

'You mean like we're . . . like we are under water?'

'A little like that. But the water-current is running *through* us. Through the land. Through all things.'

Anstil looked about her. She held out her hand. 'Through my hand?'

Scrunch nodded. 'Through your hand, yes. And through the grass and the trees and the sky and all.'

Anstil looked at him, her eyes huge. 'For *real*?'

'For real,' Scrunch said. He looked at her uncertainly, not at all sure of the wisdom of having this conversation. In his experience, human folk were simply incapable of feeling what, to humanimals, was so obvious. It was as if, in exchange for the solidity and clarity and sharp focus of mind that they possessed, human folk, in turn, sacrificed sensitivity to the deeper patterns of the world.

Anstil was staring about her. After a little, she pointed straight towards the sound of the falling water. 'That way is . . . not the way to get to the water?'

Scrunch nodded. 'Not the good way.'

'What's the . . . *good* way, then?' Anstil asked, her face screwed up in puzzlement. 'Show me.'

'I cannot,' Scrunch replied.

'Why *not*?'

'I cannot show it to you. You cannot see it. You must *feel* it. That is the only way.'

Anstil's face puckered into a frown. She closed her eyes, pivoted slowly around as she stood, her arms out, fingers open.

'What are you doing?' Scrunch asked, puzzled.

'Finding the current,' she replied.

As he watched her, Anstil turned and turned, stepping first this way then that, uncertain. She opened her eyes and looked at him. Her face was tight with disappointment.

'I can't feel it!' she said. 'It isn't there.'

'It's there,' Scrunch said.

Anstil plonked herself down upon the grass and wrapped her arms about her knees. 'I can't feel it,' she repeated. Her eyes glistened with tears. 'I *want* to feel it, Scrunch. Can't you show me how to feel it, please? I want to be like you. I want to feel the hidden current of the world.'

Scrunch did not know quite what to say. He had never imagined himself in such a position. As far as he knew, human folk no more yearned after the world's hidden under-currents than an earth-mole yearned to swim in deep waters. Yet little Anstil's grief was clearly unfeigned.

'Show me, Scrunch,' she implored him. 'Please!'

He did not know how.

'*Please!*' Anstil said through her tears.

'It is a thing of the bones and the blood,' Scrunch began haltingly. 'And of the feet. Let your feet listen and the land will talk to them. Your feet have ears.'

'My feet have *ears*,' Anstil repeated, and she giggled.

'It sounds . . . foolish,' Scrunch agreed. 'But I know of no other way to put it.' He gestured to her little feet. Like all human folk he had ever met, she wore leather shoes. 'Take off your shoes and let your feet . . . listen,' he suggested.

She regarded her shoes for a long moment, then unlaced them and flung them off. Her little woollen socks went next. She wriggled her small pale toes in the air, then stood up, placing her bare feet on the grassy ground uncertainly.

'What do I do now?' she asked.

Scrunch stayed silent. There was nothing he could tell her, and his heart misgave him. He regretted having ever brought such a subject up. It could only lead to grief, Anstil's setting her little heart on feeling the hidden depth of the world. Human folk were not made for it. Just as he was not made for fast running . . .

'What do I *do*?' Anstil insisted. 'Tell me!'

'I cannot,' Scrunch answered uncomfortably. 'Come, let us go and drink. Come.'

But Anstil stood her ground. 'I want to do it, Scrunch. Tell me how!'

Scrunch sighed. 'You must . . . must feel the depth of the world yourself . . . or not.'

She looked at him for a long moment in silence, then turned, her lips set in a thin line of determination. Hesitantly, hands out for balance like someone walking a high stretch of thin rope, she began to move about. Scrunch saw her wince as she stepped on some grass-hidden, sharp object with her soft-soled little foot. But she kept at it, moving this way and that, that way and this, circling, veering . . .

And slowly, to Scrunch's complete and delighted astonishment, she began to find the way.

Slantwise across the grassy slope she went, following the hidden contour of the land towards the softly singing water, following it uncertainly at first, then more and more surely.

Scrunch padded after, moving quietly as he could across the hummocky grass, lest he disturb her concentration.

Through the verge of the trees Anstil went, slipping along easily, following the under-current across the steepness of the slope and down to the little falls beyond. Once there, she turned to him, her eyes shining. 'I did it, didn't I?'

Scrunch nodded. 'You did it, Anstil.' He stared at her, shook his broad head. 'I don't know how, but you did do it.'

'It's not so hard,' she responded. 'I just . . . just *felt* it in my feet. Like you told me to. Like a sort of little tingling feeling. Or like heat maybe . . .' She shook her head. 'No. Not really like that. I . . .'

Anstil suddenly laughed and lifted her feet in a little flurried dance. 'Oh, Scrunch! Being with you is so . . . so *exciting*.'

Scrunch felt at a loss for what to say. He had never thought human folk capable of sensing more than the merest, dimmest echoes of the under-currents of the world – certainly never with such quick surety as little Anstil had shown. It left him a bit shaken, as if one of the trees had suddenly lifted its roots out of the earth and started to walk.

Anstil twirled about, finishing her little impromptu dance, and went to the water. The fall came gushing over a rock lip and fell as a white, gleaming cascade, forming a little foaming pool into which Anstil reached her hands, scooping up a double handful of water. She drank, splashed her face, laughing for the sheer pleasure of it.

Watching her, Scrunch felt his heart open. She was so unlike most of the human folk he had known. Human folk were closed up in themselves, tight as so many sealed barrels. It was their strength, the very thing Scrunch often envied them the most. But it was their weakness, too. Their blindness.

But Anstil . . .

Anstil, it seemed, was not blind.

Scrunch did not know quite what such a thing might mean. Was she so special, then, this one human girl-child? Was she gifted, somehow? Open like Elinor, who was a channel through whom Powers moved?

Or could it be . . . The thought came to Scrunch in a sudden flash: could it be that all human children were like this? That all were so un-blind and open when they were young, and that they had to . . . to learn how to close themselves up tight?

This was a brand new notion for Scrunch. It made his heart beat a little faster. He had thought he had understood human folk.

Anstil was looking at him. 'Is something . . . wrong, Scrunch?'

He shook his head.

'You look . . . strange, sort of.'

Scrunch smiled. 'I did not know human folk could do what you just did.'

'Feel the current, you mean.'

'Yes. That.'

Anstil laughed.

It was a bright sound, bright as the water's singing. Scrunch cherished it.

Anstil pointed to her bare feet. 'I'm never going to wear shoes again. Ever! I want to always feel the current.' She looked at him sideways. 'I don't want to go back to the Settlement, Scrunch. I want to stay here with you!'

Scrunch blinked. 'You cannot stay with me, little Anstil. What of your family? And I have a journey to make, in any case. I must go.'

'I'll go with you!'

Scrunch shook his head. 'You must return to your own folk.'

Anstil stamped her foot. 'I don't *want* to!'

Scrunch sighed. 'You must, Anstil. There is no choice. You *must*.'

She looked at him. 'But *why*?'

Scrunch gathered her close. 'You're a human girl,' he explained. 'You must live amongst human folk, and grow amongst them.'

She looked up into his face from the furred crook of his arm. *'Why?'*

'Because that's the way of the world.'

'But *why*?' She glared at him out of her bright blue eyes. 'You sound just like my daddy.'

Scrunch sighed. He had to admit to himself that he did not find his own explanations any more convincing than Anstil did.

'I want to stay with you,' she insisted. She wrapped her thin little arms tight about him, clutching at his fur.

For an instant, Scrunch was tempted. He could escape off into the wild with her easily enough. None of the human folk would ever be able to track them. He imagined himself and Anstil travelling freely through the years together, sharing the great wonder of the wild lands . . .

But no. It was a foolish notion and would spell the end to any peaceable relation between human and humanimal folk.

'You must return to your own folk,' he told her. Gently, he nudged her away from him a little.

'But I don't want—' she started.

'If you don't return, you father will become very angry. Everybody else will become very angry, too. And the humanimal and human folk will never talk to each other again.'

Anstil stared at him. 'Because of *me*?'

Scrunch nodded uneasily.

'But that's not . . . *fair*!' she said, outraged. 'I just want to stay with you. I don't want to make anybody angry.'

'But your father would be worried and angry if you did not return, Anstil. Your place is with your own folk.'

She looked at him, opened her mouth, closed it again, bit her lip. 'Can't I stay a little while?'

'I have a journey to make. I must go.'

'Now? Right away?'

'I was on my way when you found me.'

'But where are you going?'

'To see . . . to see some of my own folk.'

'Is it . . . is it *far*?'

Scrunch shrugged. 'Not so very far. A few days' travel.'

'A few *days*?'

106

He stood up. 'Come, I will see you back to the edge of the Settlement.'

Anstil hung her head. 'I don't *want* to go.' But there was no defiance left in her now. 'Everybody tells me what to do,' she complained softly. 'I never get to do what *I* want.'

Scrunch's heart went out to her, she seemed so forlorn. But there was no alternative here. 'Come,' he said, 'climb atop my back. You can ride me back.'

'All the way?' she said, brightening.

'All the way,' he agreed. 'Just don't expect me to *run* any more this day.'

She grinned. 'And when you come back from your journey . . . Will you let me ride you then, too?'

Scrunch paused for a moment, then nodded. 'Of course. But . . . but we must keep it secret, Anstil. Your father and others, they would not at all like you being here with me.'

Anstil nodded soberly. 'I know. They . . . they don't understand, do they?'

'No,' Scrunch agreed. 'They do not.'

Anstil reached for him. 'Kneel down, Scrunch, so I can climb up.'

He did so, liking the familiar little weight of her as she clambered atop his shoulders.

'Go,' she urged. 'Go, Scrunch . . .'

He went, loping along at a comfortable pace. Atop him, Anstil laughed softly. It was a nice sound.

But Scrunch felt a sore pang of doubt. His path and the path of this little human girl were inextricably tangled together now – will he or nill he. He only hoped he had not made a great, stupid mistake. For real grief could come of this, for him, for Anstil, for their two kinds . . .

And he had seen already more than enough of grief.

XI

Ziftkin sat hunched in the back of a narrow and dilapidated farmer's cart, amongst string sacks of brown market potatoes. The cart jounced and rolled along a rutted track, and he had to brace himself – along with a large black dog and three white, foot-hobbled, grumbling ducks – his shoulder pushed against the vehicle's rough wood side, cradling the bone flute carefully between his legs.

The cart driver hummed tunelessly, urging his skinny draught donkey on with an occasional flick of a string whip. 'Be there soon, now,' he called back over his shoulder to Ziftkin. He was a pudgy, white-whiskered, affable man. 'Ought to be able to see it round this next bend.'

The cart jounced past a little copse of birches where the track curved over the crest of a hill. On the far side, a new landscape opened up.

A large stone Keep stood atop a hill in the near distance, all squat grey towers and walls and slate roofs. The morning sunlight glinted off diamond-pane glass windows. Clustered about it, like a crowd of chicks about a great, brooding hen, lay a crowded jumble of wooden dwelling places.

'Actonvale,' the cart driver said. He pointed at the Keep. 'The town's no more than a couple of generations old, maybe. But Acton Keep itself goes back beyond living memory. From the Olden Days, it is. It was derelict, till Family Acton took it over. Or so the story goes. Something happened here in the Olden Days. None knows what. Something terrible, though. My old woman, now, she claims . . .'

Ziftkin gazed at the grey stone Keep uncertainly. He had never seen anything like it. Seshevrell Farm was located on the edge of the wild country, far away northwards from the lands where such ancient structures existed. It seemed a grim construction, built by folk who reckoned the world to be a dangerous place.

'. . . round these parts, do you?'

Ziftkin looked round. 'What? Sorry. I . . . I was wool-gathering.'

'I said, folk keep the Olden Days alive around here, with stories and such. Do they keep track of such things, where you're from?'

Ziftkin shrugged. 'We were always too busy with the farm work, where I was from, to worry overmuch with the doings of the past. My . . . my uncle Harst always used to say, "Work first, think later." Only there never seemed much time for thinking.'

The cartman laughed softly. 'Sounds like my old dad. He died while out in the fields, he did, ploughing. His heart just gave out. Wouldn't listen. Insisted he had to get his day's work in. My old woman, *she* told him he shouldn't ought to . . .'

The cartman's mention of his 'old dad' set Ziftkin off into uncomfortable reverie.

He had found his own father; he clung to that as a certainty. And his father had gifted him, yes. But also abandoned him, leaving him to wander alone for long days in the wilds – how many, he had no clear notion – starving and confused. He had only spotty memories of that time: him staring at the moon dying away in the sky, his heart filled with anguish; the face of some furred creature pressed close to his, and then gone; him raving at the cold rain as it soaked him; scrabbling at roots, the stringy texture of them in his mouth, the taste of earth and rock.

How he had lived through that time he had no clear idea. By rights, he ought to have died of hunger and exposure.

But died he had not.

Instead, he had come stumbling eventually out of the wild into the first of the scattered fringe farms, where kindly farmer-folk had taken pity on him and fed him and passed him on, one to the other.

Until he sat here now, in the back of this cart, headed further and yet further away from the wild that he had once thought was to be his home.

He was all alone in the wide world, with no clue as to where he might be going. All he knew – with anguished certainty – was that he had nothing to go back to, no matter how much he might wish it, dream it, yearn for it. There was only the uncertain path ahead.

The cart bounced downwards along the track, picking up speed a little now that the going was downhill. The black dog beside Ziftkin raised its head above the cart's side, sniffing. It leaped overboard, its tail wagging madly, and scampered ahead.

'Chaz!' the cartman called out. 'Chaz, you come back here!'

But Chaz just kept on going, tail up like a flag.

'Cursed mongrel dog,' the cartman grumbled. He turned back to Ziftkin, shrugged, scratched at his white whiskers. 'Always does this on market day. Out to visit the ladies, he is. Quite a lad for the ladies is our Chaz. I won't see him now till day's end.' The man sighed. 'Sometimes I wish I could trade places with him for the day. Let *him* haggle to sell the farm produce and me have a fine time nosing about after willing tail.'

Ziftkin nodded in what he hoped was a commiserating manner, but his attention now was more for the approaching town than the cartman's conversation. Shifting one of the hobbled white ducks aside, he leaned over the cart's side and gazed out ahead.

After his lone days in the wild land, what they were driving towards seemed disconcertingly loud and crowded and confusing. Everywhere there was bustle and commotion, excitement and talk. The hubbub of it filled the morning air.

Their small cart wove a way through the outskirts of things towards an open, muddy square where carts and wagons were jostling into position, drivers cursing each other with good-natured acidity. Children and dogs scampering excitedly about.

'I'll drop you here, lad, if it's all the same to you,' the cartman said. 'It'll be easier here than up there in all that press.'

Ziftkin nodded and let himself down from the cart. He walked round to the cartman and lifted his hand. 'You've been very good to me, giving me the ride and all. And me a complete stranger. I thank you.'

The cartman laid his string whip down, shook Ziftkin's proffered hand, shrugged. 'It wasn't anything special. I needed many a ride when I was your age. Besides, you may not talk much, but you more than paid for your passage by the tunes you played back there. Haven't heard such good musicking in years.' He gestured at the bone flute. 'Planning on playing that thing here, are you?'

Ziftkin shrugged, nodded.

'Best place is the Keep Market, next the Keep's West Gate. Nobody's got time to listen here to a songster in the Farmers' Market. But up near the Keep they've food stalls and such. That's the place to play. Ought to be able to make yourself a fair bit. You're more'n good enough.'

Ziftkin blinked, rolled the flute in his hands. 'Thanks,' he said. Playing here for money was a notion that had not occurred to him.

The cartman ran a hand through his whiskers. 'Well . . . Luck be with you, then, lad.' He waved farewell, picked up the little string whip, and urged his donkey onwards.

Ziftkin looked about. Folk streamed roughly past him. A woman with an armload of chickens in baskets elbowed him aside without so much as a word. A big wagon bore down on him and he had to skip aside quickly.

It was hard to get his bearings. Which way was the Keep? It had all looked so clear from a distance, but now, somehow, he could see no sign of the great stone building. It was crazy. How could such a huge structure have managed to disappear? His heart was thumping. He felt confused, overwhelmed, stifled. The wilds had seemed lonely, and he had longed, at times, for human company. But this . . . this was like a thirsty man suddenly finding himself thrown into the middle of a huge, boiling river.

He backed off towards the timber-and-wattle side of a building and stood there, back pressed against the rough plaster, shivering. He had only been in towns a handful of times in his whole life. His uncle Harst did not approve of them, and kept his family away from such places as best he could.

The thought of Harst and of Seshevrell Farm set loose a shiver of familiar anger through him. He was tired and hungry, worn and destitute. He had walked up into the wild lands and down again, alone. He stood here now, a stranger in a strange town, alone. Always alone. All thanks to Harst and his flint-hearted sons.

Ziftkin sighed. It was old anger, all too familiar, like an old pain that came and went. And old anger, as the saying went, never mended a broken pot. He shook himself. There was no point in standing here all day. The cartman's suggestion was a good one. Why not play music in this town for money? He lifted the bone flute, ran a hand caressingly along its warm smoothness. It seemed always warm, no matter what. No ordinary instrument, this.

His father's gift. Ziftkin shivered pleasantly, feeling it solid and comforting in his hold. He was only just beginning to discover how special an instrument it was, and how special a music he might make with it . . .

The Market near the Keep, when he finally found it, proved to be a far less bustling place than the Farmers' Market had been. There were folk standing about concession stands, munching on fried sausages and sipping from mugs of steaming green tea. A gaggle of younger children filled one edge of the square, squealing and flitting about in play.

Ziftkin worked his way quietly through the crowd to stand in a clear space near one of the Keep walls.

Folk began to stare at him.

He made a ragged enough figure, he knew, with clothes dirty and torn, and skin grey with long days of unwashed travel. And his hair was knotted and ragged and so stuck with twigs that he had simply wrapped it into a tangled bundle on the top of his head.

But it was not just the scruffiness of him they were staring at. Where he had once been thin, he must now appear half starved-looking, all bone and sinew and skin, big-eyed and gaunt-faced. His fingers, now, were knobbly as birch twigs. Tall as he was, his skinniness made him seem even taller.

He saw one of the children in the crowd tug at her mother's skirts and point him out, wide-eyed.

'A Fey-born lad, that,' he heard an old woman whisper. 'Fey-born and out of the deeps of the Hills.'

The word passed amongst the crowd. 'Fey-born . . .' the gathered children breathed to each other, shifting uncertainly about, caught between fascination and fear.

Ziftkin stayed as he was, quiet, unmoving, the bone flute held partly aloft, following a blind instinct that urged him to wait, to let the crowd draw closer. He felt his heart swell. Fey-born, they named him, recognizing him. Fey-born indeed he was. With his Fey-father's inheritance in hand.

Folk gravitated towards him, staring, unsure, intrigued. Mothers gathered their children in protectively, yet stayed where they were, gazing at him. 'What's he holding in his hands?' somebody asked.

'You, boy,' a man said to Ziftkin finally, stepping officiously out of the crowd. He was short, squat, florid of face, dressed in a uniform of grey trousers and tunic and grey felt cap. A short blade hung in a leather sheath at his side. 'What do you think you're doing here? Loafing about like this and causing a confusion! Have you no proper employment to keep you occupied?'

Ziftkin said nothing.

'I'm a Constable of the Keep Guard, boy,' the man said, putting one hand on the hilt of the blade at his side. 'Answer me when I ask you a question!'

In response, Ziftkin put the bone flute to his lips and blew a low, pure, drawn-out and resonant note, the lowest the bone flute could produce, low enough, almost, to be felt in the bones as well as heard in the ears.

The gathered folk shivered, uncertain.

He blew a second note, a third, a slow, rising flurry of sound, like a bird ascending.

And then, suddenly, he let the notes cascade apart into a racing, brilliant tune.

People in the crowd turned to each other in amazement. The tune was clear as birdsong, quick as rushing water. Involuntary smiles broke out amongst them. Feet began to move of their own accord, it seemed.

Ziftkin bounced into the air, kicked his heels together, and came down dancing, his long legs scissoring. Children came tumbling into the open space in the square about him in a laughing, bouncing mass. Their momentum was too great to be resisted, and soon the adults followed, and the square was awash with laughter and movement.

The bone flute was a joy to play, responsive, pure-toned. It seemed he could not put a finger wrong. The tune almost played itself.

He followed it with another fast melody, and a slightly slower one after that. And then a slow tune, letting the full, lovely voice of the flute sing melodiously through him.

And then, when the dancers began to flag, red-faced and sweating and gasping happily for breath, he tried another sort of music altogether. It was only half intentionally he did it. He was still not even sure what it was, exactly, he was doing. But, like the first time he had picked the flute up in the wild lands and *played* the trees, now he *played* the folk gathered about him.

They were people bound to the land, struggling through good harvest and famine, with aching backs and hearts paining with too much hope and too much dread. He felt it all so clear through the flute, and, through the flute, he gently pulled and pushed them through their own feelings – a flowing cascade of notes, a mournful slow shift, a tight spiral of repeated melody – bringing them to tears, to laughter, to quietness, till they stood about him, silent, rapt, and he let the melody slow and drift and finally fade away altogether.

Panting a little still, their faces flushed and wide with wonder, the people approached Ziftkin hesitantly. 'What manner of man are you,' somebody asked, 'to play like that?'

A continuous, communal crowd noise came from those gathered in the Market square. Those about Ziftkin quietened, waiting for his response, shushing those behind them.

'Fey-born . . .' could be heard suddenly from the periphery of the crowd. It was a fierce stage whisper, now unexpectedly audible in the spreading quiet. 'I told you he was a—' The whisperer stopped abruptly, embarrassed.

Ziftkin looked about him. He was shaking. The *playing* of

them had proved far more effective than he had expected . . . or intended. He was still discovering what the bone flute was capable of, and this was the first time he had attempted anything like this. Up till now, he had only *played* the wild animal folk, the little thrushes and squirrels and fierce-flying hawks.

He felt overfilled, and yet drained at the same time. His vision swirled with darkness. He could still feel the echo of these folk through the flute, though less intensely than he had while playing. He felt . . . He did not know how he felt. *Playing* them, he had done no more than mirror them to themselves. Yet he could have done more. He felt it as a sudden certainty in his guts. He could have . . .

He was not certain what he could have done.

The people gathered about shook their heads in wonder, staring at him. 'You are not like any songster we have ever seen,' they said.

A child standing before him, head craned back to look up into his face, said, 'How come you's got such big eyes? Eyes like a big funny owl you's got!'

The child was snatched back precipitously. A shiver of anxiety went through the crowd.

Ziftkin swallowed, blinked, shook himself. Taking out a little kerchief from one of his empty trouser pockets, he laid it before him on the cobblestoned ground. He made an awkward job of it, for his hands were shaking, and he kept the bone flute tucked tight under one arm, not feeling able to relinquish it.

The crowd stared at him.

Straightening up, he said, 'Anything you can spare me, friends, anything you can . . .' Halfway through the words his voice failed him. He swallowed, cleared his throat, tried again, making of the words a kind of singsong chant: 'Anything you can spare me, anything you can give . . . give in return for my poor music. Anything you can give . . .'

The faces around him eased into smiles.

This, Ziftkin knew, was something these folk would under-stand. He was in need of sustenance, must work for his living, just as they. In their eyes, he was transformed from Fey-born wonderling to more ordinary lad.

115

They laughed, dropped what poor copper coins they could spare into his spread-out kerchief, and milled about him asking a dozen questions at once. What was his name? How in the world had he ever learned to play the flute like that? And what kind of flute *was* that? From where had he come? Was he hungry? Would he like to come round to the nearest barrel-house for a drink? Would he play for them again later?

Ziftkin gathered up his chinking kerchief, laughing and spluttering, turning this way and that, not knowing where to begin. He felt overwhelmed by it all. Nothing like this had ever happened to him in his life. He wished, for an instant, that flint-hearted Mechant could be here now to see this. He would dearly love to see the look of shock and envy on Mechant's blond-bearded face as he saw his despised bastard half-brother surrounded by a crowd of such well-wishing, happy folk.

And his mother . . .

What would he not give to have Malinda witness this? She would have been thrilled to see her boy making music to such adulation.

Ziftkin had a sudden vision of a whole new life opening up for him. He would travel from town to town, making the music this wonderful flute allowed him to make, *playing* the folk of different towns, till his name became known far and wide. And then, one day, perhaps, wealthy and renowned, he would return to Seshevrell Farm . . .

From the back of the crowd, two riders came suddenly cantering in with a sparky clatter of iron-shod horses' hooves on cobblestone.

The first was a sinewy man with iron-grey hair. He wore a dark, sleeveless leather waistcoat, revealing the sleeves of an undertunic dyed a bright scarlet. Close-fitting trousers, also scarlet, were tucked into the high tops of his heeled, leather riding boots. A long iron sword hung in a plain scabbard at his side.

The second rider was a slim girl, dressed like a boy. Her trousers, leather jacket and riding boots were all dyed scarlet. The rich colour of her clothing stood out strikingly against the jet-black coat of the compact young stallion she rode, prancing and snorting under her hand.

The grey-haired man waded through the crowd ahead of the girl with his horse. She followed, ignoring those about her. The people fell silent, their eyes downcast, as she and her older companion moved through their midst.

The two riders drew their horses to a halt in front of Ziftkin. The girl sat astride the dancing, ebony stallion, slim and commanding. Oval-faced, dark-haired, with flashing dark eyes, she gazed down at Ziftkin in silence for a moment, then said, 'What is your name, songster?'

Ziftkin only stood, staring up at her. She was the most stunningly beautiful girl he had ever seen. The kerchief slipped through his fingers, the coins sprinkling out and *tinging* on the cobblestones.

The man riding with the girl dismounted and came over to her side. He reached up a hand to help her dismount, but she waved him off irritably, her eyes flashing under their dark brows. The man shrugged, bowed his head in a brief, silent motion, then backed away. The girl dismounted in one smooth, easy motion, half step, half leap, and stood there silently regarding the gangly figure of Ziftkin before her.

'Don't stare, fellow!' the man at the girl's side said sharply. 'Give her your name. This is the Lady Evadne, Lord Gault's daughter and only heir.'

Ziftkin blinked and bowed stiffly, trying to do it as he imagined it ought to be done, but managing only a graceless folding of waist and sharp elbows and knobbly knees.

The young Lady Evadne looked sidewise at her companion and snorted contemptuously.

'My na-name . . . Lady,' Ziftkin said awkwardly, 'is Ziftkin.' He fingered the flute nervously, alternating between staring at her and gazing blindly down at his own feet.

'My man-at-arms here informs me you play well on that instrument,' the young Lady Evadne said, pointing with one slim hand to the flute. 'He came especially to fetch me from the Keep so that I might hear you play.' With nonchalant elegance, she cupped her chin in the same hand she had used to point with, and gazed at Ziftkin. '*Do* you make songs upon that flute of yours as well as my man says you do?'

117

Ziftkin shrugged. 'I do not know how well your man said I played.' He smiled at her tentatively.

She did not smile back. 'Play for me.'

Ziftkin blinked, surprised by her abrupt request. She gestured impatiently towards the flute, folded her arms across her breasts, and stood waiting.

Ziftkin lifted the flute. For a moment he paused uncertainly, then he put his father's gift to his lips and filled the market square with a rich, meandering series of clear notes.

He did not attempt to *play* this young woman. He was too shaken. The very sight of her made his heart thump. He played The Rosy Dove, a lovely little tune, and played it well – he was not sure, with this wonderful flute, if he *could* play badly.

Ziftkin closed his eyes. Through the special property of the bone flute, he could *feel* something of the girl in front of him even without trying to, *feel* the manner in which she fixed on him, like a cat on cream. He played The Rosy Dove brimmingly, the individual notes rich and sad and—

'Enough,' she said.

Ziftkin's eyes snapped open, and he stared at her, the tune gone dead. 'You . . . you do not *like* my music, Lady?' he said, lowering the flute.

The Lady Evadne laughed. 'On the contrary, I like your music exceeding well.' She took a step closer to him. 'It is a gift, to be able to play as you do, songster. But why is it, I wonder, that you play such excellent songs here in the Market square for ridiculous, petty coins such as these?' With the toe of her riding boot, she flicked the kerchief on the ground before her with the few coins littered about it.

Ziftkin looked away from her and did not answer. She made him feel somehow special and stupid at the same time. He felt dizzy, as if he were standing on the lip of a great precipice.

'Well?' the Lady Evadne pressed.

Ziftkin flushed, not knowing how to respond. Nothing in his farm-boy's life had prepared him to face such a girl as this.

The Lady Evadne paused, considering the shivering, gangly figure before her. She stepped forward and reached a hand out to Ziftkin's arm in a calculated, brief touch. 'I want you to play for me, to be my special songster, at a special gathering which my father is giving, to be held soon in Gaultee.'

Ziftkin started awkwardly at her touch. 'It . . . I don't . . .' He pulled away from her, hardly knowing what he was doing, tongue-tied and confused.

'Don't just stand there gawking, boy!' the young Lady's grey-haired companion said. 'This is a golden opportunity the Lady Evadne is offering you. A once-in-a-lifetime opportunity for a no-name, wandering songster such as yourself.'

'No . . . You misunderstand. I don't . . .' Ziftkin gulped, trying to get the words out properly. 'It would be the *greatest* of pleasures, Lady, for me to accept your offer.' He bowed his clumsy bow and looked at her. 'It would be my joy to play at any gathering you host.'

The Lady Evadne nodded. 'Good. You are accepted into my service, then.'

'Perhaps,' Ziftkin said, seeing a sudden and entirely new and unexpected sort of future opening up for himself, 'your household is in need of music . . . of a songster, for more than this single gathering you have in mind?'

The Lady Evadne laughed, hands on her hips. 'What he lacks in elegance, he more than makes up for in gall,' she commented to the man at her side. Then she turned back to Ziftkin. 'Be at Acton Keep at the dining time this evening. We are guesting with Family Acton, my retinue and I. Go by the side entrance, quietly. You will be met there.'

Ziftkin looked at her quizzically.

'No questions,' the Lady Evadne said brusquely. 'You will be met and fed and looked after. You look like you need a good feeding. And a good bath, too.' With that, she swung herself back up onto the black stallion and was away through the square, her companion following, leaving Ziftkin standing awkwardly by himself in the middle of the Market, staring after her.

With the young Lady Evadne and her companion gone, folk stood about, muttering amongst themselves, casting hard looks after her. But they did not return to Ziftkin now. He was no longer theirs.

Ziftkin stared at the looming grey-stone mass of Acton Keep. Could it be this easy, then? Could the possibility of a new life open for him just like that?

He did not believe it.

He believed it.

He did not know what to think.

How beautiful she had been . . . black and cream and scarlet, like some amazing flower. His heart yearned after her.

'Be at Acton Keep at the dining time this evening,' she had told him.

Ziftkin sighed. It felt to him like it would be twenty years till then . . .

XII

Elinor crept through the forest. It was barely dawn, with the world only just beginning to take on colour. Birdsong filled the air softly. She stretched. They had been on the move since well before the first shreds of light appeared in the sky. Cautiously, she stepped across an open space between two tree trunks.

With a sudden snapping of wings, a lone blackbird flipped away through the branches overhead. She whirled, and stepped inadvertently upon a dead branch.

Krakk!

She stopped dead, her heart thumping, peering about her through the trees.

The forest stayed quiet.

She could make out fur-folk flitting past her, padding between the tree boles and through the sometime thickness of underbrush like so many shadows, moving with an easy stealth she could not even begin to emulate. When one of them beckoned, staring at her reprovingly, she continued along, quiet and careful as she possibly could be. Uncareful noise could well mean death here – or so the fur-folk insisted most sternly.

Broad-shouldered Stone appeared before her, slipping silently back through the trees. 'The camp, it liess not too far ahead,' he whispered. 'Up thiss sslope here, then down the other sside beyond.'

Elinor nodded.

The camp.

Their camp.

A young fur-man came padding up. 'Will you go down amongsst them, you, and kill them all with your sshining blade?'

121

Elinor sighed and shook her head. 'No. I only want to look. How many times do I have to say it? I need to know more before doing anything.'

Once the fur-folk had heard Gyver's telling of the bloody struggle she had been a part of, and heard about her – and the sword's – role in events, they had adopted an uncritical, almost childlike faith in her abilities.

'Sshe iss touched by the Deep Powerss,' they said of her in hushed tones. 'Wisse Cloud-Dreaming hass felt it.'

And, 'Sshe iss come here to ssave our foresst,' they told each other. 'Sshe and her sshining white blade.'

Elinor took a long breath. The faith these forest folk had in her was so touching, so unnerving. She and her blade could help them: Gyver had the right of that. They had learned hard lessons in the struggle against the Ancient Brotherhood, Gyver and she, lessons that would stand them in good stead in a situation Gyver's simple forest kin were clearly ill equipped to cope with.

Elinor gripped the bronze hilt of the sword at her side, felt the soft, uncanny pulse of it in her bones. She fingered the little warm length of the Fey-bone that hung at her throat.

Her life had once been so simple . . .

Elinor sighed. Chance or hidden design, it did not matter: they were here, Gyver and she; they were needed. But she could find no enthusiasm in her heart for such violent conflict as they looked to become embroiled in here. She had had enough of blood and grief. And she had learned that such conflict – despite what the fur-folk in their innocence might think – was never simple, and never easy.

'Thiss way,' Gyver whispered, coming back for her and gesturing along the slope. 'But go *quiet*, now.'

Elinor nodded and set off with him as softly as she possibly could.

Upslope they went, across the stony crest of a hillside and down, the fur-folk padding through the trees as alert as hunting hounds and making no more sound than the breeze.

Elinor was hungry – having had scant opportunity to break her fast in the scurry of their pre-dawn departure – and her throat was dry. She stopped to take a drink of water from the little flask she carried at her belt. Tipping her head back, she took a swallow, another, turned, and froze . . .

Through the trees there came a long, anguished wail.

The fur-folk that she could glimpse about her froze. 'What is it?' she hissed to Gyver.

He shook his head. 'I am not ssure, me. It ssoundss like . . .'

It came again, a long, ululating cry.

And suddenly Elinor knew what it sounded like. 'Phanta?' she said.

Gyver nodded uneasily.

But it was not the same cry they had heard some nights before under the moon. That had been eerie and plaintive. This held a note of genuine anguish.

Stone came back to them from where he had been ahead.

'What iss wrong?' Gyver asked him in a whisper.

'I do not know, me,' Stone replied. 'I have never heard them cry thuss.'

Once again, the cry came rolling through the trees, a long wailing that made the small hairs on the back of Elinor's neck prickle.

Stone stood for a long moment, staring off through leaf and limb in the direction the sound came from. He looked at Gyver, at Elinor. 'We musst go ssee, uss. Will you wait?'

'We will come,' Gyver said.

Stone nodded. He turned, beckoned to the fur-folk who had gathered together worriedly, and padded off.

Elinor followed after with Gyver. The fur-folk were skittish, staring about. Their unease was infectious, and she was especially careful about where she put her feet, trying to move as silently as she could. Doing so, however, was slow going, and she soon lagged behind the rest.

Gyver moved ahead, though he stayed within sight of her. It was he who gave her the first sign that they had reached something. She saw him suddenly drop down in a crouch. He waved a cautioning hand at her, and she crept forwards to his side.

The disturbing wailing had continued intermittently, and now it sounded again. This close, there was no mistaking it for anything else but a Phanta's cry.

Peering ahead through the trees, Elinor could make out a little rocky stream bed. She saw the great Phanta shapes moving about amongst the trees. Three . . . no, four of them, she counted. But she could not make out what they were doing. They seemed all to be clustered together, pushing and pulling at something on the ground wedged between two trees.

As she watched, one of them lifted up its long, flexible snout and gave vent to the cry they had been hearing.

'What are they doing?' Elinor whispered to Gyver.

He peered uncertainly ahead. 'I am not ssure, me.'

Elinor could glimpse some of the fur-folk making a careful way closer. 'Let's follow,' she suggested, pointing to the moving shapes of their companions.

Gyver nodded, but uneasily. 'Be mosst careful, you,' he cautioned. 'There iss ssomething very wrong here.'

Elinor nodded. She had no wish to move recklessly near such huge creatures when they were so clearly in an agitated state.

She and Gyver crept ahead on hands and knees, slipping carefully from one tree to the next, till they had come close enough to see clearly what it was the Phanta were preoccupied with.

Even this much closer, it took Elinor a long few moments to see it. At first, all she could make out was a dark, shapeless mass obscured by the clustered Phanta, who were pushing at it with their great heads, tugging with the flexible, long snouts. And then, suddenly, she saw what it was.

A body.

The thing the Phanta anguished over was the dead body of one of their own.

'It iss Sstarbrow,' Gyver whispered.

Elinor could make out only a bedraggled, huge carcass. 'How can you know?'

'I know Sstarbrow, me, ass well ass I know any fur-persson. We all do.'

Elinor peered ahead and made out more detail. Dead

Starbrow lay on the ground on her flank, her belly towards where Elinor and Gyver crouched hidden. The Phanta's great head pointed off to one side, her long snout limp. As Elinor watched, one of the gathered Phanta lifted up Starbrow's snout in its own and pulled at it. But the dead limb merely flopped back to the ground. The Phanta wailed desolately. It backed away, stamped its feet, then returned and lifted up Starbrow's limp snout once again, as if it could not believe its dead companion would not respond.

'What happened to her?' Elinor asked softly of Gyver.

The fur-man pointed at dead Starbrow's hindquarters. 'Look!'

Elinor looked and gasped. Starbrow's flank had been carved away, leaving a huge, gaping red trench out of which stuck a single, shattered length of bone. Flies buzzed and massed, rising up when the living Phanta disturbed them.

'She hass been hunted,' Gyver said. 'And butchered for food. Ssee? Whoever did thiss, they have taken only the besst, the eassiesst to get at meat.'

'But who . . .'

'*Them*,' Gyver said with utter, bleak certainty. 'My people, we would *never* molesst the Old Oness.'

Elinor looked uncertainly at the great carcass. She shuddered. 'But how could they kill such a huge creature?'

'They have no enemiess, the Old Oness,' Gyver answered. 'Remember Ssharp-eye? When he came to sscent uss? For all hiss power, he would never have willingly harmed uss, him. The Phanta, they are ssoft folk. They would not know to flee from hunterss. And *they* bring death with them wherever *they* go.'

Elinor stared at the group of grieving Phanta. Her heart went out to them. Whatever they might be, they were not simple beasts. Their anguish over dead Starbrow was painfully clear.

At her side, Gyver growled deep in his chest. She had never heard him make such a sound. The fur all along his back and shoulders was risen in a ruff. 'That *they* sshould do ssuch a thing . . .' he said, outraged.

Below, one of the Phanta lifted its long snout in a wail. A second joined in. Then, abruptly, they went silent.

125

'They know we are here,' Gyver said very softly. 'The wayward breeze, it hass revealed uss to them.'

The four great beasts had turned and were staring at where Elinor and Gyver crouched.

'We musst go, uss,' Gyver whispered. 'Quickly! They are not themsselvess at thiss moment. There iss no telling what they might do, them.'

Elinor nodded and turned to slip away. But before she could do more than take a single step, one of the Phanta left the group gathered about the corpse and came thumping across between the trees towards her, its snout uplifted, grumbling and growling angrily, moving swiftly for all its great bulk.

'Ssharp-eye,' Gyver said. 'He hass sseen uss!'

Elinor rose, her heart in her mouth. The creature was huge, a veritable mountain of flesh bearing down upon her. She sensed the outraged anger it radiated, like a great stove radiating heat. It was too close for her to stand any chance of outrunning it – its great legs covered too much ground at each stride. She could feel the ground tremor with its thumping footsteps. It could smash her flat.

Things had all happened so fast . . . She gripped her sword's hilt, her heart hammering, turned and made ready to dash away behind a tree in the vague hope of dodging it, at least for a little.

And then, suddenly, a small figure appeared directly before her in the Phanta's path.

It was one of the fur-folk – a young girl. Though how such a girl had come to be here, Elinor had no notion. She stared, horrified, for the little fur-girl just stood there, directly in the Phanta's way, thin arms at her sides, unmoving. The angry beast would trample her without a thought.

Elinor leaped forwards, drawing her blade . . .

But, to her astonishment, the Phanta slowed abruptly, stopped. It lowered its great head and snuffled at the fur-girl, who crooned wordlessly up at it.

Elinor felt Gyver's hand upon her arm. 'Come,' he whispered. 'Let Ssky-Flower talk to him. Come, you make the Old Oness nervouss, you. You ssmell too much like *them.*'

Elinor let herself be pulled away, sheathing her blade, staring over her shoulder at the fur-girl, dwarfed by the great bulk of the Phanta.

Gyver brought her quickly across a long slope and over a crest of cracked green stone. There, she sagged against the rock, feeling her belly tight, her heart still thumping. 'Who was that . . . that little girl?' she demanded of Gyver. 'How did she manage to *do* that?'

Gyver smiled a thin smile. 'Sshe iss Ssky-Flower. Sshe iss . . . sspecial.'

'Special indeed,' Elinor agreed. 'Where did she appear from like that, out of nowhere?'

'Sshe hass been with uss ssince we left our camp thiss morning.'

'But I never saw her amongst those with us,' Elinor said, surprised.

Gyver shrugged.

More of the fur-folk were beginning to filter in now from the surrounding trees. They had a strained look about them.

'We musst go onwardss, uss,' Stone said. He ran a furred hand across his face. 'But mosst carefully.'

Young Swift came up, his eyes burning in his face, his fur bristling stiffly. 'They musst be killed, thesse terrible sstrangerss.' He leapt upon the crest of green stone against which Elinor still leaned and brandished his barbed javelin. 'They are monssterss! Uss, we musst kill them *all*!'

A number of other young fur-men set up a growling chorus of angry agreement. Gathering in front of Swift, who was still up on the rock, they broke into an impromptu, stiff-legged dance, their hackles up.

Elinor backed away from them uneasily. These fur-folk might be exotic and different, and at times difficult for her to understand – Gyver included – but she recognized all too clearly the burning outrage in the eyes of young Swift and the rest. It was entirely human and comprehensible, and she had seen its like before. Righteous fury wedded to innocence . . . it was a deadly combination, goading folk to desperate acts of reprisal.

'We musst kill them, thesse monsstrouss sstrangerss,' Swift

repeated in fury, to the growling agreement of the other young fur-men. '*Kill* them!'

Elinor motioned to Gyver, who nodded, seeing it the same as she. But, before they could try to initiate anything to deflect the outraged young fur-men from any mad-rash course of action, Stone stepped forwards and lifted a hand for quiet.

'We musst do what musst be done,' the older fur-man said. 'But the killing fury, it will not help uss now. Do you hear me?'

Swift grunted something too low to be understandable.

'Do you *hear* me, you?' Stone demanded of him.

Swift glared. '*They* musst be killed! To cleansse the world. *Killed!*'

The other young fur-men grumbled in sullen, angry accord.

'Are you all become ssick-in-the-head perssonss like *them*, then?' Stone said. 'Kill! Kill! Kill! Iss that all your thought? Thosse who exalt death in their heartss, they die insside. You know thiss! We *all* know thiss!'

'They are monssterss, *them*!' Swift returned hotly.

Stone nodded. '*Them*, they are monssterss, yess. But uss, we are not.'

There was a long moment's silence.

Swift let out a slow, sighing breath. He looked at Stone, looked away. His hackles slowly settled. The other fur-men quieted, their heads hanging now.

At that moment, more fur-folk came padding in and the focus shifted. The young girl who had stood herself before the angry Phanta was amongst the newcomers. The fur-folk made way for her, helped her to a seat against a rock. Somebody offered her a little leather flask of water to drink from.

Elinor regarded the slight fur-girl as she sipped at the water flask, thin-limbed, big-eyed, delicately boned. Sky-Flower, Gyver had named her. It took Elinor a long moment to realize who she was: the youngster whom Elinor had seen supporting Cloud-Dreaming, the old, wounded Wise Woman.

Elinor saw that Sky-Flower's hand, as it held the water flask, was shaking in little helpless spasms. Elinor shook her head, trying to imagine what it took to stand oneself before an enraged, moving mountain.

Elinor went over to her. 'Thank you,' she said. 'Thank you for saving me.'

The girl looked up. She smiled, nodded wordlessly, shyly. Her face seemed all eyes.

'We will leave now,' Stone said, coming over to where Elinor stood. 'Now that the Phanta are calmed and Ssky-Flower, sshe iss returned.'

Elinor beckoned him away a few feet. 'Surely she's not coming with us so close to *their* camp, is she?' she said to him.

Stone nodded.

'But she's only a child,' Elinor said. 'It's dangerous, where we go.'

Stone nodded.

'But . . .' Elinor shook her head.

'Ssky-Flower, sshe iss no ordinary persson,' Stone said.

Elinor nodded. 'Obviously. But—'

'Cloud-Dreaming, sshe iss too hurt to be able to come with uss,' Gyver said, joining them. 'But we need ssomeone with the *ssight*, if we are to get closse to *their* camp. Ssky-Flower, sshe hass it.'

'The *sight*?' Elinor said.

Gyver nodded. 'The deep-sseeing beyond the world'ss ssimple face.'

Elinor looked at the girl. She had had enough strange experiences herself to be able to accept what Gyver was saying. The world had deeps to it, and there were those who could see into those deeps. But Sky-Flower seemed all wide eyes and skinny, delicate limbs, and altogether too young to be placed in such danger as they were likely to run this day.

Elinor sighed. 'She seems so . . . so vulnerable, Gyver.'

Gyver nodded. 'But there iss none other amongsst uss who can do what iss needed.'

'Come,' Stone urged them. 'We musst go now, uss.'

Softly, they went, padding off through the trees towards *their* encampment.

Elinor heard the sounds first, before getting any glimpse of the camp itself. Initially it was only the faintest of little metallic chimmerings. Then she caught a deeper kind of *thruum* that

sounded rhythmically just on the lower threshold of her
hearing.

'Do you hear, you?' broad-shouldered Stone asked at her
side.

Elinor nodded. 'What is it?'

'Protection,' said a soft, thin voice. It was Sky-Flower. 'Thiss
way,' the fur-girl whispered. Carefully, the group of them
crept further through the trees, following little Sky-Flower's
lead now – though what it was that gave the girl her cue was
beyond Elinor. The forest all looked the same to her.

Coming round down the crest of the hill, they followed a
knobbly spine of shattered rock downwards to a briar-choked
hummock of ground. Across this they crawled until, peering
cautiously round the far side, Elinor caught her first glimpse of
their camp through the tangle of the forest

At first, all she could make out was a strangely confusing,
shifting mosaic of moving forms and improbable colours. She
shook her head and blinked, feeling queerly dizzy.

'Look!' little Sky-Flower whispered in her ear. With one
thin, dark-furred arm, she pointed into the trees ahead.

Elinor squinted, seeing nothing. 'I don't . . .'

'Hanging from that tree limb. Ssee?'

Peering ahead, Elinor saw it, finally.

Secured to a branch by a length of white twine, it dangled
nearly a tall man's height above the ground. Feathers, a squat
crimson shape, the bright glint of metal . . .

Elinor strained forwards, trying to make it out clearly. She
could hear a soft, almost musical *ching ching ching* coming from
it, and a deeper *thrummm*. The more she focused on it, the
more clearly she felt the *thrumming* sound. It made the bones
of her skull ring softly, achingly.

A small, furred hand tugged at her. 'Look away from it!'
Sky-Flower hissed in her ear.

Elinor did, but found that simple act surprisingly difficult.
'What is it?' she whispered uneasily.

'Protection,' Sky-Flower answered. 'It guardss *them.* Do not
look at it sstraight for too long, you. It can be . . . dangerouss.'

Elinor felt a shiver go through her, looking down at this
wise child.

Out of the corner of her eye, she regarded the dangling

thing, taking it in in quick glances. It seemed to be some manner of long face, perhaps as long as Elinor's forearm. There were dark, staring eyes, and a mouth gaping wide open in what seemed to be a frozen wail. Now that she knew it to be there, Elinor found the bright crimson of it showed with startling brightness against the dark tree background. It twirled slowly on its length of twine, sending off little metallic flashes. A spree of lacy white feathers fluttered from its lower end. The air was filled softly with that *thrumming* sound that emanated from it, over which the metallic *chinging* rang softly.

Elinor felt Sky-Flower move away ahead towards the thing. 'Come back!' she hissed impulsively. For though the dangling face seemed to be a mere created thing, carved or fashioned somehow, it gave off an almost palpable aura of . . . Elinor was not sure what. Menace?

Stone came slipping along up to Elinor's side. 'Sshe goess to open a way for uss,' he whispered.

Elinor stared at him. 'But how can—'

'Thiss guard, and otherss like it . . . *Their* camp iss ringed with them. They make the camp difficult to ssee.' Stone gestured with one of his thick-muscled arms towards the camp.

Sure enough, as with her first glimpse, Elinor found it strangely difficult to make sense of things there. She saw flashes of bright, improbable colours and confusing movement, but could make out little else.

'And it alertss *them*, a guard ssuch ass thiss one, if any come too near the camp,' Stone said.

'Like us,' Elinor said.

'Like uss,' he repeated, nodding.

Elinor watched Sky-Flower creep towards the thing. Her hand went to her sword's hilt. 'But you can't just let her—'

'Your white blade would be of no usse againsst it,' Stone said. 'It iss not any ssimple foe. Not uss with our bowss, nor Cloud-Dreaming, nor any of the otherss of her sskillss could bring them down, thesse guardss. But Cloud-Dreaming hass learned, and hass sshown Ssky-Flower, how to make one of them blind for a little time.' Stone looked at the fur-girl. 'Sshe iss very brave, our ssmall Ssky-Flower.'

Elinor watched, her heart in her mouth, as the fur-girl

131

crawled cautiously forwards towards that dangling crimson-faced guard. It was strangely hard to keep track of Sky-Flower's movements, as if she were somehow rendering herself difficult to see. Elinor only hoped the trick – if trick it was – would work on the hanging guard. She had no notion as to what harm such an uncanny thing might be capable of causing, but the aura of menace about it was becoming clearer and clearer.

Sky-Flower had crept within a few paces now of the tree from which the thing hung. Slithering behind the tree's bole, she stood up slowly. The crimson face twirled its slow twirl, *thruumming* and *chinging* softly, seemingly oblivious. The fur-girl reached one slim hand upwards around the tree in a quick, complex movement, as if she were carving some sign into the air.

Elinor felt a collective holding of breath amongst those with her. She watched, not knowing what to expect, her heart thumping.

Slowly, the dangling face stopped twirling and settled so that the dark, staring eyes, which had been quartering the forest, now faced towards the tree only a couple of hand's spans away from it. The sounds that had been coming from it dwindled almost into inaudibility.

Sky-Flower stepped out from behind the tree then and beckoned them with a quivering hand.

Stone rushed up and put his arms about her. She smiled up at him in triumph, though she was still shaking. 'I do not know how long it will lasst, me. But we have enough time, I think.'

Stone nodded. 'Brave girl, you,' he said softly.

Elinor could not help but peer up at the dangling guard. It seemed to be carved from wood, painted, with little bronze doo-dads nailed to it and the feathers trailing. Seen up close like this, staring blindly now at the tree bole, it did not appear especially impressive. But there was a feel to it, as if there slumbered in the thing some manner of malevolent watch-fulness – held at bay somehow by Sky-Flower's strange skills.

Elinor glanced across at Gyver, who was staring up at the guard. Feeling her gaze upon him, perhaps, he turned. 'A sstrange thing, thiss,' he said softly.

Elinor nodded.

Leaving the disabled guard behind, they crept ahead with great care. On hands and knees they crawled behind the length of a half-toppled beech, until Elinor was able to peer carefully round its rotting grey torso and get her first proper look at *their* camp.

They had found a partially opened space, then felled several trees and hacked away the stumps to form a largish, oval clearing in which they had pitched a number of tents. The tents – it must have been the startling hues of the tents she had glimpsed behind the guard's uncanny interference – were of varied and improbably bright colours, with rippling stripes and swirls of bright crimson and sky blue and purple, glowing green, charcoal black, and ochre.

Smoke rose up in twisting spirals from several camp fires, and there were men moving about – ordinary enough, human-looking men.

They were short and stocky, dressed in coarse-woven clothing as multi-hued as their tents. Even their hair was unexpectedly brimming with colour: Elinor saw long green locks on one man, and an intricately pattern-shaved, bright crimson beard on another. And they painted their faces with bright streaks of colour, too. She watched one of them squatting near a fire, using a little bronze hand-mirror to apply garish purple and green face paint in broad, careful stripes.

But despite this penchant for bright hues, they were a grim, violent-looking lot. All those Elinor could see went armed with what seemed to be heavy, short-bladed bronze swords – not just bronze-hilted as hers was, but with glimmering bronze blades. She had never seen anything quite like those blades; they did not have the cold sheen of ordinary iron, nor the bright mirror radiance of her own blade.

There were long war-spears as well, with leaf-shaped bronze heads, stacked in a cone against each other in the camp's centre. And she saw several men carrying crossbows.

On the side of the camp where Elinor and the others were hidden, there was a tent bigger and more ornately colourful – if that were possible – than the rest. From out of this a man emerged. Ducking through a red and green striped door-flap, he stood for a few moments, staring into the forest. His eyes were hard and sharp, and, for an uncomfortable instant, Elinor thought he must see her and her furred companions. But no. The tree cover was too thick.

His standing there like that, however, gave her a chance to study him.

He was bull-necked, thick with muscle about the arms and shoulders, and bow-legged. A squat helmet made from polished bronze and leather covered his head. A spray of short white feathers protruded from the helm's crest, bobbing lightly as the man moved. His face was flat and hard and set, as if he were unconsciously clenching his teeth. Two wide zig-zags of dark red ran from the brim of the helm across his forehead and down his shaven cheeks and chin. His eyes had been circled in chalk white, so that his visage appeared that of a staring demon's.

He wore a short-sleeved tunic and trousers – both crimson as a sunset – and knee-high leather boots. About his thick torso, he had an intricately plated bronze cuirass. One of the short-bladed swords hung from a sheath at his side.

The man's attire was noticeably finer than that of the other occupants of the camp, and he carried himself with an arrogant swagger. Elinor picked him for leader.

As confirmation, she saw two men approach him, to whom he issued a series of peremptory instructions. Then, waving them off, he lifted the tent flap and returned inside.

Elinor shivered, staring at the multi-hued tent into which the man had disappeared. He had the look of somebody who would do *anything* to get what he desired. She had known men like him, with the same kind of set face. That sort were quite prepared to plunge the world about them into bloody chaos if it suited their notion of how things ought to progress. Seer Skolt, in Minmi had been one such. And Iryn Jagga, the mad leader of the Ancient Brotherhood of the Light, another . . .

Elinor shuddered, remembering. She was well glad to have seen the last of the likes of Iryn Jagga.

But now she looked to face another such as he – only this time she at least had the benefit of experience behind her. And this man, for all his hard appearance, seemed to her a lesser foe than Iryn Jagga had been. Or, at least, less equipped to do damage.

'Will you russh down and kill them all now, you, with your bright blade?' young Swift asked her in a breathless whisper.

The fur-folk had drawn in tightly about her. The young men clustered about Swift looked at her expectantly.

Elinor shook her head. 'I wish to look, is all,' she told them in a soft whisper. 'Just to look. Then get safely away so we can think about what needs to be done and how best to do it.'

'But we are here, uss,' young Swift said. 'Why do you not kill them all *now*?'

'Sswift!' Stone hissed.

'There would be no point in my rushing down there, even if I wanted to,' Elinor began. 'My blade isn't . . .' But she could see Swift's eyes narrow, his face clench. After hearing Gyver's recounting of what she had done, the fur-folk seemed to think of the white blade as a miracle weapon, capable of anything. Try as she might, she had not yet been able to convince them otherwise.

'Give *me* the sshining ssword, then!' Swift said fiercely. 'And me, I will go down amongsst them and cut them down and be revenged for poor Lark'ss death, and Sstarbrow'ss!' He made a quick grab towards Elinor and tried to wrest the sword from its sheath.

She slapped his grasping hands away.

'Give it me!' he hissed.

'*Sswift!*' Stone called in a hissing whisper. The older fur-man shouldered his way between Swift and Elinor. 'You are acting like a ssick-in-the-head persson again, you!'

Swift opened his mouth in an angry snarl, flashing sharp teeth in his darkly furred face, then abruptly deflated. He looked at Elinor sideways. 'I . . . I am ssorry, me. But the anger rissess in me like like hot flamess, eating me up.'

Elinor nodded. She put a hand out to him. 'I understand. The anger rises in me, too.'

'Then why will you not usse your bright blade?'

'I will use it,' she assured him, 'but when the time is right.'

Swift looked at her, his face tight.

Elinor sighed. The white-bladed sword was no such miraculous weapon as Swift and the rest thought, and confronting these invaders of the fur-folk's forest would be no straightforward matter of rushing down into their camp and killing them. The world was not a simple place. But she knew there was no way to convey any of this properly to young Swift. He was too hurt and angry, too much the innocent. 'You must trust me,' she ventured, finally, not knowing what else she could say.

Swift blinked, took a hissing breath. He stared at her, his eyes locked with hers for a long moment. Then he nodded, slowly.

The fur-folk settled.

Elinor turned and focused her attention back to the camp below. She tried to put on a calm face, but her belly was knotted up tight. There were easily fifty or sixty men down there, all well armed with weapons far more dangerous than the fur-folk's chips of sharp stone and carved bone – not to mention the dangling guard-things and whatever else kind of uncanny, hidden protection such men might possess. The fur-folk, in their forest-innocence, had no way of truly grasping what had been thrust upon them.

Which was nothing less than a war of conquest, she reckoned.

The camp down there represented some sort of advance guard, she was sure. They had exactly the look of such. There would be more coming after, in greater numbers, well organized, well armed, violent and dangerous and bent on conquest. The poor forest folk would be overwhelmed.

If she was right in this surmise, the only option Elinor could imagine at the moment that seemed to guarantee the fur-folk's continued safety was to destroy these men completely, and thus prevent them from bringing back any intelligence of this part of the wild land.

Unless they could find some way – without bloodshed – to convince these improbably colourful invaders to depart and never return.

It did not seem likely.

Elinor put a hand to her sword's hilt and sighed. She had had enough of blood and death and killing to last her a long, long time. But she had committed herself – or been committed, or been channelled, or *used* by some Power or other,

136

or . . . or something – so that she was here now and involved irrevocably. She felt her guts churn. Whatever happened, it would be neither simple nor easy. And, in all likelihood, at least some of those here with her now would not live to see the end of it.

She looked down upon the invaders' camp, but there was nothing new to see, only the startlingly multi-hued tents and the men lounging about, looking to the care of their weapons or decorating themselves, eating, or conversing quietly in groups. There seemed nothing special in the offing amongst them this morning, and the whole set-up had an unlikely air of domesticity.

In the trees behind them, the invaders' uncanny guard-thing hung, disabled for she knew not how long.

'I've seen enough,' she said softly to Gyver. 'You?'

He nodded.

'Let's go back, then.'

Gyver reached out one of his strong, slim hands and gave hers a gentle squeeze. 'What musst be, musst be,' he said. He knew – they had shared too much for him not to – the unease that she was feeling . . . the blood and grief that had been, that would be . . . She gave his hand a squeeze, grateful for his quiet understanding.

'The waterss, they flow ass they flow,' Gyver went on softly. 'And sso with uss, alsso.'

Elinor gazed into his furred face. She had grown to know it so well, the slim triangular shape of it; the way his almost-purple lips drew back from his small, sharp, white teeth when he smiled; his dog's button nose; the liquid brown of his eyes. It had grown most dear to her, that exotic face of his. It had a bruised look, now.

They were his mother's words, those he had just said to her. She remembered. 'Your mother . . .' she said gently.

He nodded. 'Sso ssaid my mother, the wisse ssoul.'

They shared a long, silent look, their hands still entwined. Gyver's eyes filled with tears. He blinked them away, and they dribbled down the sleek fur of his cheeks. Elinor reached across and hugged him silently. There was nothing to say, nothing that needed saying in words. They had known grief together already.

137

After a little, they separated.

Turning to the waiting fur-folk, Elinor said, 'Let us go.'

Silently, they all slipped off back through the trees.

XIII

Scrunch found the winding little track where it cut up across the side of a steep hill. Upthrusts of old stone showed between the trees. Rounding one of these, he saw that the track kept on over the hill's crest.

Rearing up on his hind legs, he peered ahead. Day and night, he had travelled, and now the sky was beginning to be lit by a new dawn. He was getting close; this track was proof of that. It was a humanimal track, moving with its own rhythm – where human tracks tended to barge blindly through the landscape, like human folk themselves.

Dropping down to all fours once again, Scrunch continued on. He could feel the rightness of this path. It went just so, along the impalpable way that it ought. Not the most direct route, but the rightest. One of the flow-ways, this, where currents met and became strong. Walking it, one did not tire. Walking it, one felt one's self grow solid. Walking it, one felt the world grow strong and clear inside one.

The light was growing now, and the going was easier. Long travel by night was demanding, for though he could see fairly well in the dark – better than human folk at any rate – he had to go mostly by intuition, letting his feet feel their way, letting the night into himself, keeping himself poised. It took concentration. His head throbbed.

Almost, he had missed the route to this pathway. He had been so caught up in his own mindscape at the beginning of this journey, so intent on memory – on little Anstil and the problem with the human folk and everything – so intent on gauging events against hopes and fears, that he had nearly blinded himself.

Scrunch sighed. He had been spending altogether too much time amongst human folk.

With every step along this path now, though, he felt lighter. It felt good under his feet. He felt . . . right.

The track dipped down into a little hollow and through a thicket of thorny trees. Scrunch was larger than whoever it was had originally made this track, and he had to duck his head against the prickly thorn-barbs and push a way through, relying on his thick fur to protect him. The track's current made it easy, however, and the trees seemed almost to slide obligingly aside for him.

Once on the far side he padded onwards along the hillslope, slipped between a brake of old oaks. The ground was becoming more rocky now, with the tree cover giving way to hummocky meadow scattered with shoulder-high clumps of tart-scented brush. Scrunch followed the track, which took him up over the crest of yet another hill and down slantingly to the other side. A little lake lay ahead, bordered by a fringe of trees. Near the lakeshore there was a kind of grassy grotto, rock-rimmed, with a large, rounded mass of blue-grey, lichen-carpeted stone in the middle.

Scrunch paused. There was already quite a press down there, with more coming in by the moment. He heard a flutter of wings as a large white bird-person came spiralling in. Off to his left, a small shape loped through the grass. 'Greetings, friend bear,' a voice said softly.

'Greetings to you,' Scrunch replied. For a moment, he was not quite certain who it was who had thus hailed him. Then he recognized the smallish, dark, quick-moving form of Illna, whose ancestors might once have been otters, but who detested the water herself.

And still there were more furred and feathered folk arriving.

Scrunch went down.

Those already gathered greeted him softly. He nodded and greeted them back. The feeling was subdued, quiet. It was a special place, this little grotto-by-the-lake. Hidden currents met here. Hidden Powers met. All who came here sensed such things clearly.

Perhaps three dozen humanimal folk were arrived. It was rare that so many came together in one place. It was rare that a council such as this one was called. Though this would hardly be called a 'council' in the way human folk would use the word. An ingathering, rather.

Scrunch gazed around him with interest. It was a varied group. Most here were ordinary-enough-seeming feathered or furred creatures, indistinguishable from their simpler, unmindful cousins in shape. But a number had no counterparts at all in the ordinary world – like the pale, hairless hyphons.

Scrunch knew many here, either personally or by sight, but he did not recognize all by any means. And there were some of the wild folk here, come out of the hills for this gathering – so wild, some of those, that they had never so much as seen a human being. There was even one of the great, scaly green swan-lizards, who lay silent on his belly, stubby legs tucked under him, wings quivering, blinking slowly.

There was little in the way of talk. Most waited silently, singly or in groups of two or three. For days now, Scrunch knew, they had been trickling in here to this place.

It was a good place. He felt how the deep currents of the world met here, echoing in the slow-moving rocks that thrust themselves up towards the sky, in the green-singing grass, and in themselves, mixed creatures that they were. Against the side of an upthrust of blue stone near the grotto's verge, a face had been scribed. Female it was, part-human and part-animal, long and slender of chin, pointy-eared, with overlarge eyes.

Scrunch went up to it and dipped his head in a little bowing motion. He felt the fur along his back and neck rise in a shiver as some subtle thing passed through him. 'Be with us this day, Lady,' he said softly.

Whoever had cut the Lady's image into the rock had managed to catch the sense of her in just a few lines, the deep eyes, the deepness of her entirely. Scrunch felt his heart beat a little quicker. It had been long since he had last gazed upon the Lady's image, and longer still since she had visited him in his dreams. He understood not at all who or what she might be – except that she was, somehow, the shape of their hope, of their deepest need. There were Powers and Powers. The world was no simple place.

But seeing her image like this brought back to him many things that had dimmed in his mind: the great tightness of the world that foreboded some momentous shift, the great hope they all had of finding a place for themselves, the long, hard story of humanimal existence, the precariousness of their hold upon the world, where there were so many who wished to see them destroyed. It was disturbing and exhilarating at once, that rush of renewed awareness, for he felt both the anguish and the hope, as if he walked the thin spine of some high peak, with black ruin on one side and bright thrivance on the other.

Scrunch let out a long breath, bowed his head to the image once again, and backed slowly away.

Blinking, he gazed about. There was no obvious time for such a meeting as this to begin. They could not schedule one particular instant in advance, as human folk did, as the start. When it was time to begin, they would begin. Meanwhile, they waited.

Scrunch lay down against a rock and gave himself over to basking in the warmth of the new sun, to feeling the good current of this place seep through him, to letting his mind settle into a tranquil blur.

It was an absolute pleasure to do so.

It fell, eventually, upon Scrunch to begin. He was one of the oldest here – having, he reckoned, counted his fortieth summer this season – and had had more to do with human folk, especially in the past year or so, than most.

When, eventually, the moment felt right, he clambered slowly up upon the lichen-covered rock that stood in the midst of the clearing, feeling the soft shiver of the world's current move through the stone under him, through his own bones.

It was well into the afternoon by now, with the sun half hid by clouds. There was the scent of rain in the air, but distant still. Scrunch did not know how many humanimal folk had arrived, but they filled up the little natural bowl of the grotto. He took a long breath, and another, trying to re-focus his mind to sharpness. He did not especially relish his role here as spokesperson: too many folk – human and humanimal alike – had taken to relying on him, as if his strength were always going to be enough for any task. He knew it was not so. He had seen the end of his strength once already and nearly died of it.

But there was none else here at the moment who could shepherd this gathering. 'I am Scrunch,' he said, beginning. 'Most of you know me, or know of me.'

There was a general attentive murmuring. There would be disagreement here, Scrunch knew that. But, unlike human meetings, this one would have little in the way of shouting or violent argument – for which Scrunch was properly thankful. Such mental confrontation was simply too jarring for most humanimal folk, leaving them dizzy and sick in their guts.

'We have come here because the world is changing,' Scrunch said. 'The Powers move. And we must move with them.'

'Something draws near, near, near,' a small voice spoke up.

Scrunch looked over to see who it was: Spandel. He had not known the little lamure would be here for this meeting, had not seen her in a very long time. Spandel was a Dreamer, open to the world's deeps, and most special. She had grown up in the cramped stone maze of Minmi City, Scrunch knew, companion to mad Lord Mattingly, and only Elinor's arrival had broken her free. Now she spent her days roving the wild, coasting the world's currents, dreaming her dreams.

Spandel stood on the fringe of those gathered here, reared up on her slender hind legs so that she could see above the backs of those near her, one long furred arm out for balance. 'Something draws near, near,' she repeated. The eyes in her furred face were wide and serious.

'What *ssomething*?' a voice demanded.

From the opposite side of the grotto from Spandel, a large cat emerged. He was golden-furred, with up-sticking, tufted ears and hard green eyes. A long scar marred the smoothness of his fur, running like a black crease from his cheek, down his neck, and across his shoulder to his ribs. 'What iss thiss ssomething that comess?' he repeated, his voice a soft, hissing whisper.

Spandel looked at him. 'Something terrible. Terrible and wonderful . . . a long, falling music which draws, draws us all together.'

The cat hissed softly, kneaded the sod with his clawed forehands. 'And who, then, iss this *uss* you sspeak of?'

Spandel gestured to all those about them. 'All here. All

143

those who did not, could not, would not be here. And the human folk.'

The cat spat. 'The ansswer,' he said, 'doess not lie with human folk.'

'Are we then to pretend they do not exist?' demanded one of the hairless hyphons.

'We have our own desstiny,' the cat insisted. 'We receive only grief from humanss. Can you deny that?'

'I deny it,' Scrunch said. 'We have received grief at their hands, yes. But not *only* grief.' He thought of little Anstil. 'Human folk have such solidity. We can learn from that. And they are more complex and more . . . more aware than perhaps we think.'

'We can be desstroyed by that ssolidity of theirss,' said the cat softly. 'They are like rockss againsst which we will break oursselvess.'

'What of the promise of the Lady?' one of the dogs present said. 'And Elinor Whiteblade?'

'Elinorrr Whitebladde hasss deserteddd usss!' It was one of the feathered folk who spoke, a draggle-tailed crow. 'Shee caresss noo morre forrr ourrr welfarre thannn doesss anny otherrr humann.' The crow glared at Scrunch out of one bright black eye. 'Stupiddd bearrr! She'lll onlyyy bringgg usss to griefff. I alwayss saiddd thattt!'

Scrunch shook his head. He well knew this bird. 'Not true, Otys. Elinor is the chosen of the Lady, and special.'

The crow made a *kawing* sound of derision. 'Sspeciallll? Wherre arre alll yourrr finne hoppesss, thennn?' Otys demanded. 'Isss liffe ssoo perrfecttt withhh the humannsss backk attt the Settlementtt, thennn?'

'How would you know what life with the human folk is like?' Scrunch returned. 'You who are around so seldom.'

Otys hop-flapped closer to Scrunch. 'I ammm arounddd enoughhh. I hearrr whattt goesss onnn, frienddd bearrr. Elinorrr iss gonne. The humannn folkkk risse in angerrr againsttt youu.'

To that, Scrunch said nothing.

'Elinorrr hasss deserteddd you alll! Alll yourrr hoppesss offf findinggg a placce in the worlddd alongsidde the humannn folkkk havve comme too naughttt!'

144

There was a general, uncertain murmuring from the gathered group.

'The Powers are moving,' Scrunch said by way of response. 'We all know that. We all *feel* that. There is the Lady's long promise, which we have all felt beginning to stir. And Elinor is . . .' Scrunch paused. 'Who amongst us can know what a human such as Elinor Whiteblade is. She is a focus, a channel through which currents move. Yet she is herself also, a human woman. She left us, indeed. But she had a kind of *need* upon her. We all know about such *needs* . . .'

The dog who had spoken earlier came forward. 'I say we must include the human folk in our lives. We must become more like them.'

'They are blind and deaf to the world. Do you wissh to become ass *that*?' the scarred golden cat said.

'Dim-sighted in some ways they may be, perhaps,' the dog returned. 'But they . . . they *made* us, so long ago. Have you all forgotten that? We are made in their image, at least in part. How can we ever turn our backs upon them? They hold the answer for us. They are so *solid* in themselves. We must learn from that.'

'We can be broken by that, I ssay,' the cat insisted.

'We will be broken, broken, broken by that which draws near,' said Spandel, 'if we turn our backs upon it.'

'How do *you* know sso certainly what drawss near into the world?' the cat demanded of her.

'I dream dreams,' Spandel said simply.

There was silence then, for long moments.

Then the great swan-lizard spoke up for the first time, lifting his naked green wings as he spoke. 'My folk and I have little to do with humans. And we would not wish to change that. But the world *is* changing. As the small Dreamer here has said, something draws nigh for us all. And whether or not we feel to, we must change with the world, or be lost entirely.'

'What are you suggesting, then?' somebody demanded. 'That we try to become as the humans?'

'No,' the swan-lizard said. 'There is no easy answer. But we in the wild have felt the world tremble. We are not Dreamers, but some of us have had dreams, good and bad. There is something coming. It is best we prepare ourselves.'

145

There was a disquiet stirring.

'Something is coming. Yes.' This from the furless hyphon. 'We can all feel it. The world changes. But it is not only *we* who must change. The humans must also. And will they? *Can* they?'

The hyphon turned to Scrunch. 'Friend bear, you have spent much time amongst them. What do you feel? Can the human folk change?'

Scrunch took a breath. 'I do not know. There are times . . .' he thought of angry, complaining Olundar and those that followed him, 'when I feel they are incapable of it, when I feel that their very solidness of mind renders them too brittle to change.'

'Ssee!' the scarred cat said in quick triumph. 'It iss ass I ssay. The humanss are too unbending, too hard, too blind and deaf to be of any help to uss. They will break usss if we rely upon them. I ssay we musst forssake them forever. Join our coussinss in the wildss and make a new life for oursselvess there. Free of human taint.'

A little murmur of agreement met this, but it was far from being a majority.

'We cannot simply run away,' said the dog.

'Why not?' somebody asked from the fringe.

'We have a new life building alongside this human Settlement.'

'Oh yess? And how iss thiss "new life" sso wonderful, then?' demanded the cat.

'We may come and go as we like,' the dog answered. 'None would harm us. They allow us to partake of their food—'

Otys the crow *kawwed* scathingly. 'Sso thisss wonderfulll liffe you boasttt offf amountsss too the humannsss allowinggg youu – *allowinggg* youu – to eattt theirrr fooddd. Butt attt whattt cossttt?'

Scrunch held up his forehand. 'You did not let me finish my answer,' he said. 'I was asked if I thought human folk could change.'

'And you ssaid no,' the cat put in quickly.

Scrunch shook his head. 'I said there are times when I feel human folk cannot change. But there are other times when I feel they *can*. And the young amongst them may be full of a promise that we have overlooked. On my way here, I saw one of their young find and follow the hidden contour of the land, sensing the under-current of the world.'

The gathering stared at him.

'Iss thiss . . . true?' the scarred cat demanded.

Scrunch nodded. 'I was there. I witnessed it. It . . . astonished me.'

Otys the crow *kaw-kawed*. 'Blinddd chancce!' he said.

'No.' Scrunch leaned forwards. 'She found the way, this little human girl. She found it true. There is more to human folk than I knew. And I know them better than most here. Or thought I did.'

'But this changes everything!' somebody said excitedly.

'It changess nothing,' the cat insisted. 'One human girl-child sstumbless acrosss a pathway. Sso what?'

'So the world changes,' the swan-lizard said.

'No!' the cat spat. 'The sstumblingss of one lone girl change nothing!'

Otys lifted his black wings and squawked. 'Anddd the ressttt offf the humannsss?' he demanded of Scrunch. 'Howww doo theyyy feelll aboutt thiss *sspecialll* girlll youu telll usss abouttt?'

Scrunch shifted uneasily.

Otys opened his beak and let go a raucous laugh. 'Telll usss, frienddd bearrr. Telll usss howww happyyy ittt makess the humannsss to seee thiss girlll walkk ourrr pathsss.'

'They . . .' Scrunch began. He sighed. 'They do not know. It is . . . is not simple, living with human folk.'

Otys laughed his raucous laugh once more. 'Humannsss willl nottt alterrr. Theyyy willl stoppp thiss girlll whennn theyyy find outtt. Anddd therre willl bee no thanksss too youu forrr havinggg shownnn herr the hiddennn waysss. Youu werre maddd too doo suchhh a thinggg. Onlyyy grieff cannn comme frommm ittt. Forrr thiss girlll. Forrr alll of usss!'

'Grief . . . perhaps,' Scrunch agreed soberly. 'But perhaps something else may come of it, too. Are you, then, *so* certain you know the shape of the world, Otys?'

The crow made no reply save a soft, dismissive croak.

'The world changes,' one of the dogs said.

'Changes, changes, changes,' echoed Spandel.

The gathering went quiet for a little at that, each digesting this news Scrunch had brought them, feeling the soft surge of the current of this place where they were met, feeling the mysterious tightness that was still in the world, the feeling of something borning.

'We are blind,' the cat said eventually.

'Does the bird tell the wind which way to blow?' demanded the hyphon.

To that, the cat made no answer.

Scrunch regarded the gathering. 'Is there any consensus?' he asked them.

There was no response.

'Very well, then,' Scrunch said. 'No consensus.'

In a human gathering, Scrunch knew, such a conclusion would have been entirely unsatisfactory. Human folk needed closure, needed decision, needed form and control and goals to be reached. Here, there would be none such. Here they had exchanged ideas, seen each other. It was enough. It would have to be.

Scrunch swung his head, surveying the gathering. 'Is there anything anybody else wishes to express?'

There was a little soft murmuring, nothing more.

Scrunch nodded. 'Very well, then.' He lifted his forehand. 'It has been suggested that we meet here again at the next new moon. Is this agreed?'

A general murmur of affirmation made it so.

'We are finished for this time, then,' Scrunch concluded.

At that, the humanimals began slowly to trickle away. There was no ceremony, no formal process of of disbandment. Such was not their way.

Scrunch stayed as he was, atop the blue-grey rock mound at the grotto's centre, watching them gradually disperse. He sighed softly. He felt so many ways at once, his mind was sore. Why did the world have to be such a terribly complex place? Why were there never any easy answers?

All the promise that had been implicit in their following Elinor and the rest out of the valley and into the wild hills had come to . . . what? He was not sure. Otys, in his scathing way, had set his beak to a sore spot: aside from food-sharing, what was so special about this new life of theirs? It was a life without violent bloodshed, true. At least so far. But was that all there was for them, then? Was life to be only food and the avoidance of pain?

And what of little Anstil and what she had done? And what of her parents and the other human folk – so solid and fixed in their intent – who had forbid contact between their children and the humanimals?

And what of Elinor?

And what of the . . . *something* that lay aborning in the world?

And . . .

Scrunch shook his head. There was too much. He did not know how to make sense of it all.

He wished Elinor would return. He wished the *something* that was hovering would come into the world. He wished there was not so much weighing upon him. He wished life were . . . simpler.

XIV

Ziftkin shivered, hugged himself for warmth as best he might. His back ached, his jaw did too. The wagon in which he sat lurched and rattled, and he braced himself with an elbow. Beside him, a man snored. How the fellow could sleep in this heaving vehicle was beyond him.

It was the bleakest moment before the first breath of dawn, with the sky cold and black and crackling with stars. His breath made little clouds before his face.

Three days, now, he had been travelling like this with the Lady Evadne Gault's retinue of rattling wagons and horsemen – three days, and now through the night as well. Actonvale was left far behind, and they were drawing up into a range of foothills southwards, where Gault Keep was located, with great peaks looming in the distance eastwards as they skirted the verge of the wild lands, bumping along erratic cartways and trader tracks . . .

And not once had he caught even a momentary glimpse of the beautiful Lady Evadne.

Ziftkin sighed wearily and shifted to a slightly less uncomfortable position. He stroked the smoothness of the bone flute, cherishing its faint, reassuring warmth, and tried to keep his mind from worrying at things. It was not what he had anticipated, this: nobody so much as saying a word to him, travelling hastily through the night, nearly killing the poor horses. No. Not what he had anticipated at all . . .

Gault Keep turned out to be no more than a single, squat tower of red stone. It looked old and grim, in the grey light of new-morn, perched like a spire atop a stone crest. The road wound steeply up to it like a dirty ribbon laid across the intervening slopes. The wagon-horses blew a long, sighing breath and put their shoulders into the harnesses to make the last grade homewards.

Their small cavalcade unloaded in a walled-in entrance yard. Gault Keep might be only a single squat tower, and not overlarge-looking from the distance, but Ziftkin had failed to take into account the dwarfing effect of the mountain scenery.

Gault Keep was huge.

It towered high above his head, solid as a very mountain. The big red stone blocks it was fashioned from were age-roughened and flecked with dark blotches, which, when Ziftkin examined them, turned out to be the remains of small, fantastic-looking creatures seemingly frozen into the very stone itself. He stared at one such image; like a beetle it was, but almost the size of his hand, with a ribbed carapace and hooked feelers distending from its blunt head. It made him shiver, to look at such a strange thing trapped forever in the stone.

'You, songster!' a voice called to him.

Ziftkin turned and saw a man he recognized as the Lady Evadne's grey-haired companion from Actonvale.

'There's a room prepared for you,' the man said. 'Get you to it.'

'Where is . . . where is the Lady Evadne?' Ziftkin asked.

'Busy, boy.' The man gestured Ziftkin on. 'Now be off with you. Somebody will—'

'Rath Kerri,' a voice called. 'They need you over by the East Door.'

The man nodded: 'Right. I'll be there in a moment.' He gave Ziftkin a one-armed shove, sending him reeling. 'That way. Through the door there. Now hurry!'

Ziftkin put a hand to the rough, cold stone of the Keep wall to steady himself. 'But—'

'Rather Kerri!' the voice called again. 'They need you!'

'But me no buts, boy,' the man said to Ziftkin. 'Just go!' With this, he turned and loped away.

Ziftkin stayed where he was, his heart thumping, utterly uncertain. If he could only catch a glimpse of Evadne . . . But

151

all about him there was only the chaos of unloading, horses neighing and straining against their traces to be freed, men and woman calling out, goods and wagons and freed animals tracking back and forth.

'You the songster?' somebody said to him. A lad about his own age it was, scruffy and pimply faced. 'Rath Kerri sent me to make sure you was safely put away.'

Ziftkin blinked. 'Put . . . away?'

'Aye,' the other replied. 'Got to get you hidden away right quick like. Else the surprise will be no surprise at all.'

'What . . . surprise?' Ziftkin asked uneasily.

'Why, you playing in the Great Hall, of course. For all them guests.'

'What guests?'

The other boy looked at him quizzically. 'What *are* you going on about? Tonight. In the Great Hall. It's the summer Gathering. When all the ruling Families of the Northern Dales meet. You only just managed to get here in time, you lot. Tonight's the Commencement.'

The boy shook his head: 'Travelling must've addled your head.' He shrugged. 'Well, come on, then. I'll show you to the room that's made ready for you. Where's your baggage?'

'I . . . I haven't got any.'

'Well . . .' the other said, pausing uncertainly. Then he shrugged again and gestured at the bone flute Ziftkin held cradled against his chest for safety. 'As long as you've got your instrument, nothing much can be amiss, right? I'm sure you'll be properly supplied with a costume to wear. Now come along. And be quick! Or it's *me* that'll catch the trouble. Come *on*!'

Ziftkin stumbled after him through the crowded yard.

He felt dizzy. The summer Gathering . . . He had heard about such in his days at Seshevrell Farm. But it was a distant business. Seshevrell was an independent steading, on the far northern fringes of the Dale Families' influence. But now . . .

He had never dreamed, when the Lady Evadne Gault had first commanded his services for a gathering her father was preparing, that the gathering she had in mind was this one. She must, indeed, think very, very highly of him. It was more than he could have hoped.

If a man played well before such a gathering of powerful folk, his future was made, surely. From no-account farm boy to songster to the great Families. No less than that lay ahead for him. Songster to the beautiful Lady Evadne herself. And more, perhaps. The very thought of it made his hands begin to shake.

His guide led him up a short, worn set of stone steps into the Keep. Dim and cold it was inside, with a pervasive stone chill that made Ziftkin shiver. Up more steps they went, a curving wooden staircase this time, black with age, and thence along a series of lamp-lit corridors until they came to a smallish wooden door.

'Here,' his guide said. 'This one's yours.' He swung the door open and gestured Ziftkin inside. 'Fire's lit. Food and drink on the table. Make yourself at home.'

Ziftkin stepped into the room, ducking through the low doorway.

A fire crackled in the corner fireplace, and the room was warm and scented pleasantly with the odour of burning pine. Heavy woollen hangings covered the stone walls from floor to ceiling. A pair of thick-paned, narrow windows looked out over a courtyard and stables below. There was a wooden chest against the far wall, a narrow bed across from it, and a wine-red rug strewn on the flagstone floor.

Dim in the still early morn and a-glimmer with the fire, the room seemed a cosy place, better than anything Ziftkin had experienced in a long, long while.

He turned back to his guide, but the lad was gone. Stepping out into the corridor, Ziftkin looked about. Nothing. He sighed wearily. He wished things could just somehow be . . . normal.

He returned to the room, shutting the door behind him, and went to stand in front of the fire. Its warmth was a comfort, for he was shivering with the Keep's pervasive stone-chill and with the body-memory of the long, cold, sleepless night he had just passed. He ached from the three-day journey here.

A little side-table stood near the fireplace. Upon it, he saw a flagon, and a large pewter dish of what looked like soft cheese and brown bread and butter. He drank from the flagon, finding it to contain simple water, but crisp and clean. The cheese was richly flavourful, the butter fresh as could be asked, and the bread nutty and chewsome. Altogether, he could not think of a better way to break his fast.

When he was full, he turned from the table with a yawn and went over to examine the narrow bed. It was clean, hard, and coverless. But the wooden chest against the wall proved to contain a pair of thick eiderdown blankets. He flung these over the bed and nestled in between them, the flute at his side.

He thought of the Lady Evadne, of her raven-black hair, her flashing eyes. Surely, she must think him very special to have brought him here for the summer Gathering. It seemed almost too good to be true. But what could go wrong? All he need do would be to play well. And on his father's gift-flute, he knew he could play very well indeed.

It all seemed to form a pattern of sorts, when he looked back upon events: his leaving Seshevrell was like a fledgling bird leaving its nest for the wide world. And though his dreams of finding a father had come to naught, he had come away with a future in his hands. There were far worse patrimonies. Perhaps his father was wiser than he could know.

And now the wide world had begun to welcome him. He was alone no longer, and the miseries of Seshevrell would become no more than faint memories.

A whole new future.

If only Malinda were here to see.

Poor Malinda, who lay mouldering under the black dirt, food for worms . . .

Ziftkin blinked back the tears. It did not bear thinking on, his mother's bleak life, her untimely dying. With a weary sigh, he rolled over, hugging the warm blankets about him, and let himself drop away slowly into blessed sleep.

It was mid-day when he awoke.

He ached still, and his eyes were gummed shut. But he felt better for having slept. Rolling stiffly out of the bed, he built up the fire – for the room still felt stone-chilly – then went over to the side-table and drank from the water flagon and had a bite of the remaining bread and cheese.

He had until the evening to wait. Somebody would be sent to fetch him, he supposed. And in the meantime?

He stuck his head out the door and found an armed guard standing there, a grey-grizzled man in a stout leather helm and cuirass. A short, heavy blade hung at his side.

'Back inside, boy,' the guard said, though not unpleasantly.

'But I'd like to—'

The guard pushed Ziftkin inside with the flat of his hand. 'My orders are to make sure you keep your head down and that nobody sees you. You just be a good lad and do as you're supposed to. And then neither of us will have any grief over this. You understand me?'

Ziftkin hesitated, then nodded and retreated back inside. The guard shut the door after him with finality.

Ziftkin was not sure what to think. Why such elaborate precautions to keep him here? Was he a . . . prisoner, then?

But no. Silly thought. He was to play for the great Families. Such folk had no need to to kidnap songsters. He shrugged. There must be some perfectly simple enough explanation. The ways of the great Families were complex. Everybody knew that. What mattered was that he was to play.

Ziftkin picked up the flute, feeling again the strange, faint warmth of it under his touch. Should he rehearse? What ought he to play at such a gathering as tonight's? Would the country tunes his mother had taught him be appropriate?

He had a sudden and altogether disconcerting image of himself standing before the gathered Families, and them laughing at him in his ragged clothing, laughing at his silly, simple, farm-boy tunes.

But, surely, they would have special clothing prepared for him to perform in – Family Gault would let no songster they retained perform in rags while under their patronage. And as for what he might play . . .

Ziftkin lifted the flute. The golden-ochre of the old bone caught and held the dancing light of the fire. It felt like a live thing, almost, in his hand. He could play more, far more than mere country ditties on an instrument such as this.

He lifted it to his lips and blew a soft note, another. He tried to let his mind go empty, to let the resonant notes of the bone flute come through of their own accord, if they would.

His fingers danced a slow dance . . . following his bidding, or moving as they were bid by the mysterious influence of the flute – he could not tell. But a melody began to emerge. A soft intricacy of notes interwoven like an elegant tapestry. Or like . . . like the white lace of the waves on a lake shore, moving and changing with each new wave's arrival, always changing, yet always the same interweaving pattern.

Soon he was deep in the thrall of it, lost entirely to aught else, repeating it, making it his own, fine honing the results.

'So . . .' a voice said from behind him.

Ziftkin whirled, startled. The voice belonged to a short, stout woman, swathed in a huge woollen skirt and head scarf, who stood in the open doorway of his room. 'So they weren't lying after all. I haven't *never* heard music like *that* before!' She shook her head in wonderment, looking up at him. 'Murtrude was right. You *do* look just like a heron, standing there on those long skinny legs of yours.'

Ziftkin stiffened.

'Sorry. Sorry, ducky,' the woman said hastily and made a warding sign with her fingers. 'Didn't mean no offence. You know what women's tongues are like. Murtrude, now *there's* a woman with a tongue on her. Never still, it is. She told me all about you. Heard it from one of the waggoners, she did. He's sweet on her. Brings her gifts whenever he goes out. She told me—' The woman stopped, shrugged her shoulders and smiled up at him, showing stumpy yellow teeth. 'Oh, I *do* run on so. Didn't mean to creep in on you, but I *did* knock on your door and you didn't answer, and so I opened it and there you was playing away like *anything*, and I just *couldn't* help myself really, so I stepped in, quiet like, so as not to disturb you, and just listened.'

Ziftkin said nothing. He was not at all certain what to make of this woman. And he did not know what to think of the warding sign she had made. He was not used to folk making warding signs at him.

'I was told to come here,' the woman said a little nervously, faced with Ziftkin's continued silence, 'by the Lady Evadne herself.'

'Has she asked for me, then?' Ziftkin demanded eagerly. He stepped forwards, hoping to be led into the Lady Evadne's presence, though this prattling woman seemed an odd emissary indeed. Instead of leading him anywhere, though, she bustled into the centre of the room trailing a large duffle bag behind her.

Ziftkin stood, nonplussed. 'Has the Lady Evadne asked after me?' he repeated.

The woman shrugged. 'Well . . . no. Not exactly. But she's sent me here to prepare you.'

'To see her?'

The woman nodded: 'Eventually.' She put her duffle bag down and made a little curtsey to him, surprisingly graceful for all her bulk. 'Ramona Dimphna Touree, that's my name, deary. But you can just call me Ramona.' She chuckled. 'My old mother never *could* make up her mind about anything, bless her . . .

'Now then, let's get started.'

'Started?'

'Yes,' Ramona said impatiently. 'We must get you ready for *tonight*.'

Ziftkin just stood there.

'Come *on* now, deary, don't dither me about.' All Ramona's uncertainty seemed gone now, and she fussed importantly around the room, laying out things from the bag.

'I don't . . .' Ziftkin began. 'Why are you . . .'

'Hasn't nobody told you? We've got to get you dressed up.'

Ziftkin stepped forwards. He saw she was pulling out a large sewing kit from her duffle bag, lengths of cloth, something that looked like a bundled shirt. He sighed relievedly. Everything was as he had hoped after all: he would be properly fitted out for the night's performance.

Ramona reached a hand to him and pulled him closer. 'Come on, deary. We've a *lot* to do to get you prepared.'

'. . . and one thing I've learned over the past thirty years of serving them,' Ramona was saying, taking tucks in the voluminous gold lamé pantaloons that Ziftkin stood in, 'is that Family Gault *always* have a good reason for doing what they do. And if they *insist* that you wear that tunic and these pantaloons . . . why, then, deary, you *wear* them. And no questions asked neither, mind you. *I* don't know what they have in mind but it's sure to be something *important*.'

157

Ramona stood back a moment to survey her work, then went back to it. 'This is the twenty-third Gathering of the Families I've been attendant to, deary. And the *stories* I could tell! Curl your hair, they would. Some of the things they *do* get up to . . . Touchy and quarrelsome as cats in heat, they are. There's always somebody trying to do *something* to somebody else. Keeps your head spinning, it does.

'I remember one Gathering ten years ago – or was it eleven? No, ten it was. Anyway, the Lord Ipsomn had been shamed by that sulky daughter of his. A *right* little minx she was too in those days. And she'd run off with some dandy who she shouldn't have . . . though you only needed to take one look at the young man, he was *that* handsome, and you knew straight off why she'd run away with him . . . and him, Lord Ipsomn that is, was trying to atone for the whole thing, or so it looked, but actually he was plotting to get revenged on the family for who the young gentleman—'

'Enough,' Ziftkin spluttered. 'Enough, please, Ramona. My head is reeling!'

Ramona chuckled. 'I *do* go on a bit, don't I? What was it you asked me again?'

Ziftkin sighed. 'These clothes, Ramona. Remember? I asked you why I must wear this . . . this foolish-looking costume.' He turned and looked at her where she was kneeled down at his side pinning up the pantaloons. 'Why would the Lady Evadne want me to dress in—'

'I said I don't *know*, deary,' Ramona replied exasperatedly. 'But I *do* know better than to argue with *that* one. A right *fury* when she doesn't get her own way, that Evadne. I remember once, years ago, when she was just a slip of a girl, how she—'

Ramona stopped and shrugged. 'But I'm letting my tongue get away from me again. All *I* know, deary, is that I was told to get these clothes to fit you and to have everything ready by this evening. And if I *don't* have them ready in time, the young Lady Evadne will have me boiled alive!'

Ramona tugged at the pantaloons. 'Now shush for a moment and let me concentrate on getting this hem right.'

'Me?' said Ziftkin. '*Me* be quiet?'

'Just shush,' Ramona admonished him. 'And let me get my mind straight here.'

They were silent for a time, then, while Ramona finished pinning things together. Then eased the pantaloons off Ziftkin so she could tack everything into place, leaving him standing about self-consciously in his undergarments.

Ramona kept up her steady chatter, and slowly the tunic and gold lamé pantaloons began to fit Ziftkin. The tunic was awash in gaudy, patternless, multicoloured sequins.

Was this how all the songsters in this place dressed? Ziftkin wondered. He had no experience with the ways of the Lords of the ruling Families. But his heart misgave him.

'Come on, deary,' Ramona said, bustling into his room. 'The Lady Evadne has called for you.'

It was evening, the light beginning to fade outside.

Ziftkin stood nervously ready, dressed in the pantaloons and tunic Ramona had put together. He had bathed and washed his hair, which Ramona had done up in dozens of small, beribboned plaits. A floppy felt cap of startling green perched on his head, surmounted by a wavering fan of lacy feathers. On his feet were velvet booties of a shocking scarlet, with pointy toes sporting little jingling brass bells.

He ran a hand anxiously over the outrageous, sequined tunic. 'I feel utterly foolish,' he said, turning to Ramona and gesturing at the costume.

'But it fits you so *perfectly*,' Ramona replied, smiling.

Ziftkin could not help but smile back at her. He lifted his arms, twirled slowly about. The tunic and pantaloons did indeed fit well. 'Ah, Ramona, you do have a deft hand with a needle. There's no denying that.'

'Why thank you, kind sir,' she replied and curtseyed a most exaggerated and foolish curtsey.

She laughed, and Ziftkin laughed with her. It made him feel vastly better, somehow.

'Now come *on*,' Ramona said. 'The Lady Evadne has called for you and you don't want to keep *that* one waiting. She may be only a little slip of a thing but she's got more iron in her than most men I know.'

With leaping heart, Ziftkin lifted up the flute. Ramona draped him in a long, hooded, dark travelling cloak she had brought along, and then hustled him out of his room. The guard was nowhere to be seen now. There was only the empty, lamp-lit corridor. Ramona led him through the building into the courtyard outside. The place seemed utterly deserted. There was not a sound save their own soft footfalls and the *jinkle jinkle* of Ziftkin's belled booties.

Outside, the two of them stood in silence together, shivering a little, for the darkening air was chill, and a mountain wind whined in the eaves overhead. The first stars were out now, in a velvety, blue-black sky.

From the courtyard's far side, a man drew near them: Rath Kerri, the Lady Evadne's man, dressed in an elegant, dark suit and crimson cloak.

Ziftkin swallowed. He felt himself shaking with nerves.

Ramona put a pudgy hand on his arm. 'You'll be fine, deary. Better than fine. I know you will.'

He gazed across at her pudgy, pleasant features in the star-lit dark and smiled. 'Thank you,' he said softly. 'For everything. For your kindness.'

Ramona said nothing, merely patted his arm reassuringly.

Rath Kerri came padding up. Without a word, he gestured for Ziftkin to follow.

'I'll try and sneak round to hear you play,' Ramona whispered in Ziftkin's ear. 'Good luck!'

And then Ziftkin was off, walking by Rath Kerri's side along the rim of the Keep. Rath Kerri seemed grim and ill at ease. 'You are to do exactly what you are told tonight. Do you understand, boy?'

Ziftkin nodded. His stomach was fisted into a tight, nervous knot. Under the cloak, he flexed his fingers along the flute's length, slowly, rhythmically, trying to keep them from stiffening with nervousness.

'It is most important for the Lady Evadne that you do *exactly* what you are told,' Rath Kerri repeated. 'Is that clear?'

'Clear,' Ziftkin said, nodding, working his fingers.

They skirted the immense round wall of Gault Keep in silence then, save for the soft, insistent *jinkling* of Ziftkin's booties. Through a walkway in a high wall they went, then onwards until, eventually, Rath Kerri pulled Ziftkin in after him through a small oaken door.

From a nook in the wall, Rath Kerri took down a lamp and lit it. Then, the glimmering lamp held aloft, he led the way through a series of dark corridors and stairways, upwards, always upwards, till they ascended a long spiral stair and slipped through a door into a small, empty chamber.

'Stay here and keep quiet,' Rath Kerri ordered in a harsh whisper. 'And keep the cloak about you until I return.'

Ziftkin stood where he was, uncertain, his stomach wound up upon itself in uncomfortable knots.

Peering about, he saw that the small chamber in which he stood led on to another, larger, elongated one. And one entire wall of that elongated chamber was hung with a great length of embroidered curtain, from the other side of which he could hear the sounds of people eating and drinking, and the group murmur of talk.

He shivered in a sudden nervous spasm. This must be it, then, the Gathering itself. On the far side of that curtain, his future awaited him.

Ziftkin tried to calm himself. He thought on the music he would play for them – the flowing tapestry of notes he had imbibed from the flute. It was like nothing else he had ever heard before, like nothing they had ever heard before either, he was certain.

What kind of introduction would the Lady Evadne give him? What kind of reaction would he receive?

He flexed his fingers in a quick series of impromptu exercises, feeling the joints crackle softly. The cloak about him was too warm and he began to sweat.

The noise from behind the embroidered curtain rose in volume. Ziftkin could not distinguish individual voices, just the plural hum of the group, but something had changed. There was a different quality to the voices out there now, as if one phase of the evening was over and another beginning.

Rath Kerri returned, the Lady Evadne with him. She was dressed in a long, crimson velvet gown that *whished* softly as she walked. Her black hair was done up in an elaborate coiffure, and small sharp diamonds flashed brightly in a string about her bare neck and in her ears.

'A songster will be presented soon,' she said.

Ziftkin gazed at her, entirely tongue-tied.

The Lady Evadne gestured him impatiently to the curtains. 'Watch this songster carefully here from the wings. But do not show yourself. You understand.'

Ziftkin nodded uncertainly.

'I desire,' the Lady Evadne went on, 'that you play such tunes as will make this man's contribution seem childish and dull.'

'But—' Ziftkin began, alarmed.

'Is that clear?' the Lady Evadne demanded, cutting him off. 'Is that *clear*?' There was an icy edge to her voice that stilled any questions Ziftkin may have had. He nodded slowly.

'Good,' she said, and then was gone in a crimson swirl of velvet and cold diamond-glitter.

Rath Kerri stayed behind, leaned against the wall nearby. Ziftkin turned to him, would have asked questions, but something in the man's eyes kept him silent.

Then the curtains swept open. From his corner viewpoint, Ziftkin could not see all of the Great Hall, but what he could see was one huge, open space. Enormous, glittering candelabras hung suspended from shadowed ceiling beams. There were tables arranged together to form three sides of a rectangle. The stage itself formed the fourth side.

Peering carefully from his vantage point, Ziftkin saw attendants scurrying about removing the last remnants of a feast, and the Lords and Ladies of the Great Families stretching themselves, relaxing now in preparation for the entertainment. Some strolled about briefly, and here and there little knots of people clustered together in intense conversation. Ziftkin was reminded of Ramona's comments about the constant in-fighting that was a part of such a Gathering as this, and he could not help but wonder momentarily what intrigues they might be brewing amongst themselves.

An elegant young man with a carefully curled moustache clambered up onto the stage, which was raised almost a man's full height above the level of the banquet floor. He held up his hands, and silence slowly enveloped the Hall. 'Lords, Ladies,' he called, 'Family Acton is proud to have the honour of providing the entertainment for this year's Gathering. I

162

would like to publicly thank Family Gault, who have been so generous in their role as hosts.'

The young man smiled deprecatingly, stroked his curled moustache with a finger. 'They have done quite well, considering their inexperience with such matters and the limited resources they have at their disposal here in this forsaken mountainous hinterland they are forced to call their home.'

There was a brief moment of silence, then a smattering of applause. Next to him, Ziftkin saw Rath Kerri frown.

The elegant young man on the stage went on. 'We of Family Acton have prepared a wide selection of entertainers for you this evening, the best, the most talented to be found in all the Dales.'

He paused for a spattering of more applause. Then, 'To commence the evening's entertainment, Family Acton would like to present to you a fiddle player from our own House, a songster of sublime skill. Would you welcome, please, Master Kolin Grey!'

A neat, small man, middle-aged and portly, conservatively dressed in dark, loose-fitting clothing, appeared on stage and bowed low to the audience. More applause, slightly louder now, accompanied his entrance and the young Lord Acton's exit. The songster put a fiddle to his chin and began a slow, lilting tune.

'Watch!' Rath Kerri hissed in Ziftkin's ear. 'This is the man.'

Ziftkin looked closely. The songster on stage had a lovely old fiddle, dark with age. It had a sweet tone, pure and soft, well suited to the kind of tune now being played. But the tune the man played was subtly shaky in places. He was nervous.

A good fiddler, Ziftkin decided, but not a great one. The man had good tone but his speed and clarity of intonation were not all they might have been. And, as he continued to perform, Ziftkin realized that there was a certain sameness to the kinds of tunes he had chosen to play. They fit his style of playing and the strengths of his instrument but they lacked any real variety. And they were all unimpressively traditional.

It should not be too difficult to play better than this man. But the thought made Ziftkin uneasy. It was not right, this setting of one songster against another. He tried to back away, but Rath Kerri blocked his retreat, scowling.

Which left Ziftkin small option but to stand as he was and listen.

And then, half way through the fiddler's fourth tune, the Lady Evadne appeared suddenly on the stage. She stood, hands on her hips, and glared the poor fiddler into silence in mid-note.

'Be ready!' Rath Kerri said in a whisper, lifting off Ziftkin's concealing cloak. Ziftkin felt his pulse thud in his throat. What was going on?

'My Lords and Ladies!' Lady Evadne called out. 'Young Lord Acton calls this entertainment.' She stepped closer to the edge of the stage and leaned over towards the audience. 'I call it mere *foolishness*!'

For a long moment there was silence. Then a confused murmur of sound broke out.

'Why . . .' the Lady Evadne continued, before any could really catch up with the rapid change she had initiated, 'my foolish *harlequin* can play better than this . . . this buffoon here who Family Acton call a songster! But then, it is what I would expect from a man like the younger Acton, who is himself a buffoon.'

The noise in the Hall increased. The young Lord Acton was on his feet, shouting furiously from the far corner of the tables where he and his family sat.

Lady Evadne snapped her fingers.

'Now!' Rath Kerri said to Ziftkin, giving him a hard shove that sent him reeling unexpectedly into the middle of the stage.

Titters went through the audience.

Ziftkin stood there, the little bells on his booties *jinkling*, his face suffused with a flush of mortification.

The titters turned into guffaws. The sight of Ziftkin, tall and skinny, gangly and self-consciously awkward on the stage, dressed in his extravagant and tasteless lamé and sequined garb, sent the audience into peals of cruel mirth.

'Play for us, then, harlequin!' a voice called.

'Yes, play, you silly man. Play!'

The Acton Family fiddler stood, head held erect, offended dignity writ clearly across his features. He glared at Ziftkin and sniffed haughtily.

Ziftkin could hardly breathe. The whole hall was staring at him, laughing at him. A sudden nausea spiked through him and he had to swallow, hard, to keep from being wretchedly sick all over the stage.

'Play,' the Lady Evadne hissed, her face a mask of furious intent. '*Play!*'

Haltingly, Ziftkin lifted the bone flute to his lips, tried to blow a note, but only a flatulent *floob-ub-oob* came from the flute.

Ziftkin quivered in panic. Behind him, Lord Acton's fiddler snorted disdainfully.

'Play!' the Lady Evadne repeated.

Stinging sweat runnelled down into Ziftkin's eyes. His hands shook. He felt sick. He felt utterly ridiculous. He wanted to crawl away and find a hole to hide in.

The laughing, jeering faces before him seemed to throb and sway. 'Throw him out!' somebody cried. 'Ridiculous, parti-coloured goose of a man . . .'

Goose . . .

It was the same familiar insult that Ziftkin's foster brother Mechant and the rest had goaded him with back at Seshevrell Farm. *Goose!* A sudden thrust of white anger went through him.

So they thought they could push him around and make him feel the utter fool, did they, these oh-so-fine folk? They thought he was no more than some utensil to be used for their own ends and then discarded? Well, he would show them different!

He stepped to the front of the stage, lifted the flute, and let loose a stream of furious, liquid-pouring notes, then slid into a lightning-quick version of the new melody that had come to him through the flute earlier in the day. He played faster and faster, a storm of melody, faster still . . .

Ziftkin could not see it, but behind him the Lord Acton's fiddler faltered backwards, his eyes wide. The man's face betrayed a rapid series of emotions: incredulity, amazement, then something else, something much less pleasant.

The gathering in the Great Hall had fallen into a stunned silence, mouths open, enthralled by what they were hearing. Ziftkin felt a hot thrill of triumph. He would show them!

But as Ziftkin continued to play, Lord Acton's fiddler sidled across the stage towards him, his face contorted, as if the incredible, liquid intricacy of notes pouring from Ziftkin's bone flute was physically painful for him. Creeping up from behind, he gave Ziftkin a vicious shove in the small of his back that sent him tumbling down off the stage.

It seemed to Ziftkin that the floor hove up to strike him, like a great, wood-grained fist coming out of nowhere. By desperate instinct, he tried to protect the flute, twisting awkwardly sideways, hands up and out to hold it safe. He fell heavily on his face in a stuttering burst of light and pain, and then a black vice pressed all the breath from him and he sank into empty darkness.

XV

'Here,' Rath Kerri said, dropping a small leather pouch next to Ziftkin. The pouch clinked metallically as it hit the seat of the stone bench upon which Ziftkin sat.

Ziftkin was still groggy, and not sure how he had come to be here in this small, lamp-lit room, seated on this hard and uncomfortably chill stone bench. His head hurt. His face felt like one great, throbbing bruise. His ribs flared painfully with each breath.

'You will leave,' Rath Kerri continued. 'Before the sun rises.'

Ziftkin stared at him.

'A horse is being prepared by one of the stable grooms. When it is brought, you must depart.'

Ziftkin shook his head. 'But I cannot . . .' The words dwindled away when he saw the look on Rath Kerri's face.

'See things for what they are, boy.'

Ziftkin swallowed. 'But . . .'

Rath Kerri flung a bundle of clothes at him, then turned and walked to the room's closed doorway. Unlatching a small square viewing hole, he stood there, saying nothing, his back to Ziftkin, leaning against the door and staring out through the view hole into the night.

Ziftkin stood up quickly, too quickly, and was swept by a sudden sick dizziness. He sank back down, his head held in his hands, and groaned. He looked over to Rath Kerri. 'My flute,' he moaned. 'Where is my flute?'

'Get you ready,' Rath Kerri said, turning from the door. 'The groom will be here with your mount any moment now.'

Ziftkin struggled awkwardly into the clothes Rath Kerri had provided – trousers and loose tunic and boots – thankful to be out of his ridiculous sequinned costume. 'Where is my flute?'

he demanded. 'What's going *on* here? What are you suggest-ing? That I ride out of here in the dark like some—'

'You will do as you are *told*, boy.'

Ziftkin stared. Rath Kerri's face was stone.

The older man took a step away from the door, ran a hand wearily through his grey hair. His eyes were bloodshot. 'I would not have had it like this,' he began, not ungently. He shook his head and sat down next to Ziftkin on the cold stone of the bench. 'Look, lad . . . It may not feel like it to you at this moment, but you're one of the *lucky* ones. You've been paid – *well* paid. You have your freedom. Not all those the Lady Evadne takes into her service fare so well.'

He sat in silence for a little, letting Ziftkin take this in. Then he went on. 'What happened was . . . beyond what I foresaw. But what's done is done. Leave it be, now. Take what has been given you and get out while you may.'

Rath Kerri stood up, went once more to the door and peered through the view hole.

Ziftkin stared at him. 'I have nowhere to go. There is nothing for me. *Nothing!*' He rose from the bench, white-faced and stricken. 'All my future was here. I will not leave here. I will *not!*'

'You will do as you are *told*, boy!'

'Who are *you* to be telling me what I may and may not do?' Ziftkin demanded. 'It was the Lady Evadne who enlisted my services. Not *you*! I demand to see her. How do you think she will react when she learns you are keeping me from seeing her? I *demand*—'

Rath Kerri cut him off. 'Look, boy, I do this on my own. The Lady Evadne knows nothing of your departure.' He shrugged. 'And she will be furious when she learns what I have done.'

Ziftkin blinked in confusion.

'The Lady Evadne is young, with too much of the callous-ness of youth in her still. She wields power too easily. She would break you and discard you, boy.' Rath Kerri paused and looked at Ziftkin: 'A gift such as yours deserves better.'

'Better!' Ziftkin sputtered bitterly. 'You do me no *favour* by turfing me out into the middle of nowhere like this. I have nowhere to go!'

'I will not argue with you,' Rath Kerri said. 'Go, you shall. Will you or nill you. I'll cart you out bodily myself, if so it must be.'

Ziftkin ran a hand gingerly over his bruised face, took a breath. He felt himself sway as he stood. 'Where is my flute?' he demanded.

Rath Kerri shrugged. 'It was all I could do to get *you* out of the Great Hall. I had no time to fuss about looking for your instrument.'

'No time to . . .' Ziftkin stared, stricken. 'But I *must* have my bone flute! You don't understand. I . . .'

Rath Kerri came forward, put his hands on Ziftkin's shoulders, and looked him straight. 'You've been well paid, boy. You can buy yourself another, a better instrument. Take your freedom now and *go*.' Then, in a softer voice, he added, 'It is all I can give you.'

Ziftkin wrenched himself away and collapsed back onto the bench. His head throbbed. He felt nauseous. He could not seem to think clearly. 'My flute . . . I can't go anywhere without my flute!'

With a sudden bang, the door was flung open and a man stuck his head in. 'The horse is arrived.'

'Right,' Rath Kerri said. And then, to Ziftkin, 'Time for you to leave.'

'I'm not going,' Ziftkin said.

Rath Kerri frowned. 'Don't mess me about, boy.'

'I want my flute!'

Without a word, Rath Kerri grabbed Ziftkin up, wrenching his arm painfully behind his back in a quick, practised move, and marched him outside into the night. The hold on his arm was acutely painful, and Ziftkin found himself helpless. Any attempt on his part to resist merely prompted Rath Kerri to twist a little harder.

Across a small flagstone courtyard they went, until they came to where an old mare stood sleepily with a boy holding her reins. Rath Kerri put a foot between Ziftkin's legs and spilled him onto the flagstones.

Ziftkin sat up, shivering, feeling sick and bruised. He rubbed his misused arm, staring about desperately. The Keep loomed above them, a monstrous dark shadow-shape. The pre-dawn

169

stars hung in the sky, ice-white and still. A cold breeze riffled his bruised face.

There were men standing in the shadows behind Rath Kerri now, in support of him.

Rath Kerri pointed at the horse: 'Get up.'

Ziftkin shook his head stubbornly. 'I need my flute.'

Rath Kerri swore under his breath. 'Get on the horse, boy. Or do I have to have you thrown bodily into the saddle?'

'I need my *flute*!'

Rath Kerri gestured to the men behind him, who closed in. Ziftkin swatted at them, scrambling to his feet. But he could not withstand them. After a brief, fruitless struggle, he found himself flung roughly up into the saddle. He tried to slither back down, and received a smack on his bruised face that made his vision swim.

Rath Kerri glared up at him: 'Enough of your nonsense, boy.' He flung the purse onto Ziftkin's lap, where it landed with a soft, metallic *thunk*. 'Take this. There's food and water in the saddle bags. Now go.'

Ziftkin tried to lift a leg to get down, but Rath Kerri had a sword in his hand now. The naked iron of the blade shone coldly in the starlight. 'I'm trying to do you a service here, boy,' he said, his voice hard. 'Don't force me to something regrettable. Just *go*!'

Ziftkin stared at the blade, the tip of which was aimed at his guts. He felt his heart lurch.

Rath Kerri gave the horse a slap on her withers. 'Go!' he hissed.

The mare, out of sorts at having been rousted from her warm stall and subjected to all this heaving about, nickered irritably and kicked back at him, but he skipped nimbly out of the way. 'Go, you old nag,' Rath Kerri said, and slapped her again, harder this time, with the flat of his sword.

The mare moved off then, heading in the direction Rath Kerri had driven her: across the entrance yard towards an open-doored, narrow gateway. In the silence of the night, her hooves clattered on the cobblestones.

Ziftkin felt his stomach twist up in panic. 'You can't do this to me!' he called back miserably over his shoulder at Rath Kerri. 'You can't just—'

'Shut *up*!' Rath Kerri hissed. 'Do you wish to wake everyone?' He gestured irritably with the unsheathed sword still in his hand. 'Don't be such a stupid ingrate! Go. Leave! Take what I've been able to give you and leave, quiet and quick as you can. Out the gateway. *Go!*'

Ziftkin stared, he felt his insides knot up in desperation. He reined the mare to a halt. He could not lose his bone flute. Not that! It was too much, after everything that had happened, to have that taken from him as well.

But Rath Kerri stood implacable, the naked sword out and ready. Behind him, his men stood, little more than dark shadows, but with the same grim air as Rath Kerri himself.

'Go,' Rath Kerri hissed. 'Before it is too late.'

They left him no other choice.

Ziftkin could not believe it.

How could he live with everything . . . *everything* taken from him like this?

The mare shambled on, grumbling to herself. Ziftkin slumped in the saddle, feeling his insides curdle like old milk. The reins were slack in his hands. His mind felt numbed, as if by a blow.

Outside the narrow gateway, the air was colder, and there was a wind. Ziftkin shivered. The land lay stretched in dark folds before him, empty and bleak.

The mare paused, snuffled, craned her head back to peer at her rider, as if trying to make out what manner of man it was who forced her to go traipsing about the wide world at this uncomfortable, dark time of the night. Behind them, the wooden door to the gateway creaked shut. Ziftkin heard the final *thunk* of the locking bar sliding into place.

The mare skittered forwards, and then shied abruptly to one side, nearly spilling Ziftkin from the saddle, as a figure loomed up at them from out of the darkness. Clutching at the mare's mane, Ziftkin peered about, his heart jumping.

'It's me,' a familiar voice whispered, 'Ramona.'

It took Ziftkin some little time to get the mare properly calmed. For though he had done a little riding back at Seshevrell, he was far from being a horseman.

'I've brought you something,' Ramona said, coming up

171

close to the horse, once Ziftkin had calmed her, and lifting up a wrapped bundle.

Ziftkin made no move to take it. 'You knew,' he said accusingly. 'You *knew* what was going to happen.'

'No,' Ramona replied. 'I didn't—'

'You *must* have known. Fitting me out in this . . .' He gestured at the ridiculous outfit that he still wore. It was tattered now, but the sequins of the tunic still flashed and glittered gaudily in the starshine. 'How *could* you?'

Ramona reached a hand up to him. 'Oh, deary . . . I didn't know what they . . . what *she* had in mind for you. I truly didn't! I thought your costume very fine. A bit extravagant, perhaps. But fine nevertheless. And I was flattered that the Lady Evadne would ask me, me especially, to fit you out. I didn't . . . If I'd only known.'

Ramona's eyes glistened with tears. 'I'm so sorry, deary, for what happened. So *sorry* . . .'

Ziftkin stared down at her, at a loss.

'That Evadne can be a *right* little bitch, when she's a mind to be,' Ramona said bitterly. 'You're best gone away from here, deary, as Master Rath arranged.'

'But even if . . .' Ziftkin gulped a breath. 'Even if all Rath Kerri and you say is true . . . I *can't* leave, Ramona. Not without my flute!'

Ramona lifted again the wrapped bundle she carried. 'Here. Take it, deary.'

'What is it?'

'Take it up and *see*!'

Ziftkin took it up. It was some long, slender object rolled in a woollen shawl. His heart began to shiver.

'Unwrap it,' Ramona said. 'Go *on* . . .'

Ziftkin looked down at her, at the bundle now resting on his lap, back to her again, hardly believing.

'*Unwrap* it,' Ramona repeated, her eyes shining.

Ziftkin rolled back the layers of the shawl until the object lay revealed upon his lap. It was indeed the bone flute, glowing in the starshine like a wand of soft light. He stared at it, lifted it up in shaking hands. Then, his own eyes glistening wetly, he turned to Ramona.

'No,' she said. 'Don't say anything.' She chuckled softly.

'When I saw Master Rath get his men to carry you away, I knew you'd need your flute. So I spirited it out of the Great Hall in all the confusion.'

Ramona reached up and grasped Ziftkin's hand in a brief, fierce hold. 'Will you play a last little tune on it, deary, before you go? Just for me? But softly, so those inside the Keep can't hear. Morning's upon us, almost.'

Ziftkin nodded, more than happy to oblige her. Still in the saddle, he lifted the flute to his lips, breathed a low, soft note. The instrument felt warm, with that strange warmth it always had. He felt his heart soar. He felt himself overflowing. The melody flowed out of him softly, a gentle meander of notes . . .

The Keep reared up, a great dark mountain of stone. Playing the flute, he . . . *felt* the structure, as he had *felt* the trees up in the wild lands that first morning when the flute became his.

It was like a great stone hive, filled with devious insects. Everything there was woven and re-woven into a complex interlocking tangle, the human life, the animal, the slow half-life of the very stone itself. It was an *old* place, this, and *strange*. Ziftkin felt its *strangeness*. The stone of which it was constructed was no ordinary, natural rock. Long, long ago, the stone itself had been somehow . . . *created*, brought into being by some arcane method Ziftkin could not even begin to guess at.

He only knew what he *felt* through the flute. And he could *feel* the queer history of the stone. The creatures imprisoned in it had somehow given up their lives in the process of creation, as if they were of no more account to the builders than so much chaff from a field . . . Or partially given up their lives, rather, for he could *feel* that they were not truly dead, though no longer truly alive either.

Ziftkin shuddered. It was all so . . . so twisted. What they had done to him seemed part and parcel of the greater whole here. He felt a dark anger rising up inside him. The Lady Evadne, who used him as if he were a mere utensil. Rath Kerri, who drove him out, so certain in his arrogance that he knew what was best for all concerned.

The tune Ziftkin was playing had grown more vehement, less melodic.

173

'Ziftkin?' Ramona said uneasily. 'You're playing too loud.'

But he did not soften his playing. The anger was building in him. How dare they treat him like a mere chattel? How dare they presume he would crawl away like a whipped puppy, grateful for whatever off-hand mercy they might choose to dish out?

How *dare* they?

It was a rotten, twisted, wicked place, this, inhabited by rotten, twisted, wicked folk.

All the pent-up rage and frustration and grief that was in Ziftkin came welling up like a black tide. How *dare* they treat him as they had? How *dare* the world treat him as it had? What had he ever done to merit such abuse?

Nothing! Nothing at all.

The music poured out of him through the flute, violent and jagged and harsh.

Ramona faltered back, her eyes wide, her mouth open in shocked uncertainty.

Ziftkin could *feel* the unnatural half-life of the poor creatures imprisoned in the Keep's stone walls. He played to them, played them, calling them up, feeding his own anger and outrage into them, rousing them from their somnolent stone half-lives.

It was like playing to an echo. He played the Keep, which echoed back his playing. He echoed the Keep's echo, and the great stone mass of it – and the poor half-living creatures out of, and upon which, the Keep was built – echoed back his echo.

Echo feeding upon echo . . . Building, cycling from one to the other, like a long, invisible spiral staircase of sound, going up and up, growing, growing . . .

Ziftkin could feel the stone-imprisoned creatures begin to rise up uneasily. Through the warm bone flute, he fed them his fury, echoing for them their own deep-buried anger, they who had been so mercilessly ill used.

Rising, rising, the melody spiralling into greater and greater volume.

Ramona moaned and fell to her knees, her hands pressed to her ears.

Inside the Keep, Ziftkin could *feel* folk awakening uncer-

174

tainly, unsure of what was happening but feeling the disturbance in their bellies. Ziftkin felt his being rise up exultantly on wings of rage. The Keep's stone-trapped prisoners rose up with him, stirring for the first time in great ages, coming part-way back to themselves, shuddering with a great, ancient outrage at what had been done to them.

The Keep itself shuddered.

For one single, timeless moment, the poor creatures came to themselves, no longer quite alive, yet not yet dead. They rose up in a squirming, howling mass, their selves filled with a last boil of rage and grief and whirling madness.

And then they were gone, their poor lives finally ended as they ought to have been long, long ago.

The Keep shuddered again, as if some great hand were rocking it. Then, slowly, it began to disintegrate, the red stone of which it was made crumbling like so much rotted plaster.

Ziftkin blinked, the flute dropping from his lips, the music dying. His mare had stood still during the playing, but now, with the great stone structure tumbling down upon itself before her, she bolted. Ziftkin was half thrown from the saddle, and it was all he could do simply to hang on and not drop the flute.

When, finally, he had got the horse turned round, he was shocked to see what lay before him.

Where the great squat tower had once stood, there was now only a mound of rubble. He heard wild screams coming from the wreckage. There was a loud *KRAAKK!* and a burst of sudden flame as something exploded. Dust spilled up into the morning air in a great pink cloud.

Ziftkin swallowed, stared.

Ramona lay back where he had left her, in a tangled huddle, unmoving.

The mare did not want to return, but Ziftkin forced her, using heel and rein to keep her under control. 'Ramona?' he called as the mare drew near. 'Ramona!'

She shivered, lifted herself up on one elbow, her eyes wide and shocked. 'Wha . . . what have you *done*?' she gasped, staring at the rubble that was all that remained of Gault Keep.

Ziftkin did not know what to say. He hardly knew himself

175

what he had done. He looked at the bone flute, still warm in his hand, and shuddered. His fingers, his arms, his whole body tingled uncomfortably.

Ramona struggled to her feet, white-faced and panting. 'Oh, what have you *done*?' she wailed. 'The people! What of all the folk in there? You've *killed* them! How could you *do* such a thing?'

'I . . .' Ziftkin started. 'I didn't . . .'

Ramona gaped at him. 'What manner of *creature* are you?'

A few stunned survivors were beginning to struggle out from the rubble now. A man lurched towards them. He was bruised and bleeding and white-faced. His mouth was open, his jaw working as if he were screaming, but no sound did he make. He held one arm out before him. A shard of wet white bone stuck out from it.

Ziftkin stared, horrified.

More people came staggering up. Seeing Ziftkin and Ramona, apparently unharmed and out of the danger zone, they straggled over.

'How could you? How *could* you do such a terrible, wicked thing?' Ramona was moaning hysterically. 'Those poor, *poor* folk. Look at them! Look at them, you . . . you *creature*!'

They were beginning to be surrounded, now, by a white-faced, staring crowd.

'How could you *do* such a wicked, wicked thing?' Ramona repeated.

'He did it,' somebody amongst the gathering whispered.

'Him?' somebody else responded. 'How could *he* manage to . . .'

'That flute's no ordinary instrument,' came the reply. 'I heard him play at the Gathering.'

'How could you? How *could* you?' Ramona kept wailing at Ziftkin. Her face was twisted with shock and great tears soaked her cheeks. 'All those innocent folk. They *never* did you no harm!'

'It was *him*!' the word went through the crowd, passed along to the newcomers. 'With that terrible dark-magic flute.'

'He was sent here to destroy us!' a man said.

'No!' Ziftkin said. 'You don't understand. I . . .'

176

'Wicked *creature*,' hissed a young woman.

Somebody lobbed a little hunk of rubble at Ziftkin, hitting him across the ear.

He ducked, blinking. The mare shied off, nearly slipping him from the saddle.

The crowd roared.

'Pull him down from that horse of his!' one of them shouted.

Half a dozen pairs of hands reached up. The mare whirled, frightened. She kicked out blindly, sending one man tumbling backwards with a cry. Ziftkin could only hang on, clutching the flute to his breast with one hand and gripping the saddle horn desperately with the other, his knees clenched about the mare's flanks. Then, with a snort, she bolted away.

'Stop him!' one of the crowd called. 'He's escaping!'

But the mare was off, galloping downslope as fast as her flying legs would take her. Ziftkin hung on, letting the horse have her head, as eager as she to get away from the furious crowd behind them.

The image of Ramona's stricken face haunted him: wide-eyed, white, and furious. Ramona, who had been so kind. She had turned upon him as though he were some loathsome vermin.

And that vicious, mad crowd . . .

Ziftkin tried to breathe, feeling himself dizzy and sick in his belly. He did not know how he had done what he had to create such terrible havoc. The flute was far more than he had first imagined; that was clear. Perhaps *he* was more than he had ever imagined.

The mare had slowed by now, and he reined her in to a halt. Turning in the saddle he looked back. Gault Keep showed as a mound of reddish rubble atop the hill behind them. Little figures scurried about it, made small as beetles by the distance.

Ziftkin let out a long, bitter sigh. So much for his dreams of a future at Gault Keep.

The folk there deserved what had happened to them. The Lady Evadne deserved it. He had a momentary image of her in his mind, pinned underneath the rubble, bruised and broken, knowing that it was he who had brought this retribution upon her, knowing she had made a terrible mistake in treating him the way she had.

He saw himself striding into the rubble then, plucking her free, her beautiful face turned to him in supplication.

But it was a ridiculous fantasy, that. If the Lady Evadne had died, she was crushed in her sleep, most like, never knowing anything of how it had happened.

And he, Ziftkin, was alone again, and hurting, with no place in the world to return to and no place at all to go.

XVI

Elinor sat cross-legged on the ground, her sheathed sword unhooked from her belt and balanced across her thighs. Gyver sat near her, waiting, as she was. Several bands of the fur-folk had gathered here this night, to hold council and talk war.

War.

As if they understood what war was, them. Elinor shook her head and smiled ruefully to herself; she was starting to phrase her thoughts like the fur-folk.

After long days of message-sending, three different bands were met together here, ingathered from no small distance: the Little-tree and the Longwater folk, Cloud-Dreaming called them, and her own people, Waterwisher's folk. All three bands had had bloody confrontations with the invaders. Gyver's folk, though, had had the most serious dealings, for their territory, apparently, lay directly across the track along which the invaders were penetrating into the forest.

The elders from each band sat together in a loose group closest to the fire. If Elinor had got the names right, a grizzled old fur-man named Twig, and a thin woman called Squints – who, indeed, had a perpetual squint – represented the Little-tree band. A lone, dour-faced fur-woman of middle years seemed to be the only elder present from the Longwater band. Her name was Frog and she had an intricately braided topknot of fur, died a startling green, on the crest of her skull. She had the same feel about her that Cloud-Dreaming had, and Elinor reckoned her a woman of knowledge. With Cloud-Dreaming, there sat Stone and another, older fur-woman named Sunset.

There were many bands of the fur-folk spread loosely throughout this wild forest land, Elinor had learned, but getting more than two or three bands together at one time was out of the question, for the fur-folk wandered far and wide, and never came together in truly large numbers at all; there was no simple way for them, through hunting and gathering, to feed large groups.

So there were, perhaps, fifty or sixty people here all told: men, women, and children. That was the limit, Elinor reckoned, of what she could hope for in terms of numbers: fifty or sixty. Out of which maybe three dozen might be fit to fight. It was hardly enough to swoop down and overwhelm the invaders. Especially considering the fur-folk's weaponry: sharp chips of stone and carved bone would prove of precious little use against armour and bronze blades wielded by trained fighters.

Not to mention whatever else the invaders might possess in the way of protection like their uncanny dangling sentinels. Elinor shook her head and sighed. She could see no easy answer here. Leaning back, she tipped her head up. In the dark of the night sky, the new moon hung, a shining sickle above the intricate webbery of the trees.

There was a stirring amongst those gathered here. 'Grandmother Moon,' the call went up. 'Watch over uss, your grandchildren'ss grandchildren, if it pleassess you.'

Cloud-Dreaming and Frog, the elder fur-woman with the green top-knot, lifted their furred arms to the moon in unison and called out, a long, wordlessly wailing chant that shivered through the trees.

The gathered fur-folk echoed that cry till the forest, the very wide world itself, seemed filled with it. Elinor felt it in her bones as much as her ears, a throbbing, formless sound that seemed somehow to become a part of her own beating heart's rhythm, or her heart's beating to become part of it . . .

And then there was silence.

The fur-folk gathered in together.

'We are met here thiss night, uss,' Cloud-Dreaming began, 'to hold council.'

A general murmur of assent greeted this.

'We are met to ssee our future. Dreamss and portentss, they are unclear. The world, it iss grown uncertain and sstrange. The world, it iss no longer ourss ass it once wass. We musst feel our way towardss . . . what musst be.'

A grey-grizzled fur-man stood, waiting to be acknowledged.

At a council gathering such as this, one stood to talk, waiting for formal recognition before beginning.

Cloud-Dreaming acknowledged him.

'The time,' he said, 'it iss come. Uss, we musst face thesse invaderss. There iss no denying the need. They kill our folk! They sshatter our foresst with their sshining hard bladess! They have attacked and killed the Old Oness, the Phanta! The foresst animalss, they flee. Ssoon there will be no game left. The people will sstarve!'

'Willow, he iss right!' another cried. 'We musst desstroy thesse terrible invaderss, thesse mad far-away people who paint their furlesss sskinss to cover their sshame. We musst desstroy them!'

'We musst kill them. Kill them *all*!' one of the young bucks started shouting. 'We and the sshining blade!'

'Enough!' Cloud-Dreaming cried. With the help of little Sky-Flower, who, as usual, hovered by her side, she had sat down amongst the elders by the fire when the first speaker had begun to talk. Now she struggled up again, stiff with her wounded leg and hip, and held her hand aloft for attention. 'Thiss iss a *council*!'

But there was blood-wildness in the air. 'Kill them, kill them, kill them!' the chant went up.

Some of the younger men had got up about the fire and begun an impromptu dance, leaping high into the air, whooping and shrieking and waving their weapons about madly. 'Kill them, kill them, kill them!' they chorused wildly.

'The sshining blade of death!' shouted others. 'The white-sshining blade!'

'Kill them! Kill them!'

A reedy flute took up the refrain, *sheee kaa! shee kaa!* while hand-drums added a skittering under-beat, *chikka-beeda, chikke-beeda-beee-da!* and the young men chanted their violent refrain, 'The sshining blade! The death blade! Kill them, kill them all!'

Elinor felt her heart leap instinctively to the primal rhythm of it, felt hot fury rise in her like a flood. The flutes shrieked, the hand-drums echoed like a thudding blood-pulse, the dancers whirled and leaped, their sinewy, darkly furred bodies a blur of motion, their eyes and sharp teeth flashing in the light of the flames.

Cloud-Dreaming raised both her hands. '*Sstop thiss!*' she cried, and her voice was so penetratingly, shockingly loud that the dancers stopped as one, dead still in their tracks, panting.

Elinor felt a long shudder go through her. The fury that had risen in her began abruptly to abate. Though she had not risen from her sitting position, her heart was beating hard. She put a shaking hand to her face, took a gasping breath. She heard Gyver, seated close to her, hiss.

'Thiss, it iss *madnesss*!' Cloud-Dreaming said. 'Have you all become ssick-in-the-head perssonss?'

'It iss *them* who are ssick-in-the-head perssonss!' one of the dancers returned.

'Yess!' Cloud-Dreaming said. 'But uss, we musst not, *musst not* let their killing-ssicknesss into our heartss! That, it would desstroy uss!'

'*They* will desstroy uss, Cloud-Dreaming.' It was young Swift who had spoken up. He had been one of the dancers, Elinor realized. Now he stood quiet, his hands at his sides. 'Perhapss ssuch madnesss, it iss needed.'

'No,' Cloud-Dreaming said. '*No!*'

But, 'Yess . . .' somebody responded in a soft, hissing whisper.

The crowd of erstwhile dancers shifted, uneasy, tight and tense. The air felt charged. The whole gathering quivered, as if a cold wind had blown through them.

Elinor looked across to Gyver and saw his furred face twisted with unease. She took a breath and stood up, holding the sword by its sheath in one hand.

Cloud-Dreaming regarded her. 'You wissh to sspeak, you?'

Elinor nodded: 'I wish to speak, me.'

'Let her sspeak with her blade!' somebody cried. 'Let the sshining blade of death sspeak for her!'

'Where are your mannerss, you?' Cloud-Dreaming demanded sharply.

But a wild shout went up. 'The sshining blade! Sshow uss the sshining white blade of death!'

'Quiet!' Cloud-Dreaming cried. '*Quiet!*' She pointed at

182

Elinor. 'Elinor, she waitss. Sshe iss a sstranger amongsst uss, her, yet sshe sshowss more mannerss than you! Will you *lissten* to her? Or will you continue to act like ssick-in-the-head perssonss?'

There was a general grumbling, but the shouting group subsided.

Cloud-Dreaming settled back amongst the other elders, letting herself down, stiffly, with Sky-Flower's aid.

Elinor swallowed. Every eye was upon her. She took a breath, another, gripped her sword by the sheath in both hands, uncertain how to begin. Her guts felt knotted tight. There was too much of anger here, and too much blind, blood-deep, violent excitement. And too much innocence. Fatal innocence.

'You have suffered,' she began. 'And those who have made you suffer must be dealt with.'

Quickly, before there could be any interruption, she went on: 'But I say to you that Cloud-Dreaming is right. You must not let the killing madness of these invaders into your hearts. It will only lead to your own destruction.'

A grumbling, discontented murmur greeted this.

'You do not know what manner of foe it is that you face. I have seen their like in the land from which I come. I know what they are. If you go rushing down upon them in a madness of anger, you will all die.'

'You and your white blade, you will fight with uss!' somebody returned.

Elinor shook her head. 'Me and my white blade or no, if you rush upon them in a killing madness, you will die. You cannot stand against them. They will destroy you.'

A long moment's strained silence greeted this.

One of the elders rose to her feet.

'Ssquintss, sshe wisshess to sspeak,' Cloud-Dreaming announced.

Elinor hesitated, then stepped back to sit at Gyver's side. He put a hand to her shoulder. 'Patience,' he said softly. But his face was still tight.

Squints looked about her at the gathered fur-folk, her half-shut eye making her face seem screwed up in irritation. 'Thesse invaderss . . . they may look mosst naked and ugly, and they have done terrible things, them. But ssurely it iss all a misstake of ssome ssort, no? They musst be people, them, on the insside, just ass we. They are not monsssterss.'

There was a grumbling chorus against this.

'Me, I ssay they are people. Uss, we musst not walk the path of killing madnesss. Why can we not *talk* with them?'

'You do not know, you of the Little-tree folk,' one of the young bucks shouted out. 'Uss, we have tried talk. *They* do not talk. *They* only kill!'

'Then you did not talk well enough, you,' Squints replied sharply. She shook her grey-furred head, pointed towards Elinor. 'Sshe lookss like *them*, but sshe iss ass we, under her differencess. We can talk with her. Why not with *them*?'

'They are ssick-in-the-head people, them,' Cloud-Dreaming responded. She gestured to the long scar running across her thigh and hip. 'I have tried talking with them, me. I know.'

'And I ssay,' Squints replied, 'that you did not talk well enough to them.'

Cloud-Dreaming bit her lip, but said nothing.

'It iss *you* who doess not undersstand!' young Swift cried out. '*They* will not—'

'*Sswift!*' Cloud-Dreaming snapped. 'Have you losst your mannerss *entirely*, you? Elder Ssquintss iss talking!'

Swift went silent.

'Me, I ssay there musst be ssome way to talk to thesse far-away people,' Squints insisted. 'There iss *alwayss* ssome way to talk!'

'Not with ssick-in-the-head people like *them*!' somebody said.

'What of Elinor?' one of the other elders asked, the grizzled old fur-man named Twig. 'Elinor, sshe ssayss sshe knowss thesse invaderss. What doess sshe ssay about talking with them?'

Squints paused for a moment, then gestured to Elinor. 'If you will sspeak, you, we will listen.'

Elinor nodded and stood up once again. 'I know what sort of men these invaders are. They do not wish to talk. They wish to conquer. You can no more change their course of action with simple talk than you can change the . . . the course of the sun through the sky.'

'How can you be sso ssure of thiss?' Squints demanded. 'If you are not one of them, you, then how can you be sso certain?'

'I have faced their kind,' Elinor replied, 'and know them all too well.'

She thought of Iryn Jagga and the Ancient Brotherhood of the Light, whom she had faced and fought and defeated – at least after a fashion. They were men who sought to conquer and rule absolutely their little corner of the world, who felt themselves to be vastly superior to others, and whose violent ambitions had left a bloody trail of human and humanimal wreckage behind them.

Just such were these invaders of the fur-folk's forest. She felt certain of it. It was plain to read in their armour and weapons, their violent actions, their organized and blatant war-manner.

Elinor looked at the fur-folk gathered about the fire. 'They will be an advance group, these invaders of yours,' she told them, 'sent on ahead from some home-place . . . eastwards of the mountains, it seems. Behind them somewhere is a leader who has grand, bloody ambitions, who feels himself to be special, greater than other men, who, in the name of some Power or other, will drive the rest on to wage a war of conquest. I have seen it all before.'

'We will wage war againsst *them*, uss!' a young fur-man shouted. 'We will russh upon them and sslay them all!'

A ragged cheer went up once more.

'And I tell you that you will all die!' Elinor shouted. 'You know nothing of war, you forest folk. Listen to me! You have no proper war weapons, no proper concept of what war means, no—'

'We know war,' one of the fur-men said. He rose up from behind the group of elders about the fire and stood there, a barbed-headed javelin in hand.

Dour-faced Frog, of the green top-knot, elder of the Long-water band, turned to regard him. 'Do you wissh to talk, Jumping of the Longwater folk?'

The man nodded. 'I wissh to talk, me.'

'We will lissten.'

A look and a quick, small gesture of the hand from Gyver

brought Elinor back to sit at his side again. She would just have to bide her time once more.

The fur-man stepped forwards a little. He looked at Elinor. 'You are wrong, far-away woman with no fur. We know war, uss.' Turning, he glanced quickly behind him into the group of fur-folk and called, 'Mosss . . . Mosss!'

An old man made his way slowly to the front ranks.

'Thiss,' Jumping said, 'iss Mosss-on-Rockss. He can tell you about war. He fought a war once.'

Moss-on-Rocks looked around him. 'It wass a terrible war,' he said.

'Tell uss,' somebody urged.

Moss-on-Rocks was small-boned and skinny. His fur had gone nearly all white. He stood swaying a little, scratched himself, wrapped his arms about his thin chest, and closed his eyes. He stayed like that, silent, for long moments.

Then, 'I fought in a war once,' he began, 'along with ssome otherss, long sseassonss ago when I wass a young man and sstrong. We fought that war againsst the Mountain Ssheep fur-folk in the north, uss. We thought oursselvess very bold and brave. There were five of uss, all young, three men and two women. Myself, Alwayss-Wisshing, Laughss-a-lot, and Bobbing. Laugh, he had the idea to fight that war. The lasst of uss wass Heavy-Hand, a foresst-living woman who had come down from the Peakss that sspring.'

The old man shook his head and smiled. 'A crazy woman, her, sstrong like a bear and unpredictable ass the sspring wind. But a good fighter, and very good at making love.'

Somebody laughed. 'Tell uss how sshe did it, Mosss. Wass sshe noissy like a bear, her?'

Elinor looked across at Gyver incredulously. 'They're totally losing track of what matters here!' she hissed at him.

Gyver shrugged and motioned her to further patience. 'The council, it musst run itss coursse,' he said softly.

Moss continued his story. 'It wass sspring, and the ssnow had all drained away into the earth. We fassted for many dayss, uss, and made fighting ssongs, toughening oursselvess for the war. Then we travelled northwardss. When we came to a camp of the Mountain Ssheep people, we walked towardss it sslowly, making much noisse sso they would hear uss coming.

186

' "We ssee you, People of the Mountain Ssheep," Laugh, he called out to them.

' "We ssee you, you Longwater People," they called back.

'Then we walked into their camp. It wass a big travelling band they had there, ssix or sseven handss' worth of people, women and children and men. We told them we wanted to fight a war. At firsst they did not want to, but Heavy-Hand called them sshit-for-brainss and Laugh, he pisssed on their hearth fire, and that angered them. Sso they agreed.'

'They sshould have pisssed on Laugh, them,' somebody said.

Elinor ran a hand over her face. She stared about her. Some of the gathered fur-folk had begun to laugh.

'Thiss war wass not funny,' Moss responded. The look of him silenced the rest. 'We arranged to meet them and fight the war the next morning in a little mountain valley with white high-birch all down one sside and a young sstream moving through the middle of it. Uss, we sstayed in the birchess all night, ssinging our war ssongss. When the Mountain Ssheep People came, we were ready. "We ssee you, People of the Mountain Ssheep," we called out.

' "We ssee you, you Longwater People," they called back. "Are you ready to fight thiss war now?"

' "We are ready," we ssaid, uss.'

Moss went silent for a little, standing as he was, bony arms still wrapped around his furred chest. His eyes were wide and blank now, seeing only the past he was remembering. 'Firsst we talked relationss, becausse the Mountain Ssheep people, they ssometimess marry Longwater people. And we did not wissh to kill any kin. We were not bent people, after all. We only wanted to fight that war.

'There were no kin there to either Bobbing or Laugh, sso they could kill whomever they wisshed. Bobbing laughed when sshe ssaw thiss. "I will kill you all mysself," sshe sshouted at them.

'There were three Mountain Ssheep people who thought they were kin to Alwayss-Wisshing, and we showed Alwayss to them, sso that they would know each other. There wass one persson, a tall woman, who wass kin to my ssisster'ss hussband. We were sshown to each other. Sshe wass a nice-looking woman. I remember being glad I did not have to hurt her.

'The war sstarted when Laugh walked acrosss the sstream. "Come down to me, People of the Ssheep," he ssaid to them, him. "And let me kill you."

'Two Mountain Ssheep people, they came down. One wass a very sshort man, I remember. He had blackened the fur of hiss face with fire-charcoal, and hiss eyess looked very white. He tried to sstab Laugh in the belly with hiss javelin. Laugh, he sstruck the javelin asside and hit the man on the sside of hiss head with a sstick he carried. That man, he fell to hiss kneess, crying in pain. Thiss angered the resst of the Mountain Ssheep people, and they all came russhing down towardss uss. There were more of them than there wass of uss.

'We fought that war then, and it wass very terrible indeed. One of them, he cut me on my arm. I tried to kill him but he ran away too fasst. Laugh, he wass killed. I do not know how. I did not ssee it, me. Bobbing wass hurt very badly, but sshe did not die. Alwayss wass not hurt at all. I do not know if we killed any of the Mountain Ssheep people, me, but there wass much blood in the little sstream.

'It wass a very terrible war.'

'It wass a very sstupid war,' Elder Squints said. 'What did you want to go and try to kill thosse Mountain Ssheep People for, you? You behaved like ssick-in-the-head people. You ought to have talked with them if you were angry with them.'

Moss shrugged, 'We wanted to fight a war. Laugh, he wass a perssuassive man. And we were very young. It wass not what I thought it would be. We did not feel good about it afterwardss, and we sstayed away from each other after it wass over.'

Moss ran a finger along a puckered scar that marked the grey-white fur of his left forearm. 'I have thiss, me, to remember it by.' He hung his head and sighed. 'It wass a very terrible war.'

There was a sober silence amongst the gathered fur-folk.

Jumping, the fur-man who had brought Moss-on-Rocks to speak out, turned to Elinor and said, 'Do you ssee, far-away woman? We know of war. If thesse ugly, furlesss sstrangerss wissh to bring war upon uss, we will know what to do!'

A cheer went through the gathered fur-folk. 'War! War! We will bring war upon them!'

Elinor could only stare. She did not know what to say, how to even begin to make headway against such incredible naïvete.

War?

These folk were even further removed from the reality of what had come upon them than she had thought. Such utter, fatal innocence . . .

She looked across at Gyver. His face was tight with upset. Gyver had seen enough to know what lay out there in the invaders' camp, to know that her surmises about them were, if not true in detail, accurate enough in general, and to know how pitifully unequipped his own people were to deal with such a brutal invading force.

'What are we going to *do*?' she asked of him in a whisper.

But Gyver was clearly as at a loss as she. It was simply not possible, Elinor realized, for a people to imagine a world beyond their own experience. The new and entirely strange would be re-fashioned to fit into the familiar as the fur-folk knew it. There was nothing she could tell them that would jar them out of their point of view. Most of them still believed that Gyver had wildly exaggerated when he said there were untold numbers of furless folk in the world. They went on persisting in their own sense of things, seeing the world as they expected it to be.

And that would be the end of them, for the blood and bitter anger of the confrontations that had already taken place was like an infection in them. She could see it clear. It would take so very little, now, to push these fur-folk over the edge, to transform them into sick-in-the-head people – as Cloud-Dreaming would express it – too filled with anger and bitterness and violence to do aught else but rush, howling, to their own destruction.

Gyver came up to her. 'They cannot ssee, them,' he said, echoing her own thoughts. 'They have never been out of their foresst, and they ssee only what long habit allowss them to ssee.'

'But—' Elinor began exasperatedly.

'Be patient,' Gyver urged. 'Cloud-Dreaming and thosse like

189

her, they are sspecial. They *feel* the world deeply, them. Cloud-Dreaming, sshe knowss the ssickness that iss in thesse angry men. Sshe will not let it win out.' Gyver shook his head sadly, sighing. 'We are not a sshallow folk. It iss not their fault, thiss blindnesss. All folk are like thiss. Me, I have sseen. Your folk, my folk, all folk ssee only what their habitss let them ssee.'

Elinor shook her head. 'But they cannot—' She stopped in mid-word.

'Gyver,' she said breathlessly, 'I think I see a way we can do it. I think I see a way to defeat these invaders and save your folk!'

'How?' he replied eagerly. 'How?'

Elinor smiled. ' "All folk see only what their habits let them see." Isn't that what you said?'

Gyver nodded.

'Well . . .' Elinor paused, closed her eyes, letting the new idea settle into clarity in her mind. 'These invaders, too, must have their habits, no? Their blindnesses?'

'Sso?' said Gyver.

'So . . . I think I see a way to turn their own habits against them. Listen . . .'

XVII

Towards dawn, Elinor and Gyver lay snugged up together a little apart from the rest. All was quiet now, all the wrangling and discussion finished with. Only the gentle sound of the night-breeze in the trees broke the forest stillness.

The ground under her felt chill, and Elinor curled tighter into Gyver's warmth. 'Do you think it will work, this notion of mine?' she asked him in a whisper.

Gyver said nothing for long moments. Then he let out a breath and said, 'It iss the only way.'

Elinor held him. She could feel her heart thump anxiously. It was crazy, this plan of hers. And yet . . . And yet, as Gyver said, it seemed the only way.

But it was no easy way.

'Gyver,' she said softly into his furred ear. 'When we . . . when we do this thing. Will you please be . . . careful.'

'Me, I am alwayss mosst careful,' he answered. Gently, he nuzzled the nape of her neck.

'I'm serious,' she said.

'And sso?'

'And so, will you be *careful*?'

'Ass alwayss.'

Elinor sighed. She did not know quite how to get across to him what she felt she needed to. She shifted position and put a hand on the hilt of her sword where it lay next to them. 'I have . . . protection, Gyver,' she said, hefting the sword. 'You have nothing of the sort. And sometimes . . .'

'Yess?' he said, when she went silent.

'Sometimes I feel like I shall be . . . shall be the death of you. Dragging you into things the way I always end up doing.'

'It iss not you.'

She turned and studied him. In the night's dark, with only

the soft little flicker of lapsed camp fires in the distance, it was hard to read his furred face. 'Not me who what?'

'Not you who sshapess my life.'

'But if you'd never met me, you wouldn't be—'

'If I'd never met you, me, I'd be lesss happy.'

Elinor sighed. 'Gyver, you're not listening to me! I'm *worried* for you.'

He reached for her face. 'Worry iss a little rat who eatss at our heartss.'

Elinor said, 'Hmmph!' softly. And then, 'Sounds like something your mother would say, that.'

Gyver nodded, a gesture she could just make out in the dark. 'My mother, sshe ssaid that.'

'It's all very well to talk, Gyver, but what if—'

'Elinor, my Elinor,' he said, interrupting. 'You tried to ssend me away once. Do you remember?'

Elinor nodded unhappily. 'I remember. I was convinced you'd end up splayed out on the ground somewhere, a blade in your guts. I couldn't have borne it.'

'But I am sstill here, by your sside. My gutss, they are sstill intact.'

'But—'

He put a finger softly to her lips. 'If I had lisstened, me, to the voice of your worry and gone away . . . What then? We would not be here now.' He put an arm about her. 'Life, it hass alwayss itss dangerss, my Elinor.'

'But . . .'

'No more butss. I will be careful. I ssay thiss *mosst* ssolemnly. Now pleasse, *pleasse* put asside your worry and come to me.'

Elinor sighed. 'You're right,' she said. 'It's just that . . .'

'Enough!' Gyver hissed in her ear, and then bit her on the ear lobe, a sharp, painful, sudden nip.

'Oww!' she hissed. 'What did you do *that* for?'

He laughed softly. 'It wass the only way I could think of to bring you out of your worry-sself.'

Elinor laughed with him, feeling the tight knot of unease that had been in her belly begin to loosen itself.

Gyver was using his pliant tongue now, licking the hollow of her throat in a warm, wet caress.

She reached for him.

But as they began to make slow love under the tree-laced canopy of the night-sky, she felt a desperateness seep into her. For what if this *were* to prove her last time with him? What if, despite all his careful promises, Gyver came to grief?

She felt the soft, furry warmth of him, the sinewy strength of his slim limbs. She could not bear it, to have found him against all hopes and then to lose him as she dreaded – him cut to raw dead meat by some violent stranger's blade.

She clutched him tightly to her, inhaling the muskiness of his fur, drawing him into herself in every way she knew how, the desperateness in her making her limbs shake. In the half-lit dark, she could see his eyes shining, and, against her wish, she saw him suddenly in her mind's eye, sprawled lifeless, one of his legs tucked under him at an awkward angle, one arm flung out as if he had been reaching for something, his eyes gone blind and dusty and dead, staring into an empty sky . . .

She shuddered, and Gyver held her close, murmuring wordless comfort in her ear, moving inside her softly, running his taloned fingers over her in long, gentle caresses, moving, softly moving, till the pure, blood and bone pleasure and closeness of it all brought her out of the dark vision that had overwhelmed her and she immersed herself completely in the moving body-dance they two made together, so intermingled for the instant, body and heart and spirit, that nothing else mattered for them – or indeed existed at all.

XVIII

Ziftkin tried to turn away, but the faces came at him, ribboned with glistening wet blood, screaming. There were dozens of them, pressing about him like a swarm of horrific insects, mad with pain and grief and the sudden awful soul-wrench of their own death.

The Keep shuddered, collapsing behind them, rubble splashing high into the air, while the frantic dead mauled him, clawing him with their broken and bloodied hands, screaming, screaming . . .

Ziftkin came awake with a rush, shaking, soaked with sweat. He rolled over and was sick, retching dryly.

When he was done, he pushed himself to a sitting position, wiped his mouth, swallowed. He wrapped his long arms about his knees, shuddering. 'Go away!' he muttered. 'Leave me *be*!'

It was still dark night, with starshine faintly sifting in through the trees under which he had taken shelter and the crescent of the new moon low in the sky. Ever since his departure from Gault Keep, his sleep had been invaded by the restless shades of the dead.

His dead.

'I didn't mean to kill you,' he said to the empty air. And then, angrily, 'You deserved it, anyway! You were a twisted, wicked folk.'

The only manner of response he received was the clinging memory-image of those stark, screaming faces. He shook himself, trying to shake the vision from his mind. But it was no use. The images of wailing faces clung to him as tenaciously as so many burrs.

He sighed. In the past few nights, he had found no remedy but movement for moments like this. If he stayed huddled here, those ethereal faces would haunt him to the brink of mad despair.

He levered himself stiffly to his feet. The mare whinnied at him questioningly, and he went over to her and patted her warm neck. 'It's all right, Gullie,' he reassured her. 'It's only me having bad dreams again.'

Gullie he had named her, for no especial reason other than that the name had a nice sound to it. And the mare herself seemed to like it, for she had pricked her ears up interestedly when first he had tested the name on her.

'Time to go, Gullie,' Ziftkin said, lifting up the saddle from where it lay on the grass at the mare's feet. Gullie danced sideways away from him, pulling against her tether, not at all eager to go traipsing off into the night. Ziftkin flung the saddle awkwardly across her back. Groping in the dark, he fastened the girth, giving it a good final tug with his knee against Gullie's ribs. 'Sorry, old girl,' he said, patting her, 'but they'll drive me demented if I don't get moving.'

Gullie shook her head and snorted. But she stood still enough as he clambered up into the saddle. It felt good to sit perched on her back, to feel her ribs move gently with each breath she took, to feel the warmth of her under his palms. He did not feel so alone with her as a companion.

The bone flute carefully in hand, he guided her out from under the trees.

It was rolling country beyond, grass-covered, with only scattered clumps of trees – like the little copse in which they had taken shelter for the night. Patchy clouds rolled slowly through the sky overhead, alternately hiding and revealing the stars and the thin moon. Starshine splashed across the grass in rhythm with the clouds' movements.

Ziftkin let out a long breath. He felt like the only living thing in the world, alone as could be. His heart ached. They had not needed – the Lady Evadne and Rath Kerri and the rest – to treat him so. What had he ever done to them? To offer him everything, to dangle the promise of it before his nose . . . and then to laugh at him and scorn him and thrust him out when they were done. He felt so filled with anger and anguish . . .

Gullie snorted and shied under him, bringing Ziftkin back to awareness of the world. For an instant he stared about, his heart skipping. But there was no threat to be seen. He sighed, threw his head back, took in a long lungful of the chill night air. The stars overhead hung like a bright net, a world-spanning, silent serenity of light. The night-breeze sang a soft song in the grass under Gullie's hooves.

Ziftkin breathed it all in. Despite everything, the world was still hugely, thrillingly beautiful. There was no denying it. The world spoke to him – had spoken to him all the days of his life – in a soft, mysterious, irresistible voice. His father's blood working in him, Malinda had once said, finding him as a little lad staring raptly at the sinking sun on a summer's eve. He recalled the moment clearly, for it was one of the rare occasions she made mention of his father.

Gullie blew a snorting breath, whinnied softly, and trotted out through the grass, ears up, as if she, too, in her horse's way, felt the thrill of the world's night-beauty.

Ziftkin lifted the flute. It felt warm, as always, strange thing that it was. Almost, he had thrown it from him, that first morning after the Keep's ruin. But he had found himself unable to part with it.

His lifted it to his lips and blew a long, slow note, *feeling* the clouds rolling far above him, the grass rolling below in the night breeze. The world blew through him, and he echoed the world back in music. It was the same process that had brought about the Keep's destruction, and yet not.

His music sailed through the air up into the clouds, guiding them, gathering them. He tipped his head sideways, launching a burst of melody, and the clouds jumped, flocking like so many gigantic, luminous sheep to his piping. Gullie danced under him, neighing softly. Ziftkin laughed, and the laughter, channelled through the flute, became a part of his music.

He did not know what he was become when he played through the flute – or when it played through him, which was how it truly felt at times. But he knew the thrill of it in his guts was too perfect to ever contemplate giving up.

Ziftkin played until the first glow of dawn-light began to lighten the sky and the world hung poised between night and day. He felt light-headed, empty and filled at the same moment.

When he played, he did not need to think. His mind was cleared. Memories and fears, hopes and desires, haunting faces and guilt and anger and all . . . all of it washed quite away. It was like being cleansed by a great, invisible river.

Ziftkin sighed, the flute quiescent in his lap, and gazed about at the dawning world, weary and content.

With the sun just peeping over the horizon, he guided Gullie over towards a line of trees in the near distance. Trees, he had discovered, invariably meant water in this grassy landscape. He wanted a long drink and a wash, and something solid in his belly before they went any further this day. Breakfast out of his saddlebag supplies and, afterwards perhaps, a nap.

What had appeared, in the distance, a thin line of trees turned out to be a tangle of willows and beech bordering a fair-sized river. It was the first such that Ziftkin had seen in this rolling land, and he would never have known it to be there save for the trees, for it lay deeply sunk in a fold of the land.

To get to the water, he had to dismount and lead Gullie by hand, pushing aside a tangle of branches and stumbling across rooty, uneven ground until, after a final skidding scramble down a steepish slope, they came out between two monstrous great willows onto a little sandy shingle beneath a shelf of crumbling stone that kept the tree roots at bay.

'Here we go, Gullie old girl,' Ziftkin said, wiping his forehead with the back of one hand. He was panting from the clamber down here and damp with sweat, despite the chill of the air. It was a shadowy, dim place this, with the morning sunlight obscured by the tangly leaf-cascade of the willow limbs.

Ziftkin let the mare's reins drop to the ground. 'Drink, girl. Go ahead.'

But Gullie made no move to go nearer to the water.

The river ran dark and silent. They had come down at a point where the current had carved out a kind of hollow around the stone shelf, so that the river was easily three or four times as wide here as further downstream. Except for the sandy shingle upon which they stood, the bank was mostly naked willow roots, snaking down to the water. Brown-ochre willow leaves boated along the dark surface.

Laying the bone flute carefully aside, Ziftkin squatted down at the water's verge. Save for the little sound of the current's gurgle, this shadowed place was silent as could be. He reached down and splashed a double handful of water over his face. It was so cold it stung, and set him spluttering and shivering.

From behind him, Gullie snorted. He turned and looked up at her. She snorted again, her ears pricked up, staring out at the dark water. Ziftkin turned back.

A long, rippling vee marked the river's surface as some large thing moved along smoothly beneath. It was big, whatever it was, and quick, and coming their way.

Ziftkin backstepped hastily away from the sandy verge and grabbed Gullie by the reins. But the mare reared up, her eyes wide and rolling with fear now, throwing him to the ground. He landed awkwardly on his back, the wind knocked out of him, and lay for a moment, gasping, too dazed to move.

Something surged up out of the dark water. Ziftkin heard it hit the little sandy strand with a wet *thwump*, heard the raspy bellows of its breathing. He rolled over and saw glowing eyes, a mouth full of yellow fangs, a huge, sleek, furred body . . .

Gullie screamed and tried to flee up the bank, but her reins got entangled amongst the willows and she was jerked to a stop, half falling to her knees.

The water-beast went for her in a shambling, predatory rush.

Gullie scrambled to her feet. Still screaming, she reared up and lashed out, trying to strike at the water-beast's head with her sharp-hooved front feet. It slid deftly away, quick for all its bulk.

Ziftkin struggled up to his knees, and the water-beast whirled on him. It was big, easily as big as Gullie, though shorter-legged and thinner around the body. It stank of weed and rot. It hissed at him, its wicked yellow fangs gleaming wetly.

Instinctively, Ziftkin dived for the flute.

As the water-beast came for him, he blew a single, frantic, piercing note.

The creature skidded to a halt as if it had suddenly been rammed in the guts with a pole.

Ziftkin took a gasping breath and blew another note, higher, shriller still.

The beast cringed.

Ziftkin could *feel* the creature. It was all hungering desire; it wanted blood and wet meat in its claws and the taste of quivering, warm flesh. He drove the shrill flute-note into it like a spike, *feeling* the way the special sound of it hurt the creature, feeling his own animal terror and anger channelling through the flute.

The water-beast began to whimper, making a little hurt-puppy sound.

Ziftkin bore down upon it. It was a mindlessly vicious beast, a threat to any and all who came near the water. It deserved to be eliminated. He would be making the world a better place by destroying it. For destroy it, he could; he *felt* that quite clearly. All he need do would be to drive the thrusting note he was still playing into its skull, into its mind, deeply enough to rip through the delicate membranes that held soul and flesh and mind together.

Like punching through a complex, delicate tapestry. One forceful thrust, held long enough, and the creature would never bother anybody else ever again.

Ziftkin felt anger burn hot in him. The beast would have torn poor Gullie apart, torn him apart. He thrust at it with his deadly, shrilling note, and the creature collapsed, wailing . . .

And looked, suddenly, most pitiful.

Ziftkin hesitated. He could *feel* the beast's growing agony, its blind terror at this terrible sound-force that was ripping into it like a great claw.

He remembered the faces of the dead that had been haunting him, and paused, suddenly uncertain.

It was not truly a wicked creature, this cowering thing before him. Nor a cruel one. It only was what it was. It had its place in the world, here in this shadowy-dark, chill spot. It *belonged* . . .

199

Slowly, Ziftkin let the flute drop from his lips. The water-creature blubbered. A long shiver went through it, and, for a moment, Ziftkin thought that it was too late, that the beast was already in its death throes. He felt sick remorse flood through him.

But then the creature rolled over, sluggish and weak. It took a slobbering breath, another, blinking dazedly. Lifting its head, it stared at Ziftkin. Its eyes locked with his for an instant, and Ziftkin experienced a sudden rushing vision of swirling dark water and felt the liquid joy of movement in his own limbs.

Then, with a rolling splash, the creature was gone, back into the river.

Gullie snorted, tugging at her still entangled reins, stiff-legged and anxious, and most impatient to be away from this dangerous spot. But Ziftkin stared for a long time at the dark waters of the river, the flute dangling mute in his hand. No remorse, no guilt, no anger or resentment, no uncertainty for this water-beast. No cruelty. And no agonizing over past deeds or future hopes. It was what it was, purely.

Ziftkin found himself unexpectedly envious of it.

Once more out in the rolling, grassy countryside, Ziftkin sat in the saddle, reins slack, head sunk on his breast. He let Gullie have her own head. After all, he had no place special to go. There was nowhere for him in the world. Nowhere at all . . .

He kept thinking of the water-beast's strange innocence – if that were, indeed, the right word for it. A creature so completely itself, that it belonged unquestioningly, irrevocably . . . He had never before imagined the depth of belonging that he had felt in the creature through the strange medium of the flute. It made him shiver now, just thinking on it.

It had been a part of that shadowy river place the way a leaf was a part of a tree limb.

The way he had never belonged anywhere in his life, ever.

Ziftkin breathed a long, ragged sigh. What was so wrong

with him that he could not belong anywhere? Nobody wanted him, not his kin, not his own father even . . .

He felt a shiver of bitterness – his so-wonderful gift-flute had only served to reveal to him more clearly, more deeply, more certainly than ever how totally alone and unbelonging he was.

And yet . . . Feeling the smooth warmness of the flute in his hands, he could not help but still feel that it *was* a wondrous gift. It had saved his life and Gullie's. Who knew to what it might lead him?

Ziftkin looked around him at the wide world. Somewhere, there lay a future for him, surely. But where? How? All he could see now was the blue morning sky and the seemingly endless, rolling, grassy country stretching in every direction he looked. The world was empty and silent, save for the soft sound of birdsong.

On the branch of a low bush nearby, one of the feathered songsters tilted back his head and sang: *dee-dee, tee-dee, tee-dee-ooo*. It was a smallish, blue-winged bird with a bright crimson tuft of feathers upon its narrow little head. Ziftkin dismounted, leaving Gullie to nibble contentedly enough upon the meadow grass, and walked a few paces towards the bird. Slowly, he lifted the flute to his lips and, after the bird had given forth with another burst of song, played the creature's own melody back: *tee-wee, tee-wee, tee-wee-ooo*.

The bird snapped its head around and regarded him suspiciously with one bright eye. Then it sang again its morning song: *dee-dee, tee-dee* . . .

Ziftkin played along, mirroring the bird's singing. Through the flute, he felt the small creature's surging little life, all wind and dipping flight and the good wet taste of fresh worms.

The bird leaped up into the air, and he called to it through the flute, beckoning it closer. It fluttered uncertainly, as if caught in a sudden turbulence of wind, then dipped over towards him. From somewhere another such bird appeared, and another after.

Ziftkin kept playing, repeating the basic *tee-wee tee-dee* of the original birdsong, but weaving complexity into it, threading in snatches of other birdsong he heard, or melodies that came to his fingers through the flute.

More birds appeared, and more yet, and soon he was surrounded by a fluttering, multicoloured cloud of the winged creatures, all choiring away in complex counterpoint to each other and to his own melody-making.

Ziftkin laughed, feeling light wings brush his cheek, the weight of little light-boned bodies along his shoulders. He twirled slowly, and the birds about him twirled through the air in response. It was like a kind of dance. He stepped a few paces, twirled again; the bird-cloud followed with him, surrounding him like a sort of fluttering aura.

What he had done with the water-beast had been . . . dark, somehow. He had used the flute as a weapon, thrusting the song of it into the creature's guts like a blade. But this, this was a thing of joy, calling to the wild, free-beating little hearts of the birds, bringing them all together to make song the like of which none of them had ever known.

The music seemed to lift them – man and bird alike – till they were whirling and leaping, no more than half upon the ground, no more than half aware of where song ended and beating wing and manflesh began.

And then, turning, Ziftkin looked down through the weaving of bright wings before him and saw on the grassy crest of a hill only a little distance off, a squad of mounted, armed men.

Ziftkin came down out of the air and hit the ground with a *krump*, his knees buckling, and the music ended. The birds exploded away, shrieking and keening, as if some invisible giant had kicked them with his boot. Ziftkin stood, panting and shocked, staring at the men arrayed on the hillcrest before him. It was the last thing he had expected in this deserted land, to be faced thus suddenly with a mounted squad of armed men – for he saw that they were armed with swords and lances.

'You, boy!' one of them shouted at him. 'Stand as you are!'

Ziftkin's first instinct was to make a dash for Gullie, who stood nearby with her head up and reins dangling, her ears back nervously. He could vault into the saddle and gallop off . . .

But these riders were no more than about thirty paces from him. And on more sober reflection, he did not reckon he stood any chance of outrunning them. Their mounts looked fresh and strong. And, besides, several of the men were armed with crossbows, he now realized. Two of these had their weapons trained on him.

Which left him precious little option but to stand where he was as he had been ordered.

Gullie whickered nervously, pawing the sod. He made soft, calming sounds to her, hoping she would not decide to bolt. That was all he needed, his only possible chance of escape fleeing without him . . .

He stood, his heart thumping uncertainly, his hands upon the flute clammy with sweat. He was all too aware of how ragged and travel-stained he must appear.

The horsemen were an imposing lot. They all wore identical dark trousers and tunic, severely simple, yet with a certain sombre elegance. Plate armour cuirasses sheathed their torsos, and there were iron and leather fighting helms on their heads. On each helm a crimson insignia was inscribed. They were too small for Ziftkin to quite decipher at this distance, those insignias, but one of the approaching men carried a white pennant, the pole of it booted in his stirrup, and Ziftkin could make out the design on that pennant: a stylized sun, with blood-red rays emerging to frame a pair of hands, gripped – whether in greeting or struggle, he could not tell.

The riders came down the hill slowly, drawing up about him to form into a crescent. The crossbowmen kept their weapons levelled at him.

One of the group reined his mount close up to Ziftkin. 'Who are you, boy?' he demanded. He was a stocky man with a scar running transversely across his cheek and nose like a piece of dirty string stuck to his face. He had a sword in hand, the naked iron blade pointed at Ziftkin's sternum. 'What are you doing, riding alone out here like this? And what were you doing to those birds?'

Ziftkin did not know what to say. He shifted position, put a hand to his face.

The horsemen reined their mounts nervously. One of the crossbowmen brought his weapon to bear.

They were nervous of *him*, Ziftkin realized with a shock. A dozen and three-quarters of armed and mounted men were nervous about facing him as he stood alone on the sod.

The very notion of it left him speechless.

'I asked you a question, boy. Don't get insolent with me! I'm Squad Leader here.'

'I . . . I am . . . travelling,' Ziftkin said.

Scarface laughed a short, barking laugh. 'He's *travelling*, this ragamuffin boy is,' he said over his shoulder to the gathered riders. 'Just seeing the sights, no doubt.'

The man urged his horse forwards. He looked down at Ziftkin, then turned back to his men as if he were about to say something further to them. Then, with a quick and entirely unexpected leap, he was out of the saddle and had upended Ziftkin and dumped him onto the grass.

'Do you think me *stupid*, boy?' He gave a bark of laughter. 'Well, you'd better think again.' He stood glaring at Ziftkin, who lay on the ground gasping from the shock of his landing.

'Where are they?'

Ziftkin struggled up to his knees, tried to rise to his feet.

Scarface stopped him with a menacing gesture of his blade. 'I asked you a question, boy. Where *are* they?' The man's face was alight with a fury Ziftkin could not at all make sense of.

'Answer me!'

Ziftkin blinked, shook himself. His heart was hammering. He did not understand any of this. 'Where is *who*? What are you talking about?'

'I know your sort, boy. Dirty as a sty pig, and insolent as they come. I warn you . . . Don't try to play me for a fool.'

'Then stop acting the fool!' Ziftkin snapped. 'And explain yourself properly.' The words were out before he knew it.

Scarface scowled. He brought his blade up, two-handedly. 'I warned you not to . . .'

Ziftkin saw his own death in the man's face, plain as plain. He scrambled awkwardly backwards and got to his feet. In his tumble, he had dropped the bone flute. He saw it now, half hidden in the grass.

Scarface came at him with a vicious lunge.

Ziftkin dived under the man's attack, feeling the cold *thwish* of the blade past his ear, and hit the ground hard, jarring his arm from elbow to shoulder. But the flute came to hand.

Rolling to his knees, he brought it to his lips and blew a long, breathless, piercing note.

One of the crossbowmen fired at him, his crossbow *clakking* nastily.

Hardly knowing what he did, Ziftkin *felt* the motion of the bolt through the air and played it instinctively past him with a quick flurry of notes.

Men were leaping from their horses all around him now, blades hissing from their scabbards.

Still on his knees, Ziftkin played them to a halt. He could *feel* the sudden, uncertain fearfulness his actions had engendered in them, and he took that and played it back to them, treblefold, till they stood shaking and paralysed.

He moved his head and the flute, playing a forceful little downwards snatch of melody.

The men's weapons fell from their hands.

Ziftkin laughed through the flute. These riders thought they could bully him, did they? Thought he was just a defenceless lad? Well, he was weary of being bullied, weary of other folk trying to push him about. He would teach them a lesson they would not soon forget.

Pivoting slowly, he blew a long blast of sound at them, paralysing them momentarily. Then he turned to Scarface. With a quick flurry of notes, Ziftkin set him to dancing. His feet thrashed the grass in rhythm to Ziftkin's playing, his arms jerking and whirling. The man's face was white with terror.

Which was nothing less than he deserved, Ziftkin thought with satisfaction. He had the fellow twirl about, faster and faster, faster still, till the man spun out and collapsed to the ground, vomiting helplessly.

Ziftkin allowed the music to lapse, then, lifting the bone flute from his lips and letting silence return. The men gathered about gaped at him, white-faced and shaking.

Ziftkin could not help but grin. 'Have a care, next time,' he told Scarface, who lay gasping in the grass, 'how you address strangers. They may be more than you take them for.'

Scarface made no reply. It seemed all he could do simply to get breath.

Ziftkin turned away, intending to mount Gullie and ride

out. None of the men here would try to stop him. They were too cowed – at least for the present. He got as far as grasping Gullie's saddle with one hand, but then he stopped.

Beyond the stricken men, he saw more riders upon the hillcrest.

At their fore rode one who stood out dramatically from the rest. Though he sported the same sombre breeches and tunic, he wore no armour, and he had on a long cloak that fell in dark folds from his shoulders and about his horse's withers. His dusky tunic glittered with gold interweaving, and he wore a slim gold circlet upon his head, like a glinting headband. A large golden medallion hung upon his chest.

Drawing closer to Ziftkin and those surrounding him, the man reined his horse – a white stallion – to a halt and sat in the saddle, arms crossed, silently regarding Ziftkin for long moments. He was tall, this man, robust and clean-limbed and inordinately handsome. He had long dark hair, held back by the golden circlet. His clean-shaved jaw was strong, his nose elegantly straight, his forehead high and broad. His eyes were dark and keen as a hawk's.

There wasn't the least speck of dirt about the man's clothes, nor a fold of his clothing out of place. Standing on the sod before him, Ziftkin felt every bit the rumpled, no-account vagrant.

'Well, well,' the man said eventually, and his voice was deep and smooth and resonant. He seemed unperturbed by the scene before him. 'What do we have here, then?'

The man gestured towards Scarface, who had risen shakily onto his knees by now. 'I send you ahead to reconnoitre, Squad Leader Balmot, and now I find you on your knees in the grass next to this . . . boy. Not especially impressive behaviour, Squad Leader.'

Scarface struggled to his feet, his face pale. He pointed at Ziftkin. 'He . . . I . . . You can't . . .'

'The boy bespelled us!' one of the gathered men said suddenly. 'He's . . . he is . . .' but the man lapsed into uncertain silence, obviously unsure what it was exactly that Ziftkin might be.

'It's that . . . that *instrument* he carries,' another of them put in. 'He had the rest of us paralysed with it, somehow. That terrible, writhing music . . .' The man shuddered. 'He had the poor Squad Leader dancing like a chicken.'

The man on the stallion smiled thinly.

'It's true, sir. You ought to have seen it! He had poor . . .'

'I *did* see it,' the man said. He gestured back to the hillcrest. 'From the hill. It was most instructive.' He turned his attention to Ziftkin. 'Who are you, then, songster?'

'My . . . my name is Ziftkin,' Ziftkin replied. 'As for who I am . . .' He shrugged. 'I hardly know the answer to that myself.' Self-consciously, he ran a hand over his face. He did not know why he had answered this man so directly.

The man made a formal little bow from the saddle. 'My name is Iryn Jagga. Unlike you, I know very well who I am.'

'And that . . . that would be?' Ziftkin prompted after a long few moments' silence.

The man smiled, revealing perfect, strong white teeth. 'I am leader of the Ancient Brotherhood of the Light.'

Ziftkin had never heard of any such brotherhood, and only stared at the man blankly.

Iryn Jagga shook his handsome head. 'Ah . . . such ignorance. To sorry times indeed are we come. Once, my grandfather's grandfathers ruled all these lands. Sofala was a great city and . . .'

'Sofala?' Ziftkin said.

Iryn Jagga blinked, shook his head once more, sorrowfully. 'Such an unfortunate, ignorant boy you are. Not to have heard of the great Sofala . . . One of the greatest of the ancient Domains it was – still is, and will be again.'

Somehow – he was unsure quite why – Ziftkin could not find the man's words insulting. He sounded like a doting uncle, genuinely sorrowful for Ziftkin's ignorance.

'You are from some farm steading, I imagine,' Iryn Jagga said. 'Northwards, perhaps. Near the forsaken wilder lands.'

Ziftkin nodded.

'Ah . . . That would explain your lack of perspective. No fault of yours. Come out to see the wide world, then, have you? Come to seek your fortune?'

Ziftkin shrugged self-consciously. He felt, suddenly, the utter strangeness of this situation, exchanging such small talk here with this man . . .

Iryn Jagga swung down from his stallion and walked over to stand before Ziftkin. Face to face like this, the two were of a height, but Ziftkin was all skin and bone and gangly limbs, whereas Iryn Jagga was broad-shouldered and solid. He gestured at the flute which rested quiet in Ziftkin's hold. 'An altogether extraordinary instrument. How did you come by it?'

Ziftkin shrugged noncommittally, not knowing quite how to explain things.

Iryn Jagga held out his hand. 'May I hold it?'

The outstretched hand, Ziftkin saw, was lacking the better half of three fingers. They had been sliced away, as if some great, razor-sharp carving knife had been taken to them on a chopping board. It was not a new injury, for it was fully healed, but the man's face, Ziftkin now realized, showed deep lines of pain about the dark eyes and the mouth. Ziftkin felt a stab of quick, impulsive sympathy for this Iryn Jagga. He could not help wondering what it was that had caused such a terrible wound.

But he held tight to the flute nevertheless. Did the man think him stupid, that he would just hand it over for the asking?

Iryn Jagga smiled. 'Come, boy. I mean you no harm. I saw what you did with this instrument of yours. I wish to hold it for a moment, is all.'

Ziftkin took a step away, hesitated. He found himself wanting to trust this man. There was something about him. He was obviously someone of importance, yet he treated Ziftkin with far more respect than any one else in his life had up till now.

And there was the man's impressive appearance, also. He resembled nothing so much as Ziftkin's boyhood image of a great hero: tall and square-shouldered, handsome and clear-eyed. How could one doubt the word of such a man?

But he was not about to let anyone have the flute – not even for a few moments. He lifted the instrument to his lips, determined to play this man, play them all, into paralysis so that he could make good his escape.

But the man merely smiled at him. He placed both his hands upon the golden medallion that hung upon his chest. 'Your rustic instrument would have no power over me, boy. I am protected.'

Ziftkin did not know what to think.

'It would be best not to gainsay me,' Iryn Jagga continued. He held the golden medallion up. On it, Ziftkin could make out an engraved face, a man's face, stern, commanding, handsome – not unlike Iryn Jagga's own. 'I am the emissary of a great Power, boy. You could not deal with me the way you dealt with these others.'

Ziftkin stood, the flute still raised to his lips, uncertain. He had no notion of what this man might mean – of what Power he might be emissary to, or what the engraved, golden face might represent – but there was no trace of uncertainty in Iryn Jagga. He stood calm and utterly confident as if, indeed, he faced uncanny instruments such as Ziftkin's own on a daily basis.

'I give you my word,' Iryn Jagga said. He placed his hand, palm flat, next to the gold medallion and over his heart, with a deliberate ceremoniousness. 'And the word of Iryn Jagga is no small matter. Neither you nor your instrument will come to any harm in my hands.'

Ziftkin looked about him. He was entirely surrounded by armed men now, those on horseback who had come in along with Iryn Jagga, and those on foot, who had retrieved their dropped weapons.

'Hand me the instrument, boy,' Iryn Jagga said.

If the man had used threats, Ziftkin would have found it easier to maintain his initial steadfast resistance. But despite the armed force at his disposal, Iryn Jagga made none such, merely stood, maimed hand held out patiently.

Ziftkin swallowed, glanced about again. He could still try to use the flute on them again, perhaps, and . . .

'Trust me, boy,' Iryn Jagga said. 'I mean you no ill. I only wish to hold that special instrument of yours for a little, to feel it for myself. It will be perfectly safe with me. *You* will be. Trust me.'

The man's handsome face seemed so open and resolute. He smiled, inclining his head a little, encouragingly. Ziftkin hesitated one last, long moment, then slowly handed the bone flute over.

Scarface was on him in an eyeblink, with a hard blow from behind in the kidneys and a backhand smack across the mouth that left Ziftkin on his knees swallowing blood.

Ziftkin scrambled up, tried to strike back, but his clumsy blow only bounced off the man's helm, and he was spilled to the ground where a kick across the side of his head filled his vision with dizzy blackness.

Scarface yanked Ziftkin's arms hard behind his back and started to bind them.

'Enough!' Iryn Jagga said. 'Let him up.'

Scarface hesitated.

'Loose his arms, Squad Leader,' Iryn Jagga commanded. 'And let him up.'

'But, I thought . . .' Scarface started.

'I gave my word he would not be harmed. My *word*, Squad Leader. Do you value the word of Iryn Jagga so altogether lightly, then?'

'No, of course not,' Scarface replied hastily. 'I just thought that . . . that you were planning to . . .'

Iryn Jagga regarded him coldly. 'Have a care, Squad Leader. You tread upon dangerous ground.'

The Squad Leader's face paled, and he knelt quickly at Iryn Jagga's feet.

Iryn Jagga regarded him coldly for a long moment, then gestured towards Ziftkin, still supine upon the grass. 'Help him up.'

With the scarfaced Squad Leader's aid, Ziftkin got unsteadily to his feet. His head rang and his mouth was filled with blood from a split lip.

'My apologies, songster,' Iryn Jagga said with a little formal bow. 'My man here acted . . . presumptuously. I trust you will forgive him?'

Ziftkin blinked. For a moment, he thought Iryn Jagga might be making fun of him. But no, the man seemed serious. 'I . . .' Ziftkin did not know quite what to say.

'We will say no more of it, then,' Iryn Jagga concluded. He looked across at the Squad Leader. 'Bind his hands.'

Ziftkin started: 'But I thought . . .'

The Squad Leader's ungentle hands grabbed Ziftkin again, wrenching his hands behind him.

'Gently, Squad Leader,' Iryn Jagga ordered. '*Gently*. And bind his hands in front, not behind.'

'Yes, sir,' the Squad Leader answered. 'Gently as can be, sir.' He manoeuvred Ziftkin to his knees and cinched his wrists together, too tightly for comfort. In the process, positioning himself so as to block Iryn Jagga's view, he dealt Ziftkin several painful, malicious jabs in the ribs with his elbow. When he was finished he turned to Iryn Jagga and said blandly, 'The prisoner is bound now, sir. Gently as could be, sir.'

Iryn Jagga nodded. He stood, feet braced wide apart, his dark cloak rustling gently in the breeze, studying Ziftkin. He raised the bone flute up before him, examining it curiously. 'An altogether . . . primitive-looking thing, I must say. Not at all the sort of looks I would have expected for an instrument of such obvious power.'

He looked down at Ziftkin, who was still on his knees. 'I asked you how you came by such a precious thing, but you did not answer me. Where did you get it?'

Ziftkin looked away sullenly.

'Best you answer me, boy. You do not wish to make of me an enemy, do you?'

'Make of you . . . You lied to me! And have me bound, and . . . and now you ask—'

'I have not *lied* to you, boy. You have not been harmed. I do not know who you may be . . . or even *what* you may be. Do you think I make a habit of taking reckless chances?'

Iryn Jagga came over and reached out a hand – the non-maimed one – and helped Ziftkin to stand. 'I am no enemy of yours, boy. I must take precautions is all. Prove yourself trustworthy, and I shall, in turn, trust you.'

Ziftkin was not sure what to think. Perhaps what the man said did, indeed, make a kind of sense. And he seemed so solid and believable.

'I asked you a question.' Iryn Jagga brandished the flute. 'How did you come by this?'

'It was a . . . a gift,' Ziftkin replied after a long moment's hesitation. 'From my father.'

'Ah . . .' Iryn Jagga looked back to the flute. He hefted it

211

gently, ran his unmaimed hand along its smooth bone length. 'Your father must have been a . . . special man.'

'He was,' Ziftkin said.

'Was?'

Ziftkin shrugged. He did not wish to talk about his father. For long moments, he and Iryn Jagga regarded each other in silence.

Then Iryn Jagga shrugged and made a little formal bow. 'As you wish, then. It is not necessary for me to pry into any private grief you may have.'

Ziftkin nodded. He did not know quite what to make of the man facing him. Why would a person of such obvious power and sophistication treat a ragged, vagabond songster like himself in so mannerly a fashion? He felt torn: on the one hand, a part of him wished to – already part-way did, he realized – trust this man; on the other, he was painfully suspicious. He did not think he could stand a repeat of the sort of thing that had happened to him back at Gault Keep with the Lady Evadne.

'We have a future together, songster, you and I,' Iryn Jagga was saying. 'I felt it the instant I saw you playing that instrument of yours. You are no ordinary farm lad. You are destined to do far more than grub in the dirt.'

Ziftkin was not sure how to respond.

'Great Jara himself has sent you to me in my time of need.'

'Great . . . Jara?' Ziftkin said.

Iryn Jagga shook his head. 'Such an ignorant boy.' He smiled, revealing his perfect white teeth. 'But ignorance can excuse much, can it not? Whatever you may be, believe that I mean you no harm, boy. You have my word on that. And you have seen that I keep my word.'

The man *had* kept his word, after a fashion, Ziftkin supposed. But it was no comfortable fashion. He lifted his bound hands. 'Set me free, then, if you truly mean me no harm.'

Iryn Jagga smiled again. 'Ah . . . I would like nothing so much as to do that. But, you see, I do not yet know if *you* intend *me* harm.'

'But you can't just . . .' Ziftkin took a breath and began

again. 'I give you my word that I intend neither you nor yours any harm. There. Is that enough for you?'

Iryn Jagga merely laughed. 'There is nothing so unreliable as a young man's word.'

Ziftkin stared at him. 'But . . . You expect *me* to trust *your* word, yet you refuse to trust mine.'

Iryn Jagga nodded. 'Exactly so.'

Ziftkin did not now how to respond.

Iryn Jagga came close and put his arm about Ziftkin's shoulders in an avuncular way. 'Come. I have a field camp not too very far off. You look in need of a good meal.' He sniffed and made a face, 'And a hot bath and a change of clothing, too.'

Ziftkin hesitated. He glanced round at the sombre-uniformed, armed men surrounding him. There was scant chance of his being able to get away, even if he were somehow to miraculously free his bound hands. And Iryn Jagga held his flute . . .

Perhaps the man was indeed acting in good faith, in his own convoluted manner.

Iryn Jagga guided Ziftkin over to Gullie and helped him mount – a somewhat awkward process with his hands bound as they were. Then Iryn Jagga swung onto his own white stallion. Motioning Ziftkin to accompany him, he led off across the grassy slopes. The mounted men fell into a double column behind, and they all cantered off.

Ziftkin was not sure what to think. His split lip stung where the scarfaced Squad Leader had struck him. His head still rang faintly, achingly. His bound hands chaffed and throbbed. And he noticed more than a few hard glances aimed his way by Iryn Jagga's riders, the Squad Leader not least of all.

But despite all that, he could not help feeling as if he had suddenly fallen into one of the adventurous wonder tales his foster brother Mechant had been so fond of when they were all lads together. It was surely a heady feeling – aches and pains and bound hands notwithstanding – to find himself at this imposing man's side, at the head of an armed and mounted cavalcade, cantering across the rolling grassy hills with the wind in his face.

Ziftkin felt his back straighten. Iryn Jagga looked across at him and smiled, and Ziftkin found himself smiling back. It was the strangest experience, for though he was a prisoner of this strange man, he felt like a drowning person might who, against all expectations, suddenly discovers solid land under his feet.

XIX

They stood silently in the tree shadow on a slope at the verge of the invaders' camp clearing: Elinor, Gyver, a dozen or so of the fur-folk, mostly the younger ones, but also including thick-shouldered Stone, Cloud-Dreaming, and Frog, the Longwater elder.

The day was new, with the night's coolth still in the air. They had passed carefully one of the uncanny dangling watchers – little Sky-Flower having blinded it, under Cloud-Dreaming's supervision – and now, somewhat above but within clear sight of the camp, they made no special attempt to conceal themselves. So far, none of the invaders had noticed them.

'They have no woodcraft, them,' Stone said softly. 'Like fissh out of their water.'

Elinor nodded. It was clearly true. The improbably colourful men before them were obvious interlopers here, with none of the quiet at-homeness in the woods that Gyver's folk had. For a moment, she saw the camp before her as the fur-folk must: an ugly scar on the forest, the naked stumps of felled trees protruding like so many broken bones from the trampled ground.

'Make a ssound, sso they will know, them, that we are come,' suggested one of the younger fur-men.

Gyver shook his head. 'We will wait in ssilence, uss. They will see uss ssoon enough.'

Elinor nodded her agreement. It was only a matter of time before somebody down there spotted them. 'Better to be patient and stay here quiet,' she said. 'It'll be more shocking to them if they suddenly spot us up here.'

That was what she hoped for. The greater the initial shock, the better. And the more casual this small group of theirs seemed, the better, too, for what she had in mind here.

So they stood silent, waiting.

Gazing at the camp before her, Elinor could not help but speculate about just who and what these invaders might be – and what chance the ploy she planned to use here stood of succeeding.

There seemed a raw vigour to these invaders, what with the garish paint and the bristle and brandish of their gleaming bronze weapons. They had the aura, somehow, of men who felt themselves to be on the beginning of some great path. Fanatics, maybe. Elinor shivered, remembering Sofala and the Ancient Brotherhood of the Light. Some burgeoning empire, she reckoned, stood at the back of these men.

Such was what she truly reckoned them to be, an advance party of eastern 'conquerors', sent ahead to feel out the way for others to follow. She only hoped she was right. Everything rested upon it.

A sudden stiffening amongst her companions jarred Elinor out of her thoughts. They had been spotted.

It was comical, almost. One of the invaders had come striding along in their direction across the camp clearing, glanced up, glanced away, then stopped so precipitously he nearly fell over his own feet. He would be able to make out little in the way of real detail, Elinor knew; the tree shadow in which they stood ensured that. But he would be able to see their silhouettes clear enough, and know that they were not any friends to him and his.

The man stared at them, shook his head, blinked, shook his head again, then set up a cry that startled everything in the forest. The camp erupted like a hive of anxious bees.

The man who had spotted them pointed.

Bronze weapons flashed. The men formed up hurriedly into a kind of defensive block, like a thick, multi-hued, prickly, living tapestry.

Well enough disciplined, Elinor thought, watching the speed with which they recovered from the shock of finding their forest enemy inexplicably hanging about at their camp's verge, within the boundary of their set guards.

It reassured her, that evidence of fighting discipline. They seemed, indeed, to be the sort of folk she had reckoned them to be, that she hoped them to be.

The whole of the invaders' camp was arraigned against them now, stood massed in that defensive block of theirs in the clearing. There were perhaps four or five dozens of them, dressed in startlingly bright-coloured clothing, adorned with dangling feathers and beads. They brandished their bronze-bladed weapons threateningly, short swords, long-handled war axes – the first Elinor had seen amongst them – and stout war spears with leaf-shaped blades. Their faces were painted with charcoal and bright paint in varying designs, some entirely abstract, some exaggerated into fang and snarl and staring eyes so as to make of them demon-faced creatures.

One of the men suddenly threw back his head and let out a menacing howl. The rest echoed that cry, like a pack of wild wolves in a rage.

Elinor felt some of the younger fur-folk about her shiver. 'Stay as you are,' she said softly to them. They did, and she and her little group kept to their positions, silent.

Little more than thirty paces separated the two groups, but though the invaders had crossbowmen, none of them fired their weapons. It was the uphill slope, the uncertainty of the light under the trees, or of the very situation itself that stayed their hands, Elinor reckoned. Exactly as she had hoped. She forced herself to stand unmoving, though her heart thumped in her breast wildly.

The howling dwindled. None of the invaders made any move in the direction of the fur-folk. They stayed where they were in the clearing, in their defensive block formation, tense, weapons up, obviously uncertain what to expect from an attacking enemy who simply stood in silence.

Elinor gave a signal with her hand then, and, slowly, she and the little group of fur-folk stepped out from amongst the trees and down into the camp clearing proper.

Seeing their furred enemy clear, the invaders launched into their wolf-pack howling.

Seeing Elinor, they went silent.

'A woman,' one of them said wonderingly after a long moment. 'A *human* woman!'

'A captive!' another added.

At the head of them stood a man a little taller, a little

broader, a little more grotesquely made up. He held one of the axes, elaborately decorated with feathers and scribed inlay, with a long, polished wood handle. Two wide bars of dark red zig-zagged from the brim of his bronze-and-leather fighting helm across his forehead and down his face. His eyes had been circled in chalk white, so that his expression was that of a wide-eyed, scowling demon.

Elinor recognized him as the man she had spied upon some days back as he had come out of his multi-hued tent – the man she had reckoned to be leader here.

The man waved the axe over his head. 'Run, woman!' he called. 'Quick as you can. Quick for your life. Never fear. Run! We will protect you from these beasts!'

Elinor stayed as she was.

'*Run!*'

Elinor laughed. 'Run yourself, man. I am quite content where I am.'

A little titter ran through the fur-folk.

'Her mind is gone,' one of the invaders said. 'She does not know what she speaks. They have . . . taken her mind from her by their animal brutalities.'

From amongst the block of invaders, one emerged who was different from the rest. Where they wore body armour and dressed in colourful trousers and shirt-tunics, he was un-armoured, wearing only a long drab robe; where they went armed, his hands were empty except for a black rod, from the tip of which a single white feather fluttered. Where they wore war helms, his head was bare, and bald as an egg. His face was painted entirely, starkly white, making the whites of his eyes and teeth seem yellow and his lips crimson-dark as cherries. The effect – with the egg-bald head – was a clownish face almost, but grim and eerie, too.

Elinor had spied nothing like him before this, and she was a little taken aback. Who – what – could he be?

The man stared at her and the fur-folk with yellow-white, dark-centred eyes. He lifted the black rod, brandishing it at Elinor. The white feather whirled. Slowly, he began to chant, the words in no tongue Elinor recognized. She felt a faint shimmer go through the air about her, and the small hairs along her neck prickled. In the distance, she heard – or

218

thought she heard – the soft *thrumming* she associated with the strange guardians that had been set about the camp.

But the axe-wielding leader stepped up and gave the robed man a hard shove, sending him stumbling awkwardly sideways and putting an end to the chanting.

'How dare you?' the robed man cried. '*Fool!*'

'It's *you* who are the fool!' the axe-wielder returned. He spat. 'Stupid priest!'

The other stiffened. 'Have a care how you address me, or—'

'Or what?' the axe-wielder interrupted. 'You will sing your silly songs at me?' He pointed towards Elinor and the fur-folk. 'See how effective your stupid chants are, priest? Where are your much-vaunted guardians, then, that this rabble of animals can come marching into our camp as they please, past your marvellous warders, and without so much as a breath of warning for us?'

'You understand nothing!' the priest said. 'There is something at work here. Something beyond what the ignorant eye can see.'

'I understand one thing only too well, priest,' the axe-wielder said. 'Your guardians have failed us. *You* have failed us.'

'No!' the priest cried. 'You understand *nothing*, I say!'

The other brandished his bronze-bladed axe threateningly. 'I never trusted you, priest. You nor your sort. Sneaky, back-stabbing connivers, the lot of you. I put my faith in *this* . . .' He shook his axe. 'This blade and my good strong arm. That's all I need. All your mumblings and fumblings . . .' He spat at the priest's feet. 'Get away from here, and leave this in *my* hands.'

'I will *not*!' the priest replied. 'You understand *nothing* of what you are dealing with here. There are hidden forces at work here. None could have passed my Guardians without—'

'Shut up!' the axe-wielder snapped. 'It is *I* who will deal with these presumptuous animals. You have failed in your task here. You are interfering with *my* duties. Again! From the very beginning of this expedition you have tried to sabotage things. I will make sure First-Commander Kamikal hears of it when we return. And through him, High-Lord Dalara himself. Never you doubt that.' He came forwards, his axe raised two-handedly. 'And then where will you and your precious priesthood be when High-Lord Dalara learns you have been working against his ambitions?'

'Step back!' the priest commanded. He lifted his black rod and shook it, making the white feather whirl. 'I warn you! For your soul's sake, do not threaten me.'

The axe-wielder laughed. 'My soul's sake! Save your threats for women and wide-eyed children, fool. You do not frighten me.'

'Step back, I say!' the priest repeated.

The axe-wielder came on.

For an instant, it seemed that the priest would stand his ground. But no. Under the unbending threat of the other's axe, he slunk away, muttering and fuming, his white feather fluttering impotently.

Elinor watched all this with interest. She had no real notion as to the details that might lie behind the enmity between these two men, but it was clearly an old antagonism. And it betrayed much about them. A complexity of relationships lay behind this: a brittle alliance between 'priests' – priests of what? – and warriors; a personage of authority named First-Commander Kamikal, through whom the axe-wielder would send his damaging report against the priest to a 'High-Lord' Dalara; jealousies and conflicts and a struggle for primacy, with an all-ruling Lord . . .

It seemed to fit exactly with her expectations. Elinor felt a little thrill of excitement.

The axe-wielder watched the priest slink away and laughed. 'So! And good riddance to you, fool.' He turned, then, and regarded Elinor and the fur-folk.

Elinor could see him fairly glowing with the flush of his triumph over the priest. His eyes flashed with it as he stood there, one hand fisted on his hip now, gripping the axe with the other.

'Come here, woman,' he commanded. 'And quickly, now. Enough of this nonsense. I don't know who you may be, or what you may be doing in the company of these animals, but it's over, now.'

Elinor merely looked at him.

'Come here, I say. Now!'

Neither Elinor nor any of the fur-folk stirred.

220

The axe-wielder raised his weapon two-handedly, glowering, but there was the first faint hint of what might be uncertainty in his painted face.

'Kill them!' one of the men drawn up behind him suddenly called out. 'Cut them *down*!'

In a pack, they rushed forwards, bronze-bladed weapons gleaming dully in the forest light.

The fur-folk stayed as they were, rigid, unmoving.

'Stop!' Elinor cried. '*STOP!*' And such was the force of her shout – and so strange the sight of the fur-folk standing stock still awaiting the invaders' charge – that the rushing men slowed, stumbled to an uncertain halt.

'Are you all so *stupid*, then,' Elinor demanded acidly of them, 'that you rush up here intent on killing before you even know what is happening or what brings us to your camp?'

The axe-wielding leader stood forwards. He bristled, puffed out his chest, threw back his head. 'We are warriors, woman. We live by the blade. There is glory in the warrior's life, glory in the warrior's death. We kill for glory. A man can never be covered with too much glory.'

Elinor laughed. She could not help it. He seemed so much the adolescent boy boasting in front of his adolescent comrades.

The man scowled at her. 'It is *you* who are stupid, woman, coming here as you do, with . . .' he snorted in disgust, 'with these *animals*.'

Elinor wiped the residual smile from her face. 'We are come,' she said, gesturing to herself and the fur-folk about her, 'to end the bloodshed you have started.'

The leader stared at her in hard silence. His gruesome, painted face made it impossible to read with any certainty what he might or might not be thinking.

'Why have you forced your way into the forest, bringing destruction and bloody death with you?' Elinor demanded of him. 'Surely, this has all been some sort of terrible misunderstanding. The fur-folk are a peaceable people. They would have met you with open arms, given you fish and fruit to eat, helped you. Even now, it is not too late to—'

'We need help from no man. And certainly from no *beasts*

such as these!' The axe-wielder scowled. 'We *take* what we require, woman. And none may gainsay us. We are the Chosen People. We go where we will, take what we will, by *divine right.*'

Elinor felt an uneasy stirring amongst the fur-folk. 'Ssick-in-the-head people,' she heard somebody mutter.

'I am Shosha,' the axe-wielding leader said, 'Band-Chief of the Gahilla Cohort of First-Commander Kamikal, sworn to the High-Lord Dalara, great leader of the Chosen People. In the name of great Dalara himself, I offer you asylum, woman. Forsake these beasts who have you in their brutal thrall. We will protect you. They and their kind have killed our men, ambushing them like cowards. And we will punish them for that. Punish them long and slow.'

Elinor said nothing.

Shosha stared at her for long moments, the eyes in his painted face hard as stones. Then he raised his bronze-gleaming axe and cried out, a long, ululating roar.

The invaders charged.

Before they could come to grips with the fur-folk, Elinor stepped forwards and drew her sword. Adopting the Double-tree defensive stance, shining blade held low, two-handedly, she stood poised and ready.

The invaders stumbled to a halt, staring.

'What is *this*?' Shosha demanded. He peered at Elinor, as if she had suddenly sprouted wings. 'Where did you get such a blade, woman? And what are *you* doing with it?'

'It shines white as fire,' one of the men behind him said softly, and made what was obviously a warding sign with the fingers of one hand.

Elinor felt the familiar, uncanny strength of the white blade thrill through her bones, felt herself harden into a purity of purpose that was all blade and balance and deadly movement. It had been over a year since she had last wielded the sword; it felt *good* to stand here with it in her hands, feeling her heart thump with excitement, the blade bright as a shining bar of light.

She stood here for Gyver and his folk, an act of righteous defence. But the thrill in her went deeper than that, a thing of blood and bone and instinct. She would have felt it no matter

222

whose side she fought on. It was what made the white blade both wonderful and terrible.

She kept a careful hold on herself, knowing that the thrilling strength of the blade could lead her too far if she let it, goading her into fatal extravagances of effort – and knowing, too, what blind, bloody carnage the blade could so easily cause. There had been altogether too much blood and grief already, in her own life and the lives of the fur-folk.

'Take it from her, Shosha,' one of the invaders was saying. 'No woman has the right to wield a battle blade!'

The leader came towards Elinor, stepping slow, his axe held down at his side. 'Give me the blade, woman,' he ordered, holding out his free hand, palm up, beckoning. 'You know not what you do. It is forbidden for women to wield a battle blade. And a battle blade such as *that* . . .' He stared at the shining length of it hungrily. 'You must give it to me. Be sensible now, woman. Be . . .'

Elinor had stood her ground; he was only a few paces from her now. Abruptly, he rushed forwards, clearly intending to bull her to the earth and snatch up the blade.

Elinor side-stepped his brute rush easily enough, spilled him to his knees with a thump of the blade's pommel against the side of his helmeted head – spilling his helm and sending the axe flying – and resumed the Double-tree stance, all in one smooth motion.

A low gasp went up from the gathered invaders.

Shosha scrambled to his feet with a roar. 'I tripped!' he cried to his men, hastily scooping up his axe and helm. 'I *tripped*!'

Jamming the helm back on his head, he came at Elinor again, but more slowly this time, his dully gleaming axe swinging in a low arc. 'You will regret the day you were born, woman. Nobody . . . *nobody* defies Shosha Bronze-hand and lives to laugh over it.'

Elinor stayed where she was. She set her feet carefully, maintaining the Double-tree posture, the shining blade up but entirely motionless, ready to move in any direction.

Shosha halted, squinting at her through his garish face-paint, uncertain.

'Get her, Shosha!' one of his men chided him. 'What are you waiting for?'

Elinor had never faced an axe-wielder such as this. It was different from confronting a swordsman. She could see by the way he held it that the thing had real heft. And with the long handle, its reach was comparable to that of her own blade. She did not fancy the idea of having him connect on her with such a weapon. It would cleave her like so much wet, punky wood.

He came at her suddenly, the axe swinging in a great, two-handed arc, quicker than she had expected.

But not quick enough.

Elinor pivoted, brought the white blade round, and, with all the strength and precision she could muster, cut at the axe handle as the weapon arced past her. The perfect razor edge of her blade sliced through the tough wood of the axe haft cleanly. The bronze head went tipping off through the air, a remnant of the handle left protruding from it. Shosha stumbled past her and fell flat on his face. Elinor swept through the momentum of her move and came to rest back again in the Double-tree stance.

It was cleanly, perfectly done. She felt pleased with herself.

Shosha pushed himself up on his arms, staring in startled amazement at the stump of axe handle in his fist. He had lost his helm again, and there was tree litter tangled in his hair. 'What *are* you?' he demanded of her.

'I am Elinor Whiteblade,' she answered him.

He stared at her shining blade.

'Bitch!' one of the invaders cried. 'Sorcerous *bitch*!' and flung a leaf-bladed spear at her without warning.

The white blade came up – with that almost-will of its own that it sometimes had, as if she were merely the framework by which it moved – and she deflected the cast spear deftly, dodging sideways and parrying it aside so that it snicked past to *krump* into the ground beyond her. She resumed the Double-tree stance once more.

The invaders stared at her, utterly confounded.

Elinor lowered her blade a little, but relaxed her vigilance not at all. 'You have come into this land as ignorant scoundrels,' she said, adopting the most scathing tone she could. 'Who gave you permission to molest our forest folk?'

'Permission?' Shosha the axe-wielder said incredulously. He gestured to his armed group with the stub of his axe handle.

'We need no *permission*. We are the Chosen People of the High-Lord Dalara himself. We—'

'Yes, man,' Elinor interrupted. 'So you have already said. And you take what you want by . . . "divine right", wasn't it?'

The invaders muttered amongst themselves, glaring at her.

'I repeat,' Elinor said, 'my question. Or are you too stupid to understand simple words? Who gave you permission to molest our forest folk?'

'Our?' Shosha said uncertainly. He was staring at her. 'Who is this *our* you—'

The dark-robed priest reappeared suddenly, waving his feather-tipped black rod. The eyes in his white face fairly glowed with wrath. 'Evil witch!' he cried at Elinor. The black rod shook. He began chanting, his voice a guttural growl almost. The non-words of the chant made the hair on Elinor's head lift, and she shuddered, feeling a tingling in the air about her.

The priest took a step nearer to her, another, brandishing the black rod all the while as if it were a weapon. She faltered back instinctively. He wielded powers, this man; that was plain enough. She had encountered such persons before – old Mamma Kieran and her talking raven in Long Harbour, round Tildie and fanatical Seer Skolt in Minmi, Cloud-Dreaming herself . . .

But he was a dark mystery, this stranger priest. What was he capable of accomplishing? She did not, could not know.

He was chanting louder now, rolling the black rod rhythmically. Elinor felt her heart shiver. Her skin crawled uncomfortably, as if an invisible, chill web was being spun across it. She had to do something, fast, before whatever uncanny pattern he was weaving took full effect and all her plans here died aborning. She gripped the hilt of her sword more closely, thinking to rush him, relying on speed and the blade's deadly sharpness.

But before she could move, Shosha cried, 'Go away, priest!'

The priest turned on him, and Elinor felt the invisible web about her loosen a little. 'Ignorant ruffian!' the priest snapped at Shosha. '*You* will handle this, will you? *You* will deal with this woman, with these animals?' He laughed a thin laugh. 'You dull-witted, clumsy oaf! You ignorant lout! You—'

Shosha leaped and struck the priest a vicious, back-handed blow across the head with the stump of his axe.

Elinor blinked confusedly. It had happened so fast. One instant, it seemed, the priest had been fronting her, webbing her with his uncanny chantings; the next, he lay sprawled upon the ground, unmoving, blood seeping from his bald white skull, and the invisible, chill webs about her had dissolved entirely away.

Shosha stood panting, staring down at the priest. He looked at the blood on the handle stump, shook himself, glanced about.

His men stared.

'Right . . .' he said, his voice hoarse. He coughed, swallowed. 'Right,' he repeated, clearer now. 'So much for priests meddling in affairs that do not concern them!'

'You must leave our forest folk alone,' Elinor said, picking up the thread of their talk.

'And just who,' Shosha demanded, 'might this *our* you speak of be?'

Elinor kept her face perfectly expressionless. 'Sulimon Magna and his court . . . whom *I* represent.'

'You?' Shosha said in disbelief. 'This . . . this Sulimon Magna sends a *woman* to deal with the likes of us? And a lone woman at that? Not likely!'

Elinor shrugged. 'He did not see the necessity of sending more than me.'

That stopped them cold. They stared at her, clearly half believing, half not. Painfully uncertain.

It was as she had hoped.

'This forest, and all that it contains, is part of the domain of Sulimon Magna,' she proclaimed. 'He has extended his protection to all who dwell here.' Elinor made the sternest face she could, lifting her bright blade for emphasis. 'But now *you*, ignorant outlanders as you are, come here disturbing the peace of Sulimon. What have you to say for yourselves to excuse such wanton destruction as you have wrought?'

Shosha stared at her. 'You are lying, woman. If this . . . this Sulimon Magna truly exists, why, then, did he not send

226

somebody sooner? There is nothing in these wild lands save beasts and trees – and all for the taking by those who are strong enough. You *lie*, I say!'

Elinor shrugged. 'Have it your own way, man. Bring death upon yourself and your men if you choose.'

There was a hollow muttering amongst them. 'Better hear her out, Shosha,' she heard somebody urge in a whisper.

'And just how, then,' Shosha began after a moment, pointing at her with the blood-smeared stub of his axe handle, 'do you expect to—'

Elinor laughed. 'Lay aside that . . . that *stick* first, man,' she ordered, gesturing with her blade, 'if you wish me to take you seriously.'

Shosha stared daggers at her, but dropped the stub of axe handle. 'Just how, then, do you intend to bring death upon us? You, a lone woman?'

Elinor smiled. 'I am enough to deal with the likes of *you*.'

Elinor's heart was jumping, but she found she was enjoying this charade. It pleased her to discomfit such an obvious, self-inflated arsehole as this Shosha. And from the look of growing uncertainty on his and the other painted faces of the men before her, it was beginning to look as if this ploy of hers might, indeed, be working.

'All folk see only what their habits let them see,' Gyver had said to her.

Only let these painted invaders be convinced that there was some sort of great, unknown court hidden here in the wild lands, lorded over by a leader like unto but far beyond any they served, let them feel that they could not stand against the armed might of that great leader, let them feel their own inconsequence, and . . . with any luck at all, these feckless invaders would scurry home, tails between their legs, and not bother this part of the wild again.

Such was her main hope, at any rate.

It seemed it might work.

Shosha was staring at her. 'What is it you are suggesting, then, woman?' he demanded.

'Leave these lands. Sulimon Magna commands this. If you leave immediately, your lives will be spared.'

'That is everything? We leave and you let us go?'

227

Elinor nodded. 'You need only pay fair recompense for the destruction you have caused, and you will be free to go.'

'Recompense?' Shosha cried. 'Are you mad? We will give no *recompense*! We did what we did by divine right of the great—'

Elinor raised her sword, and the man fell silent. 'Enough,' she said. 'I begin to lose patience with you. Will you abide by the command of Sulimon Magna? Or will you bring certain death upon yourselves?'

Shosha hesitated. The men clustered behind him muttered uncertainly.

'Take a moment,' Elinor suggested, 'to discuss it amongst yourselves if you wish.' She lowered the tip of her blade to the ground and leaned lightly upon the hilt, casual as could be.

This was the critical instant. Only let them truly believe that there was, indeed, a great force and a great leader backing her, like the leader they served – had to serve, being who and what they were – only a far, far greater and more powerful man than their own leader was.

The painted men withdrew a little and stood clustered, heads together in a worried conclave. Elinor could hear no more than an angry, uncertain buzz from them, but it seemed clear that the arrogance that had first marked them was wilting now. She had to keep shocking them, though, or they might recover their balance.

'Do not take all day!' she shouted at them. 'I have only so much patience.'

Shosha came out of the group and walked slowly towards her. 'We wish to meet this . . . Sulimon Magna you boast of. How do we know such a man truly exists?'

Elinor shrugged. 'If Sulimon Magna had wished to meet with you, he would have come himself. Instead, he sent me as his emissary. He has better things to do than waste time with a ragtag group of ignorant ruffians such as yourselves.'

The men bristled.

Shosha clenched his fists and glowered at her. 'Have a care how you address me, woman, or—'

'Or *what*?' Elinor asked softly, stepping towards him, blade up. 'Will you rush me again? Do you so wish to be spilled on your face in the dirt yet again?'

228

Shosha faltered.

'There is only me,' Elinor announced. 'You will see nobody else. Such is the decision of Sulimon Magna. You will recompense the forest folk for the bloody violence you have done them, and then you will depart. And by whatever honour you might possess, you will swear an oath never to return here. Either that . . .' she paused and moved the blade a little in a short, flashing arc, 'or you will die here, and none will ever hear of you again in the land from which you have come.'

'We could overwhelm you, woman,' Shosha blustered. 'Fancy shining blade or no. By sheer numbers, we could overwhelm you and bring you down like a pack of hounds. All your sneaky fighting tricks would be useless then.'

Elinor beckoned with the white blade. 'Ah . . . but which of you wishes to be first?'

Nobody seemed eager to come forward.

Elinor smiled. She felt a shiver of exaltation go through her. Her limbs thrummed with the sword's strength. It was going to work, this.

Shosha stepped towards her, his hands carefully at his sides. 'Very well, woman,' he said glumly. 'It seems we are left little choice. We accept your demands.'

Elinor gestured to the band of fur-folk behind her. 'You will recompense the forest folk? Then leave these lands forever?'

'We will,' he replied.

Having him come right out and say it like this, so simply and straightly, made Elinor uncertain. It seemed too easy, all of a sudden.

'I give you my word, woman,' Shosha was saying. 'And the word of Shosha Bronze-hand is no small matter.' He placed his hand, palm flat, over his heart with deliberate ceremoniousness. 'Spare us our lives and we shall depart this land forever.'

Elinor nodded. 'Done,' she said. 'In the name of Sulimon Magna, I accept your offer.'

Shosha stepped closer to her. 'In the land where I come from, the custom is to shake hands on agreements such as this.' He was almost within blade-reach now, and he paused. 'Lay the blade aside so that we can seal this agreement between us.'

Elinor let her blade drop. She had no intention of actually laying it aside – did the man take her for a complete fool? – but she was willing to allow him close enough to shake hands if that was what he and his men needed to close the agreement.

Shosha held out his right hand. 'Well?'

Elinor shifted the sword to her left hand, extended her right towards his, but warily. The sword felt uncomfortable in her left hand, and she hoped this hand-shaking business would be quick.

Shosha took her proffered hand in his, which was large, hard, and calloused. He gripped hers and she tensed, ready to leap away.

But he shook her hand politely enough, setting his thumb over hers, nodding his head. 'I, Shosha, Band-Chief of the Gahilla Cohort of First-Commander Kamikal, sworn to the High-Lord Dalara, great leader of the Chosen People, agree to . . .'

Behind him, his men stood abashed and silent.

Elinor let go a little relieved breath. It was going to work then, this ploy of hers.

'. . . agree to . . .' Shosha was saying, '*nothing*!'

With a hard and totally unexpected yank, he threw himself backwards, taking Elinor with him. He hit the ground on his back and flung Elinor over him so that she landed hard, face first on the ground.

The white blade went flying.

Before she could properly recover herself, he was standing over her, her own blade in his grip. From the ground, she watched the look of stunned revelation go over his painted face as he felt the sword's uncanny strength pour though him. He threw back his head and laughed.

Elinor felt her belly curdle.

'No wonder you were so arrogant, woman. With a blade like this . . .' Shosha swiped it inexpertly through the air, 'even the likes of *you* are become dangerous.' Again, he cut the air in a half-clumsy slash. 'I never thought much of swords. Too light. But this . . . *this* is a blade I could grow to love!'

From behind him, suddenly, there was the *krissh* of a bow, and a hasty arrow *krunked* against his bronze cuirass. Shosha whirled with the quick ease the sword gave to the wielder.

230

Elinor saw Gyver draw back an arrow and let fly, but Shosha lifted the sword and the arrow's stone tip shattered uselessly against the brightness of the blade. Shosha laughed.

Another arrow flew, wobbly and well wide of the mark, this time. One of the fur-men threw back his arm to cast a bone-barbed javelin.

In an eyeblink, Shosha was at Elinor's side, the blade at her throat.

Gyver took a step forwards, poised uncertainly, a new arrow nocked to his bowstring, his face puckered with dismay.

'Back away, fools!' Shosha commanded the fur-folk.

Elinor felt the blade cold and very, very sharp against her skin. It had all happened in only a few heartbeats. She had still not got her breath back properly from the hard tumble Shosha had given her. She cursed herself for a fool.

'Put your weapons down,' Shosha ordered. He pressed the blade against Elinor's throat and she felt a flash of pain and the warm wetness of blood. 'Or I will open her up like a side of meat before your eyes.'

The fur-folk faltered.

Again, Shosha laughed. He gestured to his men, who came scurrying up. 'And so you lose,' he said in Elinor's ear. 'Did you think me a complete fool, then? That I would swallow your stupid lies? That I would act like a coward and run away? Only a woman could be so stupid!'

Elinor said nothing. There was nothing to say.

A third time, Shosha laughed. 'Stupid woman,' he repeated. Grabbing Elinor by her left hand – the one nearest him – he yanked her to her feet. 'You insulted me. You shamed me with your womanish, sneaky little fighting tricks and your un-canny, flashing blade. But now it is *I* who have the upper hand!'

He twisted her arm painfully, so that she was half bent on her knees, her left hand outstretched. 'You will be sorry for the things you did. Oh, yes!' He brought the blade down close to her outstretched hand where he held it. With a quick, cold *snick*, he cut off her little finger.

The agony of it, the utter and complete unexpectedness, sent Elinor sprawling helplessly to the ground. Her hand was on fire. Her vision throbbed with a creeping blackness, and she retched sickly. There was blood everywhere.

Shosha bent over her, dangling her severed finger in his hand triumphantly. 'That for starters, woman!'

Elinor stared, sick.

Shosha did a little dance of exaltation, his painted face wide with triumph.

'Shosha! Shosha! Shosha Bronze-hand!' his men chanted.

'Shosha *Whiteblade*!' he cried, lifting the sword.

'Shosha Whiteblade!' they returned. 'Shosha Whiteblade!'

Shosha flicked Elinor's little finger at her. It bounced wetly against her cheek and fell away to the ground. She stared in horror at it lying there.

Shosha laughed once more: 'I am Shosha Whiteblade! With this weapon none can stand against me. *None!*' He cut the air in great, flashing arcs. There was no subtlety in his movements. He was obviously swinging the sword as he would have his axe, but the sword made him still most formidable. Those half-clumsy swipes of his would cut a man in two most easily, Elinor knew.

Shosha jumped high in the air, came down in a crouch. Turning to the clustered fur-folk, he gave vent to a great, screaming war cry. The fur-folk still held their weapons – having defied him in that much – but they had tried nothing, and faltered back now from him: shivering, stricken, uncertain.

Shosha's men cheered him on with wild shouts. 'Cut the animals *down*!' And, 'Blood the blade! Blood the blade!'

To delighted cheers, Shosha pivoted, raised the white blade high, brought it down in a bright arc, danced backwards, leaped high into the air with the sword's strength, spun about, raised the blade again in another great flashing stroke, leaped up, twirled . . .

And tripped coming down over his own feet and tumbled heavily to the ground, the sword flying out of his grip.

For a long instant, nobody moved.

Then Elinor was on her knees. Left hand spurting blood, she dived desperately forwards and grabbed the sword's bronze hilt, feeling the strength of it fill her. With a quick roll, she was on her feet, dizzy and shaken but master, once again, of the sword and the situation.

Shosha stared up at her in shock.

The very strength of the sword had betrayed him, as it had others before him.

Elinor welcomed that uncanny strength surging through her. Her left hand throbbed in agony. She clenched it, held it up, pressed against her shoulder, hoping to slow the flow of blood. She felt sick. But the old, familiar, hard Kess-purity filtered back into her with the sword in her hand.

She took the Wolf-fang defensive posture – not certain enough of her left hand to adopt any stance needing a two-handed grip – and stared about, her breath coming in painful heaves, not knowing quite what to do next. She felt blood seeping down her left arm, soaking the sleeve of her tunic.

'Kill her!' Shosha cried from where he lay. He scrambled to his knees. 'Shining blade or no, she's only a lone woman. And bleeding. *Kill her!*'

The men surged forwards.

Elinor took the first through the neck, a quick stab and draw back that left the man choking and throat-torn before he properly knew what had happened to him.

One of them plunged a spear at her and she skipped aside, going down on one knee to avoid the sharp bronze thrust of it. She put her left hand out to the ground to steady herself, unthinking, and a burst of searing pain went up through her arm, so sudden and sharp it took her vision away for an instant.

A man charged her, axe high above his head, too quick for her to respond. She could only stare, caught off-balance just that fraction too much, unable to bring the blade up in time, seeing his eyes light with brute triumph in his painted face, his face all blue lightning bolts across red, his mouth open in a shout, showing long yellow teeth . . .

And then he was fumbling his weapon and clawing at his face, screaming, a grey-fletched arrow protruding from his eye.

Elinor looked up, gasping, and saw Gyver nocking another arrow to his bowstring.

And then it was all a swirling, cutting, bloody tangle of men and weapons, with Elinor dancing a desperate path through

233

them, the white blade shimmering, spilling blood and slicing wet flesh with elegant, terrible precision.

But there were too many of them – just as Shosha had claimed – and she could feel her strength leaking away. Her left side was soaked with her own blood. She stood gasping, in the midst of a momentary lull. Behind her, the fur-folk clustered, ready with what arrows they still had left, shaken but determined still. Facing her, the invaders bunched together, howling and whirling about in a mad little dance, spurring themselves on for a final charge. Shosha had got another axe from somewhere, and he waved it over his head like a banner, exhorting his men.

Elinor took a gasping breath, swallowed. So much for her wonderful plan. Everything had gone so utterly wrong with such appalling suddenness. She felt sick to her bones. Her injured hand blazed with pain, as if an iron spike had been driven up into it. It was difficult for her to get breath.

The sword's hilt was slicked with blood, and she shifted her grip, trying to get a firmer hold, facing her attackers squarely.

There had always been this at the back of her mind. Try the ploy she had devised first, save lives first, if it were possible. But, finally, there was always the blade as a last resort. She had not reckoned on being so injured, though. She did not think she could survive a concerted charge.

Such a little thing . . . only the smallest of fingers, but it was like to prove the undoing of her entirely.

It was all too quick.

She felt a hand, suddenly, upon her shoulder. 'Run,' Gyver said in her ear. 'Run away! I will sshoot arrowss at them. My folk will.'

'No!' Elinor said, pushing him back. She would not abandon the fur-folk who had put their trust in her. Nor give these painted invaders the satisfaction of seeing her turn and flee. 'Go back!' she urged Gyver, trying to push him away.

'No,' he answered her. 'I will not . . .'

And then the painted invaders came for her, howling like crazed wolves, garish faces twisted in battle frenzy. The fur-folk let loose a little shower of arrows, but most shattered uselessly against armour. There was no time to say any further word to Gyver, only a single instant to imprint the image of his fine furred face in her mind for a last time – and to feel the bitterness of knowing that she had been right, that he would indeed end up here this day with a blade in his guts. Only it would be the two of them, together . . .

Stepping hastily away from him, to draw her attackers – that being all she could do for his safety's sake – she raised the sword and took her guard, prepared to go down under the angry wave of the assault.

She cut open the face of the first man upon her, and he collapsed to his knees, screaming. But the others surged up from behind him, kicking him aside and charging her in a howling swirl of dully gleaming bronze blades.

And then she heard a great, ululating cry.

The fur-folk called out in many voices.

The invaders turned in shocked confusion.

From out of the trees, huge shapes came thundering, flexible snouts held aloft, trumpeting angrily, their charging bulk making the very ground tremble.

The Phanta!

The huge beasts descended upon the invaders in a storm of great anger. Crying and squealing, they trampled the painted men underfoot, flung them into the air with their long snouts.

The invaders fled, wailing, unable to face such a giant foe, scrambling away in willy-nilly panic.

The arrows of the fur-folk took some few of them as they fled. Elinor cut down two who tried to run over her in panicky flight. The raging Phanta caught all those that were not fast enough to escape off through the trees. And those that did escape, the fur-folk hounded.

'After them!' young Swift shouted, brandishing his barbed javelin. 'Now iss the time for our revenge!' and the younger fur-folk bounded away after the fleeing survivors, intent on the hunt.

And, suddenly, the clearing was gone quiet.

Elinor stood gasping. The world seemed to pulse about her, going from too-bright to darkly dim to too-bright in a painful swirl. She felt herself reel sickly.

Gyver was there – to her huge relief. He put a supporting arm about her shoulders, and she sank into his hold, letting the sword drop. She saw again the blue-lightning face of the

235

charging spear-man, the grey-fletched arrow that had taken him – and so saved her life. She clutched at Gyver with her good hand, hardly daring to believe he was hale and whole. 'Are you . . .'

He nodded. 'I am unhurt, me.'

'And the . . . others?'

Gyver let out a breath and grinned, a quick flash of sharp white teeth in his darkly furred face. 'We are whole, uss. All of uss. We have won!' His face went tight. 'But you . . .' He gripped Elinor's mutilated hand, his furred fingers matted with her blood.

'Aye . . .' Elinor breathed, 'me.' She clenched her wounded hand, feeling a thrust of pain go up her arm. 'So much for my vaunted *plan* . . .'

Gyver said nothing, merely wrapped her in his arms. He held her wounded hand tightly, tipped upwards, trying to stop the flow of blood.

The great Phanta were still storming about, grunting and growling in harsh, deep tones. One of them came past, snorted over Elinor and Gyver, thundered on.

'Where . . . where did they *come* from?' Elinor gasped, staring about her in shock.

'They musst have followed after uss, them,' Gyver said. 'Through the gap in their watcherss that we made.' He was staring at the Phanta uncertainly.

The great beasts were gathered together now – five of them. One lifted its snout and gave vent to a great roaring, raging cry. The others joined in so that the clearing shook.

Cloud-Dreaming came limping forwards, Sky-Flower at her side. The old wise woman drew near to the gathered Phanta, raised her hands. The great beings closed towards her, still grumbling and fuming angrily. For long moments, Cloud-Dreaming stood, unmoving, leaning on little Sky-Flower's support, surrounded by the mountainous forms of the Phanta.

Then, as if some unheard message had been passed, the Phanta began to withdraw, turning and shuffling back towards the trees. One by one, they disappeared under the dimness of the tree canopy, and so were gone.

Elinor felt the world slipping away from her. Her belly heaved, and her vision was stitched with blackness. Gyver still held her wounded hand, gripped tight and tipped upwards, but blood still spilled from the stump where her little finger had once been. Elinor shifted position, caught one clear glimpse of it, a flat cross-slice of wet red flesh and a small circle of white-pink bone, blood welling wetly . . . then looked quickly aside, sick in her belly.

'Cloud-Dreaming!' Gyver cried. 'Quick! Her hand . . . Her poor hand!'

Cloud-Dreaming came hobbling stiffly over, and bent over Elinor, her silver-furred face tight with all that had transpired. She was murmuring something, her voice low and melodious, too low for any words to be clear. The old fur-woman seemed to have a strange glow about her. Her hands ran over the bloody stump of Elinor's finger, not quite touching. Elinor felt a soft tingling. Cloud-Dreaming's hands ran along her body to her face, the tingling filling her like warm liquid.

Elinor found herself looking up into Cloud-Dreaming's eyes, which were dark and deep-seeming as wells . . .

There was the world all about her, the light, the voices, the pain . . .

And then she felt herself suddenly drifting away, as if some tether had been loosed in her and she were sinking into a deep, pleasant place, the noise and light and agony of the world dwindling above her, far off, dim and gone. Leaving only the peaceful dark.

XX

Long days went by, and Ziftkin rode the hilly grasslands with the mounted cavalcade of dark-clad, sombre, armed men. They had brought him to their field-camp, as Iryn Jagga, their handsome, self-assured leader, had promised. But from there they had travelled onwards, taking him with them through the rolling green-grass sea – will he or nill he.

He was not at all sure what position he occupied amongst them. He was washed and well enough fed, his bruises tended, dressed now in a set of clean, new clothes – the same manner of sombre garments they themselves wore. Iryn Jagga treated him with unfailing courtesy. Yet none of the rest of the men would exchange even a single word with him. After the first night, his hands were no longer bound, but he slept under guard. And he had not so much as glimpsed his flute since the first day.

And the days wore on.

Gullie, the mare he had ridden from Gault Keep, kept pace well enough, but Ziftkin's limbs grew stiff and sore from the long days in the saddle.

And he got no answers to any of the questions which plagued him. Iryn Jagga – handsome and commanding and altogether mysterious – said no word about their destination, nor Ziftkin's possible fate, nor anything significant at all, deftly deflecting any questions Ziftkin tried to put to him, talking only travellers' small talk about the possibility of rain, or the quality of their breakfast, or the gait of the horses over the uneven ground. By his seeming attitude, they might have been on a pleasant afternoon's ride out from some rural Keep.

Iryn Jagga rode his white stallion in the fore, the very image of a tale-hero, the gilded circlet about his brow, the gold medallion, with its engraved, mysterious face, on his breast. A light seemed to shine upon him. But the men of this company were grim-faced and silent. There were outriders always posted, and every man in the company went helmed and armoured, with weapons to the ready.

Ziftkin did not understand. Nowhere did he see any signs of threat. The few folk they did encounter were simple farmers – who fled in terror at the sight of such an armed and mounted, grim cavalcade. Once, they came upon a village, a huddle of straw-thatched little houses which the inhabitants had deserted at their coming. Iryn Jagga commanded the place burnt to the ground and the fields trampled. Such wanton destruction made no sense. It grieved Ziftkin's farm-born heart but when he tried to protest, Iryn Jagga told him, curtly, to keep his nose out of business he could not understand.

It was all most unnerving.

And still onwards they rode, day after day . . .

Until, late one afternoon, with dark clouds piled on the horizon, they ascended a long grassy ridge. From the ridge's crest, Ziftkin gazed ahead and saw a mass of blocky-like, square stone towers set against the sky in the distance, like great blunt teeth they were.

'Sofala,' he heard one of the riders say. The men about him rose up in their stirrups and gazed ahead eagerly.

The cavalcade trotted onwards more quickly then, even the horses seeming enlivened. Despite having no notion of what it was that lay ahead for him, Ziftkin could not help but feel an echo of that same eagerness in his own breast. Here at least was some place, a destination, a change from this constant, bone-wearying ride.

Iryn Jagga had mentioned this Sofala the day of their first meeting, Ziftkin recalled. Capital of one of the great ancient Domains it was – those long-ago empires he had heard about only in wonder-tales.

Until now.

He stared ahead, straining to make out more detail. But all there was to see were the great blunt stone crests in the distance, the dark clouds piling up in the sky. Distantly, he felt a grumble of thunder.

239

Onwards they rode.

Day was dimming into evening when they finally arrived.

Sofala was surrounded by a thick wall of grey-brown stone, three times a man's height at least, ivy-choked and tumbled-down in parts, but still a truly formidable barrier. They rode along beside this wall for some little while, across rough, undulating turf, till they intersected a paved roadway. The horses' hooves made a sudden clatter as they turned onto this way, and their pace picked up, the horses blowing and snorting, the riders urging them on to a canter with eager shouts. Ziftkin hung on to Gullie wearily, while the mare kept her pace with the rest. The road bent, dipped into a little hollow. Out of this they shot, round a sharp curve and down a straight stretch leading to a large gateway.

They slowed, coming up to double wooden doors fully twice the height of a tall man, and stopped before a squad of gate-guards, the horses blowing and panting. A dark, gleaming blue, the doors before them were, ribbed with thick brass door-bindings that shone softly in the evening light. Ziftkin blinked. Against the dull grey-brown of the stone into which this entrance-way was set, the rich blue and the brass and the gleam of it all was startling.

Ziftkin saw that the doors' blue surface was pebbled by a dense mosaic of little cracks and chips. In the stone of the arch-way above, he could make out the remains of carvings, so weather-worn as to be mere convoluted lumps. He felt a shiver go through him. It was *old* this entrance-way; in its hey-day, it must have been something indeed.

A score of sombre-clothed guards, armed with long lances, stood in a double rank before the doors. One of these stepped forwards with stiff formality.

One of the horseman rode forwards alone. He held out a small gilded staff and made a kind of formal bow from the saddle. 'Gate-Captain,' he said to the guard who had stepped forward. 'I am Chief-Speaker Collis Tigh, escort to Iryn Jagga himself.'

The Gate-Captain nodded, brought his hand to his temple in a quick, clench-fisted salute. 'Pass, Chief-Speaker.' He turned to Iryn Jagga then and made a deep, formal bow, going down on one knee. The whole of his squad followed, holding the position.

The Gate-Captain made a gesture behind him, then, and the big gate-doors grated open, slowly, moved by some hidden mechanism inside the walls that squealed in rusty complaint.

'Welcome to your home, oh great Jara's favourite,' the Gate-Captain said to Iryn Jagga, rising and stepping aside to make way for their horse cavalcade.

Iryn Jagga nodded to the man, but said nothing. Slowly, they filed past the silent, kneeling guards, then through the opened gateway and into Sofala itself.

Ziftkin's heart beat hard. It truly was like being in the middle of an adventure tale, this. It was one of the ancient great Domains into which he was riding. Who would have ever thought that he – *he* – would be riding into such a place, would actually see it with his own eyes? Ziftkin smiled. His foster brother Mechant would go blue with envy, could he know. This entrance-way was only the beginning. What wonders would such a place as this hold?

Emerging through the gateway and into the city proper, he stared about eagerly.

But where he had anticipated a great open city, full of light and air and soaring architecture, he was faced, instead, with cramped, twisting streets and piles of refuse. And the place stank – worse than any ill-tended pigsty. It made the back of his throat burn.

The hooves of the horses clattered noisily on the cobble-stones of the narrow road along which they were making their way. Tattered buildings crowded them on both sides, split wooden beams showing through mouldering brick, like protruding, broken bones.

But they left this cramped way soon enough and spilled out into an open square. The air was better here, and Ziftkin breathed more easily. For the first time, he was able to make out the city's great walls from the inside. Studded with squat watch towers, they reared up protectively all around.

There were folk moving about here – the first inhabitants of this place, so far, that Ziftkin had seen. They were ragged-looking and thin, and moved silently, heads down.

Ziftkin stared, altogether discomfited.

'And so you see Sofala,' Iryn Jagga said, dropping his horse back to ride next to Ziftkin. 'And so?'

Ziftkin remained silent.

'Nothing to say?'

Ziftkin looked about him uncomfortably. 'I had imagined . . . It's just that . . .' He did not know how to go on.

'Out with it, boy.'

'I . . . I had thought one of the great ancient Domains would be more . . . more grand.'

Iryn Jagga frowned. Then he smiled sadly. 'Grand it was, once. But you are right. Grand no more. Look!' He made a sweeping, all-encompassing gesture with his arm. His handsome face darkened. 'As you can see, our once-great capital is reduced to crumbling rubble. And our proud folk to starveling poverty. And all because of *her*!'

'*Her?*' Ziftkin said, confused.

Iryn Jagga nodded. '*Her.*' He leaned closer to Ziftkin. 'There are two great forces in the world, boy: the Dark and the Light. We work tirelessly, I and mine, to eradicate the darkness that brought once-proud Sofala to its knees, to bring the Light back into the world, to bring back the greatness that once was here.' He shook his head, his face grim. 'But the Dark is not so easily dispelled. Wipe it out in one place, and it re-emerges in another. It is a plague!'

'And this . . . *her* you spoke of?' Ziftkin said.

Iryn Jagga frowned. 'Through *her*, the Dark has funnelled into the world once more and grown strong. Through *her*, abomination gathers and we are direly threatened.'

Overhead, there was a crack of sudden thunder. Ziftkin looked up, startled, having forgotten the incoming storm. A spattering of big raindrops came down. He shivered. 'I don't understand. How can this . . . this *her* be—'

But Iryn Jagga cut him off. 'No more talk of such things. This is neither the time nor the place. It has been a long ride. You must be weary.' He glanced up at the darkening sky. 'And we must be quick, if we're to beat the storm.' With that, he spurred his horse onwards and took up, once again, his position at the head of their cavalcade.

Across the open square they went at a canter, their route taking them past a complicated stone structure that had been erected in the centre. It was fully the height of three tall men, Ziftkin reckoned, the tip of it almost on a level with the great walls themselves. In the dimming day's-end light, the stone of it showed as a colourless mass.

As they drew nearer, he saw that it was composed of a series of stone platforms set in a kind of staggered pattern. Ziftkin shook his head. What possible use such a structure might have was beyond him.

The rain came again, a quick, hard skirl of cold drops. The wind picked up suddenly. Ragged Sofala folk scurried for shelter. Onwards the cavalcade went, leaving the square behind them now and clattering down a long, winding roadway that brought them, in the end, to a huge stone building, the front of which was composed of a complex array of pillars and carvings and intricate stone scrollwork.

The storm hit then, rain pelting down in a drenching, cold sheet. Ziftkin ignored it, sitting in the saddle and staring up at the building before him. Gullie did not like it and skittered under his hold, but he kept her in place, curbing her hard. Here, for the first time, was an echo of the aged magnificence he had anticipated. The building reared up like a cliff, standing well above the level of the city walls, seeming too huge to be the work of men's hands. There were statues posed above the columns and along ledges at each storey, weather-worn but still startlingly lifelike in their posture and the detail of the carvings, of men and . . . other things.

But more imposing than these varied statues was a single, enormous carved head set into the wall in a kind of recess in the building's centre. The height of two or three men above the ground, it was wrought from black stone, darkly shining, and showed the face of a man, handsome and vibrant. So lifelike was this face that Ziftkin shivered, feeling the black stone eyes staring at him.

Ziftkin realized that he was not the only one to have stopped. Despite the drenching rain, the whole of their cavalcade had halted.

243

'The image of great Jara himself,' Iryn Jagga said, dropping back once more to Ziftkin's side. He held up the golden medallion that hung at his breast.

Squinting, rain streaming down his face, Ziftkin saw that the same handsome, imposing male face that graced the building was depicted there – small and goldly shining.

'Who . . .' Ziftkin began, but a windy burst of rain took his words. Iryn Jagga's attention was gone from him in any case.

Rising stiff-legged in his stirrups, Iryn Jagga saluted the great black face above them with a ritual flourish of his arm. He held the medallion out, moved it up, down, to each side, intoning something Ziftkin could not catch. Only when this ritual of greeting was complete did Iryn Jagga motion the cavalcade onwards.

Through a great open portal they rode and, to Ziftkin's surprise, right into the building itself.

Inside, the horses' hooves echoed stutteringly off the walls and high ceiling. Bright, flickering torchlight made Ziftkin blink. Quick hands urged him down from his mount, and he was pulled, stumbling and stiff-limbed, out of the noisy chaos of the entrance chamber and through into a quiet corridor. He stopped, uncertain. Of Iryn Jagga, there was no sign. Was he to be guest or prisoner in this place?

A silent guide faced him, a thin man in the usual sombre clothing. He wore neither armour nor weapons, but there were those behind him who did. The man gestured to him. 'This way, songster.'

Ziftkin looked around. There seemed no point in resistance, so he let himself be led along, but slowly, for his legs were wooden-feeling and his lower back ached fiercely. The floor seemed to tip and tilt under him – body-memory of long days in the saddle.

They walked along a hallway, high-ceilinged, with statues of queer things set at odd angles, like creatures out of some nightmare peering down upon those who walked below. Then, through a doorway they went and thence to a long flight of steps leading both downwards and up. Chill, foetid air came from below, and Ziftkin was glad when their way led upwards.

One, two, three curving flights of steps they ascended, until Ziftkin was shown at last through a doorway and into a candle-lit room. He had hardly stepped in when the door was slammed shut behind him. Whirling, he tried to push it open, but it was locked tight.

Prisoner, then.

Yet this room did not match his notions of a prison cell. It was small but clean, with a lead-glassed window through which a flash of lightning came. The storm-rain made a flowing torrent across the glass. Thunder rattled the panes.

Closer to hand, he saw there was a bed, a table, an ornate fireplace. The stone walls were covered with dark hangings, the stone floor with a spread of different-sized rugs. A two-armed candelabra stood on a shelf near the bed, and a fire danced in the fireplace. Lightning flashed again outside. Thunder boomed. He was profoundly glad to be indoors.

There was food on the table and a carafe of some drink. His throat felt parched. He went over and took a long swig – water it was, flavoured with some herb and pleasantly chilled. The food was cold meat and dark bread.

Ziftkin ached to his bones. His eyes felt filled with grit. He had long since lost track of how many days he had spent in the saddle. His lower back felt as if someone had been at it with a club. Taking a little of the meat on a slab of bread, and the carafe of the flavoured water, he sat down with a groan on the bed.

He chewed on the bread and meat, which was stringy and flavoursome. His jaw ached – though how he had come to bruise it he could not recall. Finishing the mouthful, he took a drink of water, then plunked the carafe on the floor and collapsed backwards onto the bed.

He felt a little thrust of fear go through him. Darkness and Light, Iryn Jagga had said. A mysterious, dangerous *her*. That great dark stone face on the building-front that seemed to have living eyes . . .

What was to become of him in this strange place?

He let go a long breath and closed his eyes. His rain-drenched clothes were clammy wet upon him, but he was suddenly too tired to care, too tired to feel more than a hint of the fear, too tired to do anything but lie where he was, his aching back stretched along the bed, his head throbbing faintly, while sleep took him like a slow, dark wave.

XXI

Scrunch saw little Anstil long before she did him.

He sat waiting for her, next to a downed tree on a hummocky slope, watching her move through the forest with surprising surety, her bare feet flashing, slipping silently along the land's hidden contours.

'Scrunch!' she cried, spotting him as she drew close. She stopped, shook herself. It had rained through the night, and the forest still dripped with water. Her pale hair was plastered to her skull. 'Oh, Scrunch . . .' she said. 'I'm *so* glad to find you!' Scrambling up the little slope that separated them, she flung herself upon him, clutching handfuls of his thick fur. 'Oh, Scrunch, Scrunch . . .' she murmured. 'Oh, Scrunch . . .'

Scrunch could feel her small hands shaking. 'What is it?' he asked, gently pushing her a little away from him so that he could look into her face. This was the first he had seen of her since his return from the humanimal council. There was a bruised look about her.

'Oh, Scrunch . . .' she repeated. She shook her head, ran a small hand through her wet hair. 'Oh, everybody . . . everybody *hates* me!'

Scrunch did not know what to say. There were tears in Anstil's eyes, and her breath came in sobs now. He drew her close to him, in wordless comfort.

'None of the other children will play with me any more,' she said after a little. 'I . . . I tried to show them the . . . you know, the *current*.' She looked at him, her face clenched. 'They only laughed at me, Scrunch. And Dyll . . . stupid Dyll said I was become a crazy person, and that . . . that his daddy told him that's what happens when human people spend too much time with humanimals.'

246

Anstil took a sharp breath. 'I hit him. Made his eye all black. He cried.'

Scrunch could feel her shaking where she still leaned against him.

'I was glad, Scrunch. Glad that I'd hurt him. He's so mean and stupid. Lina and Ella and little Myr were almost going to do it, to feel the current like you showed me . . . But stupid Dyll called them names and laughed at them, and they couldn't. So I hit him. *Hard*.'

She pressed herself tighter against him. 'Oh, Scrunch! *Everybody* hates me now. All the grown-ups look at me funny, like . . . like there's something *wrong* with me. Like I have a bad smell or something. And nobody wants to play with me any more. Oh, what am I going to *do*?'

Scrunch felt his heart go out to her, small and hurt as she was. He thought of what Otys the crow had said back at the council: 'You were mad to show this human girl the hidden ways. Only grief can come from it. For her. For all of us!'

Otys had had the right of it after all. It had brought little Anstil only grief, this opening of her senses. His fault. He ought to have known better, to have thought better. He felt Anstil nestled tight against him, shaking still with soft sobs.

He could feel the world tight all about him. He could feel this as a moment of turning. It was like a great weight centred upon him. What he did here *mattered* . . .

But he was no Dreamer – like Spandel, the little lamure. No Elinor, through which Powers moved. No favoured chosen-one of the Lady. He had no special insights into the world's deep patterns, and did not know how to know what action might be for the best here. He had only his own faltering heart to guide him.

Scrunch sighed. It might have meant so much, little Anstil's learning of the land's hidden contours. No other human person, to his knowing, had ever come close to doing so. Who knew what new paths might have come into the world because of it?

Might have . . .

For poor Anstil was hurting, and – no matter all the great possibilities, no matter the tension in the world and in his guts, like an over-tight cord binding everything together – he

247

simply could not bear to see her like this. He could think of only one sure thing to do to help her in her pain.

Get out of her life.

For the human folk would give her no peace now. They had scented the difference in her – whether they yet knew it clearly in their minds or not. They would hound her, harass her, torment her. And in the end . . . they would either bring her back into the fold, the difference beaten out of her, or – he did not like to think of it – they would end by killing her, breaking her heart, or her body, or both.

She had to go back to her own folk, to become one of them again, to forget what she had experienced here in the forest. It was the only hope of peace he could see for her. He had to drop away from her life. Forever.

Scrunch took a faltering breath. He felt like a great lump of stone had been dropped into his guts. He knew first hand, and far too well, the blind, bitter hatred human folk were capable of generating towards that which was strange to them, and which frightened them in its strangeness. This trouble of Anstil's was but the merest beginning, if she did not revert safely to what she had been.

But how to explain to her? She was so young . . .

Gently, he levered her away from him a little. Her face was all puckered with crying, her eyes reddened from it. She snuffled and wiped her running nose on her sleeve.

'Oh, Scrunch . . .' she sighed.

'You must go back,' he said, knowing no other way to approach things here than by the most direct. 'They are your own folk, Anstil. You must forget me. Forget what we have done here in the forest. Go back to them.'

She only stared at him.

'A fish cannot grow wings and live in the trees,' he said softly. 'No matter how much it might wish to. Nor can you ignore what you are. You must go back. And I must go away from you.'

'No . . .' she said, her voice hardly more than a whisper. 'No. Don't . . . Not you, too.'

'Anstil,' he said, soothing as he could. 'You *must* try to understand.'

'No!' she said. She drew away from him, wrapping her thin

arms about herself. Her wet hair fell across her eyes, and she flung it back with a sharp jerk of her head.

'Anstil . . .' he began again.

'You're just like *them*!' she snapped accusingly. She was rigid with fury for a moment, then collapsed. 'Oh, why do *you* hate me, too? What's *wrong* with me?'

'Nothing's wrong with you,' Scrunch said quickly, drawing her close to him once more. 'I *don't* hate you.' He felt a rush of anguish go through him; his heart ached for her. 'Oh, Anstil, you must try to understand. You are what you are. You cannot change that. You must go back to your own folk, to who and what you were. It is the only way for you, the only way for peace. You must forget what you experienced out here in the wilds. You must forget me, put the hidden ways out of your mind.'

Anstil straight-armed herself away from him. She brandished one of her small bare feet. 'My feet won't forget!'

'They will,' Scrunch returned quietly. 'They must.'

'No . . . *No!*'

'Anstil, listen to me. Please. You have to—'

'No! I don't care what you say. I don't *care*!' She stamped her foot, shook her head. 'I won't forget. I *can't* forget. Can a . . . can a bird forget how to fly?'

'You're not a bird.'

Anstil glared at him. 'I am what I am!'

Scrunch sighed. 'Anstil—'

'You said it, Scrunch. You *said* it! "You are what you are," you said. It's *true*! I am what I am. And I feel the down-hidden currents under my feet. I *do*! And I will. Always. *Always!* How can I forget? How *ever*?'

'But Anstil—' Scrunch began again.

'It's too late,' she said quickly. 'I can't forget. Even if . . . even if I wanted to.' She held out a quivering hand to him. 'Don't you turn away from me too, Scrunch. Everybody's turned away from me. Nobody likes me . . . Don't leave me. Oh, *please* . . .'

Scrunch gathered her to him, wordlessly. He felt painfully torn. Perhaps it was as she said: perhaps she was already too changed to ever revert to what she once had been. Or perhaps it was merely a human child's wilfulness she was showing. He did not know. But there would be bad trouble if she continued like this; he felt it in his guts like a weight, felt the world's tightness cinch him.

But he could not harden his heart against her – no matter what prudence and common sense might dictate.

'Can I ride on your back, Scrunch?' she said softly. 'Please?'

He hesitated.

'Please?' Anstil repeated. *'Please?'*

He had no heart to refuse her.

So up she clambered, still shaking a little, and sat astride him. 'Not fast, Scrunch, not this time.' She sniffed. 'Can we just go slow?'

Slowly he went, letting the land's current guide his steps, feeling filled and hollow at once, cherishing the slight weight of her upon his back and dreading what was like to come of this . . .

For some time, they ambled through the forest in silence.

Scrunch's back was so broad that, when he went slowly like this, Anstil was able to stretch out lengthways on her belly, chin propped on her fists. She had stopped shaking, and lay so quietly that Scrunch began to wonder if she had somehow fallen asleep.

But after a little, she said, 'Scrunch, why are folk so blind?'

'Blind, how?' he returned, still ambling onwards.

'To the deep of the world.' He felt her shift a little. 'It's like they're all walking about on the ice of a lake in the winter. Only none of them wants to look down through the ice and see what's beneath their feet.'

Scrunch liked the image of it, put that way. And it was not unapt.

'Why, Scrunch? Why are they like that? And why do they get so angry about it?'

Scrunch stopped. There was no simple answer he could think of. He stood for a long moment, trying to get his mind focused, trying to think of some way to explain the subtle complexities of mindfulness – which he was not sure he truly grasped himself.

He took a breath, opened his mouth to begin, then froze. In the distance, suddenly, came the sound of human voices through the trees.

Scrunch felt Anstil stiffen. 'I don't want them to see me,' she said.

Scrunch was in full agreement. He did not know who it might be in the trees ahead of them, but there was likely nothing but trouble to be gained by any chance meeting here; few indeed amongst the Settlement folk would be pleased to see Anstil perched upon his back like this.

'Hold tight,' he warned her. She swung up and tucked her heels close against his sides, gripping at the fur near his neck. Once he felt her secure, he started off at a lumbering run, picking up speed as fast as he could, yet running silent for all that.

Across a long slope he went, over a stony crest and downwards, letting the under-currents give him the smoothest path, remnants of last night's rain showering down on them as he wove a fast way through the trees, Anstil swaying and bobbing astride him. He heard her laugh softly – for the sheer joy of their movement.

Behind, the voices dwindled into nothing.

'Don't stop,' Anstil said. 'Keep going.'

'We need to get you back to the Settlement,' Scrunch replied.

But, 'Keep going,' was all the answer she gave him. 'Please!'

So Scrunch kept going, quickly still, but cautious and silent as could be – just in case. He determined quietly to himself to make a long arc of his progress – without letting Anstil know of it – and thus return her to the vicinity of the Settlement that way.

Onwards they went, across another rocky ridge, the old stone of which was riven by a tangle of tree roots, then crossways down a brushy scarp. There had been lightning-fire here once, several seasons ago. Yellow fire-weed and thorny bushes crowded the slope between the charred stumps of the original trees. Saplings thrust up. The sun was warm here, out of the high cover of the old trees, and the fire-weed had been dried already of last night's rain.

Insects *thrummmed* in the thick of the greenery, went silent as Scrunch and Anstil passed, then resumed their chorus. In the distance a bird sang a three-note song, *tee-wee-too*, *tee-wee-too*.

It was a good sign; both insects and feathered folk made themselves scarce at the first evidence of anything untoward.

Scrunch slowed to a soft amble. Off to one side, there was the gurgle of water. And beyond that . . .

'What's that sound?' Anstil asked.

Scrunch stopped, head cocked to one side. There was a little twittering. Not human voices, nor birds'. Not anything he could easily identify.

'What *is* it?' Anstil asked.

'I don't know.'

'It doesn't sound . . . dangerous.'

It did not. There was even a sort of melodiousness to the sounds. The bird sang again in the distance, *tee-wee-too*, unperturbed.

'Let's go see what it is,' Anstil suggested in a soft whisper. 'Come on. Let's!' Before Scrunch could say anything, she had slid off his back and was padding off through the waist-high fire-weed in the direction from which the soft twittering was coming.

Scrunch hurried after her. The twittering sounds certainly *seemed* harmless enough. But he could not for the life of him identify them. And there were few things indeed which lived in these woods that he could not identify. He lifted his muzzle and sniffed. But the air here was still as could be, and he could detect nothing save the sweetish odour of the fire-weed itself. He felt the hackles along his spine lift, for all the seeming innocence of what lay hidden ahead of them.

'Let me go first,' he said to Anstil in a breathy whisper, and shouldered himself forwards.

A ridgeback lay ahead of them, beyond which was a steep ravine of bare brown rock, which marked the boundary of the old fire. On the other side of that, the forest began again, dark and thick. There was the sound of water more clearly now, coming from within the trees, and the twittering still. Down and across the ravine and up into the coolth of the tree-shadow Scrunch and Anstil went, soft and slow. Whatever it was ahead, Scrunch thought, it was not alone. The sound came from more than one mouth, he was certain.

Carefully, they rounded the big rough bole of one of the old trees and peered ahead. In the dimmish light, Scrunch could see a small, open hollow below them, a tumble of pale stones, a little dancing stream, a green, moss-thick slope, and . . .

He heard Anstil gasp at his side.

There were four – no, five of them, a tumble of small forms gambolling on the mossy slope, their little voices making a soft, twittering chorus. A bit beyond, the mother lay against the side of a tree, watching over them.

'What *are* they?' Anstil asked breathlessly, pulling back behind the tree round which they had been peering. 'They look like dog-puppies, but . . .'

Scrunch shook his head. Neither the mother nor the pups were ordinary dog. He peeked carefully round the tree again, thrilled by what he saw: humanimal children were all too uncommon – and five healthy, gambolling youngsters like these a rare sight indeed.

'They're humanimal folk,' he said softly.

'I've never seen humanimal babies before,' Anstil whispered. 'They're . . . *beautiful*.'

They were, indeed. The mother appeared to the eye as mostly dog, though a most exotic dog. Her fur was a dark brown, mottled with faint golden splashes, almost like a young fawn's markings. Her legs were far longer and more slender than any ordinary dog's, and the paws were equipped with stubby, blunt-clawed fingers and dextrous thumbs. Her ears were far larger than any ordinary dog's, blue-veined and quivery, her face pointed and elegant, her eyes altogether human, and green as bright wet moss.

There was no telling quite how the father of these children might have looked. The youngsters had their mother's over-large ears and long-limbed elegance of form, but their pelts were an astonishing variety of colours – dark and light, patched and mottled, and, in one case, striped. Their heads were a little blunter than their mother's, but they all had dextrous little hands like hers, stubby fingers and thumbs.

'Can we go down to them?' Anstil asked in Scrunch's ear. 'Oh, please, Scrunch. Can we?'

Scrunch hesitated, then nodded assent. There was no danger here so long as they were calm and careful.

He and Anstil had approached so carefully that both mother and gambolling youngsters still remained innocent of their presence. Slowly, Scrunch moved round the tree behind which they had hidden themselves and stood in full view.

The mother looked up immediately, her green eyes flashing alarm.

Scrunch took a slow step forwards, another, cautious, not wanting to startle either mother or youngsters. Anstil, however, went dashing down the slope, too intent on seeing the youngsters more closely to think of aught else.

The mother barked a quick, urgent word, and her children flew to her. She was on her feet in a heartbeat, her teeth bared in a snarl.

Scrunch only barely managed to insert himself between Anstil and the mother before anything nasty could happen.

'Wicked child!' the mother hissed, glaring at Anstil with her moss-green eyes. Her hackles were up in a spiky ruff all along her spine. 'Leave my babies alone.'

'I wasn't going to hurt them!' Anstil complained, peeking round Scrunch's broad, furred flank. 'Don't be so *mean*.'

Scrunch put a paw on Anstil's shoulder and gently sat her down. 'Greetings,' he said to the mother. 'My name is Scrunch.'

The mother dog nodded, but with no warmth. 'Greetings to you, Scrunch.' She gestured at Anstil with her chin. 'What is *she* doing here?'

'I can be here if I want!' Anstil said.

Scrunch gently pushed Anstil back, shushing her. 'You are blessed,' he said to the mother, gesturing at the gaggle of youngsters clustered nervously behind her.

The mother smiled a dog's loose-lipped smile, pink tongue lolling. 'Blessed indeed.'

'They're *beautiful*,' Anstil said from behind Scrunch.

The mother looked at her. 'Yes, they are.'

There was silence then, for a long moment.

'Her name is Anstil, this human child,' Scrunch said. 'And yours?'

The mother hesitated, took a breath, sighed. 'My name is . . . Rigga.'

'Can I . . . can I touch one?' Anstil asked, gesturing towards where the youngsters still crouched together behind their mother.

Rigga's hackles had settled now, but she was far from relaxed. She did not answer Anstil, merely regarded her suspiciously.

'Please?' Anstil said. 'I wouldn't hurt them. Not for anything.'

Rigga looked to Scrunch. 'I asked you what she is doing here. I have never seen one of the human children this far into the wilds. Did you find her? Was she lost, then, wandering about stupidly like they do?'

'I'm not *stupid*!' Anstil said, aggrieved. 'And I'm not lost.' She lifted one of her bare feet. 'My feet know the deep of the land. I don't get lost any more.'

'Oh, no?' Rigga said.

'No. I was out with Scrunch, walking.' Anstil put an arm upon Scrunch's broad shoulder. 'We do that, Scrunch and me. We walk the hidden deep of the land.'

Rigga's eyes went very wide, then very narrow. 'So you are good friends, then, you and Scrunch the bear?'

Anstil nodded. 'Oh, yes.'

Rigga licked her dog's thin lips, blinked. She looked Anstil up and down, her gaze lingering at the human girl's bare feet, then turned to Scrunch.

Scrunch could not help but smile. He liked the feel of little Anstil's arm upon his shoulder.

'Well?' Rigga demanded.

'We are friends, Anstil and I. As she says. We walk the deep paths of the woods together.'

'See?' Anstil said triumphantly. 'Now can I play with your children. Please?'

Rigga sat down. From behind her, her youngsters were making complaining sounds. A little voice said, 'She don't *look* wicked, Mamma.'

'What would you know of "wicked"?' Rigga snapped back, but there was no real harshness in her voice.

'We never played with a . . . a hooman, Mamma.'

'Can we have a hooman friend, Mamma? Can we?'

'*Please*, Mamma?'

They had surrounded their mother by this time, a squirming little gang of them, nipping and pulling and jumping at her.

'Please. Oh, please, Mamma. *Please!*'

Rigga stared at Anstil. 'If you hurt my babies . . .'

'I won't hurt them,' Anstil returned, meeting Rigga's hard stare levelly.

Rigga hesitated for a long moment, then sighed. 'Do you vouch for her?' she demanded of Scrunch.

'I vouch for her,' he said.

'Very well, then.' She gestured to the youngsters. 'Play with her if you will.'

In a little gang, they came tumbling over to Anstil, who first knelt, then lay down and let them crawl all over her, giggling wildly as they nipped and snuffled her in their curiosity.

Scrunch went over to Rigga and settled himself by her side. She looked thin and worn. 'You've been far?' he asked her.

She nodded, keeping her eyes on Anstil and her youngsters. 'Very far. I felt the *need*.'

Scrunch grunted. It happened sometimes to female humanimal folk. The *need*, they called it. Humanimal children were distressingly rare. For reasons none understood, mindfulness bred true; the offspring of a humanimal dog and an ordinary dog had no mindfulness. Only if both parents had the true humanimal nature would the children possess it, too. But with humanimals scattered far and wide in a world that was often deadly dangerous to their kind, it was difficult – sometimes impossibly difficult – to find a true humanimal mate.

And so the *need* would sometimes rise up in them, and humanimal females would go off on a pilgrimage in search of some suitable mate. There were times when such pilgrimages lasted years. All too often, the pilgrims returned having found no-one. Sometimes, they would settle for an ordinary male, and bring back unmindful offspring. And sometimes, they would bring back such ordinary offspring but deny that they were so, and spend anguished years trying to teach innocent, unmindful youngsters to speak.

It was fraught with far too much heartbreak for far too many, was this process of having humanimal children. Scrunch did not know this Rigga, but he was most glad to see her returned a mother. 'They are fine, mindful youngsters,' he said to her.

She smiled, still with her eye on them. 'As you say, I am blessed.'

'And the father?' Scrunch said.

Rigga was silent for a moment, then let out a long, sighing breath. 'I do not know. He is disappeared. I fear he may have been . . . taken. The dark Brothers patrol the green lands these days, right into the fringes of the wild, taking any of us they can.'

Scrunch nodded. It was an all too familiar tale.

They sat in silence for a little, then, until Rigga said, 'You were not so . . . solid, the last time I saw you.'

Scrunch blinked. 'We have met, you and I?'

Rigga nodded.

Scrunch tried to work it out in his mind, but could not.

'It was early summer,' Rigga said. 'In the good days just before the blood and fighting in the Valley . . .'

'At Margie Farm, was it?' Scrunch said.

Rigga nodded soberly. 'At Margie it was. You were . . . were nearly gone from the world. Gillien was nursing you back. I left, not knowing if you were going to return properly to the world or not.'

Scrunch sighed, remembering. 'I had seen too much of light and too much of dark. I wished no more of either.'

Rigga nodded, silent. It was something all humanimals knew of, the terrible despair of disconnection that sometimes took them, they who shared neither the unshakeable solidity of mind that human folk possessed, nor the innocence of belonging in the world that the true wild folk had.

'You have indeed returned to the world,' Rigga said softly. 'You are most solid, now.'

Scrunch shrugged. 'There is much holding me together, now.'

Rigga gestured at Anstil: 'Such as her?'

Scrunch let out a breath. 'Such as her. And others. I have become . . .' It took him a long moment to think how to

257

phrase it. 'I have become a hub about which folk turn.' It was an altogether human image, and he was not sure Rigga would understand it.

But she seemed to well enough. She looked at him, then nodded. She breathed a long sigh. 'As soon as my babes could travel, I went back there, to Margie Farm.' For the first time, she took her eyes from Anstil and her children and turned to him. 'Oh, Scrunch! The big house was burned to the ground. The fields lay in ruins.' She paused, took a snuffling breath. 'I . . . I so wanted Gillien to see my little ones.'

Scrunch nodded. 'It was the Brothers who burnt Margie.'

'I heard,' Rigga said. 'There are still some scattered few of our folk about down there.' She paused for a moment, looked at him sideways, then went on. 'I heard stories, also, about the discomfiting of the Brothers, of the shattering of an old dark image in Sofala, and of the Lady's appearance and her long promise being fulfilled. And I heard of a . . . a human woman with a terrible shining blade who is somehow the heart of all that is coming to pass.'

'Elinor,' Scrunch said. 'Elinor Whiteblade. We came here with her.'

'You *know* her?'

Scrunch nodded.

'Is it all true, then?' Rigga said eagerly. 'Is she nearby?'

Scrunch shook his head. 'She is gone away from us now. She felt her own *need*.'

Rigga nodded, understanding that.

'How did you come here, Rigga?' Scrunch asked uneasily, for if Rigga had located them, so could others.

'What few of our folk are left in the Valley tell tales, Scrunch. Tales of a place in the wild where the Lady's long promise of belonging is come true, where human and humanimal folk live and grow together in peace. Some believe it. Some do not. I came in hopes of finding a good place for my babes to grow up.'

Rigga let out a long, sighing breath. 'It was no easy journey, just me and the little ones. I did not know how to find you. My only guide was the . . . the tightness in the world.' She lifted her lips in a tentative, dog's half-smile. 'But it seems it has led me aright, finally.'

Scrunch nodded. 'It seems it has,' he agreed, relieved by her answer. No human person was likely to be able to follow such a guide.

Rigga licked her lips. 'It *is* true, then? What they say about a community here in the wild lands, about humanimal and human folk living and growing together peaceably?'

Scrunch sighed. 'We live together in peace, true enough. But grow together?' He shrugged. 'You know how desperately complicated the human folk can get. They like to argue. They don't understand us, the most of them. And they think they know more than we about everything.' Scrunch shrugged. 'Things are peaceable enough. We come and go as the need takes us, and none interferes. But . . .' He looked at Anstil, 'there are tensions. The simpler days of Margie Farm are gone forever for us, I fear.'

'Margie Farm?' Anstil said, breaking into their conversation.

She was seated on the ground, the youngsters in a panting heap about her. 'Isn't that the place that old grey-bearded Collart came from? My daddy says they were the cause of all the trouble, them at Margie.'

Rigga snorted. 'The human folk at Margie were the finest in the Valley.'

Anstil shrugged. 'Collart's . . . all right. He's a bit *serious*, though.' She ran a hand through her tousled hair. 'I like Scrunch better. He's always ready to play with me.'

Rigga blinked. Then, shaking her head, she laughed softly. 'It seems not so bad, after all,' she said to Scrunch, 'this place of yours you are creating here in the fringe wilds.'

'No,' he agreed, gazing fondly at Anstil. 'Not so bad.'

Anstil was still on the ground with Rigga's youngsters all over her. The first breathless excitement of their meeting was over now, though, and they were taking a breather. 'My name's Anstil,' she told them. 'Who are you all?'

They tried answering her all at once, and she had to shush them, laughing, and start again. 'One at a time! Or I'll never know who's who.'

One of the youngsters propped himself up on her thigh,

grasping a handful of her baggy overalls with his little forehands to steady himself, his backfeet on the ground. 'I'm Taggit,' he announced. 'I'm eldest.' He lifted his snout and snuffled. 'You smell funny.'

Anstil blinked. She opened her mouth, closed it again, then said, 'Are you a boy or a girl?'

'I'm a boy. Can't you *tell*?'

Anstil shook her head.

One of the other youngsters tried to climb up beside Taggit on Anstil's thigh. They were too big together, though, and they both tipped off.

Taggit was dark brown, his sleek fur marked only by a pale flash across his muzzle. The youngster who had knocked him over was far paler, a mixture of ochre and autumn-leaf brown. This youngster rose up and said, 'I'm Suggi, and I'm a *girl*.' She elbowed Taggit aside and clambered up on Anstil's thigh. 'And I'm stronger than Taggit is!'

'Are not!' Taggit said, scrambling to his feet.

'Are too!' Suggi replied. She turned to Taggit and growled, 'Keep back, you!'

But Taggit launched himself at her, and the two of them tumbled to the ground.

The other three leaped in, squealing with excitement, and they rolled together in a mass of little limbs and sharp white needle-teeth.

'Stop!' Anstil cried. 'You'll hurt each other.' She turned imploringly to Rigga. 'Make them stop fighting!'

But Rigga only smiled. 'They're not fighting.'

The youngsters fell away from each other, panting and giggling.

'We do this *all* the time,' one of them explained.

Taggit trotted over to Anstil. 'You could play with us, too.'

'I'm too big to play that game,' Anstil replied. 'And your teeth are too sharp.'

Taggit bared his little white teeth proudly.

'Your teeth are very nice, too,' Suggi said to Anstil. She nudged Taggit aside.

'They're very *blunt*,' one of the others said.

'That's Boe,' Suggi told Anstil. 'He's almost the youngest.'

Boe was black all along his back and side, but his legs were

260

mottled gold and his belly white. He grinned a shy dog grin at Anstil.

'I'm Korin,' said another of the youngsters. 'I'm a girl, too. Like Suggi.' She had a white coat, this one, with a myriad little spots of buff brown all over.

Anstil held up her hands. 'Wait. I'm getting confused!' She pointed at Taggit. 'You're Taggit. You're . . . Suggi.' Looking around, she gestured to Korin of the white, spotted coat. 'And you're Korin. And you're . . .' She had to think for a moment before she could remember the name of the black-backed one. 'You're Boe.'

Which left one still remaining.

Anstil turned to the remaining youngster, whose pelt was marked with stripes. 'What's your name?'

The youngster looked up at her, blinked, looked away.

'He's Grub,' Suggi explained. 'He's the youngest.'

'And the littlest,' Taggit added.

Grub was indeed the littlest of the lot, and skinny. But there was a kind of wiry energy to him. He had dark brown stripes against a golden pelt, running from his spine down transversely across his ribs and thin legs. It made for a striking effect. His eyes were big in his face, and he had long, rather floppy ears not quite like any of the others'.

He sat a little distance from Anstil and gazed at her. 'You're very . . . big,' he said in a soft voice.

'And you're not very big at all,' she returned.

Grub stiffened his shoulders and looked away from her.

Anstil swallowed. 'I . . . I like your stripes,' she said a little hesitantly.

Grub glanced up at her, then quickly down again at his forehands. He said something so softly that none could hear.

'He's shy,' Boe said.

Grub glared sideways at his brother, then he trotted determinedly up to Anstil, jumped onto her thigh, hauled himself up her front, and gave her a quick wet dog-kiss on the cheek. 'I like you,' he said softly.

With a little bound, he was back on the ground again. 'See? I am *not* shy!'

Boe leaped at him, knocking Grub off his feet, and the two of them rolled in a tangle on the ground.

'Let's play tag,' Anstil said quickly.

'What's that?' Suggi asked.

Grub and Boe looked up.

'You don't know what *tag* is?' Anstil asked in amazement.

The youngsters all shook their heads.

'One of us is *it*,' Anstil explained. 'And whoever's *it* has to touch all the rest.'

'Is that all?' Taggit asked. 'Where's the fun in *that*?'

'Let's wrestle, instead,' Korin suggested.

'No, no!' Anstil said. She got to her feet. 'I'll be *it*. I have to touch you. And you all have to try to run away from me.'

She made an abortive attempt at tagging Suggi, who was closest to her. Suggi darted away, squealing with glee.

Soon all five of the youngsters were tearing about the little mossy-sloped clearing, with Anstil in full chase.

Scrunch looked on, feeling pleased. Rigga's mother-tenseness had gone out of her, and now she seemed to feel quite comfortable with the relationship that was developing between her youngsters and Anstil.

Scrunch felt a little flutter inside him. It was something entirely new, this. Never, to his memory, had he heard of human and humanimal youngsters having such an opportunity as this to become acquainted with each other.

Rigga's children were, as far as he could gauge, only a little more than a year old, yet they were as matured as Anstil herself, or nearly, anyways. They were smaller than year-old ordinary-dog pups ought to be, who would be very nearly full-grown at that age, but humanimal young, as a rule, had a much longer childhood than their ordinary animal counterparts – though not as long as that of human folk. Human childhood seemed to go on forever, almost.

Yet for all that, humanimals and human folk lived comparably long lives. Given the chance, Anstil and the humanimal youngster could grow together through the years, their lives interlaced . . .

'That's enough, now!' Rigga called suddenly.

The youngsters and Anstil paused in their chase. It was striped-backed Grub who was *it*. He had been single-mindedly pursuing Anstil, who stood now, hands on her thighs, gasping for breath.

The daylight was beginning to wane, Scrunch realized. He had better be getting Anstil back to her home, and soon. 'Come along,' he said to her. 'Best we get you returned to your parents.'

'Oh, not yet!' Anstil complained. 'Just a little more? Please?'

Scrunch shook his head uneasily. 'If we don't start back now, we won't get you home before sunfall. And you know what would happen then.'

Anstil opened her mouth to argue, then closed it and nodded glumly. 'I've got to go,' she told the youngsters, who had gathered about her in a little crescent. 'My daddy'll get *really* mad if I'm not home soon.'

The youngsters made little sounds of disappointment, but they trotted back to their mother nevertheless when she beckoned them.

'Will you return with us?' Scrunch asked Rigga. 'You'd be most welcome at the Settlement, you and your youngsters.'

Rigga shook her head. 'No.' Then she added, 'Not yet, at any rate. Give me some time.'

Scrunch nodded. He understood her reticence. Humanimal mothers were notoriously cautious – with good reason, given the hard realities of the world.

'We'd best be off, then,' Scrunch said, getting up. 'We can find you again hereabouts?'

Rigga nodded.

'Farewell, then. We must go.' Scrunch took a few steps away, gesturing for Anstil to come with him, but she walked over to Rigga instead. 'Please, can I come and play with your children again?'

Rigga regarded her uncertainly for a long moment.

'Please?' Anstil insisted.

And, 'Please, Mamma. Oh, *please* may she?' the youngsters all said in an imploring chorus.

Rigga sighed. 'I suppose there's no harm in it.'

Anstil clapped her hands together.

'Come on, then,' Scrunch urged Anstil. 'Day is dying fast.'

Goodbyes were said all around, Rigga's youngsters flocking about Anstil. Then she and Scrunch set off. At the top edge of the clearing, Anstil paused. She looked back and waved. The youngsters waved in a chorus of small, furred hands.

'Come,' Scrunch said. 'We've a fairish ways to go.'

They set off together, Anstil walking backwards until she could no longer see any sign of Rigga or her youngsters. She turned, then, and walked along normally at Scrunch's side.

Down across the rock ravine and up through the fire-weed they went, the both of them following the inner contour of the land instinctively.

Anstil sighed and shook her head. 'Human folk get angry so *easy*, don't they, Scrunch?'

Scrunch shrugged, not knowing what to say.

'My father especially.'

They walked on a little together in silence, then, away from the burnt area and back into the dim coolth of the trees.

Watching little Anstil out of the corner of his eye, Scrunch felt both elated and disturbed. Something special had happened this day. But to what end? He had not forgot – could not forget – the bruised look Anstil had had at their meeting. Despite her joy in meeting Rigga's children, there was still the shadow of that bruising upon her. He did not know what path might be opening for her.

Onwards they went through the trees. Scrunch guided them along a different route from that which they had taken to get here, one that led more directly back to the Settlement. The land fell away before them in this direction, and there was a flow that took them down an exhilarating hillside. They took it wordlessly together, sharing the soft thrill of the good way through the trees.

Further on, the forest opened up a little, and they walked side by side.

'Do humanimal fathers shout a lot at their children?' Anstil asked abruptly.

'No,' Scrunch said. 'Why should they?'

'Why should any fathers?' Anstil replied. 'But mine shouts.' She gazed up at the fading sky through the trees for a long moment, then went on, 'I don't think my father's very happy, Scrunch. I think that's why he shouts all the time.'

'Then let's get you home, little one,' Scrunch said. 'That ought to make him happy.'

Anstil smiled. 'Race you!' she said and darted ahead.

Scrunch set off after her in a lumbering run, careful not to go too fast. She liked to think of herself as fleet of foot, did little Anstil. He was not about to hurt her feelings by catching her too easily. There was already too much in the world that could hurt her, far too much.

XXII

Three days, Ziftkin spent alone in his cell-room.

He was treated well enough: food and water were brought regularly by servants, and small buckets of soft brown coal for the fire, for the stone room took a chill in the evenings. But his door was kept locked and guarded by silent, armed guards, and none of the servants who came into the room would answer any of his questions. None would even so much as look him in the eye, and when he shouted at them one morning in a fit of uncertain anger, they slunk quickly away behind the protection of the armed guard standing at the door.

Ziftkin's aches from the long ride to Sofala grew less, and he fretted and paced restlessly, fuming and worrying, or sat upon his bed in glum frustration. This room reminded him too much of the one he had been given back at Gault Keep – and of all that had come of that. And in his dreams, still, he saw the bloodied, screaming faces of the poor souls of the Gault Keep dead, wailing at him.

He would awake sometimes in the black dead of the night, with fear like a cold lump in his guts, for he knew himself to be entirely helpless, in a strange place, without friend of any sort. Alone. And Iryn Jagga could do anything he wished.

He cursed himself for an utter fool for ever having let himself fall into the man's hands.

And then, without warning, on the afternoon of the third day, Iryn Jagga came striding through the doorway. Ziftkin glowered at him sullenly from the bed, not getting up, not greeting the man in any proper way.

Iryn Jagga made a slight, almost mocking bow. He was dressed in a velvety black over-tunic, stitched with gold in elaborate patterns, tight green-black trousers, and beautifully stitched, knee-high black leather boots. A short black cloak

266

hung from his shoulders, lined with startling crimson. His long dark hair was tied neatly back, and upon his head was a gold circlet studded with glinting white gems, a far more ornate version of the simple circlet he had worn during the long ride here. From his neck hung the golden medallion with its mysterious male face. A faint aroma of violets clung to him, and the smell of soap and of clean-washed clothing and polished leather.

Ziftkin sat up straighter, he could not help it. The man had a *presence*: handsome and imposing as he was, dressed in this sombre, regal elegance; and he moved with a total, self-composed assurance, like a man to whom the world had never said 'no'.

Iryn Jagga regarded Ziftkin and smiled a thin, ironic smile. 'You seem . . . disgruntled, songster.'

Ziftkin launched himself from the bed. 'You abducted me! You've kept me locked up here, alone, in complete ignorance, for three—'

Iryn Jagga made a little quick motion with one hand. From the open doorway behind him, two armed men abruptly appeared, bared swords in hand. Taking up protective positions flanking Iryn Jagga, they stood, silent, their faces hard as rock, the iron blades of their swords glittering coldly in naked threat.

'Have a care how you address me, boy,' Iryn Jagga said. He was still smiling, but his voice was utterly cold. 'I am no *ordinary* man, to be carped at. I am come to you here. Let that be enough for you. If you had to wait, there was good and sufficient reason for it. Do not question me, hear? *Nobody* questions the actions of Iryn Jagga. Is that *quite* clear?'

Ziftkin swallowed, looked at the dully gleaming iron blades of the menacing swords, nodded.

'You have nothing to complain of,' Iryn Jagga went on with satisfaction. He made another little hand gesture, and the swords were lowered. He smiled again. 'As I promised, neither you nor your flute have been harmed.'

Ziftkin took a breath, nodded. 'For which I . . . thank you.' The mention of his flute felt like a blow. He ached to have it back. It was like a hunger in his bones. He could almost feel the warmth of it again in his hand. But he did not think a

267

blunt demand would get him anywhere with the likes of the man he faced.

Iryn Jagga bowed his slight, formal, almost mocking bow, smiled his thin smile still.

For long moments, the two looked at each other in silence.

Ziftkin did not know what to say. There were a dozen questions he burned to ask, demands, complaints. But he could not think how to properly begin any of it.

Then Iryn Jagga lifted his hand and snapped his fingers, once.

Through the doorway at his back a man came. In his hands he held a dark cushion, upon which . . .

Ziftkin felt his heart leap.

It was his flute. Safe and intact.

Almost, he made a wild grab for it. But the still-bared swords and Iryn Jagga's look kept him in place.

Iryn Jagga reached the flute off the cushion. Holding it in one hand, he ran the fingers of his other hand – the mutilated one – along it in a kind of caress. 'It is no ordinary instrument, this flute of yours.'

Ziftkin stared, aquiver with suppressed desire, and with fury. It hurt – physically hurt – to see the man slide his fingers down the flute's smooth bone length in the casually possessive way he did.

Iryn Jagga was smiling still. 'I wanted to take it for myself. Is that what you thought?' He shrugged. 'I am not a stupid man. I could not play such an instrument. Nor could any of my men.'

He smoothed his fingers along the length of it again. 'I can feel the *power* contained in this instrument. But I cannot unlock it.'

For a long moment, he looked down at the flute in his hands in silence. Then he held it out. 'Here, take it back.'

Ziftkin stared.

'Take it, songster.'

Ziftkin made to snatch it from Iryn Jagga's hold, then stopped himself self-consciously. He let out a breath and took the flute up with as much composure as he could.

It felt *fine* to have it in his hold again. It was warm as always, apparently unaffected in any way by Iryn Jagga's over-familiar handling of it. He put it to his lips and blew a single, soft note, loving the sweet fullness of the sound.

The sword-wielding guards stiffened. Iryn Jagga's hands went to the medallion at his breast.

Ziftkin let the flute drop from his lips.

For a long moment there was a strained silence. Then the smile returned to Iryn Jagga's face. 'I gave you my word your instrument would be returned to you, songster. Did you think the word of Iryn Jagga himself is some small matter?'

Ziftkin shook his head. 'No. Of course not. Tha . . . thank you.'

'You are welcome.'

They looked at each other.

'Come,' Iryn Jagga said then. 'Let us take a walk, you and I.'

'Where?' Ziftkin said.

'You shall see.'

Ziftkin hesitated.

'Come,' Iryn Jagga said. Then, 'You are an ally I have long awaited.'

'Ally?' Ziftkin repeated, uncertain.

Iryn Jagga nodded. 'Ally indeed. I *need* such as you, boy. Come, walk with me.'

Ziftkin shivered. He looked into Iryn Jagga's handsome, strong-jawed face. *I need you.* Nobody had *ever* said anything like that to him before. He nodded, a little stunned. 'I . . . I'll come.'

Iryn Jagga nodded and smiled. 'I knew it would be so. Come walk with me, and we shall talk, you and I.'

Out of the door Iryn Jagga led, his brace of guards still flanking him, and thence along a hallway to a flight of curving steps – whether the same as those he had first ascended to come here or another set entirely, Ziftkin was not sure.

A trail of guards formed up behind them, and up the stairs they went, climbing without stop, until Ziftkin was panting and his heart thumped, though Iryn Jagga seemed not the least discomfited.

And still upwards they climbed.

Till, at last, they clambered up a narrow, steep set of wooden

269

steps – hardly more than a ladder – and a door was opened in the plank-and-beam ceiling above their heads, letting down a draught of cool air. Ziftkin scrambled up the last few steps and found himself upon a high roof-top. He gasped, catching his breath, and stared about him.

Iryn Jagga smiled. 'Impressive, is it not?'

It was indeed. The roof-top was flat, an octagonal platform perhaps ten paces in diameter, with no railing of any sort to wall one away from the distance and height and the depth on all sides. Ziftkin felt a little surge of dizziness. It was clearly the highest spot in all of Sofala, this. The city lay spread beneath them, a tumble of buildings and streets and littered rubble. Beyond the city walls, the whole of the wide world stretched away to the horizon in all directions, clear to see in the late afternoon sunlight.

Sofala, Ziftkin saw, lay surrounded by rolling grassland, like a stone island set in the midst of a green sea. All about, he could make out dotted clusters of overgrown ruins, and the blurred patterns of what must once have been fields, abandoned long since and buried under the green turf. Here and there, he could spot a still-living farm, but such were few and far between – and none close to the city.

Away off westwards, he could make out a pewter glimmer on the horizon that had to be the distant sea itself. Southwards, closer to hand than the sea, but still rendered tiny by distance, he could spy the intricate crests and spires of some other great city-domain. North – where his homeland lay somewhere – was only more rolling green sod, shading into obscurity and distance. Eastwards, he saw the humped backs of the foothills, with the blue-toothed peaks beyond, running in a long chain from south to north – wild country, far as his eye could travel. He felt a little shiver go through him. His father's country, that. His hands tingled, gripping the flute.

'What do you know of the golden years of the past?' Iryn Jagga asked abruptly.

Ziftkin blinked. He lifted his gaze from the wild hills and turned to Iryn Jagga. The guards had been left behind, he realized, and there were just the two of them up here, alone. 'Tales . . .' Ziftkin said in answer to the other's question. 'I used to hear wonder tales of great heroes and lords and seers

270

in the south. My foster-brother had an unending hunger for such tales. If half of what I heard as a lad was true, it must have been a marvellous – and a terrible – time in which to live.'

Iryn Jagga smiled his thin smile. 'Marvellous, indeed! It was a wondrous time, when men could do wondrous things. But that time passed. And do you know why?'

'The wonder tales of my boyhood . . .' Ziftkin shrugged. 'Well, they were only children's tales.'

'What did these tales relate, then?'

'War,' Ziftkin said.

Iryn Jagga nodded. 'War indeed. Each against each in a final, fatal conflict. Yet there was more than simply that. The men of the past held great power, power beyond anything we can imagine in these sorry days. We are dwarfs compared to them, ignorant dwarfs!'

Ziftkin did not know what to say. There was a dark intensity come over Iryn Jagga which was unnerving.

Iryn Jagga looked off into the distance, gesturing to the far-away city-scape on the southern horizon. 'They built great cities, the ancients . . . like Gondar away over there, and Sofala itself, and others. They took upon themselves great knowledge and great wisdom. They might have made a very paradise. Instead . . . instead, cities such as Gondar lie deserted and in ruins, and Sofala wears only a mere, patched rag of the greatness it once possessed. They brought all to ruin.'

Iryn Jagga began to pace rapidly about the small confines of the roof-top, oblivious to the great drop-off all about. His handsome face was flushed and, as he talked, his hands flashed through the air, punctuating his sentences. His crimson-lined cape fluttered and dipped. 'My grandsire's many times great-grandsire was one of those knowing ancients. His birthright is my birthright. Yet, what have I inherited? A sorry world falling into ruin and rubble all about me. The ignorant folk of these dark days understand nothing of the greatness of the past, and, in their ignorance, compound the errors that were made so many long years ago.'

Iryn Jagga stopped his pacing and went silent, turned back to Ziftkin staring down at the littered streets of Sofala below.

'What . . . errors?' Ziftkin asked uncertainly.

'There is a power in the world,' Iryn Jagga said by way of reply. He lifted his gaze and turned, arms out. The golden medallion that hung at his breast gleamed, catching a ray of sunlight. 'A great power that animates the world and all in it.'

'Do you mean the . . . Powers?' Ziftkin said, unsure where this might all be leading.

Iryn Jagga stabbed an accusing finger at Ziftkin. '*Powers?* And just what do you understand by these *powers* you name so vaguely?'

Ziftkin shrugged. 'All know of the Powers. They are the . . . the great, live forces that move the world.' He felt self-conscious, repeating what every farm-child knew. 'The Powers are like strong currents under smooth water, save that the water is the . . . the world entire.'

'And do you worship these "powers" of yours, in the untutored lands where you are from?'

Ziftkin shook his head. 'There are those who build little shrines, I suppose. But on our farm . . . Well, my uncle always said it was better to put our energy into work. He always said the Powers were greater, or lesser, than people's images of them. The Powers were – are – themselves.'

Iryn Jagga regarded Ziftkin for long moments. He shook his head sadly. 'It is a sign of the unhappy times in which we live, that such gross superstitions thrive.'

Ziftkin looked at him, confused. 'What . . . gross superstition?'

'This nonsense of *powers*.'

'But *everybody* knows the existence of the Powers!'

Iryn Jagga laughed. 'Gross superstition, I tell you.'

'But . . . what are you suggesting? What is the world, then, if it is not the manifestation of the Powers?'

'There are not *many* powers, boy. There is only one, a great, virile, single force. Without it, the basic fabric of the world would collapse entirely.' Iryn Jagga reached to the gleaming gold medallion that hung at his breast. 'We of the Ancient Brotherhood of the Light name this great, this moving force . . . Jara.'

Iryn Jagga held the medallion up so that Ziftkin could more clearly see the image of the commanding male face depicted

272

there. 'The unwashed mass of the people worship Jara at shrines. He is depicted as a handsome, robust man . . . Not unlike myself.' Iryn Jagga smiled.

'They make sacrifices to Jara, in supplication for his good-will, giving him goats or fowl or field crops. In their untutored ignorance, they believe him to be a real, existing being, whom they can ask to intercede for them in their daily lives.' Iryn Jagga laughed. 'We of the Inner Sanctions, of course, know better. He is . . . How should I put it? Mere . . . personifica-tion.' Iryn Jagga shrugged. 'But if a personification keeps them happy, who are we to deny them?'

Ziftkin did not know what to say.

Iryn Jagga stepped closer. 'But for a personification to exist, it must be a personification *of* something, must it not?'

'I . . . I suppose,' Ziftkin replied.

'You suppose?' Iryn Jagga's dark eyebrows arched. 'You *suppose*? The face of Jara may be open to interpretation, but the *force* of Jara . . . never! The power that is Jara . . . *is*!'

Iryn Jagga's face had taken on a kind of light. His eyes shone. 'The ancients knew of this force. They were able to harness it and do . . . incredible things. And so will we again, one day. We are the chosen people, songster, those who will carry on the great tradition of our forefathers. Ours is the task of recreating the world so that the greatness of the past may come to be once again.'

'We?' said Ziftkin uneasily. Iryn Jagga had the burning ferocity of a fanatic. He was beginning to sound altogether too much like Ziftkin's uncle Harst on the subject of work, back at the farm.

'The Ancient Brotherhood of the Light,' Iryn Jagga said. 'That is whom I refer to. We are an old and honourable order of dedicated souls, reaching back to the great days of old. We strive, ceaselessly, selflessly, so that a new era will dawn, so that the force of Jara will flow clear through the world once more, unsullied, as it once did, and the greatness of the past will return.'

'But how . . .'

Iryn Jagga frowned. 'Great though they were, the ancients erred, overstepping the boundaries of the vital force they served and used.'

He bent close to Ziftkin: 'The results of that ancient error sully the vital force of Jara to this day, creating . . . *impediments* in the world.'

Ziftkin shook his head uncomprehendingly.

'Such *impediments* to the Light,' Iryn Jagga explained, 'create a shadow in the world. It is thus that the Dark grows, boy. In this shadow lurk those which would oppose us. They are of the Dark, and wish the world to remain plunged in darkness and chaos and despair.'

Ziftkin shook his head. 'I don't . . . What is it you're saying?'

Iryn Jagga reached over and patted Ziftkin's shoulder avuncularly. 'Out in the fringe-land where you grew up, you remained ignorant of all this. It is not your fault. But now that you have entered civilized lands, it would be dangerous for you to cling to such ignorance. There are black dangers abroad in these lands. You were fortunate to have fallen in with me and mine rather than . . .' Iryn Jagga shrugged and went silent.

'Rather than . . . what?' Ziftkin pressed.

Iryn Jagga looked across at him, his face sober. 'We of the Ancient Brotherhood strive selflessly to bring the light of our grandsires' grandsires' wisdom and greatness back into the world. But the world is become a place of darkness, boy, filled with ignorance and folly. There are those who would raise a dark power against Jara. Mere image and wish-feeling it is, but not without a certain . . . efficacy.'

Ziftkin blinked, confused.

'The Dark confounds, boy. The Dark hides and deceives. And the Dark hates the Light. It will twist and turn like a many-headed serpent, desperate, striking here and there. Cut off one head, and others remain.'

Iryn Jagga smiled grimly: 'We have removed many of those serpent-heads, we of the Brotherhood. The Light is winning. Oh yes. But still the Dark struggles, rising through ignorant and wilfully deluded souls.'

Iryn Jagga held out his mutilated hand. 'See my hand? This was caused by such a minion of the Dark. A very serpent's head indeed, with a deadly sharp fang.'

Ziftkin shivered. 'What happened to you?'

'It was torture, boy. *This*,' Iryn Jagga flexed what was left of his hand, 'was to have been only the beginning. If I had not been able to escape, she would have had me carved to pieces, slowly, until I told her all she wished to know. Which I would not.'

Ziftkin stared at the hand. He recalled Iryn Jagga's mention of some mysterious and threatening 'her' on the afternoon of their arrival here in Sofala. 'She?' he said.

Iryn Jagga nodded. '*She*. And if she is not stopped, she – and through her the very Dark itself – will overwhelm all and bring complete and utter ruination upon this land.'

'I . . .' Ziftkin swallowed, 'I don't understand. What is there about one woman that makes her so—'

Iryn Jagga laughed. 'She is no natural woman. The Dark rises in her like a current, deforming her. She is ruthless. Heartless as a stoat. And she hungers to conquer all that remains of the great Domains of the past, the cities, the countryside. The deluded ignorant flock to her, drawn by the fatal lustre of the Dark that fills her. And many of those that follow her are not human.'

Ziftkin stared. 'Meaning?'

'She has . . . creatures in her following, creatures which resemble animals but which are . . .'

'Do you mean . . .' Ziftkin felt his heart skip excitedly. 'Do you mean those creatures folk name as . . . as humanimals?' He remembered the wondrous talking cat-creature he had encountered high in the wilds.

'You know of such creatures?' Iryn Jagga asked quickly.

Ziftkin shrugged. 'I have heard stories. I . . .' Almost, he started to tell of the cat-creature, but something stopped him.

'And what did these stories say?'

'That there are . . . beings that are animal in flesh yet human in spirit.'

'And?' Iryn Jagga said. His face was tense, and he stared at Ziftkin so intently it made Ziftkin's belly squirm.

Ziftkin looked away across into the green distance beyond the roof-top. For some reason, he felt uneasy talking about such things with Iryn Jagga. 'They were just . . . just stories is all. You know, children's wonder tales. Hu . . . humanimals they were named in the tales.'

Iryn Jagga let out a breath, nodded. 'Such tales, like many children's tales, bear a kernel of the truth. There were – are – indeed such creatures, such . . . humanimals. Once, they were creatures of Light, fashioned by my forefathers in the great days long past.'

'Fashioned?' Ziftkin said.

Iryn Jagga nodded. 'Such was the greatness of my grand-sires' grandsires that they were able to mould the very flesh of life itself to their will.'

Ziftkin blinked, trying to imagine how such a thing could be.

'It was a dangerous act my forefathers performed, this re-fashioning of the flesh. They had great wisdom and great power and greater pride . . .' Iryn Jagga let out a long, sighing breath. 'But in their pride, they overstepped. It was their great error. They brought something into the world they ought not.'

Iryn Jagga looked at Ziftkin. 'They were *made* creatures, boy, these humanimals, never intended to exist indepen-dently of their creators. While there were those around them to keep proper watch and control, such creatures posed no threat. But with the fall of the Domains, these creatures escaped far and wide and polluted the world.'

Iryn Jagga's face took on a grim cast. 'They are crippled creatures, boy, twisted, neither one thing nor the other. They are abominations, sick in their souls and deformed in their bodies. They do not belong in the world! Their very existence is an affront to Jara and all that is decent and right and honourable. They are creatures of the Dark, breeding un-checked, spreading the Dark wherever they go.

'It is our task, we of the Ancient Brotherhood, to cleanse the world of such abominations as a preparation for the Light to come. And they welcome it, these sorry half-brutes, for in their hearts they know they are become creations of the Dark. They know they are twisted creatures who ought not to be let live. They *welcome* the release from their sordid, twisted lives that we give them.'

Iryn Jagga began pacing once more. 'A return to the greatness that was once awaits us. That is our goal. To bring the Light back into the world. For this we strive unceasingly, doing all that we can, all that is needed. And slowly, we triumph. But all our efforts now are hampered, our hopes thwarted . . . by this thrice-cursed woman and her rabble of wretched followers.'

'But surely . . .' Ziftkin began. 'I mean . . . one lone woman . . .'

Iryn Jagga glared at him. 'The world is a river, boy, through which the great bright current of Jara pours. A terrible darkness has seeped into that current, polluting it. The unwashed and ignorant multitude live their lives on the river's surface, seeing only the surface, unknowing. But there are depths, boy, great depths. We are *carried* in this life by the currents in those hidden depths.'

Iryn Jagga stood to his full height, shoulders squared. He held the golden medallion in both hands before his breast. 'I . . . I am supported by such depths. I am the embodiment of the Light, of the power that is great Jara. As *she* is the embodiment of the Dark. She is no mere woman, boy, but an emissary of a force great and terrible. And she is possessed of a dark weapon, a sword like no other. Wielding it, she is all but invincible. It feeds on blood, this accursed and unnatural weapon. Its edge never dulls, and it shines like a very mirror.'

Ziftkin shivered. It was hard to take in, all of this. He felt as if one of the wonder tales of his boyhood had come suddenly true. How could such things be? Did Iryn Jagga expect him to believe it all just from the mere telling? 'I don't . . .' he began, then stopped uncertainly.

'Do you *doubt* me, boy?' Iryn Jagga said, his voice suddenly hard-edged.

Ziftkin squirmed uncomfortably. 'No, of course not. It's just that . . . Well, what you are saying *is* a little hard to . . . to just accept at face value.'

'Accept it, boy! Doubt not. This woman exists. Her shining, terrible blade exists.' Letting the medallion go, Iryn Jagga held out his maimed hand. 'How do you think *this* was done to me?'

'*She* did it?'

'With her accursed blade.'

Ziftkin did not know what to say.

'This woman must be stopped,' Iryn Jagga went on. 'She will bring all to shattered, bloody ruin if she is not successfully opposed.'

277

Iryn Jagga raised his maimed hand, flexed the stumps of his truncated fingers. 'I will stop this woman, this vessel of the Dark. There is none other, in all the land, capable of standing against her. But I cannot do it without aid.'

He looked at Ziftkin. 'And that is where *you* come in, songster.'

Ziftkin blinked. 'Me?'

Iryn Jagga nodded. 'You are no ordinary farm-boy, with pig-dirt under your fingernails. Not with *this* at your command.' He gestured at the bone flute which Ziftkin still held. 'I witnessed what you are capable of. You have power. Yet you are not a wicked boy. You only defended yourself against what you thought was an attack upon you.

'With you and your flute to aid me, songster, I can successfully destroy this woman. We can bring peace and stability to the land, you and I. We can cleanse the world of the abominable creatures that flock about her. We can triumph!'

Ziftkin felt the little hairs along the back of his neck prickle. 'But I can't . . . I never . . .'

'Don't you *see*?' Iryn Jagga said excitedly. 'Our meeting was no accident. The power that is great Jara works in most mysterious ways. I have been in great need, boy. I have meditated and fasted and prayed . . . And my need is answered. I look into your face and I see hope for this land, for the innocent and the weak, for the defenceless and the ordinary. I see peace and freedom and a bright, bright future.

'Just think on it, boy! The whole of this land at peace, that wicked woman and her abominable creatures dealt with, folk free to live their natural, proper lives once more. All because of you and I! Think on it!'

For a moment, Ziftkin felt himself caught up in the seductive picture Iryn Jagga was painting for him. He saw himself at the heart of a cheering throng, the hero of the moment, centre of all . . . belonging. Iryn Jagga beaming across at him like a proud father.

But the image faltered. 'I am no . . . no hero from a tale to come striding through and save the world,' Ziftkin said. 'I do not even know what this flute properly is, or can do. Or what I can and cannot do with it. What you say is—'

'It would be a criminal act *not* to do your best,' Iryn Jagga said quickly. 'How many men are fortunate enough to hear the call to such a high destiny? How many can say they saw their duty and saved their world from utter ruin?'

Ziftkin hesitated.

'You are no ordinary farm-lad. I tell you that with utter certainty. Just as I am no ordinary man. I speak as one Jara-touched soul to another. Take up this destiny that awaits you. Why else have we been brought together, you and I?'

Ziftkin did not know what to say.

Iryn Jagga put his maimed hand on Ziftkin's shoulder, gently. 'Listen to your heart, songster. What does it tell you? Does it say to run from this great challenge? Does it say to crawl off and hide? Does it urge you to throw away this wondrous instrument and forsake the great and generous acts you can perform with it? Does it tell you to give up all that makes life most special?

'No. Of course not! Listen to your heart, and you will hear it calling you to this great destiny. Listen to it. Only listen to it!'

Against himself, Ziftkin felt drawn. How many men, indeed, were fortunate enough to have such a clear and special destiny laid upon them? Could it be that all his unhappy boyhood, all that had followed on his mother's death, his receiving of the flute, his wanderings, all . . . all had been part of a hidden, greater pattern funnelling him to a meeting with Iryn Jagga?

He looked at the man before him, so regal with the glinting golden circlet upon his brow, the dark and sombre elegance of his clothing. No ordinary man, this. Could it really be true, then, that he, Ziftkin, was indeed destined to be more than a mere nameless farm-lad or vagabond songster? Could it be that he had been borne here by that great invisible current Iryn Jagga talked of, drawn to a place and a situation in which he could play a truly important part, where he could make all the difference? Could it be that he *belonged* here? The very thought made Ziftkin's heart beat hard with longing.

But there was a small voice in him that would not be entirely stilled. He remembered all too well how he had felt at the Lady Evadne's urging; then, too, he had had a sense of a special, wonderful future awaiting him. He was no longer the innocent he had been.

'It is the rare man,' Iryn Jagga was saying, 'who gets the opportunity to take his destiny in his own hands and shape the world. This is a most special opportunity. A once in a lifetime opportunity.'

It was the same words, nearly, that Rath Kerri had said to him back in the market at Actonvale, that first day he had met the Lady Evadne. Ziftkin shuddered.

'It is a great destiny that awaits you,' Iryn Jagga said.

'I've heard such before,' Ziftkin returned thinly.

Iryn Jagga's eyebrow went up. 'Cynicism, is it, then? World-weariness? And in one so young, too.' He shook his head, regarding Ziftkin with an intensity that made the small hairs along Ziftkin's neck prickle. 'Cynicism is the world's bane, boy! Don't you know that? It is cold and muddy water to the world's fire. It is the Dark to the world's Light. It is a sneaking, faceless, underhanded denial of all that is open and great and good.'

'But—' Ziftkin started.

'But me no buts, boy! Cynicism has ruined more lives and caused more harm than ever any blade did. Refuse this destiny that awaits you if you will. Refuse it out of craven fear if you must – sometimes a man's heart simply is not big enough for the life he is given. Or refuse it out of selfishness, and place your own ease above the salvation of others. But do not, oh, do *not* refuse it out of mere cynical suspiciousness.'

Ziftkin felt himself flush. He did not know what to say.

'Take it up!' Iryn Jagga urged. 'Take up what life offers you and live it. Live it to the fullest! Become all the man you are capable of. And one day . . . one day, you will stand beside me as the saviour of this land, and the people will cheer you. Or . . . or you will one day find yourself an old man, crippled with age, alone, waiting to die. And you will say to yourself: "Why did I not take the chance to make something special of my life? Why, oh why did I run away like a useless coward?"'

'But—'

'There is nothing worse, boy, *nothing* than knowing you once had the opportunity to do something great and good –

280

and knowing, too late, that you should never have turned your back on it.'

Iryn Jagga looked at Ziftkin, his dark eyes blazing. 'Would you do that now? Would you turn your back on the life that awaits you? Turn your back on the countless helpless folk that need you? Turn your back on *me*, who needs you no less than they?'

'I . . .' Ziftkin looked at Iryn Jagga, swallowed, looked away. He ran a hand along the warm smoothness of the bone flute, took a shaky breath. 'I . . .'

'You cannot, can you?' Iryn Jagga said triumphantly. 'You are too decent a young man to do such a cowardly thing. I know you. I know the kind of heart you have. The folk of this land can rely on you. *I* can rely on you. We will accomplish great things, you and I together. You will be like the son I never had, brought to me by the grace of great Jara.'

Ziftkin looked at Iryn Jagga and tried to resist the feeling that rose up in him: as a lad, he had dream-yearned so often for just such a moment as this, his father returned out of nowhere for him, offering him a new life, *needing* him . . .

Iryn Jagga held a hand out formally, the maimed one. 'I greet you, Ziftkin saviour.'

Ziftkin found himself taking the hand, almost as if some force stronger than he willed it. Iryn Jagga was too much. It was all too much. He felt bemused and shaken. Him a saviour? Him important and needed, with a special destiny? Part of him knew it all to be crazy-ridiculous. All this talk of Jara and the Dark and the Light . . . There was a hard intensity to Iryn Jagga at moments that made Ziftkin's guts twinge. And he did not even know, yet, what it was Iryn Jagga wanted of him, or expected he would be able to do. But he could not, somehow, bring himself to refuse. He felt a long shiver go through him. Perhaps . . . it was not impossible . . . perhaps he did belong here.

Iryn Jagga was smiling, his eyes alight. 'Together, we will triumph. Oh yes! You and I.'

Ziftkin could feel the ridge of hard scar tissue on Iryn Jagga's hand, where the fingers had once been. He felt his belly flutter. This was no boyhood tale he had been brought into. This was flesh-and-blood real. Folk were maimed and killed.

'She will stand no chance against us, boy. This Elinor of the evil-shining blade will bother our land no more.'

'Elinor?' Ziftkin said.

Iryn Jagga nodded: 'That is she. The wicked, unnatural woman who threatens this land. But her days are numbered, now.' He lifted his maimed hand from Ziftkin's, held it aloft. 'Soon, I shall be avenged!'

Ziftkin shivered.

'Elinor Whiteblade,' Iryn Jagga cried softly, staring out from the roof-top towards the grey-green tumble of the wild lands eastwards. 'Wherever you may be skulking . . .' He raised the gold medallion in both hands. 'I call the curse of great Jara upon you. A short, unhappy life may you lead from this moment onwards, and an ill death may you die!'

He turned then, letting the medallion drop, and smiled at Ziftkin. 'A great day, indeed, that brings we two together. A day minstrels will sing of. A day stories will be told about. This is the start of it all, songster. The evil Elinor Whiteblade and those abominable, disgusting creatures that flock about her will be destroyed once and for all. From this day, the world begins anew!'

Ziftkin could only nod, dizzy and overwhelmed. His heart was beating hard. He felt like a man who was rushing down a long slope, with too much momentum built up to stop.

One upon whom a door had just been slammed.

Or opened.

Standing here on the high roof-top, the great world spread out all around him and Iryn Jagga exultant at his side, he could not tell which.

XXIII

Scrunch led Rigga and her offspring softly into the Settlement early on a cloudy morn. It had been the youngsters who had forced the issue, little stripe-backed Grub especially.

They had received only the one visit from Anstil; she had not been able to get away from the Settlement to visit them since, for there was some crop or other that had come ripe in the fields that needed picking, and all human hands were set to the task. As the days had gone by with no further sign of Anstil, the youngsters had fretted and pined, giving their mother no peace until she had finally agreed to bring them down to the human Settlement – where they all hoped to find more human children for playmates.

So Rigga had related to Scrunch when, on his wanderings, he had visited them. And so here he was, guiding them in.

As they left the trees and stepped into the Settlement clearing, they were all nervous. The youngsters clustered together, all eyes and open mouths, whispering and hissing and tumbling over each other. Rigga's hackles were lifted in a stiff short ruff along her spine. Her eyes darted about, as if she expected sudden attack from any quarter, and she walked stiffly on her toe- and fingertips.

Rigga shivered, eyeing the square green mats of the fields in the dawn-light, the distant houses, the uncertain shapes of human folk moving about, half hid amongst knee-high plants. 'Perhaps this is not such a good idea,' she said.

'Be calm,' Scrunch replied softly. 'The human folk here are all right. Some may be a bit rough-tongued, is all. But you will be welcomed. You and yours have nothing to fear.'

Rigga was still peering about suspiciously. 'So you have said.'

'So I have,' Scrunch echoed, 'and it is nothing but the simple truth.'

Rigga looked at him, sighed.

'I know,' Scrunch said. 'Coming here is not easy. But it will all be fine in the end. You'll see.'

'Will I?' Rigga returned.

Scrunch nodded: 'You will.'

He put all the assurance he could into what he said, but Scrunch felt a thrust of unease in his guts. The world felt tight about them. Rigga surely felt it, too. It was as if they moved through a strong but invisible current, tugging, pushing . . . The very trees themselves seemed to shiver with it, moving and sighing as if there were a breeze – though the morning air was still as still.

It was wearying, this constant tightness of things. Something had been ready to come into the world for a long time now. But what? He felt like a person on a high, thin slope. What if . . .

But there was no point in torturing himself with doubts now. Who was he to try to know the ordering of the world? He did what he felt to do. Little Anstil pined, he knew, stuck pulling green shoots out of the ground. The youngsters were upset and discontent. Rigga looked frail. He was bringing them to where they belonged, where everybody would benefit.

Or, at least, he most profoundly hoped so.

'Come,' he urged Rigga, 'let us go on.'

She hesitated, peering about uncertainly still. There was a little sound, and she snapped her head suddenly round.

A dark shape detached itself from the trees some ways down at the edge of the clearing and came winging over. With a hop-flap, it landed on the turf before them. Rigga's youngsters scuttled back behind their mother uncertainly.

'Otys,' Scrunch said by way of greeting.

The crow stalked back and forth before them, eyeing them out of first one sharp black eye, then the other. 'Welll welll . . .' he said in his harsh-voiced manner. 'Whatt havve wee herre? Suchhh a prettty famillly. Anddd alll comme herre too bee the playtthingggsss offf humannn folkkk, thennn?'

Rigga growled at him, a half-heard tremor in her thin chest.

Otys eyed her, then lifted his dark wings and turned his

back upon her insolently. 'Orrr isss ittt hungerrr thattt bringsss youu herre, thennn?' He gazed out across the fields, where human folk were busy, then turned back. 'Alll the lovellyyy fooddd theyyy cannn givvve youu. Butt whattt willl theyyy wanttt inn returnnn? Havve youu askeddd yourrselfff thattt? Havve youu askeddd the bearrr herre?'

'Otys!' Scrunch snapped. 'Can't you leave well enough alone? Must you always be picking at everything?'

'Stupiddd bearrr!' Otys snapped. 'Can'ttt youu feelll the world'sss tightnesss?'

'Go away!' Rigga barked. She made a little rush at him, and Otys skipped back, squawking in surprise. With a flurry and snap of wings, he rose up, cawing at them indignantly.

'I can't do this!' Rigga said. 'It was a mistake to come here.' She turned to her children. 'Hurry. Hurry! We must . . .'

But it was already too late.

Otys's outcry had attracted attention. A straggle of curious human folk was headed their way.

Rigga stood poised, shivering. 'Come!' she urged her youngsters. 'Back into the forest.'

But her children – more innocent than she – spilled out from behind her, all eyes for the advancing humans.

'Calm, Rigga,' Scrunch said softly. 'They will not harm your little ones.'

Rigga looked at him, her whole body quivering. 'How can you be so *sure*? They . . . they're *human*.'

Scrunch nodded: 'And they will not harm your young.'

Rigga shivered.

The human folk drew closer.

Scrunch peered at them, trying to see who it might be. He had not talked with anywhere near all the humans in the Settlement, and recently he had not spent much of his time here . . .

Two men and a woman were striding over. Scrunch had hoped grey-bearded Collart – who was the most level-hearted man of the lot of them, and who knew humanimal nature better than any – would be one of that number, but he was disappointed. He knew only one of those coming towards them, the woman: sinewy-slim, with short-cropped grey-blonde hair. Getta, her name was. She was one of the

Settlement's hunters, though now her bow and quiver were left behind and her hands, like those of the others, were earth-stained from the field harvesting.

'What have we here?' one of the men said, drawing up first. He was tall and thin, with a long hank of sandy hair and gaunt, stubbly cheeks. He gazed at Rigga and her children in amazement.

'Puppies, of course,' Getta said, coming up behind the man. Then she looked closer and gasped. 'Humanimal youngsters!'

The second man arrived puffing. He was big-bellied and ham-thighed, and his face was flushed. 'What's this?' he said. 'What's all this?' He pushed his way past the other two humans and stared at Rigga's youngsters. 'Humanimals!' He bent forward and reached a pudgy hand towards them. The youngsters skittered away, and he pushed closer, trying to snatch one of them up.

Rigga snarled and snapped at him, nipping the flesh along the side of his grasping palm.

'Owww!' he yelped, stumbling back away from her.

'Maxil!' Getta snapped at him. 'Can't you be more *careful*!'

The big-bellied man rounded on her. 'Me? *Me* be careful? That bitch of a dog *bit* me!'

Rigga was still snarling, her lips drawn back over her yellow dog's teeth, her hackles up in a stiff ruff.

'Look at her!' Maxil said, pointing. 'She's *dangerous*, that one!'

'You went for her babies,' Getta replied.

'I . . .' Maxil shook his head. 'I wasn't going to hurt them. She . . .'

'How was she to know that, then?' Getta demanded.

Maxil sucked on his bit hand sullenly. 'She didn't have to *bite* me.'

'I'm . . . I'm sorry, Man,' Rigga said uncertainly. 'But you moved too quick.'

Maxil frowned at her in silence, his injured hand still in his mouth.

'You're Scrunch, aren't you?' the thin, sandy-haired man said abruptly.

Scrunch nodded.

'I thought I recognized you. Lorrin's my name. I've heard

286

Smitt talk of you . . .' The man, though addressing Scrunch, had turned and was gazing at Rigga's youngsters in complete fascination. 'I've never seen humanimal babies before. Where'd they *come* from?'

'From the wild,' Scrunch answered. 'Ans . . .' He had been about to say 'Anstil and I' and had to stop himself. He took a breath, not liking the feeling of telling an untruth. 'I met them in one of my wanderings.'

'They're *beautiful* . . .' Getta breathed.

Rigga looked pleased. Her hackles began to settle.

'Have they come to stay?' sandy-haired Lorrin asked.

'That depends,' Scrunch said.

'On what?' demanded Maxil.

Scrunch lifted his broad shoulders in a bear's shrug. 'On what happens.'

'They're welcome,' Getta said. She turned to Rigga. 'You and your youngsters are very welcome here to our Settlement.'

'Oh yes?' butted in Maxil. 'And who are *you* that you now speak for the whole Settlement suddenly?'

'Leave it out, Maxil,' the other man said. 'Getta's just welcoming them is all.'

'In the name of the Settlement!' Maxil returned. 'You heard her, Lorrin.'

'And so?' Lorrin returned.

Maxil glared. 'So, it ought by rights to be one of the Committee who welcomes her.'

Getta and the other man shook their heads. 'Not this again!' Getta said.

'You can scoff if you wish,' Maxil said, 'but the Committee has been rightfully established by common agreement. And as the only member in good standing here, it becomes *my* duty to act as spokesman if there's any welcoming to be done.'

'So *welcome* them, then,' Lorrin said.

Maxil only stood there, sucking on his injured hand. 'I have to bring this before the Committee first. This is a . . . a special case. It wouldn't be right for me to act here without . . .'

'What?' Getta said. She ran both hands through her short, grey-blonde hair and shook her head. '*What?*'

'The Committee has established—'

287

'Oh, don't be so *stupid*!' Getta snapped.

Maxil bristled. 'Have a care how you address me, woman, or—'

'Or *what*?' Getta returned, thrusting her face into his.

'Enough, you two!' Lorrin said, putting an arm between them.

Scrunch could see Rigga shiver. She was flicking glances behind her, and looked as if she were about to turn and flee with her youngsters back into the safety of the trees. Things were going all wrong, here. Human fracas like this always seemed to erupt with such dizzying quickness. It made his belly hurt.

'Tell this woman to behave as she ought,' Maxil was saying angrily. 'If she can't—'

'This is not the welcome,' Scrunch said, padding forward and interrupting, 'that I promised my friend here.'

The humans went silent.

'I promised her she and her youngsters would find welcome here,' Scrunch went on. 'She was uncertain. But I promised her she and hers would be safe.'

'And so they shall be,' Getta answered quickly.

'Once the Committee agrees to it,' Maxil added.

Getta glared at him. 'Oh, do shut *up*, you overweening, shit-brained little—'

'Don't you call me names, woman. Just *don't* call me names!'

Scrunch felt his belly twist up. Rigga was stiff and trembling. Any instant, she would be off – and there would be no easy way to convince her to give this another try.

The humans had gone silent for a moment, Getta and Maxil glaring at each other.

Rigga turned, motioned with her head to her youngsters, who flocked nervously about her.

Scrunch opened his mouth to say something, when, suddenly, there was a shout from the distance.

All heads turned.

From the field, a small form came running. 'Scrunch!' a voice shouted. '*Scrunch!*'

The next thing they knew, Anstil was dashing up, shouldering her way peremptorily through the grown-ups. Rigga's

288

children flew to her in a wave and she went down with them all over her, shrieking with laughter.

Other human folk began to arrive now, amongst whom, Scrunch was relieved to see, was grey-bearded Collart.

'What's all this, then?' Collart asked. He stopped in his tracks, staring at Rigga and her children in amazement. Then a huge smile lit his face. 'Youngsters!' he gasped. He knelt down and watched as Anstil and Rigga's children rolled over each other. 'And such fine youngsters, too.'

He looked over at Rigga and made a little gesture of welcome. 'You and yours are *most* welcome here. These are the first new-borns we have seen this season. And such fine, *fine* youngsters, too. Welcome indeed!'

Rigga blinked, looking at him. She could not, Scrunch was pleased to see, help herself from smiling. Scrunch let out a relieved breath. With Collart here now, all would go well.

But Maxil had not finished. 'Who are you to speak for the Settlement?' he demanded of Collart as he had of Getta. 'Only the Committee . . .'

'Hang that precious Committee of yours!' Getta snapped irritably.

'Now, Getta,' Collart said. He got to his feet. 'The Committee—'

'Is more trouble than it's worth!' Getta interrupted. 'It just makes everything more complicated, that's all!'

Collart sighed. 'We all agreed it was necessary to have some form of permanent organization.'

Getta shook her head. 'We don't need . . .'

But whatever she had been about to say was drowned out in the growing murmur of those gathered about.

More children had arrived now, and one boy was venturing out of the swelling crowd towards where Anstil and Rigga's youngsters were still gambolling about each other.

'Be careful!' Maxil cried. 'She bit me, that one did. For no reason!'

'Tam!' one of the grownups called to the boy. 'Don't you dare go near those . . .'

But the boy was already there.

'Do they . . . bite?' he asked Anstil, kneeling down.

'Only in fun,' Anstil replied.

Two of the humanimal youngsters had come over to investigate him. One of them – Taggit it was, the eldest, dark brown of fur with a pale splash across his muzzle – leaped into the boy's lap and stuck his dog's wet nose into the boy's face.

The boy laughed.

'I'm Taggit,' the humanimal youngster said. 'I'm eldest.'

'I . . . I'm Tam,' the boy replied. For long moments, he stared down at little Taggit, still stiff and uncertain. He put a hand tentatively on Taggit's back, felt the soft dog-puppy fur. A big smile opened his face.

'Do you know how to play tag?' Taggit asked.

There were more children about now. A little girl, younger than either Tam or Anstil, had one of Rigga's youngsters cradled in her lap. Two more human children – a boy and a girl – slipped themselves past the grownups and joined the growing throng on the grass.

The grownups shifted about uneasily. 'Come back here, Tam,' a male voice called. And, 'Kallie, you get away from there.' But Tam and little Kallie and the rest were completely enthralled and deaf to their parents' voices.

Scrunch regarded the humanimal youngsters and the human children, massed together in a contented, giggling group. It was as it had been with Anstil the first time: the children, human and humanimal, took to each other with an immediacy that was quite startling. It warmed him to see it.

But the human adults were clearly uneasy. They stood in a crescent, stiff and uncertain.

Somebody pushed his way to the front suddenly, a thick-shouldered man, bearded and short, with an angry face. 'Anstil!' he shouted. 'Anstil, you come here this instant!'

'Leave her be, Olundar,' Getta said. 'Can't you see she's having fun?'

'You stay out of this!' Olundar snapped at her.

'That one bit me!' Maxil chimed in, pointing accusingly at Rigga. 'For no reason, either. Just bit me!'

Olundar beckoned to his daughter. 'Come *here*!'

'Leave her be, can't you?' Getta said. 'She and the others are only—'

'Anstil's *my* daughter,' Olundar said. 'She'll do as *I* say.' He turned his back on Getta and called to Anstil, 'Come *here*, girl. At once, do you hear!'

Anstil looked at him, her face puckered in distress.

'Anstil!' her father shouted and took a step towards her, reaching out.

Little Grub was in Anstil's lap. He whimpered at the shout, but, as Olundar reached for his daughter, Grub growled and snapped his little needle teeth.

'Get away, stupid beast!' Olundar hissed. He raised his hand, as if to slap little Grub out of Anstil's lap.

Rigga growled and sprang forwards.

Only a quick move on Scrunch's part saved things from a nasty conclusion. He thrust himself hastily forwards, coming to stand between the man and Rigga, and between him and Anstil and Grub.

'Peace!' Scrunch said to them. He felt his heart thumping. His belly was tight. Human folk filled him with despair at times, they were so intractable and troublous.

'Peace,' he repeated, looking from one to the other. 'There is no need for fighting.'

'There'll be peace once I get my daughter back,' Olundar spat. 'Anstil, come *here*!'

Anstil looked up, tears starting in her eyes. 'But I only . . .'

'Don't try the crying jag on me now!' her father said. 'Just do as you're told. Hear? *Now!*'

Anstil laid Grub slowly aside. He whimpered and nuzzled her hand, uncertain.

Anstil's father beckoned impatiently. '*Now*, I said.'

Grub cowered at the whiplash tone of his voice. Anstil bent down to his little face and whispered something. Then she stood slowly up, walked around past Scrunch, and went to her father.

Who gave her a hard slap across the thigh. 'Next time, do as you're told, girl!'

Anstil quivered, but bit her lip and uttered not a sound.

Looking on, Scrunch felt a thrust of anger go through him. Little Anstil deserved no such brutality. What was wrong with the man that he behaved so? He took a step forwards . . . and then stopped himself. No good could come of his placing himself between a human father and his child.

But Getta seemed to feel no such compunction. 'You're a brute, Olundar,' she said. 'A rotten, bloody-minded brute!'

Olundar pushed Anstil away, thrusting hard against her shoulders so that she stumbled. 'Off to the fields with you, girl. And be quick about it. There's a pile of work still left to do before day's end.' Then he turned to Getta. 'And you . . . you mind your own business, woman. What do *you* know of children?'

'More than you, man.'

'Oh yes?' Olundar gestured about him. 'And where are *your* children, then? You who spend all your time off in the woods with that bow of yours? You dress like a man, act like a man . . . No wonder no real man will have you.'

Getta paled. 'I had children . . .' she said, her voice shaking. 'They were killed. The Brothers . . . I saw my boy, Len, cut down before my very eyes.'

Olundar looked at her.

'I never once,' Getta said, 'hit any child of mine.'

'More fool you, then,' Olundar returned. 'Hard hand makes for good character, my old dad always said.'

Getta blinked, took a breath.

At which point, Collart slipped between the two of them. 'Leave it be, you two,' he said. He put a calming hand on Getta's arm. 'We've other matters here to deal with.'

Getta cast a venomous look at Olundar. 'Shit for brains,' she murmured, then sighed and nodded.

Rigga, meanwhile, had gathered her brood about her. The human children had all been dragged away by their parents, two with hard slaps and tears. Rigga stood, stiff and uneasy, protectively between her young and the crowd, staring with deep suspicion at the press of human folk about her.

Scrunch felt his heart sink. Nothing was going right here. The way Rigga was poised, the littlest thing now might send her fleeing off. He wanted out of here himself; the sharp quickness of human conflict made him – made all his kind – dizzy and sick-feeling.

But Collart walked over to Rigga, slow and gentle, and made

292

a little sort of bow. 'Please accept my apologies,' he said. 'I know how disturbing human disputes can be to the Free Folk. You are most welcome to stay amongst us if it pleases you to do so.'

'And if the Committee so decrees,' Maxil spoke up.

'Aye,' Olundar agreed.

Getta whirled as if to make a hard reply, but Collart hushed her with a motion of his hand. He sighed and turned back to Rigga. 'We are a noisy folk. But we mean well nonetheless. Please forgive us our harshness.'

Rigga regarded him in silence for a long moment, then nodded slowly.

'My name is Collart.'

'I am Rigga,' Rigga replied after a moment. 'And my youngsters are Taggit, Suggi, Boe, Korin, and Grub.'

'Well, Rigga,' Collart said, 'and Taggit, Suggi, Boe, Korin, and Grub . . .'

The youngsters swirled excitedly about behind their mother, hearing their own names.

'You are all most welcome here in the Settlement. And as for the Committee . . .' Collart looked round at Maxil. 'I'm quite sure that the Committee will welcome you as we all do. Isn't that right, Maxil? There's no reason in the world for the Committee to refuse her and her youngsters welcome, is there?'

Maxil shrugged. He held his injured hand up before his face, examining it. 'Probably . . . not.'

'Especially not now that they're here and welcome amongst us anyway,' Getta added.

Maxil glared sidelong at her.

Collart held up both his hands, palms out. 'Enough . . . enough for now. We've more than sufficient to keep us occupied without wasting our energy snapping at each other.' He gestured to the fields from which they had all come. 'The day is passing and we've still much to harvest.'

'Aye!' Olundar said. 'We've few enough hands as is. And we waste what precious time we have standing about here gawking at puppies and arguing uselessly. Let's to work!'

There was a general muttering of agreement.

'What about *them*?' somebody asked, pointing at Scrunch, Rigga, and her children.

'Let them join in on the harvest if they wish a welcome here,' Olundar said. 'They've hands, haven't they? Let them work if they want to be part of this community.'

'You can't make the Free Folk work like that,' Collart said quickly. 'Everybody knows—'

'All *I* know,' Olundar cut in, 'is that my back aches and I have a long, weary day ahead of me. While *them* . . .' he glared at the humanimals, 'they'll spend the day swanning about in the shade of the trees more than likely. Then show up when the work's finished, demanding a share in the harvest. Well, I say—'

'Nobody *cares* what you say,' Getta interrupted.

Scrunch saw Rigga back away, drawing her youngsters with her. It was about to break out all over again. Scrunch felt his hackles stiffen. What was *wrong* with human folk?

But Collart calmed them, as he had before. 'Enough! Enough, I say . . . Fighting amongst ourselves will get us nowhere. Let's to work, as Olundar says, and use up our energy that way.'

'And *them*?' somebody insisted, meaning the humanimals.

Collart sighed. 'The Free Folk have their path and we ours.'

'And ours leads to the fields,' Getta put in. 'Let's to it, then.'

There was a moment's uneasy pause. Then they began to filter off, muttering and murmuring, some of them, but going nonetheless.

Scrunch watched them leave with relief.

Collart, the last to go, stepped over and ducked his head close to Scrunch's. 'Keep them out of sight for a while if you can,' he said softly, gesturing to Rigga and her children with his bearded chin. 'Just to be on the safe side.'

Scrunch nodded. It agreed with his own instincts, that. Human folk were too unpredictable, and all too capable of blind, hard acts when roused.

Rigga looked at them uneasily, perhaps having heard Collart's whispered suggestion.

'We'll see this clear,' Collart assured her. 'It just takes time, sometimes, for us human folk to adjust to new developments. You'll see, though. Everything will be fine.'

294

Rigga said nothing.

'Well,' Collart concluded, 'I'd best join the rest. We've a long day's work ahead.' With that, he headed off back to the fields, where Scrunch could see the rest already beginning to go back to the work of harvesting.

If anybody could see things through, it would be Collart, Scrunch thought. He wished Elinor were returned, though. Since her departure, things here at the Settlement seemed to have got more complicated. All this talk of the Committee – whatever exactly that might be.

Rigga was gathering her brood together. 'Come,' he heard her say. 'Time to go.'

'But not too far,' Scrunch said. 'You heard what Collart said. Everything will be fine here. Human folk are just a bit . . . pricklish is all. We will come back again later.'

'Oh, yes, Mamma!' one of the youngsters said.

'It was so much fun,' another piped up, 'to have human children to play with!'

Rigga gestured them towards the trees at the edge of the Settlement clearing, and they began trotting in a ragged group in that direction. With them a little ahead of her, she turned and looked at the human folk hunched over in the fields. 'They do not like children, here,' she said softly to Scrunch.

'It will be *fine* here, Rigga. You'll see.'

'Perhaps,' she replied, but there was no conviction in her voice.

'It *will* be,' Scrunch insisted.

But Rigga merely shrugged and went after her youngsters, who were drawing close to the shadow-cover of the trees now.

Scrunch went after her. It would be fine, he told himself. Those like Collart and Getta would see that it would be fine. It was only a question of waiting a little till the human folk adjusted to this new thing.

The way the human children and Rigga's youngsters had come together so easily, despite all the tension and snapping of the adults, boded well.

Only a little time was all, and then things would come together, and the possibility of a new pattern would come into the world, humanimal and human bonded together as never before. And who knew where that might lead?

Only a question of time . . .

At least, he fervently hoped so.

XXIV

'Come,' Iryn Jagga ordered Ziftkin, sweeping into the room, bringing with him the scent of violets and rainy outside air. He wore a rain-cloak, water-spotted, under which he was clad in a dark shirt and pleated trousers. At his waist, a broad leather belt supported a short sword in an ornately inlaid brass scabbard. His hair was damp, and the golden circlet upon his head shone wetly. He left muddy-wet footprints behind on the floor, his shining dark boots spattered with yellow mud. 'Quickly now!' he said, 'Come *on*!'

'Where?' Ziftkin replied. 'Where have you *been* all this while?'

Ziftkin sat on the bed in his cell-room. The rain splattering on the glass panes of the window behind him made a soft tattoo. He had been listening to it all morning.

After all Iryn Jagga's stirring roof-top talk, Ziftkin had been left languishing alone for a day and a half in his cell-room, with the door barred and guarded from the outside – prey to a parade of fears and hopes, his dreams haunted still (though less than before, it was true) by the nagging Gault Keep dead. He was sick and tired of all of it.

And now Iryn Jagga came swaggering in, issuing his commands. 'Why have I been—' Ziftkin began.

Iryn Jagga held up his hand in a peremptory gesture to silence. 'I have told you, boy. Never question me. What I do, I do for the good of all. Do you think you are the only care I have?'

Ziftkin looked at him sullenly. 'Why am I locked up here like a . . . a *prisoner*?'

Iryn Jagga regarded Ziftkin coldly, his face going hard. Then he let out a breath, shook his head, and smiled thinly – for all the world like a doting father with a wayward child. 'You are a guest, songster. My very own special guest. Is the food brought to you not of the finest quality? Are the bed linens not changed daily? Were you not given soft soap and hot water to wash with?'

'Why is the door locked and guarded, then?' Ziftkin returned. 'If I am a *guest*?'

Iryn Jagga's face went serious. 'There are dangers, songster. *She* has minions everywhere. I keep you here under guard for your own protection.'

Ziftkin blinked, uncertain.

Iryn Jagga snapped his fingers impatiently, and a man came out of nowhere and knelt hastily, produced a little bowl and a wet cloth, and began carefully wiping the mud from Iryn Jagga's boots. 'You are in danger, boy. It is the truth. You have my word on it. I would like nothing better than to give you free rein of the city and allow you to poke your nose about wherever you wish. But it is simply too dangerous. You are too *important* to place at risk like that.'

'But what if I . . .'

Iryn Jagga silenced him with a wave of his hand. 'Enough! The issue is closed. Trust me on this. I know best. And now . . .' he beckoned Ziftkin off the bed, 'come! There is something I wish to show you.'

'What?' Ziftkin demanded.

'Come and see. Unless . . .' Iryn Jagga smiled a mocking smile, 'unless you would rather spend the day here, slumped upon your little bed like some sulking, silly child.'

Ziftkin glared at him, stung.

'Come, then,' Iryn Jagga repeated.

Ziftkin swallowed his anger and got up.

'Good.' Iryn Jagga waved away the man who had been cleaning his boots – who had finished now in any case. 'Follow me. And bring your instrument.'

The flute was already in Ziftkin's hands; he was not about to go anywhere without it.

Without another word, Iryn Jagga turned and marched out of the room. Ziftkin followed after, still bubbling with resentment, but curious also. And a little anxious-excited. To what was he being taken?

*

Groundwards Iryn Jagga went this time, leading Ziftkin down flight after flight of steps. A handful of the dour-faced guards accompanied them, armed with both pikes and swords – Iryn Jagga never went anywhere, it seemed, without a gang of such guards grouped about him.

The building through which they moved was dim and utterly silent. Ziftkin shivered. It was unnerving, a structure as vast as this one – with floor after floor, the whole place ornate with carvings and pillars and elaborate stone furnitures – and yet with no sign of life. The last time through, on his way up to the roof-top, he had been too uncertain, too preoccupied with the effort of upwards climbing to notice. Now, it grated on his nerves, this silent emptiness.

'Where . . . where *is* everybody?' he asked finally. Iryn Jagga, descending before him, either did not hear or chose to ignore him. Ziftkin felt a spasm of irritation. He swallowed it and continued on. There seemed little other choice.

Downwards they went until the air began to be chill and damp. There were no windows here, and the light was dim. Two of the guards lit hand-torches and walked, one ahead, one behind, holding the torches high so that their hissing, flickering flames cast whirling shadows across the walls and upon the tiers of steps dwindling into obscurity above and below them.

And still their way was down, flight after flight of endless stairs until, at last, Iryn Jagga gestured them off into a series of branching corridors. The place stank of mould and old decay, and there was a clamminess to the air that made Ziftkin shiver.

Along a low-ceilinged corridor they went. From ahead, there came soft sounds. At first, Ziftkin was not sure if he was really hearing them or only imagining. But as they continued onwards, the sounds became clearer. Moans and sighs, groans and mumblings, the creak and shuffle of bodies moving.

Round a sharp bend Iryn Jagga led, then along a passage-way lined with squat wooden doors – from behind which came the sounds.

Iryn Jagga motioned to one of the guards, who unbolted a door and pulled it open. The lead torch-bearer stepped forwards into the room beyond, first ducking through the low doorway, then holding his light high.

Iryn Jagga went next. 'Phawg!' he muttered, holding his hand to his nose. He gestured Ziftkin in impatiently.

Ziftkin ducked uncertainly into the room. The air was thick with a stench that stung his nostrils – a mix of excrement and decay and mouldy damp, bad enough, almost, to make his eyes water. He stared about him in confusion. 'Wha— What,' he began.

Iryn Jagga gestured.

Against the back wall, Ziftkin made out a huddled shape. The room was perhaps five paces square, the floor littered with sticky, discoloured straw. In the uncertain torchlight, Ziftkin could not make out clearly what it was that lay against the far wall, for it was tucked in upon itself and part-way buried in a matted straw-clump. He was not sure he wanted to see any more clearly what it might be. He felt sick in his belly, being in a place such as this.

He rounded on Iryn Jagga. 'Why have you brought me here?'

'Look,' Iryn Jagga said by way of reply. He pointed at the huddled form against the back wall. '*Look!*'

Ziftkin swallowed and took a few steps, gingerly, through the filthy straw. The guard held his torch higher. In the dance of the flame, Ziftkin saw that there was some manner of furred creature there, curled in upon itself, legs tucked close under it.

Ziftkin blinked. It was large, perhaps as much as waist high when standing, he reckoned, and seemed to be some sort of dog, though unlike any dog he had ever seen before. It seemed to have legs far longer than any normal dog's, and its fur was startlingly striped, dark brown against what might have once been a golden-ochre pelt, running from its spine down transversely across its ribcage and thin legs. It had long, drooping ears and dark eyes that seemed very big in its face, half closed now and vacantly staring.

Ziftkin bent forwards a little, to look at it more closely, uncertain – though it had showed no response at all to their presence here so far.

A hand yanked him back.

'Careful,' Iryn Jagga warned. 'These creatures can be dangerous.'

From behind, two more guards stepped forwards into the room, one with a pike ready, the other with a sword. The swordsman flipped a clot of matted straw away from the dog-creature with his blade's tip.

Ziftkin stared, maintaining a discreet distance, though he could not imagine how this poor, starveling, huddled being could be dangerous. It ribs showed clearly through fur that was thin and lustreless, and its breath came in snuffling gasps. There was a raw, open sore along its flank, with flies buzzing and darting about it. Ziftkin swallowed. 'What . . . what has happened to the poor thing?'

'Poor thing?' Iryn Jagga laughed. 'This . . . *thing* is a monstrosity. An abomination. Look at it!'

Ziftkin looked, but all he could see was a starved and ill-treated, queer-looking dog.

Iryn Jagga motioned to the pike-man, and the man prodded the dog-creature with the butt end of his weapon. His first prod had no effect, and the pike-man reversed his weapon and jabbed with the blade, bringing blood. The dog groaned and shivered. One of its front legs came flailing out, and, to his amazement, Ziftkin saw that it ended in fingers and a kind of stubby thumb. The creature's eyes opened fully for the first time.

Ziftkin gasped.

A dog this creature might look to be – or a sort of dog, at any rate. But its eyes . . . Ziftkin shivered. Its eyes were utterly human.

Looking into them, he could read all the misery and pain and terror the poor creature must have experienced in this terrible place. His heart went out to it instinctively – Iryn Jagga's warning or no – and he knelt down and tried to reach out.

One of the guards shoved him away.

'Do not be fooled, boy,' Iryn Jagga warned. 'This *thing* is nothing worthy of your pity.'

The poor dog looked up at Ziftkin and made a little plaintive sound.

'Silence, you!' Iryn Jagga snapped.

The dog lowered its head weakly.

'I don't . . .' Ziftkin began. He shuddered, looked away, swallowed, working to get enough breath in the foul air. 'Why did you bring me here?'

'To allow you to see, first hand, what it is we must confront, you and I. Do you see what a foul thing it is? What a travesty? No honest dog in shape at all. And those eyes?' Iryn Jagga pointed at the creature's expressive human eyes. 'An unholy mixture. A forcing together of that which should never have been joined in union. Abomination!'

Ziftkin did not know what to say.

'So now you know,' Iryn Jagga went on. 'Now you have seen.' He motioned the guards back a little and stepped back himself. 'And now *I* wish to see what power your instrument has over such.'

Ziftkin blinked, taken by surprise. 'What is it you expect me to . . . do?'

'I have seen you control others with that instrument of yours. Such a creature as this is a *made* thing. It ought to be easy enough to control such. I care not what you do to it. Only make clear for me how much you can reach this creature, how much control you can assert over it.'

Iryn Jagga stepped closer and reached a hand to Ziftkin's shoulder. 'Do not be fooled by it. They can have a certain . . . seductiveness, these creatures. I see the look in your eyes. You are too soft-hearted. It is a *thing*, nothing more. A *made* thing that has got beyond control and needs to be destroyed, or it and its like will bring utter ruin into the world.'

Ziftkin stared at the poor dog-creature, licked his lips, lifted the flute, let it drop again.

'Play, songster,' Iryn Jagga ordered. 'Play!'

Ziftkin lifted the flute and played a slow, mournful skirl of notes.

The dog-creature raised its head weakly and gazed at him in surprise.

Through the mysterious medium of the flute, Ziftkin *felt* the creature's pain and misery washing through him. And despair. Such a blackness of despair as nearly took all the breath from him.

He channelled the creature's pain through him with the

flute, feeling the dark current of it flow into wrenching, melody.

The creature howled.

Ziftkin could sense its agony and utter weariness of spirit.

And more . . .

Understanding flowed through him in a rush.

As with the water-beast that had attacked him and his mare by the side of the dark stream, he could *feel* this suffering being's inner shape. The water-beast had *belonged* in its little section of the world, totally and completely. This dog-being was caught . . . between.

The water-beast had been virtually mindless, a creature of blood and hunger and dark intuition, with no uncertainties, no guilt, no confusions. The dog-being *felt* something like that, immersed a little way into the same sort of seamless, mindless world of the water-beast, but only enough to have the flavour of it, not the fulfilment. For the dog-being was irrevocably mindful, looking on at the world and at itself, separate and self-aware, yet tormented by the promise of a belonging to which human folk were blind – like a fish stranded irrevocably upon the surface of a river, unable to submerge itself properly into the beckoning water, no matter how it might yearn to.

Iryn Jagga was right, then. This poor being was a kind of unnatural, uncomfortable, painful mixing. But there was nothing . . . *monstrous* about it. Ziftkin could summon none of the repugnance that Iryn Jagga so obviously felt, and could not imagine what it could have done to merit such brutal treatment. All he felt for it was sympathy. The poor creature was so utterly . . . *lonesome*.

After his encounter with the water-beast, Ziftkin had envied the mindless, complete *belonging* that defined the beast's nature. He had never before imagined belonging like that, and the realization of it had left him shaken. The poor dog-being before him felt the hidden promise of just such a belonging in its bones and blood every moment of every day, but could never achieve it.

Ziftkin's heart went out to it. He shivered, playing a slow, complex pattern of notes on the flute, *feeling* the dog-creature's nature as a part of himself . . . And as he played, something began to emerge in his mind, some thread of the dog-being's experience woven into momentary clarity amongst the flute notes: a bursting image of green-sod slope and free running, of the sky a shade of pale colour he could not name, the feel of long muscles in his thighs as he ran, the land itself somehow guiding his steps . . .

And another such dog-being gambolling in the grass – a female whose dark brown fur was mottled with faint golden splashes, almost like a young fawn's markings. She pranced and leaped with a gazelle's light-foot grace, her legs far longer and more slender than any ordinary dog's. Her ears were large, blue-veined, quivery, her face pointed and elegant, her eyes green as bright wet moss, expressively human, and filled with tenderness.

Ziftkin felt a shiver of vicarious joy go through him. For an instant he *was* the dog-being, leaping and laughing, coupling in moving ecstasy, making new life, feeling completely at one with the long-legged female, belonging with her, with the world entire.

But that momentary joy died, ousted by pain.

Ziftkin *felt* the dog-being shudder, racked with memory and body-agony and a blackness of despair that was completely overwhelming. It was at the bitter end of its strength, beyond help, beyond hope, exhausted, empty, broken and alone and yearning with a desperate and bitter desire for . . .

Release.

Ziftkin remembered how, with the water-beast, he had played a single, desperate, long-held, piercing note. How he had nearly killed the beast with it: all he would have needed to do would have been to drive the keening note he had been playing deeply enough into it to rip through the delicate membranes that held soul and flesh and mind together.

And so end its life.

It would have been a . . . a cruel thing to have done then.

But here . . . here he suddenly felt the cruelty would lie in turning his back upon this poor dog-creature and condemning it to live on in the pitiful, suffering manner it now did. It *yearned* so for release.

Ziftkin shivered. He felt that yearning so acutely it was an agony almost as hard as the other agonies the poor wretch suffered. Soothing dark and release . . . and absence of pain. Coolth and emptiness and release. Blessed non-being.

Hardly knowing what he did, Ziftkin slipped from the almost-tune he was playing and blew a single, wavering note. Slowly, he inserted that note, the power of the note . . . a vibrating shiver of energy that, somehow, had a realness to it as much as any length of wood or metal.

Slowly, he inserted the vibrating energy of that note into the poor being's centre, pushing through until he sensed the very core of it, the place where everything met, where spirit and flesh, mind and soul, sense and pain and hope and self, idea and image and the intricate landscape of memory all intermingled.

It was all so indescribably complex, a moving webbery of shining, dripping, quivering delicacy. And *so* intricately balanced, one thing interwoven with another and an-other . . .

Like a man undoing a complex knot, Ziftkin reached in with the flute-note and severed the core.

In a heartbeat, it all unravelled.

He felt the spirit go, like a rush of water escaping from a suddenly ruptured bag, leaving only the sagging, damp remains of the empty bag behind. But so quick was it, so weakly held-together had the poor creature been, that, as if he had been pushing hard against somebody who suddenly collapsed backwards, Ziftkin felt himself flung off balance and plunging downwards into empty dark.

The dog-being's released spirit was whirling away like an autumn leaf in the wind. Ziftkin sensed himself, also, being drawn off, drawn apart, like earth dissolving in a strong current of moving water. He felt darkness all about and, in the unclear distance, glimpsed a hint of dim landscape, hills and plains.

A snatch of old verse came into his memory:

> Bitter ash and leaf and thorn,
> The Darkling Hills lie seer and worn . . .

Blind terror came over him then, for what he sensed could be nothing less than the Shadowlands themselves, the realm of the dead, and he was somehow being sucked along after the departing spirit he had released with the flute's uncanny music.

He fought desperately against his own impending dissolution, caught in that terrible dark current, struggling not to drown in the darkness, trying with every shred of will he had left to hold himself together, to bring the world back, himself back.

A spasm of white-hot agony went through him. Ziftkin cried out, shuddered, opened his eyes, found himself abruptly back in the torch-lit, stinking room.

He took a faltering breath of the bad air, another. The flute was still in his hands, but he had taken it from his lips – when, he could not recall – and he stood, his limbs stiff and quivering, his heart hammering painfully.

He stared at the pitiable, huddled form of the dead being before him, his eyes stinging with tears. For long moments, it was all he could do just to breathe, to stand without falling, to still the painful thumping of his heart. Then he turned and staggered out of the room.

Outside in the corridor, he collapsed against the chill, damp stone of the wall and stood there, panting, eyes unfocused. His knees felt weak as water.

'Well done!' Iryn Jagga said, coming after him. '*Well* done! Better than ever I could have hoped.'

Ziftkin blinked. He felt sick. He did not know how he felt.

'Would that it were only this easy,' Iryn Jagga was saying. His face was lit by a triumphant smile. 'Would that I had all of their accursed kind here, so you could play death upon them all so efficiently.'

Ziftkin felt a long shudder go through him.

'We will be famous, songster, you and I.' Iryn Jagga rubbed his hands together. 'There is nothing can stop us now! We will destroy this Elinor and rid the world of the abomination these creatures represent. And then . . . *then* the great days of the past will return again!'

Ziftkin opened his mouth, took a breath, could find nothing to say. He shuddered, recalling the dark, the dim, seer hills, the utter terror of spirt that had gripped him as he felt his very self beginning to unravel.

He thought of the poor souls back at Gault Keep, trapped and smashed by the falling walls . . . souls whirled away into that waiting dark, as he still saw in his dreams. It had been a . . . a kindness he had done here, at least of sorts, to grant the poor dog-being the release it so yearned for. And the destruction of those wailing souls back at Gault Keep had been altogether unintentional on his part. But to kill and go on killing as Iryn Jagga urged, to purposefully destroy how many? Dozens? Scores? of such creatures . . .

Unnatural such beings might be, as Iryn Jagga said. But their pain and aloneness were altogether too recognizable. No. He could do no such thing as Iryn Jagga demanded. There was too much of death upon him already. He felt it too nakedly. He could not bear to be steeped in more, no matter how noble or how necessary for the world's greater future.

He looked down at the flute and felt a creeping horror go through him that such a beauteous thing, a thing capable of producing such perfect, moving melody, could be the cause of death . . . that *he* could be such a cause.

'Come, boy,' Iryn Jagga coaxed. 'Pull yourself together. What you did here today is a necessary thing. A *good* thing. And it is only the beginning. You must steel yourself. You must harden your will. There is much work to be done yet before the world is freed of the taint of such abominable creatures.'

'No,' Ziftkin said. 'No!'

'No . . . *what*?' returned Iryn Jagga, his handsome face going abruptly stiff.

'I cannot do as you want.'

Iryn Jagga leaned forwards. 'Now you listen to me, boy! There is a high destiny upon you. What you will or no is of no matter. You must be *strong*. We must do what is necessary, you and I. We must do what we must . . . for the sake of the world.'

Ziftkin shook his head. 'You do not understand! I cannot—'

'Cannot? *Cannot?*' Iryn Jagga grabbed him by the shoulder, spun him about so that they were standing nose to nose. 'There is no *cannot*. Do you hear me? Men like you and I, songster, we must do what we must. Ours is no easy road. We must—'

'You don't *understand*!' Ziftkin interrupted. He was panting. His skin felt chilled and clammy and his guts were churning. 'I . . . I cannot play death upon these creatures as you wish me to.'

'*Cannot* again! I tell you, boy, there is no such thing as *cannot*. You can and *will* do all that is necessary!'

'Listen to me!' Ziftkin cried. '*Listen* to me. It is . . . I . . .' He tried desperately to think of what to say. Iryn Jagga would accept no mere excuse. 'It's not . . . not a question of whether I wish to or not. I *cannot*! The creature in the cell *wished* to die. Do you hear? I released its spirit because it *wished* for such. It *wanted* death. But I . . . I could not bring such release upon any creature that did not want it so.'

Iryn Jagga eyed him coldly: 'Is this the truth?'

'It is,' Ziftkin lied – or thought he lied. Perhaps this spur-of-the-moment untruth was not so short of the mark after all. Or perhaps not . . . He did not know how to know, save by trying to play death upon some being again. His guts churned at the very thought.

Iryn Jagga stood staring at him, eyes hard as a hawk's. 'So . . .' he said after a long few moments. 'So . . .' He scowled, his gaze going blank, his forehead puckered in thought. Then he shook himself and said, 'Come.' Turning, he swept out the door and back along the route they had taken to get here.

Ziftkin followed, only too glad to get away from this sad, foul place.

XXV

Ziftkin stood before a long wall-mirror, staring at his own image: he could hardly recognize himself in the figure he saw there.

He was dressed in a long-sleeved shirt and loose-fitting trousers, both of a deep wine-red so dark as to be almost black. The shirt was drawn in at his waist with a slim, silver-buckled, black leather belt, and its long tails fell nearly to his knees in neat, elegant folds. On his feet were a pair of black leather boots. A long dress-cloak hung from his shoulders, a rich blue-black, lined with pure white silk that glistened as if it were wet.

The boots, which came almost to his knees, were stitched with crimson thread in spiral patterns. The tops had a little flare which opened out on each side, from which hung a single, winking ruby. They were surprisingly comfortable on his feet and silent when he walked – altogether the most remarkable footwear he had ever worn.

The trousers and shirt were equally elegant, and astonishingly soft against his skin. The dark wine colour of them was mesmerizing almost, the way it soaked in the light so richly and so subtly.

It was altogether elegant and beauteous clothing. Iryn Jagga himself possessed none better. And Ziftkin was bathed and scrubbed and perfumed, with his carefully braided hair so clean it shone. Dressed in clothes such as these, he could feel himself to be a . . . a person of importance.

Part of him wanted desperately to cling to that feeling. Who he was mattered were in Sofala. Against all expectation, he had found a place where he was important, where he could belong.

But, looking at his new self, he felt sick in his guts. What was the price of such elegance? Of such belonging?

He made a little bow to himself in the mirror, wafting the bone flute – which, as always, he carried with him – like a baton, trying to make the bow as grandly elegant as he could, imagining, with a little stab of satisfaction, the bitter envy his foster brother Mechant would feel to see him as he now was. But it was a vain and pointless gesture.

Ziftkin turned from the mirror with a long sigh. Try as he might, he could not get the feel of the poor humanimal dog-being out of his mind.

Abomination. An unnatural thing that ought to be destroyed for the betterment of the world . . . So said Iryn Jagga. But Ziftkin could not find it in himself to regard the dog-being so. He felt too much of . . . kinship with it. He knew too well, himself, the sense of aloneness from which it suffered. The flute had shown him. His own life had shown him.

He pictured Iryn Jagga, the man's handsome face enlivened with the passion of his belief, pacing back and forth, declaiming: 'The world must be freed from the taint of such abominable creatures. *Made* things that pollute the world with their very being. They are of the Dark, spreading the Dark wherever they go . . .'

Ziftkin shook his head. He could not do it. He could not bring himself to embrace Iryn Jagga's claims. He had *felt* the dog-being's inner shape. There was nothing abominable about it. What is was evoked only sympathy from him, and it had done nothing, as far as he could make out, to merit the foul, cruel treatment it had received at the hands of Iryn Jagga and his ilk.

Ziftkin looked about him with a sigh. No more was he confined to his original cell-room. Now he had a two-roomed suite, with an opulent, marbled bath and eider-down bed – such luxury as he, a farm-boy, had hardly ever dreamed of. Candles danced in gilded wall sconces. Out the room's ornate double window, he could see the lights of Sofala twinkle in the night's dark below. He fingered the sumptuous soft cloth of his shirt sleeve, lifted a foot to feel the comfortable glove-leather fit of the boots. The irony of his situation was bitter. He *did* have a place here, a future. The figure before him in the mirror seemed – *seemed* – to be all he had ever hoped for as a lad.

But Iryn Jagga was too much like his uncle Harst, bloody-minded and single-visioned. And he would not, *could* not bring himself to do as the leader of the Ancient Brotherhood required. He would not be a part of the wholesale destruction of such creatures as the humanimal dog-being he had encountered this morning.

Which meant he must flee this place at the first available opportunity . . . find some way over the city wall and thence away into the wild lands. Alone once more, pursued perhaps. Likely pursued. Iryn Jagga was not a man to brook opposition to his will lightly.

But no such flight would be possible this night.

Ziftkin looked at his oh-so-elegant image in the mirror once more. 'A festive gala such as has not been seen in Sofala for many a year,' Iryn Jagga had said. 'To celebrate the bright new future that awaits us all.'

And so he was dressed in this finery and he would be introduced deeper into Sofala, to know more intimately what it was he was abandoning.

He looked down at the flute in his hands and damned it, and blessed it, and sighed a long sigh. At least back in Seshevrell farm life had been . . . simple.

Down a long corridor, Ziftkin followed the dark-robed servant who had come to fetch him. Not a word had the man said. Beckoning Ziftkin respectfully from his room, he had led the way down a series of corridors and stairways and thence, eventually, to a long, candle-lit hall, at the end of which stood an ornate, open doorway. A brace of sombre-clothed guards stood to attention before it, armed with long, gilded pikes. The servant stopped, silently bowing Ziftkin on ahead.

Ziftkin glanced at the guards – who regarded him blankly – took a breath, straightened his cloak, went on through.

And stopped dead after no more than three paces.

The floor was smooth white stone, the walls of what seemed a sort of mottled green marble, veined with startling red and purple. Overhead was cloud-studded, open blue sky – blue sky in the middle of the night. For a long instant he was completely flummoxed.

Then he realized it was a painted ceiling above him, so incredibly well executed that it had truly seemed like an open, lightly clouded sky.

He swallowed, shook himself, realized that he was on a short flight of steps leading down to a room lit with a vast array of candles: in chandeliers, in gilded wall sconces, in upright candelabras resembling trees, or buildings, or queer-looking men . . .

A rumbling buzz of sound enveloped him. The room was filled with a moving tapestry of people. And such people . . . They swirled about as if some invisible current were slowly sweeping the room, women aglitter with colour and scintillating jewellery, the men no less glittering, though their clothing was all of sombre colours. And everywhere there were attentive, silent, dark-robed servants.

Ziftkin stood self-consciously on the verge of it all, staring, his heart beating uncertainly. Nothing he had witnessed thus far in Sofala had prepared him for a scene of such opulent elegance as this. His clothing felt strange and uncomfortable suddenly, the long dress-cloak unmanageable. He feared to move, lest he get it all tangled up between his legs and sprawl forward across the floor and make an utter and complete ass of himself.

Suddenly, Iryn Jagga was at his side. The leader of the Ancient Brotherhood of the Light was dressed in his usual sombre elegance, with the golden circlet upon his brow. This evening his long dark hair was twined in a queue, threaded with gold, and he fairly dripped with precious stones, rubies and emeralds sewn into his tunic, bright yellow diamonds, blue topaz. On the index finger of each hand was a gold ring set with black onyx. 'Welcome, Ziftkin Salvator,' he said.

Ziftkin looked at him, disconcerted.

'It is to be your name,' Iryn Jagga explained. '*Salvator*. It comes from a word in an old language meaning "saviour". For you will be the saviour of Sofala and all it stands for.' He smiled and gestured to the elegant throng of people. 'A gala in your honour.'

Ziftkin swallowed. 'Muhh . . . *my* honour? But you never said . . .'

Iryn Jagga smiled. 'My little secret. But you have become a

person of *importance* now, you know. We must have a proper *bringing-in* for you.' He gestured to the throng of people. 'Here before you, you see Sofala's brightest and best.'

Ziftkin did not know what to say. He was shaken by the blunt magnificence of everything, and by the hard irony of the situation – such a lavish welcome for one who would soon be gone.

He turned uncomfortably from Iryn Jagga and looked at the room. All along one wall was an array of food and drink, shining goblets and plates of silver and gold, mounds of glistening fruits and sweet-meats. At each end of the table there stood an enormous candelabra, shaped like a gilded tree, alight with a multitude of white, smokeless candles.

A small orchestra was seated in the corner of the room beyond the table: a group of immaculately attired men; two flute players, a drummer, a fiddler, and a man plying a long-necked, fretted stringed instrument unlike anything Ziftkin had ever seen before. As he watched, the orchestra began to play, and the air rang with the pleasant, soft music they made.

The high, clear voices of the flutes were a pleasure to hear – and equally a pleasure to look at, all creamy ivory and dark wood and scintillating gold. They made him think of the beautiful flute his mother had given him. And that led back to a complex of recollections he did not at all wish to dwell upon.

'Come,' Iryn Jagga said. 'Let me introduce you to the company.' Taking Ziftkin lightly by the elbow, he led him forwards, guiding him first to a group of silver-haired, distinguished-looking men, standing together sipping from small golden tumblers.

Ziftkin moved with self-conscious stiffness, one hand gripping the flute, the other trying to keep his wayward dress-cloak in check. No matter that he was set to leave Sofala the instant he could: he was determined not to make a bumbling, farm-lad fool of himself here.

'Gentlemen,' Iryn Jagga said, drawing near, 'let me present to you Ziftkin Salvator, of whom you have all heard so much.'

The men turned and bowed to Ziftkin as one, a graceful bending from the waist, arms across their chests. Not so much as one drop was spilled from the little golden tumblers.

Ziftkin bowed back, keeping the flute and the cloak in check

313

as best he could, and was pleased to find that he was able to pull it off. Iryn Jagga nodded in paternal approval, and Ziftkin felt a ridiculous little surge of pride. If Mechant could only see him now, he could not help thinking.

'First-Speaker Orilion Tarnay,' Iryn Jagga was saying, beginning the introductions. 'High-Captain Itho . . .'

Ziftkin was almost immediately lost in the swirl of it all. Too many names, too many faces, all elegantly alike, all gazes fixed on him. From one group to the next he was led, meeting the men first, then the women, knowing he had no chance of remembering anyone's name aright, knowing that it did not matter.

And then the round of introductions was complete and he found himself standing with a little group of younger men, Iryn Jagga having gone off somewhere else suddenly to attend to something. Ziftkin did not know what to say, and simply stood where he was, trying to look as dignified and self-possessed as he could.

'Drink?' one of the men near him asked.

He nodded.

The man made a complex motion at one of the many dark-robed servants who circulated about; the servant disappeared, then promptly returned with a small silver tray containing little crystal goblets of amber liquid.

Ziftkin took a sip of his when it was handed to him, found it fiery and sweet and delicious. He tipped back his head and drank it all in two gulps, then took a gasping breath, for the stuff burned all the way down to his belly and left him with a pleasant tingle. The cloak had fallen from his shoulder and he shrugged it awkwardly back in place.

The man next to him, who had commanded the drinks, lifted one elegant eyebrow. He had merely sipped delicately at his goblet. 'Another?'

Ziftkin swallowed, nodded. He felt the blood singing in his ears. Another glass appeared in his hand. This one, self-consciously, he sipped from as those around him did – a farm-boy out of his element and feeling it mortally at the moment.

The orchestra had gone silent for a little. Now they began an intricate, slow dance tune, a wash of many notes interwoven

314

with each other in a manner Ziftkin had never heard before; like a fall of water it was, all splash and sparkle, yet carefully controlled for all that.

Suddenly, a woman was standing before him. She was tall, almost Ziftkin's own height, and dressed in a long, body-hugging dress of shimmering scarlet silk, embroidered with gold and black. Her hair was startling white-blonde, done up in an elaborate coiffure, her eyes lined dramatically with dark make-up. She was clearly older than he, but by how much he was hard put to tell.

'Do you dance, in the far-away land from which you come, oh young Salvator?' she asked in a deep, melodic voice.

Ziftkin realized that the company had begun a dance as complex as the music that accompanied it, an interweaving of lines of dancers, male and female alternating, hands held high. 'Nuh . . . no,' he stammered. 'Not like this, at any rate.'

He expected the woman to laugh at him, or sneer. She had such an aristocratic elegance about her – like an older version of the young Lady Evadne. He faced her with instinctive dread.

But she neither laughed nor sneered. She regarded him with interest. 'You are the talk of the city. Did you know that, songster?'

Ziftkin blinked and took a sip of the fiery amber liquor in his goblet. He had had no idea.

'Oh yes,' she said. She gestured to the bone flute. 'May I . . . touch it?'

Ziftkin did not know what to say. He felt his thoughts all run together liquidly. He wanted to keep his instrument away from *anybody's* hands, but to deny her such an innocent request – for what could be the harm in her merely touching it while it was still held firmly in his own hands? – seemed churlish.

'Please, may I?' she asked, looking at the flute. 'Such an indelicate, powerful-looking thing it is. No decoration upon it at all. I imagined it would be more . . .' She lifted her shoulders in an elegant shrug to complete the thought. 'It *does* have a certain rough, simple beauty, though.' She smiled at him: 'I would be so . . . *thrilled* to feel it.'

She put a hand upon his arm and gazed at him with imploring eyes, 'Please may I?'

How could he say no? He nodded.

She let him go and reached to the flute, running her fingers along its smooth, simple bone length in a slow and somehow intimate caress. 'It's so big and hard,' she breathed softly, smiling at him. 'And *warm* . . .' Her eyes twinkled and, for a moment, he was uncertain if she were mocking him or not.

But the moment was gone, for Iryn Jagga came marching up, a trail of the usual armed guards tagging along behind. 'Leave the boy be, Talla,' he said to the woman.

Talla blushed slightly and hung her head. 'Yes, great Jagga. But he is a . . . beautiful boy.'

Iryn Jagga frowned at her, then smiled suddenly. 'Get you gone,' he commanded. 'We have more pressing things to do than play your woman's games this evening.'

Talla curtseyed quickly and turned away into the crowd. Ziftkin caught one last glimpse of her face, turned towards him, smiling, and then she was gone.

'Come,' Iryn Jagga said to him. 'Follow me.' Before Ziftkin could say anything by way of reply, Iryn Jagga had removed the little crystal goblet of fiery liquor from his hand and taken him by the arm. Around the dancers Iryn Jagga guided him, and thence towards an open doorway at the room's far end.

Ziftkin followed none too steadily, stumbling when the cloak caught between his legs. He felt a fiery stab of irritation. He was grown entirely fed up with Iryn Jagga grabbing him abruptly like this and yanking him off without explanations. 'Where are we going?' he demanded.

'You'll see.'

Ziftkin tried to pull back. 'I want to know where we are going!' he said, too loudly, his blood still singing with the liquor he had drunk.

A little open space had formed about them in the crowded room. People were staring.

'There is something you need to see, boy. Now come *on*!'

'But can't it wait?' Ziftkin complained. 'You're always dragging me off to—'

316

'Enough!' Iryn Jagga said. 'You will follow me. Now. No more talk. What I have to show you will explain all. Now come!'

Ziftkin swallowed, nodded. Iryn Jagga's face had gone hard. Resisting him would only create trouble.

Through a side doorway they went. Beyond lay an outdoor patio. Large potted shrubs stood here and there, with benches about them. The night air was fresh and chill, and filled with the delicate, astringent aroma of the shrubs. Ziftkin took a breath and shivered, feeling his head clear.

'Come,' Iryn Jagga urged, pulling him past the shrubs towards the patio's far edge. A train of armed guards formed up about them, emerging silently from amongst the potted shrubbery. An open staircase lay ahead. Iryn Jagga led the way groundwards.

The stairway laced down the outside of the building. Following Iryn Jagga, Ziftkin could make out a lantern-lit courtyard below, enclosed by a thick wall, beyond which lay the Sofala streets. The night's dark on the other side of the wall was lit only erratically. Ziftkin peered down at the night-maze of the streets and shuddered.

After the immaculate opulence indoors, what lay beyond the wall below seemed startlingly grim and blighted: tumble-down buildings, littered streets, dirty-smoking torchlight. In the near distance he could see a small square, lit uncertainly by the smoking torches. Ragged folk milled about in it, some staring upwards at him and the party he was with, exposed as they were descending the building's stairway. The faces of the folk below seemed white and stark as bone in the uncertain light, and their eyes shone blankly in the torchlight like the eyes of wild creatures.

Ziftkin looked away from them with a little shiver.

Down the stairs he and the rest continued, their feet slapping softly on the step's wooden risers. Soon they were low enough so that the wall cut off further view of what lay beyond.

And then they were in the courtyard. Lanterns hung in brackets from the wall before a thick-planked door. Three pairs of armed guards stood before this door, grim-faced, bared swords in hand.

Ziftkin felt a quick stab of cold unease go through his guts, seeing the naked iron.

'This way,' Iryn Jagga said, and pushed forwards, opening the door. Ziftkin hesitated for an instant, then followed.

Inside, there was a smallish room, candle-lit. For a long few moments, Ziftkin could not make any sense of what confronted him. The air was thick with an odour he could not place. There were people about, but there was something utterly *wrong* with them . . .

And then he recognized what it was he faced: death. The room was thick with the stink of it.

'Look!' Iryn Jagga ordered. '*Look!*'

Ziftkin stared.

There were five of them, three women and two men. One of the women was white-haired, old. The other two were – had been – young. Both men were of middle years. The white-haired woman's belly had been ripped open. Her guts hung out in a knot of muddy, bloody pink coils.

Ziftkin tried to look away.

Iryn Jagga took him by the shoulders. 'Look!' he ordered.

So held as he was, Ziftkin had little choice. The throat of one man had been torn out. The whole of his front was sticky-dark with his own blood. His eyes were blind-staring, his mouth wide open as if in a scream. The other man had great gouges ripped from him, as if some demented creature had been at him with a razor-edged, forked hoe. Both the younger women had been so mauled that they were a mass of wet red flesh, torn, blood-stained clothing, and shreds of pale skin. One woman's head lolled loosely on a broken neck – like some pitiful rag-doll's.

Ziftkin felt he was going to be sick. He turned away, swallowed, trying to keep the bile from rising in his throat. 'Why . . . why have you brought me here?' he demanded weakly.

'To see what manner of foul things *they* are capable of,' Iryn Jagga replied. He stood, hands on hips, seemingly unaffected by the bloody ruin that lay before him. '*Look!*'

'I *have* looked!' Ziftkin snapped. 'Why are you doing this to me?'

'To make you understand, boy. *They* did this.'

'*They?*' Ziftkin repeated, uncertain.

Iryn Jagga nodded impatiently. '*They* indeed. Creatures of the Dark. Abominations!'

'Do you mean the . . . the *humanimals*?' Ziftkin said.

'Yes! Those foul creatures you feel so much sympathy for.' Ziftkin blinked.

'You wear your heart on your sleeve, boy. How you feel is plain for anybody to see. I warned you these creatures had a certain dark seductiveness to them. You were taken in, weren't you?'

Ziftkin did not know what to say.

Iryn Jagga motioned to the poor dead that lay in the room. '*Now* do you believe me when I tell you such creatures are dangerous? *Now* do you believe me when I say that such creatures are not worthy of your sympathy?'

Iryn Jagga shook his head and sighed. 'They were simple farmer folk, these poor victims, a family party, travelling in all innocence to Sofala to trade their farm produce, when they were viciously and needlessly attacked by a marauding band of *them*.'

Ziftkin stared, shaken to his bones. 'All were . . . killed like this? Wantonly?'

'One member of the party escaped. How, we are not sure.' Iryn Jagga beckoned Ziftkin out of the room. Across the courtyard they went and through a little door on the far side. Inside, somebody was weeping.

Along a short hallway they went and thence into a little room containing a single bed in which a small boy huddled. His torso and both his arms were wrapped in thick, blood-stained bandages. His face was white and stricken, and he rocked back and forth, weeping breathlessly. A woman sat next to him, stroking him, trying to calm his crying, but to no avail. His eyes stared white and blank and terrified.

'This is the lone survivor,' Iryn Jagga said. 'See what beasts it is we must face, that they would do this to a child . . . a defenceless *child*!'

Ziftkin felt his guts twist. The poor little lad . . .

'These violent creatures must be stopped, songster,' Iryn Jagga said. 'Do you see? Do you *see*?'

Ziftkin shuddered. Could the dog-creature he had faced be capable of such an act of bloody, mindless ferocity as this?

'They are part human, true,' Iryn Jagga was saying. 'But only part. You and I, we are entirely, fully human. But the main part of *them* is beast. And so tormented are they by their unnatural state, that the bloody beast in them drives them to violent madness. It is only a matter of time before this happens to them. And so now you see, first hand, the terrible danger they represent, and why it is so vital that they be destroyed. Such an abomination spreads destruction and ruin into the world, polluting it.'

Ziftkin felt sick and stricken. He had felt so . . . so *close* to the suffering dog-creature. He had thought he had understood it. But now . . .

'It is their twisted, unnatural nature,' Iryn Jagga said. 'They are neither one thing nor the other. And the terrible tension of it tears them apart. They are made things, and cannot help being what they are. But what they are is an abomination!'

Made creatures. Terrible internal tension. Neither one thing nor another . . . Ziftkin shuddered. He had felt that tension, sympathized with it.

The hurt lad in the bed was still weeping, unchecked, gasping for breath and rocking back and forth mindlessly. What had the poor little soul witnessed? It did not bear thinking on.

'*This* is what we fight, songster,' Iryn Jagga said. 'The creatures that attacked this poor child and his family must be destroyed. As long as they live, none are truly safe. It is the great error of my forefathers, that they came into the world. It is the great responsibility of me and mine to put that error right.'

Iryn Jagga had come close to Ziftkin. Now he put a hand out, his maimed one. 'And *she*, this Elinor Whiteblade, uses such creatures, sets them on, loosing them against innocent folk. She, too, must be stopped. She and all the foul breed that follow her. *This* is what you must help me do, songster. *This* is what must be done so that the world can be cleansed and the greatness that once was return again.'

320

Ziftkin found it suddenly hard to draw breath. He felt as if the very ground had been yanked out from under him. How could he have been so utterly wrong in his understanding of things?

'It is not your fault,' Iryn Jagga said.

Ziftkin started, for Iryn Jagga's remark seemed in direct answer to his own thoughts.

'You could not have known what manner of creature they are,' Iryn Jagga continued, 'without witnessing something like this. Others, too, have been taken in by them, by their seeming . . . vulnerability. But they are an *abomination*, boy. Make no doubt of that. Save whatever sympathy you may have for worthier objects. And help me and mine now to rid the world of such foul, violent, *twisted* creatures. It's what is best for them, in the end, to loose them from their unnatural life and put them out of their misery. And it is absolutely necessary for the protection of others.'

Ziftkin glanced at the still-weeping boy on the bed. The image of the pitiful, murdered men and women he had seen in the other room was burnt painfully into his mind.

He remembered a day, years ago now, when Massy, one of the Seshevrell farm dogs, had come staggering into the main yard, mad-eyed, frothing at the mouth.

'It's the Rage,' his uncle Harst had said, and before young Ziftkin could properly gather his wits, Harst had killed poor Massy with a pitchfork.

Ziftkin shuddered, remembering. He had wept and railed for days, for Massy had been his special favourite of all the dogs. But even in the worst of his grief, he had known in his heart that Harst had acted rightly. 'Best to put the beast out of his misery,' Harst had said. 'And we've got to protect the stock.'

Ziftkin still mourned poor Massy, whenever he thought of him. Never again, after that, had he ever been really close with any of the farm dogs. Ziftkin sighed. He wished the world were not such a blunt, cruel place.

'Songster?' Iryn Jagga said. 'Are you with me, songster? I *need* you in this.'

Ziftkin shivered.

'Songster?'

321

'Aye,' Ziftkin said softly. 'I'm with you. What I can do to help, I will.'

Iryn Jagga smiled. He put a hand – the maimed one – upon Ziftkin's shoulder in a fatherly gesture. 'I knew I could count on you. You have too good a heart to turn your back on those that need you.'

'But what . . .' Ziftkin held up his flute. 'What is it you expect me to be able to do with *this* against such vicious creatures? I do not . . .' He let out a long, shuddering breath, remembering the Shadowland dark. 'I do not think I could play death upon them, even given . . . even with what I have witnessed here this night. I am not . . . able for it.'

Iryn Jagga nodded. 'Perhaps not. But there is something you *can* do.'

'And that is?'

'Come with me, and I will explain.' Iryn Jagga turned and strode out, motioning for Ziftkin to accompany him.

Casting one last glance back at the weeping boy, Ziftkin followed after.

XXVI

Scrunch the bear sat at the edge of the human folk and looked on, along with a double handful of other humanimals – though not Rigga and her youngsters.

Virtually the whole of the human population of the Settlement was gathered here, women, men, children. Scrunch was not good with numbers, but he reckoned there must be something like seven or eight dozens of people, perhaps more, all clustered together in one large group, chattering and milling about.

On a makeshift platform fashioned of squat, upright logs and hand-hewn planks, three men sat upon stools. Scrunch recognized only one of them: big-bellied Maxil, whom Rigga had nipped the day Scrunch had led her and her youngsters into the Settlement. The man's hand was wrapped with a large white bandage.

'This meeting of the Settlement Committee will now come to order!' one of the three up on the platform called out. He was an older man with a pouchy, pale face, grey chin whiskers, and no head-hair except for a straggly grey fringe about his ears. 'To order!' he repeated. In his hand he held a short staff, with which he thumped the plank platform, *krack, krack, krack!*

The general murmur and bustle subsided.

'This Committee meeting is now officially in session!' the grey-whiskered man called out. 'We are met here in accordance with established precedent in order to arrive at a decision that affects the whole of the Settlement. Let this hearing commence!'

'Hearing?' a voice called out. 'Established precedent? What are you talking about?'

Scrunch saw that it was Getta, bow in hand. She stood in a

323

little group which included grey-bearded Collart, bald Passaly, young Smitt with his thick black beard and sharp eyes, several others – all of them part of the original group that had formed about Elinor in the dark days when the struggle against the Ancient Brotherhood had begun.

Scrunch found it difficult to follow the complicated ins-and-outs of human relationships, but he could see that Collart and Getta and their companions stood slightly separated from most of the human folk here, at the fringe of the gathering, nearest the humanimals. The three men up on the platform, and those clustered close to it, were all of that portion of the human folk who had taken little part in the fighting which Elinor had been at the head of, and that had had the least contact with the humanimals since the departure from the Valley last year.

For the first time, Scrunch saw clearly that the human side of the Settlement was not a single entity. It came as a bit of a shock to him that he had been quite blind to this before, for it now seemed suddenly so obvious. There were three separate groups: Getta and Collart and their companions; the men on the platform and those near them; and those in between the two groups.

One of the men on the platform had risen. He was tall and thin and clean-shaven, with a long face, a beaky nose and small, bright eyes. 'You,' he said to Getta, 'are interrupting an official enquiry.'

Getta bristled. 'Official *enquiry*? We're supposed to be met here to give welcome to Rigga and her youngsters.'

'And where *is* this Rigga, then?' big-bellied Maxil demanded from his place on the platform.

Getta looked about. 'You've most like scared her away with all this stupid ruckus you've organized.'

'And that,' interjected the third member of the Committee, the older, grey-whiskered man, 'is one of the questions we wish to have answered.'

Getta looked at him, frowning in puzzlement.

'Why,' the grey-whiskered man went on, 'would this Rigga appear so suddenly and mysteriously as she did, and then simply disappear, eh? Have you asked yourself *that*, woman? What were her *real* motives in coming here?'

Getta blinked, opened her mouth to respond, but was given no time to say anything.

'You are far too trusting, the most of you,' the tall, clean-shaven man with the beaky nose said. He was still standing, glaring down at Getta from his place on the platform. 'This creature's actions are most suspicious. That is why we have launched this official enquiry.'

'Suspicious?' Grey-bearded Collart had come to stand beside Getta. 'What are you talking about, man? Rigga came here to become a part of our community, bringing her youngsters with her. What's suspicious about *that*?'

'We are gathered here to make an official enquiry,' the grey-whiskered man went on. 'All will be given a chance to have their say. For now . . .' he pointed at Getta with his staff, 'you will kindly go back to your place and wait your turn along with all the rest. We must have order here! Nothing will be accomplished if we act like irresponsible rabble.'

'Shit for brains,' Getta muttered, glaring at him.

'What?' he demanded. 'What did you say, woman?'

Getta merely glared back at him.

'Come on,' Collart said, putting a hand on Getta's arm, 'nothing's to be gained by antagonizing them.' He pulled her back to their little group at the fringe.

'Good!' the grey-whiskered man said. 'And now, if there are no further interruptions . . .' he looked pointedly about, 'perhaps we can begin.' He turned to his tall, beaky-nosed companion, who was still standing, and said, 'Kymsa?'

The beaky-nosed man nodded and returned to his stool. He coughed softly behind his hand and straightened his sleeves. 'We are met here this day . . .' he began.

'Get *on* with it, Kymsa!' a voice called out from the crowd. 'We haven't got all day.'

Soft laughter greeted this remark.

Kymsa frowned. 'This is an *official* enquiry,' he said. 'And, as such, *not* something to be rushed.' He glared at the gathering with offended dignity, straightened his sleeves once again, and went on. 'We are gathered here this day to conduct an official enquiry into whether or not the Committee – as the properly sanctioned voice of our community – will officially welcome the humanimal Rigga and her offspring into our Settlement.'

'They've already *been* welcomed,' Getta returned.

'But not officially by the Committee.'

'So welcome them, then,' black-bearded Smitt called out from his place alongside Getta and Collart.

'It's not so easy as all that,' the grey-whiskered man replied. 'There is serious question as to this Rigga's motives in coming here.'

'Motives such as what?' bald Passaly demanded. He stood at Collart's right hand and had, so far, been quiet. Now he stabbed a finger at the grey-whiskered man on the platform and frowned. 'Just what are you suggesting, Acker? What manner of reasons do you think she had for coming to us?'

'We don't know,' beaky-nosed Kymsa said. 'That is *exactly* why we have convened this Committee meeting.'

'So how do you intend to find out what her motives might be, then?' somebody called out.

The speaker was a tall, thin man with a long hank of sandy hair and gaunt, stubbly cheeks. Scrunch recognized him as one of those who had first greeted Rigga and her youngster on the day of their arrival into the Settlement.

'This Rigga's not here,' the man was saying, 'so just how do you expect to find out why she wanted to come here?'

'The fact that she is not here doesn't speak in her favour,' somebody else put in. It was the man named Olundar, Scrunch saw, little Anstil's father, standing close to the Committee's platform.

'You were there when she and her youngsters first arrived,' the sandy-haired man said to Olundar. 'You saw her. As I did. There was nothing . . . suspicious about her behaviour.'

'Then why has nobody seen her since?' Olundar demanded.

'Because people like *you* threatened her!' Getta spoke up.

'I did not threaten her!' Olundar responded. 'It was *she* who did the threatening. She *bit* poor Maxil here.'

'For no good reason!' Maxil put in from his place upon the raised platform. 'She bit me in a completely unprovoked attack. She's *dangerous*, that one!'

The human crowd was beginning to argue amongst itself now, and grey-whiskered Acker resorted to his staff again: *krack, krack!* 'Order!' he called. '*Order!*'

'Why not let Scrunch here speak for her?' Collart suggested

once folk were sufficiently quiet. 'After all, Scrunch was the one who first found her and brought her in to us. If anyone can explain to us what she wanted in coming here, it ought to be him, surely.'

'Let Scrunch the bear speak,' several voices piped up.

The three men on the platform looked at each other. Grey-whiskered Acker held up his hand. 'We will conduct this enquiry in an orderly manner. All will have a turn to speak.'

There were some murmurings of discontent from the gathered crowd.

'An *orderly* manner,' Acker repeated. He looked over at beaky-nosed Kymsa, who coughed into his hand.

'The humanimal, Rigga, appeared in our midst with no warning, and disappeared equally as quickly,' Kymsa said. 'The question is: why? In order to arrive at an answer, we will proceed by interviewing those who interacted with her.'

Grey-whiskered Acker nodded: 'Call the first witness.'

Kymsa turned to Maxil. 'Maxil, once of Tarnoth Farm, did you interact with the humanimal in question?'

Big-bellied Maxil nodded. 'I did.'

'And what was the nature of that interaction?'

'She bit me on the hand.'

'Did you provoke her in any way?'

Maxil shook his head. 'I reached out my hand in a gesture of good will. She bit me for no good reason. Out of pure spite, perhaps. Or perhaps she is, by nature, violent and unpredictable.'

'That's stupid!' a man called out. 'I was there. I saw—'

'Quiet!' Acker shouted. He thumped his staff, glaring at the man who had spoken up, at that portion of the crowd that had begun to mutter and shift about restlessly. 'You threaten the stability of our community with your antics. This is an orderly enquiry conducted by a properly ordained Committee. If we cannot do this without falling into chaos and pointless argument, then we are a sorry excuse for a community indeed! What has happened to all our great hopes of prospering here, then? Are we to end up a mere shouting rabble?'

The crowd shuffled and murmured and gradually went silent.

327

Acker nodded. 'Good. Now . . . Is there anybody here,' he said formally, 'who can corroborate Maxil's testimony?'

Olundar raised his hand. 'I can.'

'This is a *farce*!' Getta shouted.

Acker glared at her. Some of the human folk muttered disparagingly at her interruption. One man hissed something Scrunch could not catch but which made Getta whirl angrily and start forward.

Collart pulled her back, and she retreated, fuming and red-faced.

On the platform, grey-whiskered Acker turned to Olundar. 'You say you can confirm Maxil's testimony?'

Olundar nodded. 'Yes, sir. I saw the humanimal, Rigga, bite Maxil on the hand. It was an unprovoked attack.'

There was a murmuring from the crowd. Acker raised his staff. 'Order!'

Acker said to Olundar: 'Why, in your opinion, would this Rigga commit such a violent act?'

'I believe they are naturally violent, her sort,' Olundar replied. 'One of the puppies went to bite me as I was trying to rescue my little daughter – I was afraid they would do some damage to her, they were so rough, the way they trod all over her and pushed her about so – and Rigga attempted to attack me. In my opinion, they are violent and dangerous animals.'

Again, the crowd erupted into discordant mutterings.

Acker thumped his staff for order.

'Let Scrunch the bear speak!' somebody called out over the confusion.

'Yes!' others agreed. 'Scrunch hasn't had his chance to say anything yet.'

'Let Scrunch speak for this Rigga.'

'Let Scrunch have his say!'

The members of the Committee looked at each other. Acker shrugged. 'Let Scrunch the bear speak, then,' he said after a moment. He looked over at Scrunch once the crowd had settled. 'Where has this Rigga come from, then? What were her motives in coming here?'

'Why did she attack people?' Maxil added. 'And where has she disappeared to?'

All eyes turned on Scrunch.

Uncertainly, Scrunch looked about him. There were too many different questions . . . Which should he answer first? What ought he to say? He was too unbalanced by this sudden shift which had brought him into the centre of things.

Rigga had felt her *need*, had wandered far to find a sire for her children. But the humanimal *need* was not something one talked of with human folk.

She had come following the rumour of Elinor and her white blade, hoping to find a home for her children, a community where humanimal and human folk could live harmoniously together. And she had bit Maxil because, as an anxious mother, she had deemed his actions threatening.

Easily enough put to himself. But how to put anything to this suspicious, squabbling human crowd?

'Well?' Acker was demanding impatiently from the platform. 'This is your chance to have your say, bear. Speak up, then!'

Scrunch took a breath. 'Rigga came here to . . . She was following rumours of Elinor. She had heard . . .'

'Elinor . . .' somebody said. 'Elinor has left us.'

'Abandoned us,' added another.

An uneasy shifting swept the crowd.

'Elinor has *not* abandoned us,' Collart said.

'Says *you*!' somebody returned.

'She will return,' Collart insisted.

'If she does, she'll find things here changed,' Olundar said with some satisfaction. He glared at Getta and Collart and the rest standing near them. 'You and your little clique have been lording it over the rest of us for far too long now. Your precious Elinor has abandoned us, and it's time the rest of us – the *sensible* ones amongst us – took matters into our own hands and . . .'

The crowd erupted once more.

Getta started shouting, but Scrunch saw only a look of dismayed surprise on Collart's face.

'Enough!' Acker cried from the platform. He thumped his staff for order. 'Enough of this!'

When the crowd had settled once more, he motioned towards Scrunch with his staff. 'We must continue in an orderly fashion. The bear will have his proper chance to speak.'

Scrunch blinked. He was having trouble keeping up with the swiftness of things. Something was happening here – had already happened. Some cleavage between people. He felt like he was in the midst of a hive of grabbing bees, set against each other in ways he could not quite grasp clearly. There was such complex animosity in the air that it was like a dark fog.

'Well, bear?' Acker said from the platform. 'Why did this Rigga come here?'

'She came . . .' Scrunch paused, took a breath. 'She came in hopes of finding a . . . a home.'

'Then why did she *attack* me?' Maxil demanded from the stage.

'She did not . . . attack you, Man,' Scrunch replied. 'She was . . .' He stopped. How could he explain? Human folk had no clear notion of the world humanimals lived in, of the dire, hard threats that lurked everywhere, of the anxieties of humanimal motherhood.

'She was *what*?' Acker demanded.

Scrunch swallowed, licked his lips uneasily. 'She was . . . anxious for her children.'

'I see,' Acker responded. 'A man reaches out to her in a gesture of goodwill . . .' He looked across to Maxil. 'Wasn't that how you put it?'

Maxil nodded.

'A man reaches out to her in *goodwill*,' Acker went on, 'and this Rigga bites him viciously because she is . . . *anxious* for her children. Such . . . *anxiety* seems dangerous to those around her – whether they are good-willed or not.'

'No,' Scrunch said. 'You don't understand.'

'I understand one thing only too well,' Maxil interrupted. 'I reached out to her in all innocence, and she *attacked* me!' He held up his bandaged hand. 'I went to her in peace, and she bit me cruelly!'

'Maybe that'll teach you to stop putting your hand where it's not wanted,' a young woman called out.

The crowd murmured. One or two people laughed.

'Enough of that!' Acker admonished, thumping his staff. He motioned the other two members of the Committee in closer.

Heads together, the three men whispered amongst themselves, while the crowd waited restively.

Scrunch felt all twisted up inside. There was more he wished to say. They had it all wrong, these men. He cleared his throat, tried to say something. But it was too late. His chance had come and gone.

Acker stood up and thumped his staff officiously upon the wooden planks of the platform: *krack, krack!* 'Upon the due presentation of proper evidence,' he announced, 'this Committee finds the humanimal Rigga and her pups to be of too violent and unpredictable a nature to be welcome here amongst us. She and her sort represent a danger to us, to our children, to our way of life. It is our official decree that she be repulsed if she ever tries to return again within our borders.'

There was an unquiet murmur from the human crowd, and a few voices raised in complaint, but most seemed to be nodding their heads in satisfaction.

Scrunch felt the humanimals near him quiver with the shock of such a judgement. They stared at the human folk, wide-eyed and uncertain.

Acker was still standing. 'As there is no further business, I now call this meeting to a—'

But before he could finish his announcement, a small body came barging through the crowd and burst out into the cleared space before the platform.

Little Anstil.

She stood, hands on her hips, white-faced and shaking. 'You can't make Rigga and Grub and them all stay away! You *can't*!'

Acker and the other members of the Committee glared down at Anstil.

'Quiet, girl!' beaky-nosed Kymsa ordered.

'Anstil!' Olundar shouted.

'Is this girl yours?' Acker demanded.

Olundar nodded.

'Then get her away from here, at once!'

'Yes, sir,' Olundar replied. He turned to his daughter. 'You heard the man, Anstil. Go back to your mother.'

But Anstil stood where she was, defying him. 'I won't let you send Grub away. I *won't*!'

'You'll do as you're told!' Olundar responded.

'I want Grub. I want to be with Grub!'

'I forbid you,' Olundar said, 'to ever see that animal again!'

Anstil glared up at him. 'You're so . . . so *mean*!'

'Me?' her father said, outraged. 'Me *mean*?' He leant down, took Anstil by the shoulders, and shook her. 'Now you listen to me, my girl. If you want an ordinary, normal dog, I'll get you one. You hear? Old Magan just had pups. She's a fine, *normal* dog. Have one of her pups. I'll arrange to get you one.'

'I want Grub,' Anstil said stubbornly, yanking away from her father's hard grip. 'Not some stupid *dog*.'

'Well you can't have Grub. I forbid it! I won't have any daughter of mine seen traipsing about with one of *them* as a pet. What will folk think?'

'Grub's not a . . . a pet!' Anstil replied, outraged. 'He's my *friend*.'

Olundar shook his head. 'Friend? How can you be friends with one of *them*? Besides, what kind of a name is "Grub" anyway? They're all *strange*, I tell you. No knowing what one of them might be capable of doing.'

Olundar looked around him. He ran a hand through his hair self-consciously, the centre of everybody's attention. 'I will *not* discuss this with you here, girl. Do you hear?'

'What's the harm in her being friends with one of Rigga's youngsters?' Getta called out suddenly. 'The humanimals have never hurt any of us.'

'What's the *harm*?' Olundar threw his arms up. 'Have you and those like you gone completely *mad*, then? Humanimals are unstable. Everyone knows that. They flit in and out of our lands here like so many feckless birds, eating what they can – without working for it, I might add – and then flitting off again. The Powers alone know what strange places they visit or what queer acts they get up to. Or *can* get up to.'

'You know nothing about them!' Getta cried.

Olundar glared at her. 'Humanimals are dangerous, I tell you, and I will not have any daughter of mine exposed to such danger! Are you trying to tell me I don't have a right to my own judgement? I have a family to look out for, and I will do what I think is needful for their safety. Would you come between me and my own family?'

None said a word.

'Good!' Olundar nodded. 'So you're not that far gone past common sense at any rate.' He softened a little. 'I have nothing against the humanimal folk. Everybody here knows that. It's just . . . just that human folk and humanimals are different is all. You wouldn't expect a . . . a dog and a cat to go about keeping company together, would you? Well, it's the same here. It just isn't *natural*, I tell you.'

Getta shook her head. 'There's more at stake here than just you and your precious family, Olundar.'

'Oh, aye?' Olundar returned.

'Aye.' Getta gestured past the Settlement clearing towards the enclosing forest, the chains of mountains beyond. 'There's a whole big world out there, Olundar. And we have to find a place in it.'

'We *have* a place,' Acker said from the platform. He pointed to the greening fields. 'We can make this place nearly as good as the Valley was, one day. If we work hard and look out for ourselves carefully, and—'

'You miss the point entirely,' Collart said.

Acker glared at him.

'A place in the world,' Getta said.

'Our fields *are* in the world,' Olundar replied.

Getta sighed. 'The wider world that includes us human folk and the humanimals and all else, too.'

Acker shook his head. 'What are you talking about?'

'There are those of us,' Collart said, 'who are beginning to feel that friendship between our children and Rigga's bodes well for the future.'

Olundar shook his head, scowling.

'We need each other,' Collart said. 'Human folk and humanimals both. Together we can do things which, alone, would be impossible. What better way to cement the bond between us than to encourage it at an early age?'

'Ignorance is the greatest threat,' Getta added.

Olundar frowned. 'Are you calling me *ignorant*?'

'No, of course she isn't,' Collart said quickly. 'It's just that—'

'Enough!' Olundar cried. 'Calling me names and trying to tell me what I ought to do for my daughter . . . my own flesh and blood, as if *you* know better. Enough, I say!' He glared at them. 'My daughter will have nothing to do with the humanimal kind.'

Anstil let out a little wail of angry despair.

'Be quiet!' Olundar snapped at her.

'Olundar,' a female voice said, and Olundar's wife came out of the crowd and gathered Anstil up in her arms. 'Do you have to be so—'

Olundar bristled. 'I'm the head of this household, woman! I'm Anstil's father. I know what's best for—'

'You're mean, mean, *mean*!' Anstil wailed. Wrenching herself from her mother's grip, she fled away through the crowd.

'Anstil!' Olundar yelled. 'You come back here! At once, do you hear me? Come *back* here!'

The human crowd was in an uproar by now, with folk shouting and arguing amongst themselves.

'Silence!' Acker shouted from his place upon the platform. He thumped his staff. 'Order!'

Scrunch had had enough. His head was reeling and he felt sick in the pit of his belly. Turning, he began walking away. The other humanimals, he saw, were spilling away too. Behind him, the human crowd was still boiling, like a nest of agitated insects.

'Scrunch!' somebody called.

He continued on, ignoring the voice. He had had more than enough to do with human folk for the moment. He wanted well away from them and into the deep green silence of the wild.

But the voice persisted, 'Scrunch! *Scrunch!*'

He slowed, and, turning, saw it was Getta calling after him, with Collart and the rest of that group along with her. They, too, had abandoned the meeting, it seemed. Scrunch sat down to wait till they caught up with him.

'They're leaving?' Collart said worriedly as they drew up. He gestured to the last of the other humanimals who were drifting away by now into the sheltering trees. Scrunch glanced after them enviously.

'They *will* come back, won't they?' Collart said.

Scrunch lifted his broad shoulders in a bear's shrug, looked away. 'They will do what they will do, Man.'

Collart stiffened. 'Scrunch . . . Scrunch! It's me, Collart. We've shared too much to let something like this come between us. Surely, Scrunch . . .'

Scrunch sighed. His insides felt pinched and swollen. His mind ached. 'You are right,' he said slowly.

Human folk were so exhausting, so utterly overwhelming. He felt bruised and aching, as if he had just been beaten, and sickly replete with painful human complexity. But he could not help but feel a warmth towards this group before him. Collart was right. They had shared too much together, from the beginning alongside Elinor and her shining blade, through the winter past.

Elinor. Where was she now that they needed her so? If she had been here, none of this would have come to pass, he felt sure.

Scrunch felt the world's tightness still in his belly and bones. Immersed in the complex swirl of human affairs, he all too easily lost his sense of the larger world. Now it was seeping back. He shivered. Was it the tightness that presaged things coming apart? Like the tightness in the air before a great storm?

'Word will spread quickly about what has taken place here,' he said to the human group before him.

'And?' Collart said worriedly. 'How will your folk react?'

Scrunch shrugged tiredly. He yearned to be away from here and deep into the soothing quiet of the wild. 'It is hard to say.'

'Olundar's an arsehole!' Getta snapped disgustedly. 'Him and all the rest like him.'

'He's a man trying to do what he thinks best for the security of his family,' Collart said.

'Are you on *his* side, then?' Black-bearded Smitt spoke up.

Collart shook his head. 'No. Of course not! But I . . . I understand his feelings.'

Getta opened her mouth, closed it again, made an angry sound in her throat. She looked back at the crowd, which was still busily engaged with itself. 'They've ruined *everything* we've tried to build here. Somebody ought to shoot that Committee!'

They all stared back.

'What do we do now, then?' bald Passaly said softly.

None of them, it seemed, had any answer to that.

XXVII

Elinor stood atop a small promontory. Like a ship's prow it was, a wedge of grassy-stony land hove up over the rest. She looked westwards, high enough here to see across the tops of the trees undulating away in a great, grey-green tapestry into the distance of the morning. Somewhere out in that direction, amongst the trees, beyond them, lay the Settlement. Many a long day's walk away, it was. Hidden and distant.

It hardly seemed real to her. The faces, the fields, the houses . . .

Elinor sighed. Her finger throbbed, a flaring of pain with each pulse of blood. She looked at her maimed hand. Old Cloud-Dreaming's healing ministrations had made it heal with astonishing quickness. But the scar on the nub of the missing finger was stiff and tender, with raw edges still, and it hurt to flex the hand.

A part of her was gone forever.

So much of her seemed gone, now.

For long days she had lain in convalescence, filled with pain and dreams and flitting, confused memories . . . The Settlement seemed to be part of another world, and when she had tried to remember her former life back in Long Harbour, to recreate the sound and the smell of the streets she had once known so well, she could not. She tried to see her mother's face, but could not. All she could bring to mind with any clarity was the memory of her mother's sharp, complaining voice – and her step-father's shouting.

Elinor shivered. The Long Harbour life she had once led seemed so utterly *distant* now.

It frightened her, a little, that she was so changed, that the things that had once meant so much to her now hardly touched her at all. She felt like a plant with no roots. She imagined a butterfly must feel much the same, looking back upon its former caterpillar-self. Save that she was no butterfly . . .

What she might be, though, she did not know.

Gently, she massaged the throbbing stump of her finger. The invaders of this forest land might be defeated, but neither the greater world nor her belly were surely settled yet. There was still some obscure thing aborning, and the world felt poised. Here, alone in the great silence of the wild, she could almost hear it throb, a deep pulse at one with her own heartbeat.

She was weary of the feeling.

Westwards, the sky was pale blue, striped with low clouds. How were they faring in the Settlement without her? she wondered. Grey-bearded Collart and sharp-tongued Getta with her bow. Bald Passaly and dark-eyed, dark-bearded young Smitt. And little Spandel and sharp-beaked Otys, the crow, and Scrunch and the rest.

She had a sudden image of herself connected by only the slimmest of threads to the Settlement and all it held. A little more distance, a mere turning of her back, and that slim thread would snap, leaving her . . . where?

Elinor sighed. She had found a home with the Settlement folk, humanimal and human alike. Perhaps it had been a fatal mistake to leave them behind and come on this journey with Gyver.

For no doubt they were getting along just fine back there in her absence. More than a few had been glad to see the back of her, she was sure. She had long been aware of the dark glances some of the human folk gave her when they thought she was not looking. What use was she to them, anyway? She and her shining blade – which made ordinary folk uneasy and skitterish. She felt the thought like a little fish, gnawing at her guts. They were farmers. They did not need her and her blade to till fields or harvest or to thresh grain. And Iryn Jagga and his dark Brotherhood would never find them now. The Settlement was too well hid, too far into the wild. She was useless to them, now.

Staring off at the far-away, westwards clouds, Elinor let out a long, sighing, weary breath. All that was as it might be. But whether the Settlement needed her or not, there was this . . . something that would not let her go. She could feel it like an invisible web upon her, pulling, pulling. But the direction was not clear. Westwards? She could not tell. Stay here? Leave? She did not know. There was just the unease in her belly that would not let her ever rest completely, that had driven her to come up here, alone, far off from camp, hurt finger throbbing, torn every which way by confusion.

It was not fair. She had played her part in events, done all that was required and more. She and Gyver and his folk had *won*. There ought to be peace for her, now. But there was none. 'Let me *alone*!' she hissed, at the sky, the earth, the air itself. 'Just let me alone, can't you?'

Elinor shivered tiredly. Her hand hurt. She had been on her feet too long. Cloud-Dreaming had warned her: 'You musst resst sstill, you. Do not walk too far too ssoon . . .' Elinor smiled a little, thinking on the old fur-woman – who possessed healing hands and a soul deep as an old well.

An altogether remarkable people, Gyver's fur-folk. And Gyver himself not least of all . . .

A sudden, unexpected sound in the woods at her back made Elinor whirl, heart jumping. Her right hand went to where the sword ought to hang at her belt – but it was not there. Life here in the quiet woods amongst Gyver's folk these past days, now that the violent invaders of their land were gone, felt so utterly without threat, and the sword felt so completely foreign to everything here, that she had taken to leaving it in its scabbard leaned against a tree back at camp.

Peering uncertainly into the shadowy thickness of the trees, she cursed herself under her breath for a brainless fool. The world was a dangerous place. She had learned that to her cost. Coming out here as she was, alone, still far from her full strength, away from camp and without weapon of any sort . . . What had she been thinking?

The noise came again, a soft *kruppling*. Something moving with care through the trees . . .

Elinor glanced hastily about, gauging her chances. She might flee across the rocky promontory upon which she stood, for there was a long, bare slope on the further side, and, beyond that, more trees, where she might find shelter. But the slope was humpy, treacherous ground, and anybody standing where she was now would have clear sight of her and an open shot, if they were armed.

She caught a glimpse of movement now, and froze. Shadows flickered as some large body padded behind a screen of branches. A very large body . . .

One of the Phanta, Elinor suddenly realized.

The creature eased its way out of the trees. Elinor stared, her heart thumping. They were so huge, these creatures. One forgot.

It came towards her, moving with a loose-kneed, silent gait. Incredible that such a great beast could move so softly. It held its strange, flexible snout up, snuffling softly.

Elinor stayed exactly as she was. She had no idea what this great being might want. It came closer towards her, closer still and stopped so near that the snout brushed her belly.

Elinor felt her heart hammering – each beat echoing as a stab of pain in her truncated finger. She felt like a rabbit faced with some huge and dangerous beast, and wanted, like the rabbit, to turn and flee madly away, zigging and zagging, to safety.

But there was no such way out left to her here. Any way she might turn to run, the creature before her could head her off. She had seen them run. She stood no chance of fleeing to safety.

The snout was flicking softly over her face now. She tried not to flinch. Her nose was full of the Phanta's scent – a melding of wet black mud and roses. It let out a long, snorting breath. She heard its belly burble, softly.

Still she stood, feeling the fear sweat trickle down her ribs.

The Phanta stepped back from her, one pace, two . . . Then it hunched forwards, bending its front knees so that its great head came down close to her. It regarded her out of one large, dark eye.

The eye was thick-lashed as a cow's, but with none of a cow's bland gentleness. The gaze it directed at her held . . . she was not certain what. It made her shiver. There was a deepness of thought there, but of thoughts never read by a human mind.

340

It lifted its long snout, and gave vent to a series of whistling snorts. Then, gently, it put the fleshy tip of that snout against her face again.

'What do you want of me?' Elinor asked uneasily.

The moist lips of its snout slid across her cheek. She could feel the delicate tickle of its breath. The large eye stared at her, unblinking.

'What do you *want*?'

It lifted its snout from her and snorted. Then, softly, it turned and padded away.

'Wait!' she called after it. 'What do you *want* of me?'

But it was gone.

Had it had been one of the Phanta that had charged down upon the painted men in such wrath? Or a wild one? Had it come to communicate something to her, and then changed its mind? Had it found her somehow . . . lacking?

She did not know. How could she know what manner of sense such a strange and mysterious creature made of the world? There was so much in the world that seemed to have roots going down into depths she could not understand. Elinor sighed and rubbed her hurt hand. She felt bereft, somehow, at the Phanta's departure.

The world was too full of mystery, her life too full of uncertainty. She was weary of it.

She stood where she was for a long while, staring about her, trying to will something to happen, some sign, some event, anything at all that might let her know in which direction her life might be headed. But there was only the high sky and the endless trees softly whispering secrets amongst themselves.

She turned, eventually, and headed back towards camp, to Gyver's warmth. It was all there was left for her to do. In all the uncertainty, she at least had him as the one sure thing. Her rock. Her anchor. She did not know where she would be, now, without him.

XXVIII

Ziftkin stood alone upon the parapet that rimmed one of the squat octagonal towers set into the eastwards flank of the Sofala wall. Though not as high as he had been upon the roof-top with Iryn Jagga, he was still high enough here to have the country spread out all about him like a great brown-green tapestry, a complexity of fields and occasional little houses huddled together in the distance, of dark ribbons of rivers and grey-green clumps of trees. Beyond all of which lay the foothills, rolling upwards in complex waves of forest and rock. And beyond them, the great stone peaks of the eastwards mountains.

Wild land, that. Fey land. His father's land . . .

And the dwelling place, according to Iryn Jagga, of those who must be brought in.

'They have been skulking about in the far-away wild lands to the east for more than a year now,' Iryn Jagga had told him.

Ziftkin and the leader of the Ancient Brotherhood had been standing upon an outdoor balcony in the half-light of dawn, the dirty maze of Sofala's streets below them. Ziftkin felt himself weary and sick, the memory of the humanimal murder victims still too fresh in his mind.

'Over a year ago now, it was,' Iryn Jagga said. 'They broke into the city, killing and destroying. Wantonly, viciously! We had done nothing to them. It was *her* instigation, *her* ambition that drove them.'

Iryn Jagga clenched his fists. 'We beat them back, and they fled away into the wilds, like the cowards they are at heart. We hunted after them, throughout the grasslands first, then up into the wild foothills. But though we heard rumours, we could locate no clear sign of them.'

Iryn Jagga placed his hand upon the balcony's stone balustrade, the amputated nubs of what was left of his fingers showing clearly. 'But they are out there still, this I know. *She* is out there, nursing her hate and her dark designs, planning our destruction. She is *of* the Dark, songster. She and the unholy, mixed rabble that follow her, human and not. Make no mistake about that.'

Iryn Jagga flexed his maimed hand, let out a hissing breath. 'I *owe* her. But we cannot find her. And we are vulnerable here to any surprise attack she might mount. She and the violent folk and vicious creatures that follow her could appear at any moment and descend upon us in a bloody fury.'

Iryn Jagga shook his head, the golden circlet he wore gleaming softly in the dawning light. 'We will never find them by sending out search parties. So far, the only thing of worth such searching has brought in is you.'

Ziftkin blinked. 'Me?'

'What did you imagine I was doing out there in that forsaken landscape when we first met?'

There was silence between them for a few moments, then Iryn Jagga went on. 'So, we cannot find them by searching for them, and we are vulnerable to attack so long as they remain at large. But . . .'

'But?' Ziftkin echoed, when Iryn Jagga went quiet.

'I remember the first time I saw you in the distance, songster. You were surrounded by a mass of fluttering birds you had called up from the wild grass with that instrument of yours. I have been recollecting that day, recently. I see now how you can help us to victory. Great Jara does indeed work in mysterious ways.'

Ziftkin looked at him uneasily: 'I don't see how I can . . .' He held up the flute. 'This instrument is not a weapon. I cannot use it again to bring death upon any creature.'

To Ziftkin's rather surprised relief, Iryn Jagga nodded agreement. 'I accept now the weakness of your instrument. When I first saw what you were able to do to the dog-creature in the cell, I became, shall we say . . . overeager. I should have realized. Such an instrument as you carry is, as you say, no

343

true weapon. I can accept that. But it has *power*, songster. There's no denying it. And I have seen a way to use that power.'

'And that is?'

'You will use your instrument to call them to us. It is that simple! You will bring them here to us in Sofala – human and humanimal alike – and we will deal with them as they so properly deserve, so they will never pose threat to any again. As you called up the birds that day, so will you call up *her* and *her* followers.'

'But . . .' Ziftkin said quickly. 'I don't know any of her human followers, how they look, or . . . or *anything* about them! And as for the humanimals . . .'

'You have met one such creature already, and dealt with it. You now know the type. I refuse to believe that an intelligent and gifted person such as yourself cannot find a way to do what is necessary.' Iryn Jagga leaned forwards. 'I am counting on you for this, songster. The whole city of Sofala is counting on you. Without you, we are helpless. *She* and her horde can come sweeping down upon us at any moment. You have seen the sort of mad viciousness of which humanimals are capable. And that was but a small, marauding pack. Imagine the bloody destruction they could wreak with miscreant humans as their allies and *her* and her uncanny white blade leading them.'

Iryn Jagga shuddered. 'It does not bear thinking on. We must destroy her before she destroys us and plunges the world irrevocably into the Dark.'

Ziftkin hugged himself, shivering, not wanting to envision what a maddened horde of such creatures allied with violent humans might be capable of under the cruel direction of somebody like this Elinor.

'You can do this, songster,' Iryn Jagga said. He put his hand on Ziftkin's arm in a fatherly gesture. 'You *will* do it. And when we have triumphed, a great re-birth will come upon Sofala. The days of old will return and all . . . *all* folk here will know whom to thank. Songs will be made telling of Ziftkin Salvator, the songster who ended the scourge of the white blade and brought back the greatness of old . . .'

*

Ziftkin stood atop the parapet, remembering. He had come here alone, refusing all company, wanting no distractions . . .

Here to save a city. It hardly seemed possible. He did not know quite how he felt. Six ways at once . . .

It was evening now, with the first few faint stars already twinkling into visibility in the fading sky. The sun's dying light came from his back, and Sofala cast a long shadow over the lands before him. The world was hushed, poised between day and night, light and dark, neither and both. Barriers were fading, distances dwindling into haze.

Ziftkin took a breath, brought the bone flute to his lips, felt the little warm pulse of it in his bones. If he was to do this thing, now was surely the moment, with the world poised as it was in the *between* of twilight.

But he let the flute drop. He did not have any notion at all of how to do what Iryn Jagga demanded of him. He had only met one single humanimal. How was he to summon up whole groups of them? He felt a shiver of cold futility go through him. It was impossible.

And he could not quite suppress a shiver of stubborn sympathy. It was, after all, to their own certain destruction that he was summoning these poor creatures.

But he thought, also, of the dead he had seen, and the poor weeping lad, of a whole city threatened by such terrible, bloody violence. And he remembered his uncle Harst's words as he had killed poor mad Massy: 'Best to put the beast out of his misery. We've got to protect the stock.'

To protect . . .

Ziftkin looked at the bone flute in his hands and let out a long, sighing breath. As Iryn Jagga had said, he held the only sure key to preventing any further such bloody misdeeds as he had been witness to.

For long, uncertain moments he stood as he was on the parapet, alone, staring out at the green-grey tumble of the wild lands. Then, slowly, he lifted the flute and blew a tentative note, trying to feel his way into this thing he must do, trying to recall the feel of the dog-creature whose spirit he had sent into the Shadowlands, trying to imagine what others of that kind might be like . . .

He felt the note he was blowing go out in a long, slow coil of questing sound, further and further ... In some strange manner, as his breath blew the note, so a part of himself seemed to go with it, outwards and away ... Almost, he jerked back from the feeling, for it was like a long falling, making his heart jump and his belly cramp up.

But he could not stop now. Ignoring his lurching heart, he went with the flute's pull, letting the note he blew take him spiralling away, searching, searching ...

It was like ... like being a blind fish swimming through undiscovered waters, *feeling* a way. He could somehow sense the world all about him, but not the world as he ordinarily knew it. A complex of patterns, sound and rhythm and movement, little hummings and snatches of melody, tree-song like he had heard the day he first received the flute, the whirling notes of the wind, the great, slow, bass chanting of the mountains ... with small bursts of melody here and there, melody like light, or light like melody, he could not tell which.

It was impossible for him to interpret what he was sensing in terms of the ordinary world. Time had ceased to exist: heartbeats or days, it made no difference. Direction, distance, location, all meant nothing in this strange mode of flute-guided perception he had fallen into. There was only the melodious, interweaving complexity.

And then, suddenly, he *felt* a familiar tension.

Like a cluster of little throbbing stars they were, or glowing fruits, little spirals of repeating melody. He recognized the uneasy balance of them, like oil and water.

Humanimals. He felt certain of it. A loose grouping of them, milling and spilling about, but interconnected nevertheless. And near them, there was something else: tied with them in a threaded tangle like a complex melody, or a net woven of thin light. Other beings, more solid and singular ... wholly human.

Was this, in fact, the group he was questing for? How would he know? But, as his perception focused more sharply, he could *feel* such a complex of animosity about them that it was like a dark fog.

It must be them, then.

But what of this Elinor? He could sense no single presence

amongst or near the humanimals or their human companions, no glow of uncanniness that might be the power of the white blade she carried.

Unless . . .

Faint and far, there was a little echo . . . It was as if the slimmest of threads linked the humanimals to a far-distant, white-pulsing mote that was one – no, two beings of some sort, so faint he could not properly make them out.

But the connection was there, joining the humanimals with . . . *her*. If she were, indeed, a part of that faint dual form he could just sense. But distance was no true barrier, he realized, not for what he was attempting. All he need do was to summon the humanimals, and those others, nearby or far-distant, would be caught up in the summoning by virtue of the interconnected pattern that netted them all together.

Slowly, Ziftkin let the long, questing note he was playing spill over into the beginnings of a melody, a calling melody, a falling melody, like a long chute of water rushing, carrying all in its path along with it . . .

XXIX

Elinor came up out of sleep with a rush, sweat-soaked and shaking, her heart thumping in her breast. She stared about into the thin, pre-dawn light, trying to make sense of where she was . . .

There had been a long slope, a long, *pulling* slope, and she had been stumbling down it, urged along by the slope's steepness, faster and faster, tripping and stumbling over the uneven ground, unable to stop herself or halt the growing momentum of her downwards plunge. And through it all, there had been a soft, falling, beauteous music, like flowing water all about, a falling, calling music, the notes of it like insistent small fingers hooking into her guts and pulling her along.

She could still hear the echo of that strange music in her head.

Elinor shuddered, wrapped her arms about herself. There was no such slope as she had found herself upon, no music. It had all been a dream. She was here, in the forest, in the world, with a new day dawning. She shivered, for the air still held its night-chill, and turned over to snuggle into Gyver's furred warmth.

But Gyver was not there.

Elinor scrambled to her feet, her heart thumping.

It was ridiculous to be worried, she told herself. There were half a dozen places he might be – and all perfectly safe.

But the dream had left in her a residue of . . . she was not altogether sure what. Her belly was clenched with a kind of shadowy dread, as if it knew of some dreadful thing coming that her mind could not yet perceive.

She looked about at the fur-folk camp, but all seemed well. Little tendrils of dawn mist floated here and there through the trees. There were dark huddles and clusters of sleeping folk curled up together. Two or three were up already, gathered about a little twinkling fire.

But nowhere could she see any sign of Gyver.

'Have you seen Gyver?' she demanded of those squatting about the fire. But they merely shook their heads.

'Be calm,' she told herself. She stood, staring about, rubbing at the stump of her amputated finger, which throbbed uneasily. 'There's nothing to worry about.' But her beating heart said otherwise. Where could Gyver be?

She headed off away from the camp and into the trees, not knowing where she was going, only needing to move, to walk off the anxiety the dream had provoked in her, to search.

She called Gyver's name, but there was no response.

In the dim dawn light, the big trees seemed like a solid mass. She felt as if she were in a dark maze. 'Gyver,' she called. 'Gyver!' But still there came no response.

Over a rocky hump she went, across the further slope and along that, and further still, impelled by some obscure urge that would not let her rest until, finally, the ground fell away before her and she found herself atop a small, stony bluff. She stood, panting a little, her hand pulsing with pain, leaned against the peeling trunk of an ancient birch. She was looking westwards, she realized, with the sun climbing into the sky behind her. There was a small vale beneath her, and she was high enough here to see across it to the rise of trees on the further side.

Again, she seemed to hear the strange, calling music in her mind. The world seemed unnaturally still, as if poised, tense and waiting for something about to happen.

The bluff upon which she stood fell away on either side in rocky, shrubbery-tangled slopes. As Elinor's gaze fell from the distance and focused on things nearer to hand, she spied a figure at the base of the slope on her right. One of the fur-folk it was, standing still as still, staring blindly westwards.

She skipped down the slope and made her way over, hoping desperately that it might be Gyver.

It was.

But as she drew near he did not turn his head, nor acknowledge her in any way.

'Gyver?' she said uneasily as she approached him. 'Gyver!'

Still, he did not turn. His gaze was locked westwards and he stood utterly still, hardly breathing even, like one in a trance.

'*Gyver!*' Elinor said, and reached a hand to him and gave him a push.

Still he did not respond.

She pushed him harder, knocking him off balance.

Only then did he turn and blink and notice her. 'Elinor!' he said. 'I did not ssee you, me. I wass—'

'You were standing here like a stupid statue!' she replied in a surge of mingled relief and irritation. 'Didn't you hear me calling to you? What's wrong with you?'

He blinked at her, like a night-owl startled by sudden, glaring sunlight.

'What's wrong, Gyver?' Elinor put her hand upon his slim, furred arm. 'Something's *wrong.*'

She felt him shudder. 'Me, I do not . . .' But the words dwindled into silence, and he turned from her and gazed westwards once more.

'Gyver . . . *Gyver!*' She shook him. 'Look at me!'

He turned to her, still blinking owlishly. 'Do you hear it, you?' he said softly.

'Hear what?'

'The . . . the falling mussic.'

Elinor stiffened.

'I . . . I dreamed, me,' Gyver went on. 'I wass on a long sslope, running, running . . . I could not sstop. And all the while, a sstrange . . .' He lapsed into troubled silence.

Elinor felt her limbs tremble. 'A strange . . . calling music,' she finished.

He looked at her sharply. 'How did you . . .'

'I dreamed the same dream,' she said.

He blinked, his furred face troubled. 'What can it mean?'

'I do not know,' Elinor replied.

Gyver drew her close to him. 'I . . . Me, I thought I wass in the dream . . . But I awoke to find mysself sstanding here, alone on the cold hill'ss sside. I . . . I walked here assleep. What iss happening to me, my Elinor?'

She put her arms about his slim chest and hugged him.

350

He was staring westwards again. 'The world iss sso tight,' he murmured. 'Sso tight, it hurtss . . .'

Old Cloud-Dreaming regarded them seriously.

'And none of your folk have sensed anything?' Elinor asked.

Cloud-Dreaming shook her head. 'A few, they had an uneasse in their belliess. But none that I know of have heard thiss . . . mussic.'

'Not even you?' Gyver asked.

Cloud-Dreaming shrugged. 'My dreamingss are not ssuch ass yourss. I . . . am aware, me, of many thingss. I heard thiss mussic, yess. But it wass a far-away thing, not meant for me or mine. It iss not a path we foresst-folk musst walk.'

Gyver regarded her uneasily. 'But why, then, iss thiss mussic for me? Even Elinor, sshe doess not hear it like I do. I can hear it now, Cloud-Dreaming, like a little inssect buzzing about my head.' He ran a furred hand shakily over his eyes. 'I feel, me, ass if I am sstanding on a sslope, and every sstep I take iss uphill, ssave . . .' he gestured westwards, 'ssave in that direction. What doess it *mean*, Cloud-Dreaming?'

The old fur-woman sat silent for long moments.

'It iss a . . . calling,' she said finally. 'It iss a dream come into the world. When ssuch a dream comess, you musst walk itss path.'

'But we are not true-dreamerss, Elinor and I, ssuch ass you are,' Gyver said.

Cloud-Dreaming reached a hand to him. 'The world, it iss tight. It . . . pullss wesstwardss. The dream, it iss *in* the world now, a calling.'

'A calling to what?' Elinor demanded. 'And why does Gyver feel it so much more strongly than I? This is his homeland, here. If it is to be either of us, surely it ought to be *me* who feels such a westwards calling – if calling it is. *I* am the one who came from those westwards lands.'

Gyver was fidgeting, and kept glancing westwards.

'Look at him!' Elinor said. 'He can't keep his attention on anything else for more than a few heartbeats at a time.'

351

Gyver shrugged sheepishly. 'It iss . . . Me, I feel it *pulling* . . .'

Cloud-Dreaming motioned Elinor closer. 'You carry a . . . a hidden token, you.'

For a moment, Elinor could not think what the old wise woman might mean. The sword? No, not that. Then it hit her: the Fey-bone, Cloud-Dreaming must mean. She had all but forgotten it. Her hand went reflexively to it where it still hung from its thong about her neck.

'Give it to me for a few momentss,' Cloud-Dreaming said.

Elinor drew back.

'Give it to me,' Cloud-Dreaming insisted. She smiled, showing ivory teeth through her thin purple lips. 'And calm yoursself, girl. Me, I do not wissh it for mysself . . . But it iss a Fey-gift, thiss token, and it hass some virtue. Perhapss, it . . . protectss you.'

Elinor reached uncertainly for the little bone. It was oddly warm to her touch, as always – perhaps warmer than usual now. Reluctantly, she slipped the thong over her head. She did not feel to give the thing over, but if what Cloud-Dreaming said was true – and it certainly might be – then she had to know. With a little uncertain shiver, she dropped the bone into the old fur-woman's wrinkled, dark-skinned palm.

And felt a sudden dizzying rush of . . . She did not know quite how to explain it to herself. It was not simple music; rather, it was like the echo of a far-away melody brought to her through her bones. She stood up, entranced, uneasy. The ground seemed to tip under her, as if the world entire had been abruptly tilted. Every way seemed a fruitless struggle except one. Only in that direction was movement easy; in *that* direction, it took no effort at all to move. One step, two, and she had covered half the distance out of the camp and into the trees. The falling, calling melody was clearer now, as she walked into it. Three steps, four . . .

She felt something tugging at her and shrugged it off impatiently.

Elinor!' a voice called. '*Elinor!*'

And suddenly she was sprawled upon the ground in a tangle of limbs, and a furred face was pressed into hers. '*Elinor!*'

She shuddered, pulled herself together. The uncanny music echoed all about her, and she put both hands to her ears. But it did no use. The notes reverberated in her skull, calling, calling . . .

'Here,' somebody said. 'Give it back to her.'

Elinor felt a little length of warm bone pressed into her palm.

The music dwindled.

She took a long, relieved breath, another. Looking about her, she saw Gyver, Cloud-Dreaming, a little cluster of anxious fur-folk. Gyver was shivering.

'How . . . how can you . . . resist it?' she asked him. She felt faint and sick, her limbs all quivery.

Gyver shrugged, blinked, hugged himself. 'I do not think I can, me.'

Elinor put a hand upon him, knowing now what he was enduring. Struggle as he might, in the end, he could no more resist a pull such as she had experienced than a minnow could resist a strong river's current.

She looked down at the Fey-bone and shivered. 'Did they . . . know, the Fey?' she asked. '*Could* they know?'

Cloud-Dreaming shrugged. 'Who can tell what the Fey know or do not. They are beyond our undersstanding, them. But thiss gift, it protectss you, girl.'

Elinor hugged herself, feeling her mutilated hand throb. What were they to do now? Follow that calling? Try to resist it somehow? 'I don't understand any of this,' she said.

'Ssomething, it netss the two of you together,' Cloud-Dreaming said. She pointed. 'Ssomething from the wessternnesss you left behind. It . . . *reachess*.'

Elinor and Gyver looked at each other.

'The Brothers!' Elinor said, feeling a cold shudder of sudden certainty go through her. 'But how could they . . .'

Cloud-Dreaming closed her eyes and was silent for long moments. 'Me, I can *feel* the thread that tiess you,' she said, eyes still closed. 'Faint, it iss, but clear enough. Along that tie, the calling comess, through the . . . how do you call them? The little folk with the knowing heartss.'

'The . . . humanimals?' Elinor said.

Cloud-Dreaming opened her eyes, nodded slowly. 'Them.

We know them here, though we have few here in thiss land. It iss them who are called, and, through your tie to them, you.'

Elinor shook her head. 'I don't understand . . .'

Cloud-Dreaming looked at her. 'The dream hass come to you. The world, it iss tight. Clear iss the call. You musst go, you two.'

Elinor blinked, swallowed. 'And so we . . . leave? Just like that? Right now?'

Cloud-Dreaming gestured to Gyver, who was shivering, gazing blindly westwards. 'Him, he hass little choice to sstay.'

Elinor stared about her. The fur-folk lived a loosely structured life, coming and going freely. Few indeed were the times when all were in this camp together. Cloud-Dreaming was here, but others – young Swift, solid, thick-shouldered Stone, little Sky-Flower – were not. 'But we can't just leave!' Elinor said. 'Not without saying goodbye or . . .'

Cloud-Dreaming gestured at Gyver, who was edging away westwards, one shaky step at a time. He looked at Elinor imploringly, his limbs shaking with strain.

'You are called,' Cloud-Dreaming said softly.

Elinor looked about her, her fists clenched, resisting.

But Gyver's face was rigid with effort. There would be no staying.

'Go, girl,' Cloud-Dreaming urged. 'The dream hass come alive. The sslope of the world, it drawss you.'

Elinor hesitated for a last moment. All this talk of dreams and paths . . . But Cloud-Dreaming's certainty was somehow reassuring. The old fur-woman *knew* things. Elinor had had enough dealings with such wise women to trust their certainties.

Gyver had both arms about a tree now, holding on as best he could. With clumsy haste, Elinor belted on her sword and snatched up her travel bag. 'Can you say our goodbyes,' she asked Cloud-Dreaming, 'to those who are not here.'

The old fur-woman nodded.

'Here,' one of the fur-folk said, coming up to Elinor and handing her a little leaf-wrapped package. 'Journey food.' It was Stream, Gyver's mother's sister.

354

Elinor thanked her and tucked the food package away into her travel bag.

Stream held Elinor's arm a moment. 'Look after him,' she said, gesturing to Gyver. 'Bring him back to uss.'

Elinor nodded, but she felt her guts clench up. This was all too heart-wrenchingly sudden, hauled out of sleep and propelled away westwards without even knowing the why of it. It all seemed so . . . *impossible*.

The fur-folk in camp stood in a little crescent, looking on gravely. They seemed to accept fully the necessity of what was happening.

'Fare well, you,' Cloud-Dreaming said to Elinor and came over and gave her a calm hug. 'You came to uss in our time of need, and we thank you alwayss, uss.' Then she limped over to where Gyver was hanging on to the tree, grim-lipped and shaking, and raised her hand over him in benediction. 'Return to uss, Gyver, when you can.'

Gyver nodded, his eyes wet with sudden tears, clutching at his tree as if he were drowning.

'Go now,' Cloud-Dreaming said.

The old fur-woman's voice was calm, but Elinor saw there were tears in her eyes.

Elinor felt her belly lurch, but there was no time to do or say anything further. Even with the protection of the Fey-bone, Elinor could feel the echo of that uncanny calling. Gyver was slipping away, as if a strong current were tugging at him.

'Goodbye!' Elinor called back unhappily.

The fur-folk waved, silent and sober.

Gyver was gone already, drawn away through the trees.

Elinor followed after.

Gyver might have been able to hold on back in camp, but now that he had started to move, he went like a hound unleashed.

'Gyver!' Elinor called, seeing him flit ahead through the trees. But it was no use. She muttered a curse under her breath, put a steadying hand upon her sword's hilt, hitched up her travelling bag, and ran.

Dodging through the trees she went, skidding across tangly slopes. Coming over the crest of a wooded ridge, she glimpsed him ahead. By now, she had little breath left for calling out. Seeing him was enough. She bent her head and ran on.

And on.

Until she could keep it up no more. Leaned against a tree, she took great gasping breaths, feeling her heart crashing against her ribs.

'Gyver!' she called, when she had her voice back. *'Gyver!'*

But there was no sign of him.

She went on, slower now, casting about for some sign of him. But she was not yet nearly as woodwise as he, and could see no evidence of any spoor. It was little things she must look for, she knew: a trace of fur-hair, a broken bit of branch, a half-obliterated footprint in the leaf mould. But there was no time to stoop and scrutinize each little section of the forest.

She paused, slipped the cord holding the Fey-bone up over her head, and hung it momentarily from a dangling branch. The full force of the calling music nearly pulled her off her feet. But it gave her an indisputably clear direction – the one Gyver would be drawn along.

Snatching up the Fey-bone before she could be pulled away entirely, she dragged it over her head and set off again.

And after a little, she saw movement ahead through the trees, a furred shape. 'Gyver!' she called. 'Gyver, wait up!'

But he slowed not at all.

With a gasped curse, Elinor sprinted on, determined to catch up.

It was a hard course, rocky ground and steep, with clumps of thorny bushes here and there where the trees were thin. She vaulted a crumbly ridge of stone, half stumbled, kept on.

And then, there he was! No more than a dim figure glimpsed through the trees, but close now. Close . . . She sprinted after, too short of breath to call out, running with the last dregs of her strength until, bursting through a thicket, she flung herself upon him, dragging him to the ground.

Only.

Only it was not Gyver.

The fur-person beneath her tried to twist away. Whoever it was, was smaller and lighter than Gyver. Elinor shook herself, her vision blurry, her heart labouring. She pulled back, turned her face, and looked into the eyes of . . .

Sky-Flower, Cloud-Dreaming's young girl apprentice.

'Wha . . . what are *you* doing here?' Elinor gasped.

Sky-Flower shivered, panting, her tongue hanging like a dog's.

Elinor let the fur-girl go, then rolled back to sit on her haunches, straightening her sword, trying to get breath. Her mutilated finger stung like fire. 'What are you *doing* here?' she repeated. 'Have you seen Gyver?'

Sky-Flower blinked. 'I . . . I dreamed, me.'

'Of *music*?' Elinor demanded quickly.

But Sky-Flower only stared. 'Mussic? No. Not of mussic.'

Elinor shook her head. 'You hear no . . . calling music?'

'No.'

Elinor could still hear the insistent echoes in her mind; every moment she spent here with this girl was one more moment for Gyver to be pulled further away from her by that uncanny calling. 'I must go,' she said curtly, getting to her feet.

Sky-Flower stared, her dark eyes wide.

'Good . . . goodbye,' Elinor said, lamely, and turned to leave.

But Sky-Flower came after. 'I will go with you, me.'

'What?' Elinor whirled. 'This isn't . . . Why should you . . .'

'Me, I will go with you,' Sky-Flower repeated. 'Thiss, it iss in the dream.'

'What dream?'

'My dream.'

Elinor let out an exasperated breath. More dream talk. And every heartbeat, Gyver grew further away. 'I have to go,' Elinor explained. 'Gyver and I, we are . . . called. We must—'

'I know,' Sky-Flower interrupted. 'The calling, it pullss you both. I dreamed thiss, me. And . . .' She shivered. 'And a great dead place filled with fear.' The little fur-girl went silent for a long moment. 'In my dream, I am . . . in thiss great dead place.'

'But . . .' Elinor shook her head. 'What "great dead place"? What are you talking about? It's just a dream!'

Sky-Flower looked at her, sober and serious. 'Never *jusst* a dream.'

Elinor did not know quite what to say.

'Thosse ssuch ass Cloud-Dreaming and I,' Sky-Flower explained, 'we . . . *live* our dreamss. When the dreamss, they come to uss, they are the pathss we musst walk.'

Elinor swallowed. She looked ahead through the trees, where Gyver was forging on without her.

'I will go with you, me,' Sky-Flower insisted. 'Thiss iss the dream I musst walk.' She stood, hands at her sides, clothed in nothing but her fur, carrying nothing at all, a small, determined figure.

Elinor hesitated. Sky-Flower was only a girl. 'What about your family?' she demanded. 'What will they say if you disappear like this?'

Sky-Flower lifted her slim, furred shoulders in a shrug. 'They will undersstand, them. Me, I am what I am. It iss the dream. It musst be.'

Part of Elinor felt this was all craziness, all this talk of dreams and such. But Cloud-Dreaming, for all her strangenesses, was no crazy person. And there was something in Sky-Flower's voice, some irrevocability, that settled Elinor's doubts suddenly. The world, after all, was full of strangenesses. 'Come, then,' she said. 'Let us go on together. Gyver is somewhere ahead, getting further off by the instant.'

Sky-Flower nodded. 'I wass following hiss sspoor, me.' She gestured. 'Gyver, he went thiss way, running.'

Elinor felt a quick surge of relief. By so much, then, would this journeying be made easier. With the fur-girl as guide, she would not lose Gyver. 'Let's away, then,' she said.

Sky-Flower nodded and flitted ahead along Gyver's track.

XXX

High on the wild slopes, well away from the Settlement, Scrunch had laid himself down in a sheltering thicket to sleep. A balmy, late-summer evening it had been, stars softly emerging in the darkening sky, the gentle buzz of the last bees returning to their hives, the sweet smell of ripening berries . . . all of it balm to his aching mind after too much of human complexity, too much of human tussling, too much of the hard edge of human mindfulness.

And then he had been dreaming.

Music . . . music all about, filling the air like a dancing mist, seeping into his mind as the mist might seep into his lungs, echoing through him, a calling, falling music, pulling at him, and him on a long, drawing-down slope . . .

The last of the trees were well behind him now. Ahead lay a rolling stretch of grassy-hilly land. He was tired. He wanted to rest. His paws were raw, his legs ached, but his feet kept padding along, padding along.

The falling, calling music . . .

Scrunch did not understand any of this. Every way but this one seemed . . . upslope. And *this* way – out of the safety of the wild lands and back to where human folk made their habitations – was the last path he would have chosen for himself.

Long, weary days now . . . that uncanny music echoing in his mind, louder or softer, growing so slight at times it seemed but the memory of a whisper. But never was he entirely free from it. Scrunch shook his head irritably, snorted. Asleep or awake, he felt the unremitting nag of it, pulling him ever onwards out of the wild.

Up a long hillslope he was drawn now, his claws digging into the sod for traction, the long muscles in his legs burning with the strain of the climb, his breath coming in hard pants. Cresting the brow of the hill, he saw the blunt, rearing shape of a human city ahead.

Sofala.

Scrunch shuddered, recognizing it. All humanimals knew this place: home of the Ancient Brotherhood it was. Scrunch had once abandoned himself to the Brothers' ungentle clutches. To this city they had taken him – or tried to. It would have been the death of him, had he completed that journey into the Brothers' ancient stone stronghold.

He remembered all too clearly the despair that had gripped him then; he had been finished with life, ready for the Brothers to set his paining spirit free in their violent way.

And then Elinor had come along.

Elinor . . .

Where was she now?

Scrunch sat down. It took a huge effort to do so. The uncanny calling music was so strong now. Every bit of him strained to go onwards, across the lumpy grass hills and so to cruel Sofala.

What was *wrong* with him? He did not want to go down into that dark stone place. He absolutely did not wish to have anything to do with the hard-handed Brothers. He wanted free of this terrible, uncanny compulsion that had him in its grip.

But it was so forceful now it hurt. There was no resisting it. Sitting still here felt like clinging to a cliff face, limbs straining to the limit, with no way upwards and down the only direction to go.

So 'down' he went, drawn irrevocably towards dark Sofala, the uncanny, falling, calling melody pulling him in like a hook sunk into his flesh.

It was evening before he drew close to the city wall. The look of the place chilled him, it was so huge and bleak. A thick mat of living greenery hid much of the cold stone of the wall, but the place nevertheless felt dead.

The wild lands were alive, in every rock and stream, every

cloud and sky-borne breeze, each breathing, flying, swimming, running creature. But here . . .

Dead stone walls. Dead stone structures inside. The ground had been scraped bare. The place stank of death. It felt to Scrunch like he was entering into a black pit. He tried to stop once again, but it strained his aching joints to remain still.

And then, off to his left, he saw something that made his heart lurch. Moving through the grass, bounding . . . One of the hairless, pale-skinned hyphons, it was. They were sedate creatures, hyphons, when left on their own. But this one was moving with a kind of manic speed, leaping and staggering erratically. With an effort that left him dizzy and shaking, Scrunch managed to hold himself still. The hyphon passed him close by. There was a raw wound along its shoulder, he saw. As it passed him, Scrunch could make out its face clearly in the waning evening light – haggard, the eyes staring, the mouth open, ribbons of spittle trailing down its bare chin. There was terror in that face, and utter incomprehension. The poor soul hurled itself past Scrunch, mewling like a sick kitten.

And there were others. Scrunch saw them now. The grass was alive with them.

It made him feel sick.

Up till now, it had never occurred to him that any but himself might be affected by this uncanny music, for it had, after all, taken him while he had been in the wild, alone. But now, everywhere he looked, it seemed, he saw humanimals throwing themselves towards Sofala's dark bulk. And he among them – will he or nill he. What could it mean?

Scrunch could keep himself still no longer. He growled deep in his chest, hating this, his limbs quivering painfully with strain. But there was nothing he could do save follow the call. So onwards he went with the rest, funnelling towards the dark bulk of dead-feeling Sofala.

The sun was slipping away in the west, now, and darkness was encroaching upon the world. With the sun sunk behind it, the Sofala wall seemed a high cliff of blackness as Scrunch approached it. He had to crane his head back to take it all in, amazed and daunted by how high men could build.

What was to happen now? he wondered uneasily. Would the uncanny music drive him straight into the wall? He had a momentary, unsettling vision of himself plastered against the wall's unyielding face, trying to claw his way blindly through the naked stone and dying of hopeless exhaustion in the attempt.

But there was some sort of light ahead now, and he heard the sound of human voices, and something else, too . . .

Up till this point, the uncanny music that had drawn him had seemed entirely ethereal – echoing in his mind but not in the world. Now . . . now he heard the music with his ears, faintly at first, then clearer as he drew near.

It made the fur along his spine crackle, that music. He felt it pulling at him like so many tiny-strong, invisible, tireless fingers. His head buzzed. His eyesight flared and dwindled strangely. Instinctively, he fought it, rearing up on his hind legs, growling and roaring inarticulately.

But there was no way to resist it. He had not the strength. The incessant flow of notes pulled him down to all fours again and drew him along, closer and closer to the black city wall. The light ahead, he now saw, was from a brace of lanterns hung over a small doorway. As he drew unwillingly nearer, he saw a lone humanimal dog go limping through that doorway, accompanied by the sound of cruel human laughter.

Scrunch could make out human figures now, outlined against more light coming from the inner side of the doorway through the wall. They were Brothers, sure enough. He had seen enough – more than enough – of them to recognize the type: dark-clothed, dour-faced, armoured and armed. They stood flanking the doorway, which became a sort of tunnel leading through the stone thickness of the wall. As the humanimals were drawn in, the Brothers laughed triumphantly. Some of them shouted taunts. Others urged the hapless in-comers on with kicks and prods of their pike butts.

When Scrunch's turn came, the men went momentarily silent, daunted by his size.

Despite all his struggle to resist, he had accomplished nothing save to make his entrance into the doorway a little slower than others'. But he fought for all the slowness he could, panting and gasping, growling still and shaking his head, determined to resist in any and every way he might.

'Hurry along, *animal*!' one of the Brothers taunted him. The

362

man raised his pike and gave Scrunch a *thwack* across the flank.

Scrunch whirled and grabbed for the man, moving quickly despite all the debilitating drag upon him. For an instant only, he felt man-flesh under his talons, and he tried to grip and draw the man closer. But something gave – flesh or clothing, he could not tell – and the man fell back, screaming.

Then Scrunch was gone inside, drawn irrevocably on through, the doorway lanterns left behind, blind in utter blackness . . .

Until, re-emerging at the far end, he found himself in Sofala.

An impact of light and noise hit him, human voices shouting, the uncanny music stitching all together still, drawing him irresistibly onwards. He made out more men, the dark shapes of the Brothers. A painful flash of bright torchlight in his face blinded him. He felt the sharp prod of a pike, herding him along. He would have turned to rend the pike-wielder, but something stabbed painfully into his flank and prevented him. He snarled and struggled, but between the music and the sharp pricking of the men's weapons he was helpless.

Along a kind of chute they drove him. He heard shrieks and cries, the harsh laughter of the men on all sides. A small body skittered desperately past him, moaning, and plunged on. There were others further ahead; he could hear them clearly now, crying and mewing. The place stank of fear.

His feet were unsteady, and he left bloody footprints behind, his flanks seeping wet blood where he had been prodded and pricked onwards.

Round a last bend they herded him, and, suddenly, despite the pain and the compulsion that drove him on, despite all the shrieking and wailing and the press of hysterical bodies that flowed about him . . . despite everything, he stopped, rearing up upon his hind legs.

Ahead, the chute down which he and the other humani-mals were being driven emptied into another dark doorway. Those before him disappeared into it. But above that doorway there was a kind of high stone ledge. And perched atop that ledge there was a man.

But no ordinary man . . .

He was dressed in the Brothers' dark clothing, but he wore no armour, no weapons. Instead, as he stood there upon the ledge, he held a bone flute to his lips and blew a flow of stronger melody.

The music of it hit Scrunch like a solid thing.

'Drive the beast onwards!' Scrunch heard some man shout from behind him, and a sudden hard blow upon his spine toppled him to his knees.

'Onwards!' the man-voice ordered, and more sharp blows fell upon him.

The music bit at him, drawing him on. But for an instant, just before he was plunged into the darkness of the doorway ahead, Scrunch looked up . . . and locked gazes unexpectedly with the man above.

The music faltered. The man stared down at Scrunch, his face tight, his eyes wide and suddenly unsure.

For that brief instant, something passed between them, a connection too uncertain to be put clearly into words. But, in some manner Scrunch could not fathom, he felt . . . comforted. It made no sense. Clearly, it was the man above him who had drawn them all helplessly here. Clearly, he was some manner of terrible human sorcerer.

And yet . . . And yet that man was no Brother. There was not the same darkness of spirit to him. He was somehow more *alive* than they. Scrunch felt, somehow, a momentary, inexplicable connection between himself and the man . . . It lasted no more than a few heartbeats, and then Scrunch was driven through the doorway and into the darkness beyond. But he took that unexpectedly comforting moment of connectedness with him.

Stumbling onwards in utter dark, he found himself at the head of a flight of human steps. Confused and weary, he tumbled awkwardly down them and landed with a painful thump at the bottom. So spent and lacerated and bruised was he, he just lay there, gasping.

Only when some body thumped heavily into him from above did he gather up the strength to shift himself away from the stairs' foot. It was too dark to see anything about him, but he could hear – moans, sighs, the awkward shifting of bodies in the dark. Some creature came spilling down the stairs, shrieking, and Scrunch backed further away. He stepped on something soft, and somebody wailed.

'Who are you?' a shaky voice demanded from the dark.

But Scrunch was too weary to even bother responding. With his last shreds of strength he managed to force himself through the press of bodies and up against a wall. Sinking down there, he curled up upon himself and laid his head upon his forearms. Utter weariness came over him like a wave of dark earth, and, music or no, he passed away into exhausted sleep.

XXXI

'Where is Elinor of the white blade?' Iryn Jagga demanded.

Ziftkin stood, head hanging, his arms quivering with fatigue. 'I don't know. She's out there. I can . . . *feel* a kind of presence.'

Iryn Jagga was dressed all in black this day, sombre as a starless midnight, with only the golden medallion that hung from his neck and the gilded circlet upon his brow to break the dark solidity of his appearance. He glared at Ziftkin. 'I must have her! Do you hear? The rest are only so much chaff. But *her*—'

'I'm trying the best I know how!' Ziftkin snapped.

He stood with Iryn Jagga upon the high parapet of the same squat octagonal tower from which Ziftkin had been calling for long days and nights now. He was learning as he went, weaving that calling into more and more solidity in the strange *otherplace* his flute-guided perception laid open for him, so that, even when he slept, the calling echoes of his playing remained alive.

But he had not slept much; Iryn Jagga had seen to that. Ziftkin rubbed wearily at his eyes with one hand. Perched up here on the city's high edge, he was far enough removed from Sofala's inhabitants that they could not readily hear the sound of his musicking, and the *summons* of it they felt only as a faint unease, if at all, for it was not directed towards them.

He had summoned in the original humanimal group he had discovered, and any wandering others he sensed along the way, *feeling* them flock to his call and spill across the land towards Sofala. The human folk with whom the humanimal group was connected had been drawn irrevocably along in the humanimals' wake, like so many leaves pulled by a strong current. He had *felt*, also, the distant, white-pulsing mote that was – must be – this Elinor, had played her, trying to draw in her and the companion – or was it companions? He was not sure – travelling with her. But there was some strangeness about them; one or the other always seemed unreachable, as if shielded somehow.

Ziftkin looked wearily across at Iryn Jagga. 'All but the last few stragglers are drawn in now, humanimal and human. What threat is this Elinor to you without her followers?'

'You must call her to me!' Iryn Jagga insisted vehemently. 'Without her, all this is but a hollow victory.'

Ziftkin took a shaky breath. It was mid-morning. He had been up here most of the night, playing, playing. He felt himself quivery-weak with exhaustion. Save for a night and a day, when the humanimals had arrived in a flood and Iryn Jagga had had him down in the pens fluting them in, Ziftkin had stood here playing for so long he could no longer keep clear track of the days. He wanted an end to it.

But Iryn Jagga was implacable. The leader of the Ancient Brotherhood appeared to have unlimited reserves. He was always busy, striding this way or that to deal with some issue or other, showing up unexpectedly on this tower-top in the dark middle of the night, urging Ziftkin to more effort, as full of energy as if he had just risen from a long sleep.

Sleep . . .

Ziftkin let out a weary breath. His eyes felt gritty. He ached to stretch out on a bed and fall away into soothing sleep. But there would be no arguing with Iryn Jagga once he had set his will. Might as well dispute with the wind.

Iryn Jagga regarded Ziftkin in silence for long moments, then, reaching over, he patted Ziftkin on the shoulder. 'You have done well, songster. There is no denying it. And I can see you are weary. Time for a respite, I think. Come, follow me.'

Ziftkin blinked. 'Where?'

'You will see.' Beckoning Ziftkin to follow, Iryn Jagga led the way down the tower's internal steps, a long, winding stairwell that made Ziftkin spin-dizzy.

'You must leave your instrument behind,' the leader of the Ancient Brotherhood said over his shoulder as they neared the bottom.

Ziftkin gripped his flute. 'Why?'

'Where we are going, it would not be . . . appropriate.'

They had reached the bottom of the stairs now. Ziftkin stood his ground. 'I . . . I cannot . . .'

'You can and will,' Iryn Jagga said. 'There will be no problem, I assure you. Your instrument will be kept safe and sound, ready for your return.'

'But why must I leave it?'

Iryn Jagga smiled. 'We go to see the fruits of your labours . . . the wretched, miscreant people you have summoned here for me. *Her* followers. Are you not curious to see them? I have waited till they were properly ingathered to treat with them. The time has now come.

'I wish you with me as I do what I must this day. But to have such a crowd as we shall face see the very instrument of their retribution flaunted before them . . . No. I think not.'

Ziftkin shivered. 'What are you planning to do with them?' For a moment, he felt his belly clench. The humanimals' fate was sealed – a hard fate, maybe, but a necessary one. But the human folk . . . he had assumed unthinkingly, engrossed as he had been with the calling-in, that Iryn Jagga would mete out some punishment. But what – the thought hit him with sudden bleak force – what if Iryn Jagga intended for the human folk to suffer the same hard fate as the humanimals? Was the man capable of such an act? No, Ziftkin told himself. *No.*

He looked at Iryn Jagga. 'What will you *do* to them?'

The leader of the Ancient Brotherhood smiled. 'Don't worry so, songster. I can see it in your face. I am the shepherd, not the wolf. They will be punished, these misguided folk. But then they will be brought back into the fold, like the lost sheep they are.'

Ziftkin took a breath, nodded.

Iryn Jagga lifted his hand and a squad of the ever-present guards formed up about them. 'Come, then,' he said and strode off.

Along a last stretch of corridor Iryn Jagga led, pausing at a thick, barred door at the end to wait for Ziftkin to catch up.

Their accompanying guards had swelled now, to fully a score at least. Ziftkin rubbed his empty hands – the flute had been left behind, under special security, on a silken cushion – and followed after Iryn Jagga uneasily.

The door was unbarred and pushed open, and they filed through.

The room they came into was high-ceilinged and large, with sunlight slanting in from long, narrow windows set in the upper half of the walls. The place throbbed with the echoing sound of voices, a confused hum of noise that seemed to come from everywhere at once. All Ziftkin could see, however, was a double line of armed and armoured guards, the side of a man-high, raised wooden platform, and a set of steps.

Iryn Jagga mounted the steps, gesturing for Ziftkin to follow.

At the top, Ziftkin found himself upon a platform of new planking, more guards spaced out along the platform's back and side. A further double rank of guards – armed with long-handled pikes – was formed up on the stone floor, like a hedge, in front of the platform. And beyond those . . .

'Behold, your success!' Iryn Jagga said, gesturing to what lay before them.

The wooden platform had been erected at one end of a large hall. From wall to wall, the place was filled with a milling crowd of people, at least four or five score of them, Ziftkin reckoned, ragged and weary-looking, clothing torn, bruised, white-faced, confused and angry and frightened.

Seeing Iryn Jagga and Ziftkin and their guards upon the platform, the crowd burst into a storm of shouts and cries. Ziftkin shied back, but Iryn Jagga strode to the platform's leading edge, arms crossed below the golden medallion that hung at his breast, surveying them. The crowd went gradually, sullenly quiet.

'So . . .' he said into the silence. He smiled, and on his face showed an expression of enormous satisfaction. 'So . . . the wayward sheep are returned to the fold.'

There was no response to this save the shuffling of feet. Somebody coughed. All eyes were upon Iryn Jagga.

Ziftkin felt most uncomfortable standing about up here,

empty-handed and helpless-feeling, surrounded by dour-faced, armed guards. He shivered, gazing down at the crowd of folk that were *her* followers.

They appeared altogether ordinary-looking, with white-faced children – he had never expected children – clinging to exhausted mothers and folk leaning wearily on each other for support. Ziftkin's heart misgave him. They seemed such poor, starveling folk, so shaken and so . . . innocent-looking.

It made him think of that creature, the bear he had seen the night the humanimals had come washing up into the city in a confused wave.

'They are not as they seem,' Iryn Jagga kept insisting. 'They are an *abomination*!'

But though he ought to know better by now, perhaps, Ziftkin had sensed nothing of such *abomination* in the bear-creature. Through the bone flute, he had *felt* only fear and anger and hurt. The bear had seemed just another soul in anguish, and, perched above it, flute in hand, he had felt sick at the terror and pain he had caused – necessary or not.

And he had felt, for the brief moments he had locked gazes with the bear-being, a sense of something like . . . kinship. As he had with the dog-creature he had played into the Shadow-lands. The memory of it nagged at him. He tried not to dwell upon it.

On the platform, Iryn Jagga had raised his arms: 'Error and rebellion and foolishness,' he was crying, his voice reverberating throughout the hall. 'Wayward sheep are you all indeed. And now . . . *now* . . .' He opened his arms in a gesture that encompassed all before him. 'What am I to do with you?'

He paused, looking at them.

An uneasy murmuring went up.

'Quiet!' Iryn Jagga shouted, his face suddenly gone darkly stern. 'I have not given you permission to speak.'

'We are not yours to give permission to!' a voice cried. A woman stepped to the front of the crowd. She was sinewy thin, with short-cropped, grey-blonde hair. She stood, hands on hips, glaring up at Iryn Jagga. 'We are a free people. By what right do you keep us here, without food, without water?

370

What wicked, unnatural thing did you employ to have us *brought* here?'

A confused cry went up: 'Water . . . *water*!'

'By what right,' the thin woman demanded, 'do you shout orders at us. We are not chattels!'

Iryn Jagga laughed. 'Chattels? Yes, chattels indeed. And mine to do with as I wish.'

The woman approached the hedge of pike-armed guards that separated the platform from the captive crowd. 'I demand,' she said, calling out over the heads of the guards, 'that you—'

Iryn Jagga made a quick motion with his hand and several of the guards stepped forwards. With quick, brutal efficiency, they attacked the woman with their pike hafts. A raining storm of hard blows, and she was left in a moaning heap, blood seeping from her face.

The crowd fell silent, shocked and staring. Ziftkin, too, stared. It had all happened with such mind-numbing, violent speed. He felt sick, looking at the poor woman as she lay there alone and broken.

'Do you see where stupid rashness gets you?' Iryn Jagga shouted at the crowd. 'Let there be no mistake about this. You are *mine*. Every one of you. To do with as *I* see fit.'

The crowd shivered in dismay, shifting this way and that in fruitless unease. A murmur like the wind in the leaves went up.

'Quiet!' Iryn Jagga shouted. 'Or must I send my guards in amongst you to show you the cost of disobedience?'

The folk below froze, staring white-eyed at the pike-armed guards. In the sudden silence a young child began to cry. The sound was quickly hushed.

Iryn Jagga nodded with satisfaction. He put a hand to his brow, adjusting the set of the golden circlet. 'Good,' he said. 'You are not so stupid after all.' He came to the very edge of the raised wooden platform. 'You have learned an important lesson here this morning.'

He motioned two-handedly to the guards, who moved forwards in a line, compressing the crowd back, so as to leave a cleared place on the stone floor between their armed ranks and the platform. The woman they had beaten lay in that cleared space behind them, like something thrown up by an invisible tide. A puddle of blood had begun to form on the flagstone under her cheek.

Iryn Jagga leaped down from the platform, landed lightly on the floor, and walked over to stand at her side. 'Let this woman here be remembered by you all. She tried to defy me.' He knelt down and lifted her head and shoulders. Her face was blue and swollen and bleeding. She stared up at him and moaned through broken teeth.

Iryn Jagga stroked the woman's hair with one hand, the way one might stroke the hair of an ailing child. He shook his head sadly. 'Stupid, wilful woman. I *did* warn you.' He took out a gleaming little knife from somewhere beneath his cloak. With a quick sideways slash, he opened the woman's throat.

Skipping neatly aside, he stood and watched.

The woman collapsed backwards, gasping and choking as blood welled up in a flood through her sliced throat.

'No!' Ziftkin cried, horrified. '*No!*'

Iryn Jagga didn't spare him a glance.

A great, wordless heave of noise came from the crowd and they surged forwards. The guards beat them back amidst screams and shouts.

When it was finished, many were bruised and beaten, moaning and crying. The woman lay still and white and bloodless, her life poured out in a sticky pool on the floor all about her.

Ziftkin felt he was going to be sick. He staggered over against the wall at one end of the wooden platform for support, three cold-eyed guards close about him. Pressing his cheek against the chill stone of the wall, he swallowed hard, trying to keep his belly down. He kept seeing the woman's throat opening like a ripped sleeve, blood gushing. He had known Iryn Jagga to be iron-willed, but the man had performed the bloody deed with such cold precision.

The leader of the Ancient Brotherhood, meanwhile, stood just as he was, arms half crossed across his breast, the bloodied knife held loosely in one hand. Calmly, he reached up and adjusted the set of the golden circlet once again, gazing upon the moiling, weeping, panicky crowd.

'*Silence!*' he shouted. '*SILENCE!*'

The room stilled.

'I will have order here!' Iryn Jagga announced. 'Who speaks for you?'

No one replied.

'Who speaks for you? I say. Who are your leaders?'

'The Committee,' several voices called out after a little. 'The Committee . . .'

'Let the members of this Committee step forth, then,' Iryn Jagga said. 'I wish to treat with them.' He stood, arms partway crossed, waiting. The little knife dripping a last few drops of blood upon the floor beside him.

Nobody came forth.

'What?' Iryn Jagga called. 'Is there nobody who would face me? Are you all such cravens, then? Where is this "Committee" you speak of? Who are its members?'

The crowd shivered.

One lone man stepped forwards, elbowing his way through the press. From his vantage point upon the platform, Ziftkin saw several people try to pull him back, but the man kept on resolutely.

'Ah . . .' Iryn Jagga said, seeing the man emerge. 'You are head of this Committee, then?'

The man shook his head. 'I am no part of the Committee.'

'Then why do you stand before me?' Iryn Jagga demanded.

The man shrugged. He was grey-haired and grey-bearded, no longer young. His clothes were in tatters and his face white with exhaustion.

Ziftkin felt a pang of sudden sympathy for this grey-haired man. He seemed such an ordinary fellow, and brave, not at all the sort of evil, violent scoundrel Iryn Jagga had made his like out to be. And Iryn Jagga . . . Ziftkin shivered.

'My name,' the grey-haired man was saying, 'is Collart. I can speak for those here.'

'On whose authority?' Iryn Jagga asked.

'My own,' Collart returned.

Iryn Jagga turned his gaze to the crowd. 'You allow this man to speak for you, then?'

There was some muttering, some little pushing and whispering and grunts of 'the Committee', but nobody came forth.

'I see,' Iryn Jagga said.

'What do you wish of us?' grey-haired Collart asked in a weary voice.

But Iryn Jagga merely stood, regarding Collart.

'Well?' Collart said.

'You are a man others look to, I think,' Iryn Jagga said. His voice was not especially loud, but it carried clearly through the hall nevertheless. 'Perhaps *the* man this rabble looks to. Is that not so?'

Collart shrugged. 'I am one amongst many, that's all. Some listen to me. Some don't.'

Iryn Jagga smiled a thin smile. 'I think you are too modest. I think you are more to this rag-tag mob than you let on. Perhaps more than you know yourself. Where are you from, fellow?'

'Out of the wild lands.'

Iryn Jagga shook his head impatiently. 'Before you fled there. Where are you from in the Valley?'

The grey-haired man regarded Iryn Jagga for a long moment. 'I lived at Margie Farm, before . . . before you and yours burnt it to the ground.'

Iryn Jagga nodded. 'So . . .'

'What do you want of us?' grey-haired Collart demanded.

But Iryn Jagga merely looked at him.

'In the name of these folk, I demand that you—'

'You *demand* nothing!' Iryn Jagga snapped. He stepped back a quick pace, lifted his hand, snapped his fingers. There was a sudden *krakk!* from somewhere at the edge of the platform, followed by a soft, wet *crump* sound.

Collart grunted, staggered back, clutched at his chest with both hands. He stared down in horror at his sternum, where the nub of a crossbow bolt protruded.

Iryn Jagga snapped his fingers again, twice this time.

Krakk! Krakk!

Collart spun about, one bolt sideways through his ribs, the third skewering him in the neck just above his collar bone, the bloody tip of it thrust out his back between his shoulder blades. He slumped to the ground with a little mewling sound.

The guards held Ziftkin tight, hard hands gripping his arms.

The hall erupted, then went quiet as a tomb.

'Another lesson,' Iryn Jagga said softly into the silence. 'I am the power and the right. I, it is, who says whether you live or die. All of you. Each of you. Is that clear?' He glowered at them. 'Is that *clear*?'

There was a shaken murmur of assent.

Iryn Jagga nodded. 'Good.' He lifted the golden medallion that hung from his neck and held it up. It winked in the room's light, the male face imaged on it standing out clearly for all to see. 'You are *mine*!' he cried to the crowd. 'But I am merely the humble spokesman of great Jara. It is *He* who has determined your fate. The great force that is Jara flows through the world. But it has been stopped, bound up, impeded by the wickedness of these times in which we live.'

For long moments, Iryn Jagga stood as he was, statue-still, medallion raised. Then he slowly let his hands drop and smiled. 'I will tell you how it is. You were farmer folk once, here in our lands, before you shattered our peace by breaking out into lawless and bloody rebellion.'

'It was *you* who . . .' somebody began impetuously.

'*Silence!*' Iryn Jagga shouted. 'The next one of you who speaks out of turn is a dead man.'

The crowd fell stiffly silent.

Iryn Jagga nodded. 'That is better. Now, as I was saying . . . This lawless rebellion of yours has caused untold destruction and suffering. Many were the innocent folk that died because of your unthinking acts! But we of the Ancient Brotherhood are merciful. *I* am merciful.

'Before you broke out into this wilful, pointless, *wicked* rebellion, you were a farmer folk.' Iryn Jagga regarded the crowd a moment. 'And you can be again, if you wish.'

The crowd murmured.

'We need dependable folk to work the farms in our lands. Many is the field that lies fallow, now, from lack of hands to work it.' Iryn Jagga gestured to the crowd. 'I offer you forgiveness. I offer you a productive future once again. I offer you your farms back.'

The murmuring rose in a shocked crescendo.

'Your own farms to live on, to plant and harvest as you did in the past.'

The crowd surged.

'Speak,' Iryn Jagga told them. 'I give you permission.' He

pointed to a thick-set, bearded man near the crowd's leading edge. 'You. What do you say to this generous offer of mine?'

The man shifted from foot to foot. He started to speak, cleared his throat, cast anxious glances at the guards that hemmed the crowd all about.

'Speak up!' Iryn Jagga commanded.

The man coughed nervously, then said, 'We can . . . can have our own lands . . . back again? Our farms?'

Iryn Jagga nodded.

'But . . .' the man began confusedly. 'I don't . . .'

'You will be returned to your farms,' Iryn Jagga said. 'Do you see how mistaken you have all been? There was no need for bloody rebellion. It was only this woman . . . this Elinor of the wicked blade who poisoned your minds. She blinded you, twisted your wits with bitter untruths. With you I have no more quarrel. You may return to your farms. But with *her* . . .'

The crowd had burst into confused chattering. Folk were shaking their heads in amazement, smiling and gasping and arguing amongst each other whether it could really be true, what Iryn Jagga had offered.

'Silence!' he cried, and they settled quickly.

A woman came forward hesitantly, short, grey-haired, weary of face, dressed in torn trousers and shirt. 'May I . . . may I speak?' she asked.

Iryn Jagga nodded.

'I . . .' The woman had to swallow and clear her throat before continuing. 'I am Lessie, of Sutton Farm,' she said. 'Are you . . . are you saying that I and mine can return there, to Sutton, and work it as we used to.'

'Absolutely,' Iryn Jagga replied.

The woman stared at him, mouth open. She took a breath, closed her mouth, opened it again. 'We can all return to our own farms and work them as we used to? And things will go back to the way they were before . . . before—'

'Before Elinor Whiteblade tore it all uselessly apart with her wicked lies,' Iryn Jagga finished for her. 'Yes. Exactly. You may all return to your farms, and everything will be the same as it was.' He smiled his thin smile. 'Except for one small matter, of course.'

'And that . . . is?' the woman said uncertainly.

'The ownerships of the farms have been forfeited.' Iryn Jagga shrugged. 'Naturally.'

A shock went through the crowd, then they erupted into confused chatter.

'Silence!' Iryn Jagga warned.

The people settled stiffly.

'You rebelled against your rightful lord . . .' Iryn Jagga began.

'We were *free* farmers!' somebody shouted from the back.

Iryn Jagga frowned. 'You were . . . and *are* a rebellious rabble. By your violent and bloody acts, you have forfeited any rights as land-owners you might once have had – *which* were held only by the good graces of we here in Sofala in the first place, for the land you farmed has been under our benediction and our control for many generations of men.'

The crowd rumbled.

'You are free to return to your farms,' Iryn Jagga said.

'As tenant farmers on our own property,' somebody returned bitterly.

'On *my* property!' Iryn Jagga responded. 'As properly ordained leader of the Ancient Brotherhood, and as recognized inheritor of the long bloodline of the Lords of Sofala, it is *I* who decide the fate of the lands hereabouts.' He gestured about him at the phalanx of armed and armoured guards. 'I have the *right*, and I have the *power*!'

The crowd shifted and grumbled, like a large, uncontent beast.

'And what—' a man started to demand, and then went silent as one of the guards approached him threateningly.

Iryn Jagga waved the guard off. 'Speak!' he commanded the man.

The man looked about him nervously, swallowed. 'What if . . . if any of us do not wish your offer? What happens to us then?'

Iryn Jagga regarded the man calmly. 'I will force nothing upon any of you here. You may take up your farms again under the conditions I offer. Or not. The choice is yours, freely.'

'And if,' said the man who had already spoken up, 'we do not wish to become tenant farmers to you? What then?'

'You will die,' Iryn Jagga said calmly.

The crowd erupted once more, surging against the walls, everybody crying questions and confusions.

'Silence!' Iryn Jagga commanded. '*Silence!* Or I will send the guards in amongst you.'

That quieted them.

'You are rebellious subjects,' Iryn Jagga went on, once silence had settled upon the hall again. 'You have forfeited whatever rights you once may have had by your rank and bloody deeds. Now . . . *now* there remains for you only mercy or justice. I offer you both. It is your decision as to which you will accept.'

The crowd stared at him.

Iryn Jagga smiled. 'I will give you a little time to discuss this amongst yourselves. Surely this . . . Committee of yours, composed as it is of prudent men who do not like to risk themselves unnecessarily, will see the wisdom in what I am offering you. You may all return to your old lives. With only the one small difference.'

'We become land slaves!' somebody shouted from the back of the hall.

Iryn Jagga sighed. 'Not at all. You become the proper subjects of Sofala, under the benediction and protection of the great Jara himself.'

'It's not fair!' a woman complained. 'I and mine sweated for twenty years to build what we had.'

'And you threw it all away by your bloody deeds!' Iryn Jagga responded.

'It was *you* who did the killing!' another man cried. 'I watched your armed men put my farm to the torch and kill two of my sons!'

'The proper wages for rebellion,' Iryn Jagga replied.

'It was *you* who started the—' somebody began.

'*Enough!*' Iryn Jagga shouted. 'I did not come here to *debate* with you. I will give you some little time to discuss amongst yourselves what you deem is best to do.'

With that, he turned from them and vaulted lightly back up upon the wooden platform. He gestured towards Ziftkin, who still stood against the wall at the platform's edge, shaken and sick-feeling in his belly. The guards at Ziftkin's side urged him

378

forcefully along, and he found himself part of a little procession that filed out through the door at the back of the platform and left the hall.

Behind them, the door was shut, barred, and guarded.

Down a long hallway Iryn Jagga strode, then through into a little wood-panelled room. The guards stayed outside at the entrance, leaving Ziftkin to follow.

Against one wall of the room was a sideboard, on which sat a wash basin, several towels neatly folded next to it. A round wooden table stood in the room's centre, surrounded by a scatter of low chairs with thick, elaborately embroidered seat-cushions. Upon the table was a silver tray containing a crystal decanter filled with amber liquor and two small glass cups.

Iryn Jagga went to the basin on the sideboard and carefully washed his hands, then dried them. The basin water was pink when he had done, Ziftkin saw, pink with the last remains of the poor dead woman's blood. The knife he had used was nowhere to be seen.

Striding over to the table in the centre of the room, Iryn Jagga lifted the decanter, poured himself a glass of the amber liquor, and downed it in two gulps. He smacked his lips lightly in satisfaction and poured himself another. Glass in hand, he went to one of the chairs and sat down with a sigh. 'Help yourself,' he said to Ziftkin, waving at the decanter and the remaining glass.

Ziftkin stayed as he was, near the room's entrance, so clotted with fury and sick confusion that he still felt like he wanted to vomit.

Iryn Jagga smiled and took a sip from his glass. 'You look discontent, songster.'

Ziftkin walked towards the table. He suppressed the urge to kick it, to lash out at the chairs with their fancy embroidery. He felt betrayed and terrified and furious, all at once. Iryn Jagga had done monstrous things, yet he sat there as composed and immaculate as ever, legs crossed casually at the ankles, sipping from his elegant clear-glass cup.

The man was . . . He did not know *what* the man was.

'Sit,' Iryn Jagga said, pointing to the chair next to him.

'I'd rather stand,' Ziftkin replied, tight-lipped.

Iryn Jagga laughed. 'You disapprove of me, boy?'

379

Ziftkin opened his mouth, closed it.

'I though you might. That's why I brought you along with me, to be a witness.' Iryn Jagga put his glass down on a little table next to his chair. His face was gone dead serious. 'This is no *game* we play here, boy.'

'I know!' Ziftkin snapped. 'Two people lie *dead* back there in that hall. At your hand!'

'Ah . . .' Iryn Jagga breathed. 'So that's it, is it? Your soft heart is showing.'

'At least I *have* a heart!'

'And I do not?' Iryn Jagga shook his head. 'You understand nothing, boy.'

Ziftkin bristled. 'I understand that you slit that woman's throat as if she were some poor farm sow ready for the autumn slaughter!'

'And thus saved the lives of all the rest!'

Ziftkin stared at him.

'You do not,' Iryn Jagga said, 'understand.' Again, he motioned for Ziftkin to sit next to him. 'Sit!'

This time, Ziftkin obeyed.

'They are a wild and dangerous group, that lot,' Iryn Jagga began.

'They looked nothing of the sort,' Ziftkin countered. 'There were *children* amongst them!'

The leader of the Ancient Brotherhood shook his head. 'Don't be naive, boy! Children mean nothing. In that hall, they were contained, cowed. But only let them break loose for one instant . . . They have committed terrible and bloody deeds, those folk.'

'So you have said.'

'For what they have done,' Iryn Jagga went on, ignoring Ziftkin's comment, 'these folk deserve the severest of punishment. But I want them *back*, boy! Do you understand? We need such folk as they. Sofala is on none too secure a footing. We . . . struggle. They were good farmer folk once, before this foul Elinor and her madness descended upon them. They have been deluded.'

'And you intend to . . . to *un-delude* them by killing them piecemeal?'

Iryn Jagga shook his head. 'Not at all. One does not . . .

380

un-delude people, as you put it. It is a misguided waste of time and effort. Does any right-minded father argue with a young child about issues that concern that child's safety and future? No! A father does what he deems best for his child – and the child thrives.'

'But—'

'Listen to me, boy! You have brought back these wayward sheep to me. But now I have to make them *mine* again.'

'By killing them?'

Iryn Jagga nodded soberly. 'By killing a few if need be, yes. I had to establish my authority over them. Do you think it was easy for me to do what I did? Do you think I enjoyed the killing?'

Ziftkin did not know quite what to say. He felt the sick confusion of fury in him dwindling. Iryn Jagga's handsome face seemed so open and candid.

'I have liberated the spirits of two troubled people,' Iryn Jagga said. 'They have by now met their just rewards at great Jara's hands. Is that so terrible? And by their deaths, I have saved the lives of all the rest. Do you think they will refuse my offer, those we left back there in the hall?'

Ziftkin shrugged. 'No. Only a fool or a hero could refuse.'

'Exactly so,' Iryn Jagga agreed. 'And I have already dealt with the two potential heroes amongst them.'

Ziftkin blinked.

'I am not a stupid man,' Iryn Jagga said very softly.

Ziftkin sat back in his chair, no longer sure quite how he felt.

'It is hard times in which we live, songster,' Iryn Jagga said, leaning forwards. 'Trust me. If I must sometimes do hard things, ruthless things, it is because the times call for it. But everything I do is in aid of a great cause. Think on it! The ancient greatness restored. For that, if I must, I will harden my heart and do whatever is required. One or two lives against many. It is no easy choice. But I am prepared to make such choices. I do what I *must* in order to bring about a great destiny . . . As do you.'

'I have not killed any . . .' Ziftkin started to say. But it was, of course, untrue. He had killed people. In a hurt fury and by accident, not knowing his own capabilities. But his hands were really no cleaner than Iryn Jagga's. The Gault Keep dead still haunted his dreams. He shivered, thinking of the poor woman's blood spilling across the floor, the woman whom *he* had summoned to such a cruel death. What new nightmares was he building for himself here?

'Every act of mine is part of a larger pattern,' Iryn Jagga was saying. 'It all fits together. And one day . . . one day, all will come to fruition.' He downed the last of his glass and stood up. 'In the meantime, you must trust me. You have a good heart, and it pains you to see the hard things in life. But I brought you with me here today so that you could see exactly what you have seen . . . and so that you could understand the proper *significance* of all you have seen.'

Reaching a hand down, he helped Ziftkin up out of his chair. 'I need your support, songster. I need you on *my* side. It may not always be easy, but we fight the good fight, you and I.'

Iryn Jagga looked at Ziftkin as they stood, eye to eye. His handsome face was intent, his eyes clear and bright. 'Are you with me, boy?' He offered his good hand for Ziftkin to take again. 'Are you *with* me?'

Ziftkin hesitated. Part of him wanted nothing more than to be far, far away from all of this. But it was too late. The bitter irony of it was like gall. He had wanted so much to belong somewhere, to be needed somewhere. Well, his desire had come to be, but he felt like a man who had walked down a clear-looking path, step by step, only to discover himself abruptly faced with a precipice – and no way back.

His actions had created what had come to pass this day. He could not undo what he had done. Ziftkin shivered. 'No more will die?' he asked.

Iryn Jagga nodded. 'No more. Unless they bring it upon themselves.'

Still Ziftkin hesitated.

'We are part of a larger whole, songster,' Iryn Jagga said. 'All our actions form a part of a great pattern. Can you not sense it? Our meeting, what you have done. We cannot – we *must not* stop now. Faintheartedness would be fatal.'

Iryn Jagga held out his hand. 'Are you with me, then?'

Ziftkin swallowed. What other path was left him? Only a fool or a hero would stand against Iryn Jagga. And slinking off into the wilderness would do no good. He took Iryn Jagga's proffered hand, feeling the strength of the man's grip.

So be it, then.

But he could not quiet the sick feeling in the pit of his belly.

'Good,' Iryn Jagga said. 'Now come along. We have unfinished business still.'

'With . . . *them*?' Ziftkin said, meaning the crowd they had left back in the hall.

'With *them*, yes. They ought to have arrived at their answer by now.'

'Already?'

'Close enough. Too much time and they will merely confuse each other. Let us go. And *trust* me, boy. There are still hard things left to do. But all . . . *all* I do is in the aid of greater things. Now come.' With that, he strode out of the room, Ziftkin tagging along behind.

The hall was throbbing with noise when they stepped through the door behind the raised platform.

'Any difficulties?' Iryn Jagga asked a guard captain standing at the foot of the short flight of steps leading up to the raised platform.

The man shook his head.

'Good,' Iryn Jagga said, and advanced up the steps.

When they saw him upon the platform, the crowd went quickly silent.

'So . . .' Iryn Jagga said. He leaped down. The bodies of the dead man and woman had been removed, but the floor was still discoloured with their blood. Iryn Jagga walked close to the crowd, stepping carefully round the blood stains. 'Have you arrived at a decision?' he demanded of them.

Silence.

'Where is this . . . Committee, then? Let the members of this Committee step forwards to face me.'

There was a general muttering and shuffling of feet, but nobody stepped forwards.

Iryn Jagga regarded them, unsmiling. 'Do not try my patience too far.'

From his vantage point on the platform, Ziftkin saw three men come forth hesitantly through the crowd. One had grey chin whiskers, and a fringe of fluffy grey hair about his ears; one was big-bellied and ham-thighed, with a flushed and anxious face; the third was tall and thin, with little eyes and a beak of a nose.

'We,' said the man with the grey hair and whiskers, 'are the . . .' his voice was unsteady, 'the Committee.'

'So . . .' Iryn Jagga said. He regarded the men scornfully. 'You finally show yourselves.'

The three men flushed, but none said a word.

'Men of . . . prudence. That is good. I like prudent men. They are so . . . How shall I put it? So willing to *adjust* themselves.'

Iryn Jagga crossed his arms below the golden Jara medallion. 'And so? Have you reached a decision as to my offer?'

The grey-whiskered man nodded. 'We have . . . uhh . . . respected sir.'

There was a little commotion at the back of the crowd, fierce whispers, the soft, fleshy noise of a blow.

Iryn Jagga regarded the proceedings with apparent interest. 'Not a *unanimous* decision, I see.'

'It is, sir. It is indeed unanimous,' the big-bellied man said with quick earnestness.

'Oh, yes?' Iryn Jagga replied.

'Yes, sir,' the grey-haired man said. 'We have decided to accept your most generous offer. We will go back to our farms quietly, if you let us. And we will make no more trouble.'

Iryn Jagga nodded. 'Good. Good. I thought you might.' He turned and addressed the crowd in general. 'The arrangement is agreed upon, then. But I will force it upon nobody. Any who wish to refuse my offer are welcome to.'

'And be killed!' somebody shouted bitterly from the crowd's rear.

Iryn Jagga nodded. 'As is only fair and right.'

There was silence, then.

Iryn Jagga glanced back at Ziftkin, raised an eyebrow as if to

384

say: See? I told you so. Turning back to the crowd, he regarded them with obvious satisfaction. 'The wayward flock returns, then.'

The three men of the Committee were still standing before him, fidgeting anxiously. 'May we . . .' the tall, beaky-nosed one began, 'may we leave this hall, then? Will there be water and food for us?'

'Of course,' Iryn Jagga replied. 'All will be taken care of in due course. There is, however, one last small thing remaining. In order for me to feel . . . confident in your actions, I require each of you who chooses to accept my offer to perform a symbolic action to prove your change of heart.'

'And that is?' the grey-whiskered man asked hesitantly.

Iryn Jagga faced the crowd. 'There are, as you well know, abominations amongst us, creatures that masquerade their humanness.'

'Humanimals . . .' several voices chorused softly.

'Call them what you will,' Iryn Jagga said, 'they are an *abomination*! Until they are removed from the world, all will remain in chaos and disrepair.'

The crowd muttered uncomfortably.

'Silence!' Iryn Jagga cried. 'The time for these creatures to exist is past. They must be *eradicated*! And you . . . *you* will aid in that task.'

They stared at him in confusion.

'Each of you who accepts my offer,' Iryn Jagga went on, 'will be given the opportunity to personally remove one of these *creatures* from the world.'

'Kill the humanimals?' a voice said from the crowd.

'No!' somebody else cried. 'We will not do such a thing.'

'If you wish to live and return to your farms, you will,' Iryn Jagga said. 'Each of you will.'

The crowd erupted into confusion.

'*SILENCE!*' Iryn Jagga shouted.

The crowd stilled.

From out of it, suddenly, stepped a thick-shouldered man. 'I will do it,' he said to Iryn Jagga. 'I have a family, a wife and little daughter. I want my farm back! These *creatures* never did me or mine any favours. The world is better off without them, far as I'm concerned.'

'No!' a child's voice cried in anguish. 'You *can't*!' A small girl tried to struggle out of the crowd, but a woman – obviously her mother – dragged her back and shushed her desperately.

Iryn Jagga looked at the man. 'You spoke without my leave,' he said.

The man paled but stood his ground, rigid.

Iryn Jagga regarded him for long moments, his face stern, then nodded. 'So be it. I am not without feeling. You have a family. I forgive you.'

The man let out a breath, went a little less rigid.

'Your name, fellow?' Iryn Jagga demanded of him.

'Olundar.'

'I will remember you, Olundar.' Iryn Jagga turned to the crowd. 'And the rest of you? Who else will follow in this man's footsteps and accept my generous offer?'

Several men started to come forwards, but a new commotion broke out in the crowd's midst. Voices were raised. A confused scuffle broke out.

Iryn Jagga turned and vaulted back up onto the platform. 'Hear me!' he cried through his hands. '*HEAR ME!*'

The crowd turned.

'You have received my offer. The choice is now yours.'

Silence.

'I will return. When I do, each of you will be given a chance to make his or her decision, young and old, weak and strong.' He looked at the crowd for a long moment, then turned and swept off the platform and out of the hall.

Back in the wood-panelled room, Ziftkin sat down unsteadily. He felt shaken to his guts.

Iryn Jagga leaned back in his chair and smiled, sipping another glass of the amber liquor. 'They will talk themselves into it. I only needed to turn one of them. The first – that Olundar – was the important one. He will turn the rest.'

Ziftkin stared at Iryn Jagga. The flute was back in his hands once again, but he felt no comfort from it.

'Do you think me cruel, boy?'

Ziftkin let out a breath. 'I . . . I don't . . .'

'It was necessary. You must *trust* me. I know what I am doing. I must bind these people to me. There is no surer way.'

'Than making them *kill*? The young and the old alike?'

Iryn Jagga sat up in his chair. 'The *creatures* they will eliminate – you ought to know this by now, boy! – such creatures are no more than a mere tormented mimicry of true life. They are not truly alive and not worthy of your pity – noble sentiment though it may be.'

Ziftkin shifted uneasily. This was all too brutal.

'It is *she* who is at the root of all this, songster. Without her wanton and bloody interference, I would not be forced into doing any of the hard things I must. If you wish to apportion blame, place it upon *her*!'

'Elinor?'

Iryn Jagga nodded. 'Elinor indeed. Bring her to me, songster! Call her forth as you have called the rest. Until *she* is in my hands, all else matters little. There will be no true peace while *she* is still at large.'

'And if I manage to call her in?' Ziftkin said.

Iryn Jagga smiled. 'Then peace will settle on this land and we will begin a new age. You will see! All our hard decisions now will be made clear in the days to come. And all the world will remember what you and I did.' He raised his glass. 'To the glorious future that awaits us, to peace and prosperity and the revival of all that once was.' He drank the contents of the glass in one long gulp.

Ziftkin said nothing. He sank back into his chair and closed his eyes, trying to think of the future rather than the present, of the vision Iryn Jagga was offering him.

But he could find little comfort in it. He kept seeing that poor woman's throat opened up, the hurt look in the bear-creature's eyes, the white faces of frightened children.

'No great destiny is ever achieved easily,' Iryn Jagga said.

Ziftkin kept silent, holding the bone flute on his lap, feeling the warmth of it through his fingers.

'Bring this Elinor to me!' Iryn Jagga said.

Ziftkin nodded. He would do it, if he could. What else was there left him? Let her destruction bring about an end to the violence. He had had enough.

387

He ached, suddenly, for Seshevrell Farm, for his little room atop the barn, for his dead mother, for all that his life had once been . . . and would never be again.

XXXII

Elinor, Gyver and Sky-Flower came down out of the hills early one morning, drawn by the implacable calling that was upon them, and found themselves in all too familiar territory.

Off in the distance westwards, Elinor could see rolling, grassy hills, and, beyond, at the distant edge of her sight, she made out a mass of blocky, square stone towers set against the horizon like great blunt teeth.

Sofala.

Her heart sank. She had hoped there might be some other explanation for what was happening. *Any* other explanation . . .

Gyver, at her side, was hunched down, panting like a dog, clutching handfuls of the rough grass, limbs quivering with the strain of holding himself still.

'Here,' Elinor said to him. She lifted the Fey-bone from around her neck. 'It's your turn.'

He shook his head. 'No. I can hang on, me, for a little longer.'

'Gyver, take it,' Elinor insisted. 'You've been too long without.' She slipped the thong over her head and handed him the Fey-bone. He hesitated, but she forced it into his palm until he took it.

The full, bruising impact of the uncanny calling music hit Elinor with enough force to make her reel. Her feet began to move of their own accord and she struggled to hold herself back.

Gyver held her, anchoring her. She felt the long muscles of her legs quiver. Her scarred leg ached fiercely. For days, now, after she and Sky-Flower had caught up with Gyver, the three of them had been on the move, the calling music that pulled them growing or diminishing, but always there. She and

389

Gyver had shared the Fey-bone turn and turn about, and so lessened the impact of that terrible music a little. There were times when it had dropped to a mere half-sensed whisper, and they had been able to sleep a little. But always it was there, weaker or stronger, drawing them along unremittingly.

And now they were here, sprawled wearily on a hill crest, staring down at the dark silhouette of Sofala in the distance.

Elinor dug her heels into the sod, braced herself. 'I am all right,' she told Gyver, 'you can let me go.'

He regarded her uncertainly.

'I am all right, I tell you!' she snapped, pushing him from her, sharper with him than she had intended. The insidious pull of the music was enough to drive one to fits. She fought it grimly, biting her lip till she tasted the salt-iron of blood, finding her balance for the moment, resisting. Though how long she could hold out remained to be seen.

Gyver sat back on his heels. Uneasily, he turned his gaze on distant Sofala. 'It *iss* the Brotherss, then,' he said, hoarse-voiced. He let out a long, slow breath with the ease the Fey-bone granted.

Elinor nodded. She felt a cold emptiness hit her guts. 'That is where the Settlement must have gone, then. Drawn the same way as us.'

Gyver nodded grimly.

They had passed through the Settlement some days back – how many, she was unsure. The fields had been ragged, deer-ravaged, choked by new weeds. In the houses, they had found tables overturned, clay crockery shattered. The door to one house hung half off its hinges. In another, they had disturbed a gang of rats feasting on the remains from a grain basket. No bodies, no sign of fighting . . .

They had not understood at the time, or had not wanted to understand, rather.

Now she knew. She rested her hand upon the sword that hung at her side. It was not over, then. Iryn Jagga . . . Whatever terrible, uncanny force was at work here, *he* must be at the heart of it somehow; she was convinced of it.

'When we draw closser, uss,' Gyver said, 'you musst let me go on alone.'

'And I,' little Sky-Flower added.

'No!' Elinor panted, struggling against the pull on her to stay still. '*No!*'

'You *musst*!' Gyver insisted. He lifted the Fey-bone, offering it back to her. 'Thiss you musst wear.'

She pushed it away. 'But you—'

'I will be drawn in, me,' Gyver said softly.

'And me, I go with him,' put in Sky-Flower.

'No!' Elinor insisted. She glared at the fur-girl, who was thin and travel-worn. 'This is none of your concern! Why don't you just go *back*?'

But Sky-Flower only shook her head. She looked away from Elinor, combing her fingers through a stretch of fur on her thigh that had become matted with dirt. 'I cannot.'

'You *can*!' Elinor replied angrily. 'The calling isn't for you. You can walk away any time you—' Elinor had dug her hands into the sod for purchase against the pull upon her, forgetting her maimed finger. She felt a sudden flare of pain so sharp it took her breath away.

What with that pain, and the unrelenting, nagging pull upon her, and her frustration at Sky-Flower's blind insistence, she felt like screaming.

'It iss—' the little fur-girl began.

'It is the *dream*,' Elinor finished for her. 'I know.' Elinor sighed. It was an old dispute, this. It would achieve nothing to replay it yet another time.

'I musst go into the place of sstone dark,' Sky-Flower was saying. 'It iss my path, thiss.'

Elinor looked imploringly at Gyver, but he only nodded agreement to what Sky-Flower had said. All along, he had accepted her motivation. She felt like slapping the pair of them, hard. They were so . . .

She did not know what they were. Fatally innocent. Very brave. Both.

'I will go onwardss, me,' Gyver said. 'And Ssky-Flower. And you . . . you will come after and ssave uss.' He held the Fey-bone out towards her again. 'But you musst not let yourrself be drawn in helplesssly.'

Elinor struggled to get a clear breath. 'I can't just let you . . . walk in there defenceless!'

'You musst. You will,' Gyver insisted.

'We have no other choice, uss,' Sky-Flower said. She looked at the stone crest of Sofala in the distance and shivered. 'We will go down to the place of sstone dark, Gyver and me.'

'We will . . . ssurvive,' Gyver said. 'Until you come for uss.'

Elinor stared at the two of them.

'It iss the way the world pusshess,' Sky-Flower said softly. 'It iss the *way*.'

Elinor swallowed. She felt sick at the thought of Gyver and little Sky-Flower in Sofala. It was crazy, them doing this. 'You don't understand,' she said. 'You don't know what sort of place Sofala is.'

Gyver shivered: 'We will find out, uss.'

'Gyver,' she said, looking into his face. But the words failed her. He was so . . . open. Always had been. She could see how weary he was, could see the fear in him writ clear in his eyes, as she could see it in Sky-Flower's. But he would do what he said. Little Sky-Flower would.

She reached for him, tears in her own eyes, angry and shaking and filled with fear, hating her own helplessness.

'You will ssave me,' he said softly. 'Little Ssky-Flower and me. You and your sshining blade.'

'Yes,' she returned. But as she gazed past his shoulder at the dark, angular outline of the city in the distance, her heart misgave her.

Gyver kissed her, a soft, passionless brushing of his lips across hers. Then he let her go, and, without a word, handed the Fey-bone back.

Three together, they started downwards towards Sofala.

XXXIII

It was dark and hot, and the air was so thick with stink it was hard to breathe comfortably. Scrunch lay on his side, panting. He hurt. The fur on his back and sides was crusted with dried blood. His tongue was swollen and dry as a stone.

Around and about him, the others lay in like ways.

He heard a soft whimper and opened his eyes. To his surprise, he saw Grub, Rigga's youngest, struggling across the stone floor. The poor little fellow could hardly stand. His tongue hung out of his mouth slackly, and his eyes were bright and staring.

'Grub!' Scrunch heard Rigga call hoarsely.

But Grub kept struggling on and did not respond.

Rigga tried to get up to fetch him, but was too weak. 'Grub! *Grub!*' she cried hysterically.

Scrunch roused himself. Poor Rigga was entirely heart-broken. Only three of her five pups were with her – two now, without Grub.

'Grub!' she moaned.

Scrunch got stiffly to his feet. He grunted, feeling a stab of sharp pain as the scabs along his side ripped open. He did not know how far he could manage to move . . .

But little Grub, it turned out, straggled over towards him.

'You must go back to your mother,' Scrunch told him as he drew near. 'Don't you hear her calling you?'

Grub made no reply, merely struggled onwards, his small face set. Over the prostrate form of a hyphon he clambered, panting and shaking, and tumbled heavily to the floor.

'Grub!' Rigga cried.

Grub got shakily to his feet and continued on.

'Go back,' Scrunch said.

But Grub came on till he was only a few paces away. There,

he sat down with a tired thump and said, 'Talk to them. Why don't you talk to them?'

'Talk to who?' Scrunch said.

'To the human folk! You know human folk. You can talk to them. Tell them we didn't *do* anything. Tell them we'll be good. Tell them . . .'

Scrunch felt his inside contract with mingled rage and pity. *Talk to them*.

They had been here, in this dark stone hole, for none of them knew how long. After the first flood of bodies down the stairs, there had been an intermittent flow, then a trickle. It seemed like a long time now since any had come in. The uncanny music was still there, dropping away at times almost to nothing, then swelling into torment. But the terrible pull of it was gone. It was like a swirling current all around them, dizzying . . .

No water, no food had they received, and no contact with anything or anybody outside here.

'They're going to leave us here to die,' somebody said in a hoarse voice.

Scrunch shivered. It was a thought he had had himself. Most of the humanimal population as they knew it was crammed into this stone prison. He did not understand what was happening, how they had been brought here. But he knew, as did they all, that it boded nothing but ill for them. They were in Sofala – a place whose very name chilled one's blood.

'Please,' little Grub said. '*Talk* to them.'

Scrunch did not know how to respond. They had cried out, at the beginning, shouting through the thick-planked door at the top of the stairs. All to no avail.

'There's nobody to talk to,' he said to Grub. 'And they wouldn't listen anyway.'

'Try . . .' Grub said in his little hoarse voice. '*Try!*'

'Go back to your mother,' Scrunch replied softly.

'You *know* human folk,' Grub insisted. 'You can talk to them. Why won't you do it?'

'Grub!' Rigga called out. She had dragged herself a little ways over, but was torn now between her other two pups, who had stayed as they were, and Grub.

'Go back to your mother,' Scrunch said again.

'Why won't you try?' Grub insisted. 'Why is nobody *trying*?'

Scrunch looked around. It was a broad, low-ceilinged stone cellar they were trapped in. The place was crammed with bodies, panting and moaning, It was too much for some, this: the uncanny, irresistible compulsion that had brought them here, this terrible, dank stone prison, the misery of their discomforts and hurts. Scrunch felt his own, the scabbed cuts and bruises, his cracked tongue, empty belly . . .

'We tried,' he said softly to Grub.

'Then try *again*,' Grub returned.

Scrunch blinked.

'*Try!*'

Perhaps his mind had been loosened by all that had occurred, but it seemed to Scrunch suddenly as if little Grub were a torch burning brightly, a small but steady flame that lit his own insides somehow with faint warmth.

He opened his mouth, closed it, turned to the stone steps leading upwards to the door . . .

And stared in astonishment.

The door creaked open slowly. A human head appeared round it.

There was an uneasy flutter and stir amongst the humanimals.

The man – for man it was – slipped past the door and stood at the top of the stairs. In his hand he carried a length of pale bone.

Scrunch knew him. It was the flute player, the man who had called them all here, for what fell purpose he alone knew.

Furred and feathered folk dragged themselves desperately away from the stairs.

Scrunch could feel little Grub's eyes upon him. He forced himself stiffly forwards till he was standing at the foot of the steps. 'Man,' he called up, 'why have you brought us here? What have we done to you and yours that you treat us so?'

The man above only stared at him, an unmoving figure outlined by the brightness that flowed in through the half-opened door.

'Talk to me, Man,' Scrunch said. 'What do you wish of us?'

He remembered the moment of unexpected contact there had

been between this man and him, and the sense of inexplicable connection, the night he had entered into Sofala, and he felt a little flare of hope. In league with the dark Brothers this man might be, but he was not of them. He smelled of . . . *betweenness* in a way Scrunch had never perceived in a man before.

The eyes in the man's pale face were large and dark. He held the bone flute in both hands, cradled to his breast, as if it were as precious to him as a babe to its mother.

'What have we done that you thrust us into this terrible dark place?' Scrunch asked him, taking a step up the stairs. '*Talk* to me, Man!'

But the man only stared, at Scrunch, at the mass of huddled bodies that lay thickly in the stone gloom. Then he turned and fled, slamming the door solidly shut behind him.

Humanimal voices called out, in supplication, in anger. One of the humanimal-dogs scrabbled up the steps and flung himself at the shut door, again and again, weeping and wailing. Scrunch staggered back, away from the steps.

Little Grub lay in a heap, sobbing.

Scrunch went over and lay down next to him. Nodding reassurance at Rigga, he gathered Grub close in the crook of his forearm. He could feel Grub's small ribs heave with each sob. He searched for some words of comfort . . . anything.

But there was no comfort.

There was only dark stone walls, the tight-shut door, thick air . . . and the numb throb of a dull, helpless fury in his guts.

XXXIV

Ziftkin sat on the edge of his eider-down bed in the chill greyness of pre-dawn, staring at the wall of his opulent room. There was a silver flagon of tart wine and a bowl of cheese placed on a little table near the bedside by one of the servants. He took a sip of the wine, sighed. His back ached, his head did. His eyes were dry and stinging. He had been up the entire night, trying to call *her* in with the flute – without success. Two last non-human stragglers had been all he had managed to summon up. He rubbed his sore eyes, ran a hand along the warm smoothness of the flute where it lay on the bed by his side, and shivered.

Just before dawn, he had left his perch upon Sofala's wall and crept down through the city's bowels to the dungeon where the in-called humanimals were imprisoned. A foolish thing to do, perhaps, but he had been drawn by a sudden irresistible impulse to look upon the creatures he had summoned. Now, he could not shake the vision of it from his mind: the poor, huddled animal shapes in that stinking subterranean place. And he had seen the bear-creature again – the one he had locked gazes with as it entered Sofala. He was sure it was the same one. 'What have we done to you and yours that you treat us so?' it had demanded of him. 'Talk to me, Man. What have we done? *Talk* to me!'

Ziftkin heard Iryn Jagga's voice in his mind: 'Do not be fooled, boy. They are an unholy mixture, and not worthy of your pity, a forcing together of that which should never have been joined in union, and so tormented by their unnatural state, that the bloody beast in them drives them to acts of violent madness!'

Ziftkin sighed. He had seen the evidence of such bloody humanimal madness with his own eyes. But despite such hard facts, he could not, somehow, quite bring himself to embrace Iryn Jagga's convictions. He could not *feel* the 'abomination' in them.

Seeing the poor misused bear-creature, he had felt only instinctive sympathy and pity.

And guilt.

Faced with the bear's entreaties, he had bolted, unable to meet the creature's sad eyes, unable to bear the blinding stink of the place, unable to face what he had done.

Ziftkin slumped backwards onto the softness of his eider-down-covered bed. What he had done was necessary, he told himself. A hard task but a needed one.

But he wished he had never met Iryn Jagga. He wished he could undo everything that had happened since he had left Seshevrell Farm . . .

He rolled over and put his arms over his head. He did not want to think about it any more. He was too weary, and the world too complicated. He pulled the eider-down blanket over him, fully dressed still. He just wished for sleep to take him, sleep that would knit up his ravelled nerves, sleep that would let him sink blessedly away from the nagging uncertainties he could not silence.

Krakk!

Ziftkin twisted about.

'Come!' Iryn Jagga said, flinging the door back and striding into the room. 'And be quick!'

Ziftkin levered himself groggily up. He rubbed his eyes, exhausted and irritated. 'Leave me *be*!' he grumbled.

But, 'Up!' Iryn Jagga cried, and ripped the eider-down blanket away from him. 'Come *along*!'

Ziftkin glared at him. 'I've been on the wall all night, doing *your* bidding. What's the rush, now?'

Iryn Jagga smiled. 'You'll see. Now come along!'

Down through the building Iryn Jagga strode, with the inevitable guards following along, and then out across a large courtyard. Ziftkin scrambled to keep up, clutching his flute awkwardly.

Something went *tling tlang* and Ziftkin turned quickly to

398

look. The pewter dawn-light made everything dim and hard to see, but he could make out a group of men struggling to pull some large contrivance out through a narrow gateway at the courtyard's far end.

'What're they doing?' he asked Iryn Jagga.

'Do not concern yourself with it,' Iryn Jagga replied.

But Ziftkin could not help but feel a little stab of curiosity. Whatever object it was the men were wrestling with, it did not resemble anything he had ever seen. Peering through the uncertain light, he made out spoked wheels, some kind of narrow carriage, and . . . he was not sure quite what it was. A cylinder, it seemed, long as a man was tall, but slimmer than any man. Of cast bronze. Or so he guessed, for the thing had the dull gleam of bronze, and it was clearly very heavy, for the men struggled and grunted, trying to wheel it through the gateway.

Ziftkin looked closer and saw that the cylinder was cast in the image of a dragon, mouth open and gaping in a roar, stubby legs forming a clutch into which the wheeled carriage fit.

'What *is* it?' Ziftkin pressed Iryn Jagga.

'A new invention,' Iryn Jagga said. 'Or, rather, a revival of some of the old learning.' He reached a hand and pulled Ziftkin sharply onwards. 'Nothing to concern you, songster. Now come along.'

'Where are you taking me?'

'You will see. Come *on*!'

Ziftkin was grown tired of Iryn Jagga constantly dragging him here and there, never telling him what it was he was being taken to. But, as he had learned, there was no arguing with the man.

He followed after.

Inside the building once again, they descended a flight of curving steps, the guards still accompanying them, and emerged into a long subterranean hallway. Torches flickered from iron sconces set in the walls. At the far end, a group of men stood waiting, mostly composed of more sombrely clad armed and armoured guards. But amongst them there stood also a number of men Ziftkin recognized from the night of the gala. It was easy to recognize such men; their clothing, their arms, their stance, all were far more elegant than the aspect of the more lowly guardsmen.

They bowed to Iryn Jagga and nodded to Ziftkin, those elegant men, but stayed silent. Despite the early hour, there was an alertness, a suppressed eagerness about the waiting group that made Ziftkin pause.

And then he saw that one amongst them was different from the rest, raggedly clothed. It was one of the . . . Ziftkin was not sure how to call them. One of the followers of Elinor White-blade that he had called in along with the humanimals.

'Good,' Iryn Jagga said, looking at the ragged man. 'They have brought you quickly.'

The man bowed and nodded, wringing his hands nervously. 'What is it you wish of me . . . great sir?'

'You will see,' Iryn Jagga responded. 'I told you I would remember you, and I have. Now come.' With that, he snatched the nearest torch from its wall bracket and strode off round the corner and further down the hallway. The whole party, guardsmen, notability, Ziftkin and all, followed after. The ragged man, Ziftkin noticed, had an escort of six guards who stayed tight close to him.

They did not go far before Iryn Jagga stopped at a barred and guarded door. At a motion from him, the guards lifted the locking bar and flung the door open. Iryn Jagga swept through, torch in hand, the rest of the company following.

In the waver of the torchlight, Ziftkin saw that their party stood upon a narrow gallery. Below them was a large, high-ceilinged room with windowless stone walls, a flagstone floor, bare of any furniture. And huddled against the far corner of that room . . .

Ziftkin gasped.

It was a human form. No . . . two human forms, one smaller than the other. But for all the humanness of their limbs, they were covered in thick, dark fur like a beast's. They sat, arms about each other, staring with big eyes that caught the flicker of the torchlight like those of a cat.

Ziftkin had never seen – never imagined – any such creatures as these.

During the long days and nights of his calling-in, he had *felt* those he summoned through the flute as they drew nigh. But they had been like bobbing lights in the dark to him. Except for that one night when he had encountered the bear-creature, when the humanimals had come in such a sudden flood that he had been forced to shepherd them through the city gate, he had seldom actually seen in the flesh any of those he summoned – certainly not these two . . . Though it might, perhaps, have been them that he had *felt* drawing in this night past.

'What *are* they?' he asked of Iryn Jagga.

'I do not know,' Iryn Jagga replied. He beckoned to the ragged man who had been one of Elinor's followers. 'You! Olundar, is it?'

The man nodded eagerly. 'Yes, great sir.'

'I am wondering, Olundar, if you might be able to enlighten us concerning these . . . creatures.'

Olundar looked at the two furred beings huddled against the wall below.

'Well?' Iryn Jagga said.

'That one, I know.' Olundar pointed to the larger of the two. 'The other . . .' He shrugged. 'I've never seen it before.'

'And the one you know?'

'He is called Gyver. He was . . . is Elinor's . . . lover.'

Iryn Jagga's eyebrows lifted. 'Really?' He stared at the fur-man. 'You are sure of this, Olundar?'

'Oh yes, great sir. Everybody knew of it. Elinor and he . . . they have been lovers ever since she . . .' Olundar stopped, bit his lip, went on. 'Ever since she began her struggle against you and yours, great sir.'

'How . . . interesting,' Iryn Jagga said softly. 'And the other one?'

'I don't know, great sir. I thought . . . I never knew if this Gyver were a . . . a sort of freak or if he came from a group of creatures the same as he. There must be others like him, then. But I swear to you I have never seen any but him before.'

Iryn Jagga gazed down upon the two huddled fur-people and smiled a self-satisfied smile, like a cat eyeing a trapped sparrow. 'Songster,' he said, 'you called these two in last night. Play them for me now. Show me what command you have over them.'

Ziftkin hesitated. The two fur-people had neither moved nor spoken. They sat pressed against the wall with arms tight about each other, like twin statues save for their glistening eyes. He did not know whether or not they could follow the conversation. Were they human inside? If they were, indeed, the two he had called in last night, they had felt to him no different from the many humanimals who had passed in. But that might have been his failing, for he had been so very weary.

'Well, *do* something!' Iryn Jagga snapped impatiently. 'I haven't got all morning.'

Ziftkin shot him a look of irritation.

'Don't mess me about, songster,' Iryn Jagga snapped. 'This is *important*! I want—'

A sudden commotion interrupted him. From the door a man came running. 'She's here!' he panted. 'She's come to the wall.'

'*She?*' Iryn Jagga said.

The man nodded excitedly. 'Elinor Whiteblade!'

'Come!' Iryn Jagga cried. 'To the wall!' He pointed at Olundar. 'Send him back.' Then he swept aside those before him and strode for the door. 'Bring that creature along,' he called back, gesturing at the bigger of the two huddled fur-people. 'But make sure it's not in any shape to cause trouble. And you, songster, hurry *up*!'

And then he was gone, out the door and away down the hall.

Ziftkin was not certain what he had expected to see. An older woman, certainly. A man-faced woman with a dark fury in her eyes and wild hair. But what fronted him was nothing of the sort.

She stood half a bowshot off from the wall. They were high here upon the wall's crest, but he could still see her clearly enough to tell that she was young, hardly very much older than himself, it seemed. And she was comely, with shoulder-length dark hair and large blue eyes. She wore loose-fitting, nondescript forest clothes, worn and stained by hard travel. The sword at her side, in its crimson scabbard, seemed too big for her.

'Do not let yourself be fooled by appearances,' Iryn Jagga said in Ziftkin's ear. 'She is more than she seems to be.'

Ziftkin blinked.

'Be warned!' Iryn Jagga went on. 'She is an enemy both powerful and subtle. And utterly ruthless.' He lifted his maimed hand before Ziftkin's face. 'Look! It was *she* who did this.'

Ziftkin stared at Elinor. He did not know what to think. She did not look capable of doing any of the terrible things Iryn Jagga claimed for her.

'Play her to me,' Iryn Jagga commanded.

Ziftkin turned.

The leader of the Ancient Brotherhood was tense as a hound, his fists and jaw clenched. 'Call her in, songster!'

Ziftkin lifted the flute to his lips and blew a few enticing notes, a little uncertain as to exactly how to do this.

Flute in hand, he tried to focus on Elinor. His fingers danced, and a quick flurry of notes followed. A little involuntary shudder went through him. He opened himself, extended himself, sharpened himself, and *felt* her . . .

He was ready, once he had got the sense of her, to try to net her with his music the way he had the rest, weaving a calling, falling melody that drew them as water was drawn down a steep slope, using their own rhythms to form the melody, their own strengths to keep it strong.

He *felt* after her, waiting for the moment when he had her.

But as his awareness of her deepened, he could *feel* a . . . a depth to her the like of which he had never before experienced. It was as if she were a . . . a sort of channel through which invisible currents swirled. He did not understand. She felt larger than she ought to.

The calling-tune Ziftkin had begun lapsed. The flute slipped from his lips. Elinor stood, looking up at him, and, for a long moment, despite the distance, their eyes locked. He could see her quiver, *feel* the echo of that quivering in his own limbs. He felt as if he had lifted a rock, expecting to find some loathsome grub, and, instead, had found . . . he did not know quite what.

A sharp jab in his ribs brought him up short.

'Play, songster. Play!' Iryn Jagga commanded. 'What is wrong with you? Play before she has a chance to escape!'

Ziftkin hesitated.

Iryn Jagga's dark eyes were lit with anger. 'I *warned* you! Do *not* let her appearance fool you. This is the *enemy*. This is the one who will bring us all down if we do not stand against her. In her poisonous spite, she will destroy everything I and mine have fought so long and so hard for, all the future we have striven to create, the future that you, too, shall be a part of.' Iryn Jagga reached a hand to Ziftkin's shoulder and shook him. 'She will *destroy* you, boy, if you do not wake up! She will suck you into her web, chew you up, then spit out the pieces!'

Ziftkin swallowed.

'Call her, songster. Or you will ruin *everything*!' Iryn Jagga shook Ziftkin, rattling his teeth: 'Call her!'

But Ziftkin still stood, shaken and uncertain, staring at Elinor in the distance.

Iryn Jagga shook his mutilated hand in Ziftkin's face. 'Remember what I have told you! She sliced the fingers from my hand one at a time with that cursed bright blade of hers, laughing while she did so. Fair she may seem to you. But she is foul underneath that seeming. Foul and most deadly dangerous.'

Iryn Jagga took Ziftkin by the shoulders and brought him close, so that their two faces were nearly pressed together. 'Call her up!' he ordered in a hissing whisper. 'Call her here to me with that instrument of yours. Or do you wish to plunge the world into bloody chaos? Call her up to me. Do it. Now! *Do it!*'

Haltingly, Ziftkin turned, lifted the flute to his lips once again and blew a long, beckoning note. He could *feel* Elinor more clearly now, sense the strange swirling of force that was all about her, within and without her. Iryn Jagga must be right. Surely this was no ordinary, innocent young woman.

She stood there, one hand upon the glinting hilt of her sword, staring at him. He closed his eyes, shivering, and played, the notes flying into a complex melody, calling, calling, enticing her forwards, one step, another, pulling her

404

into a slow come-hither dance that would bring her, eventually, into Iryn Jagga's hands.

It was the only way. This woman was dangerous. Iryn Jagga had said it, and he could *feel* the danger in her now. For she was like a moving storm, a focus of power, a bottleneck through which events must pass . . .

He played her, trying to feel his way down to the heart of her and summon her as he had the humanimals and the folk she had drawn into the wilderness with her, played her as he might play the birds or the clouds or the very wind itself, played her forwards, pulling her like a stream downhill . . .

But she did not come.

Opening his eyes, Ziftkin saw her standing where she was, one hand still upon the hilt of her sword, the other clutching something that hung on a cord from about her neck, staring at him.

'What is *wrong*?' Iryn Jagga demanded. 'Why have you stopped playing? Why does she not come?'

Ziftkin shook his head. 'I don't know. I can't . . . reach her somehow.' He opened his mouth, closed it again. He felt a rush of dizziness, as if the world had suddenly side-shifted under his feet.

'Fool!' Iryn Jagga hissed. 'Useless, tootling *fool* . . .'

XXXV

Elinor stared up at the crest of the Sofala wall, shivering.

She had been gazing at the figures there, only moments before, trying to recognize whom she might.

And then . . .

She had been plunged deep into the same calling, falling melody that had haunted her, waking and sleeping, all the long journey here. This close, she had felt the incredibly powerful, insidious tug of it like a great tidal current, and had gripped the Fey-bone desperately, resisting. Even with that anchor, though, she had felt her feet move – one, two, three steps before she could stop them.

But the Fey-bone had held her safe and now there was silence.

Elinor stared up at the figures clustered along the wall's parapet. There was no mistaking Iryn Jagga, tall and darkly handsome and arrogant, even in his posture. But next to him stood a younger man, unarmoured and without the usual fighting helm the Brothers wore, his hair long and dark and frazzled. His face was pale, with big light eyes. He held something in his hand, but it was no weapon – a slim length of some ochre stuff, like a wand of wood or bone. She could see him staring at her, and the small hairs on the back of her neck prickled.

It was a flute he held, she realized. He it was who had been making the uncanny calling music . . . So that was the explanation of what had emptied the Settlement and drawn her and Gyver here.

Elinor stared at him, shivering, trying to see him more closely. But she could make out only what she had already: a young man dressed in the Brothers' sombre clothing, helmless and unarmed, pale-faced, with big eyes.

No ordinary man could accomplish such uncanny things as he had. Elinor felt her guts twist. Why had he called them into Iryn Jagga's ungentle hands? She did not understand where such a man had come from, or by what process he had become enemy to her and hers – complete strangers to him.

She waited uneasily for him to lift the flute to his lips again. It had been so completely powerful, that playing of his, that she was not sure she could resist another such attack, even with the Fey-bone to aid her.

But he made no such move, merely stood there, staring.

It was Iryn Jagga who moved, coming to stand at the very brink of the wall's parapet. 'Come closer, woman,' he called down to her.

Elinor was not about to do any such thing. The area around her was clear; she had made sure of that. Those she faced were all safely cooped up behind their walls, and there would be no sudden ambushing of her from behind. She was safe enough here, so long as she stayed at least half a good bowshot away from the wall – using her blade, she could easily deflect any arrow shot at her from such a distance.

So she stood, one hand on her sword's hilt, looking up at Iryn Jagga where he stood upon the wall-top. Just looking at the man made her pulse beat with balked fury. Why could he not leave well enough alone? Why must he always be twisting the world, twisting lives and hopes and dreams to his own dark ends?

And where was Gyver? The thought of him in Iryn Jagga's ungentle hands made her belly tight. She felt a trickle of nervous sweat down her ribs. There had to be some way to get Gyver out of there. *Had* to be.

'Come closer, I say,' Iryn Jagga called from his perch.

Elinor stayed where she was, silent.

'Come to me, woman,' Iryn Jagga called. 'I wish only to talk with you. That was all I ever wanted. It is why I had you and yours called to me. Talk to me. You will be safe. Only come a little closer, so we do not have to shout so.'

Elinor laughed. 'I am quite content where I am,' she called.

'Do not bait me, woman!' Iryn Jagga returned.

Elinor said nothing.

407

Iryn Jagga looked at her, his hands upon his hips. Then he shook his head and called, 'It is over, woman. *Over.*'

Elinor said nothing.

'I have all your followers in my hands. You have no support. What can you do, you, a lone woman?'

By way of reply, Elinor drew the sword, lifting the bright blade so that it shone in the early morning sunlight. She felt the thrill of the sword go through her bones. 'There is still much I can do!' she cried to him. 'Things are *not* over.'

The little throng on the wall's top surged forwards and then back as she drew the white blade. She heard them muttering in consternation amongst themselves and felt her heart leap with the satisfaction of causing them such discomfort.

But Iryn Jagga merely glared at her. 'Give the blade up to me, woman, and I shall let you go free.'

Elinor laughed.

'Give the blade up to me,' he repeated.

With a little flashing flourish, Elinor sheathed the sword and stood there, arms crossed across her breast. It was all the answer she would give him.

Iryn Jagga looked at her for a long moment, then made a peremptory gesture behind him. Several men came up through the group upon the wall. It took Elinor a little time to realize what was happening.

It was Gyver they brought forth. His head lolled and he stumbled groggily. His arms were cinched tightly behind his back in a manner that must have been acutely painful. As far as she could see, though, he did not appear to have taken any fatal harm.

Elinor breathed a long sigh of thankful relief that he was still alive and unmaimed. But her heart was thumping in earnest now. It was one thing to know he had been taken, and quite another to actually see him in Iryn Jagga's hold.

'Give the white blade up to me, woman,' Iryn Jagga shouted, 'and I will give you your freedom.' He lifted a hand and gestured towards Gyver. 'And the freedom of this . . . creature you choose to share your wilderness bed with.'

Elinor swallowed.

'He is *mine*!' Iryn Jagga called. 'To do with as I wish. Do you remember the deep chambers, woman? Do you remember the time you spent there?'

Elinor shuddered, remembering only too well. The 'deep chambers' Iryn Jagga called them, but they were torture chambers, dank and evil-smelling and reeking with the pain and the misery of those poor souls imprisoned there.

'It will be the deep chambers for him,' Iryn Jagga was saying. 'And a long, slow, *painful* stay for him. Think on it, woman. *Think on it!* And it will be *your* fault if he suffers. For he need *not*! Only render up the blade to me and the two of you shall go free. You may walk away together, leave our lands forever, live however you like in the far-away wild lands. It matters not to me. Only give up the blade. The choice is yours!'

Elinor stared at Gyver, whose head still lolled. She felt sick at the grim possibilities her mind painted.

'The choice is *yours*!' Iryn Jagga repeated. 'I give you my word, woman – and the word of Iryn Jagga is no small thing – that neither you nor this . . . this creature will be harmed. Nor will any of your misguided followers. They have already been forgiven their trespasses. They will be returned to their farms and resume their former lives. Only give up the blade to me and all will be well.'

Despite everything, Elinor could feel herself tempted by the seductive possibility of what Iryn Jagga offered. Perhaps it was truth – or near enough to truth – he was speaking. Perhaps those of the Settlement had reached a kind of peace with the Brothers. She imagined walking off with Gyver, free . . .

She felt the weight of the blade in its sheath at her hip. The thing was curse as much as gift. She had done too many terrible things with it. And since it had come to her, her life had been painfully complex, and she knew not what it was that guided her: herself, or the blade, or some other, far more obscure something. Life would be so much more simple if she could just let the sword go, just walk off, with Gyver, as Iryn Jagga suggested, and turn her back on this whole complicated, painful episode of her life. Just walk away and begin afresh. A new life . . .

A new life. Oh, yes.

But she knew better. Iryn Jagga was no more trustworthy

than Shosha Bronze-hand, the leader of the painted men who had invaded Gyver's homeland. She remembered the moment she had stood, about to take Shosha's outstretched hand, having accepted his reassurances. Her amputated finger throbbed, a painful reminder of what had come of that moment of misplaced trust . . .

Iryn Jagga was another such. Ruthlessly self-serving, concerned only with the power he might wield over others. She would believe nothing such a man said.

And there were the humanimals to consider, as well as the human folk. And little Sky-Flower somewhere in Sofala as well . . .

Elinor sighed. Much as a part of her might like to, there was no taking of the easy path out of here. And Iryn Jagga was not about to relinquish Gyver so easily. Nor the rest. Nor was he likely to relinquish *her*.

But looking up at Gyver, helpless in the Brothers' hands, she did not know what she might do. A terrible feeling of hopelessness filled her. She would not – could not – accept Iryn Jagga's offer. Which meant that poor Gyver . . . It did not bear thinking on. How could she doom him to such an agonizing fate?

What other option did she have?

She felt sick with it.

'Give up the blade to me,' Iryn Jagga repeated, 'and all will be well. None will come to harm.'

Elinor wished she could believe him. She remembered the persuasive power of him; even now, at this distance, she could hear the calm, fatherly assurance in his voice. If only . . .

'Give it up!' he urged her.

At that moment, she saw Gyver shift.

It was just a little movement, a twisting of the shoulders, a shaking of the head, but it made her heart beat to see it.

'Gyver!' she cried impetuously.

He lifted his head.

'Here!' she called.

He tried to shake himself free of the guards holding him, but to no avail. They began to haul him backwards, away from the wall's brink.

Iryn Jagga motioned them to stop. 'He is still intact,' he

called down to Elinor. 'As you can plainly see.' With a gesture, he commanded Gyver's guards to bring the fur-man back towards the wall's brink. 'But his safety lies now entirely in *your* hands.' Iryn Jagga stepped forwards so that he stood next to Gyver. 'You can save him any . . . discomfort. Only give up the blade to me—'

'No!' Gyver shouted. 'Do not, Elinor. *Do not!*'

Iryn Jagga motioned, and one of the guards struck Gyver across the face, rocking his head painfully.

Elinor took a step forwards, unthinkingly.

'Good!' Iryn Jagga called to her. 'Come here with it. Bring it to me. I have given you my word, woman. Give it up to me and all will be well!'

'No!' Gyver called again, his voice a hoarse shout.

'Be quiet, *animal*!' Iryn Jagga snapped.

Gyver ignored him. 'Do not ssurrender it, your blade!' he called down to Elinor. 'He iss not to be trusstted, thiss dark man!'

Iryn Jagga motioned angrily. 'I told you to shut your mouth!'

Once again, one of the guards struck Gyver, who struggled now in their hold. With a sudden lurch, he managed to get partially free from one of them. Twisting about, he sank his sharp teeth into the nearest guard's neck, above the armoured cuirass. The man shrieked. Gyver flung himself backwards, wrenching at the hands that tried to grip him.

For a moment, he stumbled free.

There was a faint *clakk* and Elinor saw a crossbow bolt suddenly appear in Gyver's thigh – like a conjuring trick: only fur, then a thin black bolt protruding suddenly.

Gyver crumpled over, groaning.

Iryn Jagga barked a quick order and the fur-man was swept away out of sight on the inner side of the wall.

'Do you see what happens when you ignore what I ask?' Iryn Jagga called to her irately. 'It was *your* fault he was hurt so. Only do as I ask and he will be treated well, his wound carefully cleaned and oiled and bound with fresh linen. It is still not too late. Do not damn him to a painful fate!'

Elinor stood, shaking, silent. There was nothing she could bring herself to say.

411

Iryn Jagga shook his head. 'Do not be *cruel* to him, woman.'

Elinor bit her lip.

'So be it,' Iryn Jagga said. 'You condemn him to a slow agony, then. But *I* am merciful, even if *you* are not. I shall give you till this time tomorrow to repent of your harshness. If you persist, then, in acting thus cruelly . . . then your animal paramour here shall die, but it shall be slow, woman, a slow, hard death indeed. And all *your* fault!'

With that Iryn Jagga turned and strode away, sweeping the rest of the company with him as if they were all attached to him by strings. Only the flute player lingered, for a long moment, to stare down at her.

Then they were all gone and she was left alone on the grassy slope, her heart quivering.

XXXVI

Elinor prowled about the vine-cloaked, high stone wall all that day. She met not a living soul, and found no way into Sofala. As the day slowly died, she felt progressively more and more desperate, trying not to dwell on what awful things might be happening to poor Gyver – Iryn Jagga's assurances of a day's grace or not.

Iryn Jagga . . . The man was a stone-hearted lunatic! The very thought of him made her feel sick with impotent fury.

By evening, she was standing close upon one section of the impenetrable wall, staring up at it bitterly in the dimming light, her belly knotted with balked fury and desperate worry.

Along her left side, the wall reared up like a cliff choked with trailing ivy. She turned from it, having come from that direction, and headed off. Something in the ivy caught her eye, though, and she stopped. She pulled at the trailing greenery with one hand, and it shifted like a curtain. Bending closer, she saw a small doorway, the lintel hardly high enough for head-room. She tried the handle, her heart beating hard, imagining herself let loose in Sofala, she and her blade . . .

But the door gave not at all. She pushed against it with her shoulder, kicked at it, even tried a couple of hacks with the sword, but all to no account. The old wood was solid as so much iron.

She stood panting, fuming with frustration, helpless. Then, having no other option, she turned from the useless door and continued morosely on her way.

And heard, from behind her, the sudden soft sound of booted feet on the grass. No bluster, no bravado, and no warning beyond that soft sound of feet . . . and they were sprinting at her from all sides out of the gathering dark.

She had a single, frozen instant to see them, a thin, dark wave of armoured men and glimmering iron, an instant to draw the sword, take stance . . .

And then they crashed upon her and she was caught up in the whirl and cut and thrust of it, ducking and parrying desperately, trying to be everywhere at once, trying to keep them from cornering her and using the force of their numbers to bring her down.

Men screamed and cursed. The white blade sang against iron. All the impotent fury in her came surging out, and, in the panting, bloody confusion, the sword moved in her hold almost as if it had a life of its own.

She cut one man down at the knees, leaving him screaming, and came up ready for the next, who leaped his fallen comrade and came at her with a heavy, two-handed broadsword. Her own weapon came up and parried his attack in a quick *klang* and *shrassp* of blade against blade. Before he could recover his balance for a second stroke, the white blade had taken him through the neck, a lightning thrust that left him gasping and clutching at his sliced throat, sword forgotten, blood welling through his fingers, his face frozen in sudden horror to feel his own death come upon him so utterly quick.

Elinor took the next, the sword moving in a deadly blur, and the next after, and the one after that, till her attackers broke apart in terror and fled.

She chased after, cutting them down as they ran, for she was filled with a blood-lust, a black desire to deal death and more death, to carve her way through these men, through the whole of the dark Brotherhood, and so come at last to Iryn Jagga.

And make him pay.

Every man she emptied of life was one step closer to Iryn Jagga, every one a small revenge.

She took as many as she could.

Eventually, Elinor found herself alone in the dark. She stood, trying to calm her own panting breath and to listen. She heard a man call softly off in the distance. From somewhere inside the wall came muffled calls. But there was nothing close to her.

Overhead, the sky was spangled with stars. A whirl of cloud passed by, blown by a wind too high to touch the grass where she stood. Starlight and cloud-shadow danced across the turfed slope, the Sofala wall, the dim bulk of the city itself.

Elinor threw back her head and howled.

She had not intended to do anything of the sort. But the starlight, the free-funnelling cloud, the fact of herself alone here, blood-spattered and panting, on the outside of the wall . . . She felt herself suddenly to be some sort of fell, wild creature.

Again she howled, a wild challenge, whirling the bright, bloody blade of the sword above her head so that it caught the starshine and formed a whirring, pale oval of radiance about her. She felt her heart beating hard, her jaw, her guts clenched. It was like a kind of madness come upon her. Only let them leave the protection of their wall and come at her . . . and she would destroy them! Destroy them all!

She howled once more, triumphantly.

Faint sounds came from behind the wall, men calling to each other in consternation.

She felt a kind of fire sloosh through her veins. Throwing back her head, she laughed and howled and shrieked till her throat was raw and her lungs ached.

In Sofala, now, there was only silence.

XXXVII

'I will not be held penned up in my own city like this!' Iryn Jagga shouted. 'Do you hear me? Not by a lone woman. I will *not*!'

Ziftkin, standing in the doorway, stayed quiet. He had never seen Iryn Jagga quite like this before. The man was actually dishevelled-looking, his hair a bit awry, his eyes flashing darkly.

Three sombrely clad officers stood before him, armed and armoured, with badges of rank on their fighting helms. The middle one said, 'We've lost those two squads entire, sir. The first last night, and the second just before dawn. She cut them down. Elites, they were, too, but she scattered them and hounded them across the fields.'

'We could see some of it from the wall,' one of the other men put in. He shook his head. 'That cursed blade of hers shone like very lighting in the dawn light. Not a man survived.'

Iryn Jagga hissed. 'One lone woman. Howling at my gates like some demented beast all night. *Alone* . . . and all of you put together cannot—'

Turning, he saw Ziftkin in the doorway for the first time. His face clenched. He opened his mouth, closed it, straightened himself, took a long breath. 'Songster,' he said. 'I was not expecting you so soon.'

Ziftkin shrugged. 'I was up already and well awake when the summons came. I, too, heard the . . . howling out there.'

Iryn Jagga nodded. 'What have I been telling you? She is an enemy fell and bloody.'

Ziftkin shuddered. It had seemed hardly human, that night-howling. He had got no sleep and felt exhausted and shivery.

Iryn Jagga looked at the three men facing him and shook his

head. 'These minions of mine tell me there is nothing they can do against her. They send out their best men and she cuts them down.'

'It is that cursed shining sword of hers, sir,' one of the three officers said. 'With that in her hands, she is all but unbeatable by any ordinary man.'

'Or group of ordinary men,' added another. 'There's nothing we can do against her. She can turn arrows or spears with it . . .'

'What about the . . . the animal-man you hold captive, sir?' the third man offered.

Ziftkin had been shocked by Iryn Jagga's ploy on the wall the day before – to threaten torture like that as he had seemed to . . . But now Ziftkin was not so certain. The short hairs along his scalp still prickled with the memory of Elinor's night-howls. A fell and brutal enemy indeed she seemed. 'Can you use this . . . fur-man to stop her?' he asked Iryn Jagga.

The leader of the Ancient Brotherhood ran his hands over his eyes, shrugged. 'Having that animal-man captive will yet work to my advantage. But the woman hardly seems in a fit state of mind to parley at the moment. It would be a waste of a counter on my part to play him too soon. No . . . I think I will keep the creature in reserve yet, just in case.'

Iryn Jagga's long dark hair had come part-loose from the neat queue he normally tied it in and he swept the wayward strands back from his face irritably. He regarded Ziftkin, gestured towards the three men still standing before him. 'These officers of mine, and the men they command, have failed me.'

The three men stood motionless, blank-faced, tense.

Iryn Jagga lifted his good hand and snapped his fingers.

Ziftkin flinched, remembering the last time the leader of the Ancient Brotherhood had snapped his fingers like that. But now all that happened was a quick-scurrying servant darted into the room and handed Iryn Jagga a fist-sized golden goblet of some liquid which he downed in two long gulps. Handing the goblet back to the servant, he dismissed the man, who scurried off.

Iryn Jagga licked his lips, let out a breath, straightened himself. 'Well . . .' he said, smoothing his tunic. 'So we have

417

ourselves a . . . difficulty, with this Elinor and her white blade.' He turned and looked at Ziftkin. 'Who, as these men of mine keep reminding me, no ordinary man can stand against.' Iryn Jagga smiled. 'Which is why I have sent for you, songster.'

Ziftkin swallowed.

'You are no ordinary man, songster.'

Ziftkin felt a little tremor go through him. 'What are you suggesting . . .?'

'You,' said Iryn Jagga softly, 'could succeed where others have failed.' He came over and put an arm about Ziftkin's shoulders, as a doting uncle might with a favourite nephew. Ziftkin could smell the sweetish aroma of the liquor he had just drunk. 'You have brought all the rest in, songster. Thanks to you, we can begin to undo the wickedness this Elinor of the white blade has wrought. But if she remains free outside Sofala, to prowl and murder as she wishes . . . then all you have done so far with that instrument of yours is for nothing!'

Ziftkin glanced self-consciously at the bone flute, which, as always, he had with him. He shrugged out of Iryn Jagga's hold uneasily. 'What do you expect me to do against such a . . . against an enemy of such violent strength?'

'You must face her, songster,' Iryn Jagga said. 'Only you have the power and the gift. Only *you*!'

Ziftkin opened his mouth, closed it.

'There is no other hope for Sofala, save you, Ziftkin Salvator,' Iryn Jagga said.

Ziftkin shook his head. 'Send out a great force and over-whelm her!'

'She would only fade away into the wild lands, to return again and murder again. No, *you* are our hope now. Bring her close. Bring her out in the open before the city wall and face her.'

Ziftkin swallowed.

'Separate her from that fell blade of hers, if you can. But bring her into the open before the wall and hold her, however you may. I and mine will then do the rest.'

'But—' Ziftkin began.

'Trust me. I have seen into this.' Iryn Jagga lifted the golden

418

medallion that hung from his neck. 'The power of great Jara has not deserted us. He works in more ways than one.'

Ziftkin regarded the golden image-face of Jara – so like Iryn Jagga – uneasily.

'You must do this, songster. For the saving of Sofala. For your own saving, and mine. For all the helpless folk who otherwise will fall before this mad, violent woman. She must be brought down! She must be stopped! Do it, and all the world will remember and say, "*He* it was who saved Sofala. *He* it was who risked life and limb to bring about a return to the greatness that once was." Salvator, they shall call you. And the name will be on men's lips for generations to come. Salvator. *Ziftkin Salvator!*'

XXXVIII

The small watch-door shut behind him with a solid *krunk*, and Ziftkin found himself standing alone outside the Sofala wall.

It was still early morn, and he could feel the coolth of the mass of stone and hanging greenery at his back. The thick grass underfoot was dew-soaked, and each step he took away from the door sent tiny shining droplets spinning.

He walked a ways off from the wall and stopped, uncertain. Behind him, he could see the double portals of the gateway: not the blue-doored city entrance through which he had first entered Sofala, but one near as large, oaken and dark with age and stone-solid, with the outline of the little watch-door through which he had stepped clear to be seen on the right-hand portal. Somewhere behind that tight-locked gateway and the vine-hung wall, Iryn Jagga and the rest were hidden, lest their presence disturb things – but ready, Iryn Jagga had assured him.

Ziftkin shivered uneasily. He could see nothing save the stone wall and the rolling green turf. Elinor Whiteblade might be anywhere at all out here, prowling about as she had been doing all through the night – stealthy, violent, murderous . . .

He stood utterly exposed, staring about, his heart thumping.

The world was quiet. Nothing howled. There was no sign of her.

Slowly, he lifted the flute to his lips and began to play. No calling tune this time. He knew better than to expect such a ploy to work on *her*. But the music would carry on the air. She would hear him, and come to him – or so he reckoned.

He blew a simple tune, such as he was wont to play back on Seshevrell Farm, making no effort to put into it any of the deep power he had been imbuing his music with. It was a relief to play simply again, to take joy in the rise and fall of the melody, to be out of the dusty stone confines of Sofala, to feel the morning breeze tease his hair and the shining blue sky open up above him.

Almost, he fell so deep in thrall to the music that he forgot his purpose . . .

Until he glanced up and saw *her* striding towards him over the rolling sward, flashing blade in hand.

There was such an aura of menace about her that he reacted with an instinctive thrust of hard melody.

She faltered a little, and he thrust at her again, driving the spike of the melody into her as he had once done with the water-creature.

She reeled.

Could it be this easy? he wondered for a fleeting moment.

But no. She had recovered now, and stood her ground.

They looked at each other.

Elinor Whiteblade was ragged and dishevelled, her clothing torn and stained, her hair a bird's nest of tangles. There were dark smudges under her eyes, and her face was gaunt and clenched like a fist. Her gaze was one of unblinking menace, with eyes slitted and glittering like a serpent's. She stood with the naked white blade in one hand, the other clutching something that hung from her throat on a cord.

No more than twenty paces separated them now.

One step she took towards him. Another.

Ziftkin shot a burst of sharp melody at her.

She shivered but came on.

He tried again, letting his awareness sink under the ordinary shapes of the world so that he could *feel* her coming towards him through the medium of the flute. Once again, he *felt* the uncanny largeness of her, the manner in which some impossible current seemed to surge through her.

She was closer now . . .

He tried to *feel* a way to get at her. *Separate her from the blade*, Iryn Jagga had said. Ziftkin tried, *feeling* after the substance of her uncanny weapon. He had made trees and clouds dance. It ought to be possible to dance the weapon right out of her hands.

But though the flurry of melody he aimed at it made the

bright blade quiver in Elinor's hold, it did not succeed in wresting it loose.

Closer still, she came.

He tried to push her back, creating a solid, intricate wall of moving sound.

She faltered, stopped.

He played faster, weaving, binding, feeling himself getting the upper hand now. One struggling step she took, two, this way and that. He *felt* the uncertainty in her and played it back, twisting it into a hurry-flurry of whirling, netting notes.

She lifted the sword, as if he had physically attacked her, and brought it whistling round in a quick, elegant pattern of sharp strokes.

And severed the melody in mid-note.

Ziftkin gasped, shaken.

She looked at him wildly, her feet planted wide apart, the blade up in a two-handed grip. She was holding something between her teeth he saw, thin cords dangling from it down around her neck. A little slim length of some pale stuff it was, like bone or peeled wood.

He took a gasping breath and flung a hard series of notes at her.

She arced the blade before her like a moving shield. It glittered and hummed, sending stuttering flashes of brightness across the turf.

He played harder, panting, shooting sharp spikes of melody at her, trying to break the uncanny protectiveness of that blade, seeing it shiver and shimmy and falter a little . . . but always recover.

She was still coming for him across the grass, step by slow step, forcing her way against the melody he hurled at her like a person wading against the current of a strong river.

Closer . . .

Where was Iryn Jagga? Ziftkin glanced back desperately at the gateway.

Nothing.

He gasped out more notes, feeling his heart labouring now, like a frantic, out-of-beat drum to the binding melody he was trying to play.

Closer still she drew. Her blue eyes were filled with a cold fury.

Ziftkin felt a sudden rush of icy fear go through him. He saw his own death in her cold, unblinking eyes. Her face was implacable as that of a sky-storm's. She came at him, the flashing blade up, ready for the killing stroke.

The gateway was still tight shut, the wall empty and silent. What was Iryn Jagga playing at?

She was only a few paces off from him now, implacable, furious, deadly.

Ziftkin felt his legs buckle, and he fell to his knees upon the sward. But he continued playing. It was his death not to.

This close, he could *feel* so clearly the fury in Elinor, like a swirling, cold fire. The white blade shone, and he *felt* the strength that was in it, and how it fed her. There was nothing he could do against *that*, he realized sickly. He felt like a rabbit facing a deadly-fanged serpent. There was nothing for him to do save flee.

But it was too late for that. Too late for anything.

The flute fell away from his lips. On his knees, he stared up at her, frozen, feeling his heart falter, feeling this for his last moment in the world, seeing the green of the grass under her feet like sharded emeralds, the blue of the sky shining like purest light, feeling his own self shiver like a leaf in the wind and his soul shudder, waiting for the blow that would send him reeling away into the final darkness of the Shadowlands . . .

423

XXXIX

Elinor stood, the sword raised above her head two-handed. She could feel the thrill of its strength in her blood, feel the throb of the fury in her gut. The Fey-bone between her teeth was still vibrating, even though the punishing music was stopped now. The songster, on his knees, stared up at her with big, dark, frightened eyes.

One quick, hard stroke, and he would never again trouble the world with his horrible music.

She looked down at him, gathering herself for that killing stroke. But she was saner than she had been during the night. Or simply more weary, perhaps. She hesitated. His face was turned full towards her, narrow, sharp-chinned, beardless, with a mass of dark hair and big dark eyes. The fear in those eyes was clear to read. He was far younger than she would have thought.

The flute with which he had made his uncanny music lay across his knees, a deceptively simple-looking thing seen this close, a length of old bone with a line of holes piercing it. It was an ochre-ivory colour. The same colour, in fact, as the bit of Fey-bone she herself carried.

Her Fey-bone was still vibrating, faintly but uncomfortably, against her teeth, and she spat it out, letting it drop to her breast on its cord. She took a step closer, setting her stance just so, gripping the sword for the quick killing stroke of the Viper's Thrust.

The songster stared at her, shivering, and she felt a pang of uncertainty. He seemed so completely helpless kneeling there before her. She let the sword falter a little.

But then she caught herself. This was ridiculous! This was the man who had wrought such misery for them all with his terrible music. She took another step closer and readied herself for the two-handed stroke that would loose him from the world.

He stared, unmoving, frozen before the face of his own death.

And then, from the Sofala wall, there was a sudden commotion.

Glancing over, Elinor saw a vine-framed gateway, double portals of age-darkened wood. They swung open and something came trundling out.

A narrow carriage of some sort, it was, with a pair of spoked wheels, supporting a dully gleaming bronze cylinder, long as a man was tall. The contraption was clearly heavy, for six men struggled and grunted, trying to wheel it out hastily through the gateway.

Elinor had never seen anything like it, and she had no idea at all as to what it might be. She hesitated, puzzled and uncertain.

The bronze cylinder was cast in the image of a dragon, mouth open and gaping in a frozen roar, stubby legs gripping the wheeled carriage under its belly. The men manoeuvred it so that the gaping dragon-mouth was pointing directly at her and the songster.

A phalanx of sombre-clad, heavily armed Brothers formed up behind the wheeled dragon-thing. From out of their midst, Iryn Jagga stepped.

'Help me!' the songster cried out in a ragged voice.

The leader of the Ancient Brotherhood regarded him for a moment, then looked away disdainfully.

Elinor heard the songster take a sharp, stricken breath.

Iryn Jagga raised a hand over his head. From out of the armed ranks behind him, a man stepped, holding a little sparky torch.

Iryn Jagga smiled a sudden, thin smile. Wordlessly, he brought his hand down.

The man with the torch stepped forwards and touched it to the tail end of the wheeled, bronze dragon-thing. For a long moment, nothing happened.

Then the dragon belched sudden fire from its mouth with a sharp clap of thunder.

Elinor was never certain if she actually saw what it was that came hissing through the air at them, fire-spat by that metal dragon, or if she only imagined it. Like a spurt of hot-metal rain, it seemed, but deadly, for it would have torn scaldingly through flesh and bone like a hot poker through butter.

But the very instant the flame erupted from the dragon's mouth, the songster took up his flute and blew a blast of melody so seeringly sharp it sent a flash of agony through the bones in Elinor's skull. She felt a disorienting throb of sound go through her, heard the air hiss threateningly on all sides, felt a little hot stab of something along the edge of her left shoulder . . .

And then the music stopped, and she found herself standing, alive and whole still, at the songster's side.

Iryn Jagga was staring at them, mouth agape.

Elinor heard the songster laugh a little shaken laugh. She turned and saw that he was trembling, the flute slack in his hands. A trickle of bright blood ran down his temple where he had been cut by something. Her own shoulder burned, and, craning her head to glance at it, she saw a raw streak there through cloth and flesh, as if she had been whipped with a a red-hot wire.

'Wh . . . what *was* it?' she gasped.

The songster shook his head. 'I don't know. It . . . it spat something at us, little hot metal things. I . . . I turned them away past us.'

'With . . .' Elinor gestured to the flute in his shaking hands.

He nodded.

She stared at him.

At the gate now, there was a sudden commotion. Iryn Jagga barked frantic instructions. A little group of men were swarming over the dragon-thing, trying to stuff something down its bronze throat.

With a wild cry, Elinor leaped at them, the white blade up and shining balefully.

For a frozen instant, the men working over the dragon-thing stood their ground. Then they turned and fled backwards through the gateway and into the safety of the city. The rest of those formed up in the gateway followed after, clawing over each other in panicky haste, shouting and shrieking. Iryn Jagga, too, turned and fled, hastily as the rest.

Only just did they make it, slamming the oaken gateway portals in Elinor's face, leaving her balked and furious.

She turned and looked at the dragon-thing. It stank of some burnt stuff she had never smelled before. An utterly strange and deadly contraption . . .

Out on the sod beyond it, the songster stood, staring at her uncertainly. She took a step towards him.

He backed away.

She had been ready to kill this man. And now . . .

He had saved her life, surely, with his uncanny musicking.

But he had saved his own, too. And they had been standing so close, she and he, that he could hardly have saved himself without saving her as well.

Which left her . . . where?

She looked at him, and their gazes locked. He seemed so young. And so very much . . . simpler than she would have expected from such a man as he, an ally of pitiless Iryn Jagga and the Ancient Brotherhood, a man who wielded power such as few were able to.

The songster's glance suddenly flicked in alarm to something above and behind her. Whirling, Elinor saw a string of bowmen appear atop the Sofala wall. They drew, sighted on her, let loose their shafts, all in a heartbeat.

The white blade leaped up, flashing, and swept aside the speeding arrows so that they went twirling and skipping away to rip into the turf behind her. Elinor saw the songster staring at her, and she laughed. He was not the only one who knew how to turn an attack.

Another shower of arrows came down, and Elinor dashed away from the dragon-thing and the wall, dodging and whirling, slashing aside those shafts that came too close. The Songster flinched as she came near him, lifting his flute in defence. But she motioned at him reassuringly with her free hand. 'Run,' she said. 'You're still within bowshot.'

A *kwirring* shaft spun past his ear, and he blinked, shook himself. Elinor was already past him, sprinting to put distance between her and the archers on the wall – whose shafts she could not keep deflecting forever.

The songster paused, staring back at the Sofala wall. An

arrow *kripped* into the grass next to his knee. He whirled and took to his heels after her.

Elinor sat hunkered down against a curve of rough rock, well away from Sofala for the moment. She shifted her left shoulder, which was stinging painfully where the dragon-spat projectile had nicked her and sticky with drying blood. Her breath came in heaving gusts from running, and she could still feel her pulse thudding in her throat.

The songster crouched a little ways off from her, panting.

What now? she wondered uneasily, examining him out of the corner of her eye, trying not to be too obvious about it.

He apparently felt no such reticence, and was staring at her with an uneasy fixity, fidgeting nervously with his flute.

The sword was still naked in her hand. Should she sheathe it perhaps, to set him more at ease? But without the blade in her hand, she knew the rush of exhaustion that would hit her. She had been on the move for too many days, and could not remember the last good night's sleep she had had; she needed the sword's borrowed strength too much.

She was still breathing hard, and her heart had not settled properly. Her head was throbbing. It was as if the air about her were somehow becoming denser, pushing upon her from all sides. Her ears buzzed. She felt her limbs quivering. The world under her seemed to tip, spilling her sideways . . .

Abruptly, she knew this feeling. She had been so entirely caught up in the struggle with the songster's calling music over recent days that she had all but forgotten about the tightness that was in the world, in her belly, that had been there for long weeks.

It was as strong now as she had ever felt it. Her heart laboured with it. Her guts shivered. The world seemed to slope down, down, leaving her only the one way to move.

Towards the songster . . .

His music, she began to realize, had been a part of the tightness somehow, or the tightness had been a part of his music, or . . . something. It made her dizzy, thinking on it, for there was such a *depth* to the feeling that gripped her.

She knew the subterranean surge of power that underlay

that *depth*, like giant, groping currents thrusting her that way and this. She *hated* the feeling. As if she were some utensil to be used . . .

She wanted no more to do with it. What she wished was her Gyver back, safe out of Sofala with no more bloodshed. She wished the humanimals and the Settlement folk safe. She wished this conflict finished. Most of all, what she wished was to be far away from here, she and Gyver, to be free to make her own choices and guide her own life as she wanted without being pushed and pulled about by forces beyond her.

But the shiver in her guts told her otherwise.

She looked over at the songster and sighed. There would be no peace for her till she did what she had to. But that was what? She gripped her sword. Kill him . . .?

The moment for that seemed past. Iryn Jagga, for whatever reasons, had clearly turned against him; the explosive dragon-thing, and the archers' arrows, had been aimed against the both of them, the songster included.

He was so entirely and completely different from what she had expected: an old man with a mossy beard, an age-wrinkled face, and the eyes of a hungry crow would not have surprised her. Another suave, self-inflated madman like Iryn Jagga maybe. But he seemed a mere boy, almost, this oh-so-powerful wizardish songster. And . . . innocent-looking, too, despite that he was dressed in the elegant, sombre garb of the Brothers.

She sighed, unsure.

He was still staring at her.

She motioned at him with her blade, a little put out by the rude insistency of his gaze.

He flinched, shifted backwards, glanced quickly about as if looking for aid. But they were alone, the two of them. He raised his flute to his mouth with quivering hands.

Elinor rose, lifting her blade in instinctive defence. She felt the small hairs on the nape of her neck prickle. The air seemed charged, and it was hard for her to get a good breath.

They faced each other, poised.

But Elinor let her blade drop. She could not, somehow, find it in herself to attack him. 'I am no danger to you,' she said.

The songster regarded her with silent suspicion.

'If I'd intended you harm, I could have attacked you already,' she said a little irritably.

He just kept staring at her.

'Well, say something!' she snapped.

'Iryn Jagga told me all about you.'

Elinor blinked. 'Oh yes? And what did Iryn Jagga say, then?'

'Fell and bloody, he said you were. No ordinary woman at all. He told me how you and your followers descended upon Sofala violently. How you tried to . . . to force all under your yoke. How you . . .'

Elinor glared at him. 'How *I* attacked Sofala?'

The songster nodded, gripping his flute tightly. 'You and your rabble of violent followers, human and . . . not.'

She looked at him, silent.

'Iryn Jagga says—' he began.

'Iryn Jagga,' Elinor interrupted, 'is a liar.'

'Says *you*.'

'I *know* him. I've had more than enough dealings with him in the past.'

The songster nodded. 'Yes . . . he told me how you tortured him.'

'He told you *what*?'

'He told me all. How you severed the fingers from his hand with that blade of yours, one at a time, until he managed to escape you and—'

'What?' Elinor gasped. She did not know whether to laugh or shriek. 'He lost those fingers because of his own blind greed. He tried to snatch up the sword by its blade.'

The songster scowled at her.

'It's the *truth* I'm telling you!' Elinor said. 'Iryn Jagga *lies*. It was *he* who had *me* tortured and beaten!'

The songster's face was clenched tight.

'Iryn Jagga,' Elinor said, 'tried to have you killed.'

The songster blinked, shook his head. 'He . . .'

'He *what*? Made that dragon-thing fire its . . . its hot-metal killing rain at you by *mistake*? Had his archers loose their shafts at you *accidentally*?'

The songster stared at her for long moments in silence. Then, 'I . . . I can . . . feel the world when I play this,' he said,

430

hefting the bone flute. 'I can sense into things, people . . .' His hands, where they clutched the flute, were quivering. 'What . . . *are* you?'

Elinor blinked. She felt a cold shiver go through her. She did not know how to respond to such a question.

The songster was staring at her as if he expected she might suddenly sprout wings and dripping fangs. 'All Iryn Jagga said, and last night – that wild howling. But now, here, you are not . . .' He shivered. 'There is something that . . . *flows* in you. I do not know what you may be. How can I believe you?'

Elinor took a long breath. The air about her felt thick and shivery. Her guts were churned up. The Fey-bone that hung on her breast was still vibrating ever so faintly. She fingered it, feeling the nub of her amputated finger throb, feeling the bone warm to her touch.

'I suppose,' the songster said, 'that you will try to tell me that Iryn Jagga took your finger off?'

Elinor shook her head. 'That was something else entirely.'

He stared at her, uncertain, then, 'What *is* that?' he asked, pointing at the little length of the ochre Fey-bone on its cord about her neck.

Elinor hesitated. How could she tell him? Ought she to tell him? After all, she was still entirely unsure of his intentions – and the Fey-bone was the only thing that had kept her safe from his uncanny musicking.

But something prompted her to answer. 'It was a gift. From . . .' she swallowed, 'from one of the Fey.'

He stared at her. 'You're lying.'

'Why would I lie about such a thing?' Elinor returned hotly. 'And who are *you* to put yourself up as an expert on the truth, you who swallowed the lies Iryn Jagga fed you like a greedy little bird swallowing worms from its mother?'

He glared at her. 'He told me you were an angry, arrogant woman. And he was right enough about that!'

'Oh *yes*?' Elinor gripped her sword. Little sparkles of radiance seemed to fill the thick air between them. She took a step towards him, the sword coming up.

He stood his ground, raising the bone flute.

With an effort, Elinor stopped herself. 'And Iryn Jagga is a master of humility, is he?' she said. 'And you? You're a humble saint, I suppose, you who call up innocent folk and dance them to their own deaths.'

The songster frowned. 'Not to their deaths. Not the human folk. They will all be given their lands to work again. Iryn Jagga promised. I was there. I heard him.'

'Iryn Jagga *promised*!' Elinor mocked. 'And you believed every word he told you, like a good little boy. Well, he lied about me, and he lied to those folk.'

'So you keep insisting.'

'He's a dangerous, lying, violent madman, is Iryn Jagga,' Elinor said, feeling herself fill with outrage. 'He'll kill Gyver, and anyone else who gets in his way. And all the humanimals as well . . . that *you* so obligingly called in for him. They will be murdered, each and every one of them. *Your* doing, that! You, Iryn Jagga's faithful and obedient retriever!'

'They . . . it's best they go from the world.'

Elinor stared at him. 'What are you saying?'

'They're . . . stricken. Their very natures make them dangerous and violent.'

'Says who?' Elinor demanded. 'Iryn Jagga?'

The songster hesitated a moment, then said, 'I've *felt* the unbalance of them. And I've seen, first-hand, the bloody violence they do.'

'What bloody violence?'

'I saw a whole family murdered, torn and clawed. Innocent people.'

Elinor stared at him. 'What are you saying?'

'Humanimals are deadly dangerous.'

'No.'

'Yes! I have seen this with my own eyes. I have *felt* it. They are neither one thing nor another, such creatures. And so tormented are they by their unnatural state, that the bloody beast in them drives them to violent madness.'

'You don't know what you're speaking of!' Elinor said angrily. 'I have lived with them. I *know*. They are not as you say.'

'I have seen the results of their violence,' the songster insisted. 'A whole family ruthlessly murdered.'

'You *saw* the humanimals do this, did you?' Elinor asked.

The songster hesitated, shook his head.

432

'Then how do you know it was humanimals that murdered these people?'

'It was . . .' the songster began. 'I . . .' He stopped, took a breath. 'Iryn Jagga told me.'

Elinor laughed mirthlessly. 'Iryn Jagga? And you *believed* him?'

The songster stared at her, open-mouthed. 'No . . .' He took a shuddering breath, another. His mouth closed so sharply she heard his jaw click shut. He shook his head, sat down suddenly upon the turf, hard.

Elinor looked at him. 'Iryn Jagga has deceived you,' she said. 'Humanimals are two-natured, perhaps, but they do not kill mindlessly. They are not mad, violent creatures.'

He was shaking now. 'How . . . how can I believe you? You could be lying to me. Iryn Jagga warned me . . .' He looked at her with dread uncertainty.

'Iryn Jagga,' Elinor said, 'is a ruthless, fanatical man. He is capable of—'

'No!' The songster shook his head vehemently. 'Not that! Not a whole family. Not the poor hurt child.'

'Even that,' Elinor insisted. 'You do not know him if you think him incapable of such an act, knowing it would suit his purposes.'

He stared at her out of bruised eyes, opened his mouth, closed it, ran a hand across his face.

Elinor felt the air about them prickle uncomfortably. Her guts throbbed. She was not sure what to do. He looked like a man ready to collapse, hunched in upon himself, his flute hanging in one hand. Now was a perfect chance. If she rushed him now, she could wrest the flute out of his grasp, render him helpless . . .

But she could not bring herself to do it. He seemed so stricken, she could not help but feel for him. He had the look of a man who had swallowed something he could not digest. She saw a long shudder go through him. He stood up, turned about, stared at Sofala off in the distance, fidgeted with the flute, sat down again.

He looked at her, his eyes going to the Fey-bone on its cord around her neck. 'Is it . . . really true,' he said suddenly, 'what you told me about . . .' he pointed at the Fey-bone, 'about *that*?'

433

Elinor nodded.

'It truly came to you from the Fey?'

'Truly. It gave me protection from your calling music. That was how I was able to resist.'

The songster shivered. He looked down at his bone flute for long moments in silence. Then he glanced up and said, 'So did this, also, come from the Fey. From my . . . father.'

It took Elinor a few instants before she understood. 'Your father is one of . . . *them*?'

The songster nodded.

It was Elinor's turn to stare. She had had no idea that such a thing could be.

'Do you think me a liar?' he said.

'No,' she replied quickly. Somehow, what he said made complete sense to her. She could see it in him. He was such a tall, thin boy, long-fingered and long-toed, with those big dark eyes of his. Like the big dark eyes she had seen on the Fey that night of the Phanta's moon-dance. 'I . . . I can see it in you,' she said to him.

'See what?'

'The . . . feyness. You are no ordinary person.'

'Nor you.'

Elinor shrugged, nodded. She took a step towards him, but he shied away, uncertain of her still. She sheathed the sword then, willing to take the rush of exhaustion that would follow in order to set him more at ease.

To her surprise, however, it was not near so bad as she had expected. She went closer to him, her legs shaking only a little. 'We need not be enemies,' she said softly. 'We are . . . the same, somehow, you and I.'

'Fey-gifted,' he said, his voice breathless. He was staring at her.

Elinor nodded. 'Strangers brought together by forces deeper than we can easily perceive, perhaps.'

The songster shivered. He looked at her, looked around at the world bemusedly.

'The . . . the old Seers who once ruled this land, back in far-gone days . . .' Elinor began, 'they attained much knowledge and such power.'

'So Iryn Jagga said,' the songster returned. 'And we have

434

stories of those far-gone elder days, where I am from. It is the greatness of old, the greatness of the ancient Seers, that Iryn Jagga wants to bring back into the world.'

Elinor nodded. 'But that . . . "greatness" that was theirs, it was too much. In their purblind wilfulness, they upset the multifold balances of the world.' Elinor shivered. 'And now . . . now the world is beset by a great, blind backlash, a re-balancing of Power and Power. And it . . . it may be that we are not met haphazardly, you and I.'

He could only stare at her.

'There are Powers . . .' Elinor said.

The songster nodded: 'The Powers that move the world.'

'And those who walk the world, sometimes,' Elinor said.

He looked unsure.

Elinor did not know what further to say. She was hardly sure she understood it herself. But she felt in her gut the certainty that she and this songster were tied somehow. On sudden impulse, she held her hand out in an offer of friendship.

Ziftkin gazed at that proffered hand for a long, hesitant moment. 'This is the *last* thing I expected to happen this day,' he said bemusedly.

Elinor shrugged and smiled, 'Me as well.' She kept her hand out.

The songster lifted his Fey-bone flute, ran a finger along it, looked at her. 'It is like seeing a wicked serpent turn to a butterfly before my very eyes . . .'

Slowly, he stepped forwards and took her hand.

They looked at each other, hands clasped. He was taller than she, and Elinor had to look up into his face. For the space of a few heartbeats, something seemed to flow through them. Elinor felt a little prickle go up her spine.

They let each other go, self-conscious.

'My name,' the songster said after a little, 'is Ziftkin, once of Seshevrell Farm, north of here.'

'I, too, come from the north,' Elinor returned, surprised. 'From Long Harbour, on the seacoast. I had thought you were one of the Brothers, or . . . something.'

The songster blinked. 'And I thought you native to this southern land.'

'I . . . I ran away from Long Harbour years ago,' Elinor said to the question in his face. 'Things didn't exactly work out between me and my family. My father left us when I was a little girl. I never saw him again . . .'

There was something in that that hit him. She could see him flinch.

'I . . . I never knew my father,' he said softly.

They looked at each other in silence, uncertain.

Ziftkin took a breath, let it out. 'What . . . now?' he said after a little.

'That depends,' Elinor answered. 'Me, I have to find some way into Sofala.' She stared soberly at the blocky outline of the city in the distance. It looked a darksome, forbidding place, the city walls a mass of looming, ivy-choked stone set in the rolling turf all about. 'Things are far from finished for me here.'

Ziftkin, too, stared at the city. Emotions came and went across his face, too quick for Elinor to be able to follow. He bit his lip, his face pale. 'Perhaps,' he said to her, 'I can be of help.'

XXXX

Through darkness, Elinor and the songster crept. It was raining, a constant, chill downpour. Sunfall was only a little time gone, but the wafting curtains of rain and the clouds overhead made this first beginning of the night so obscure that Sofala was a only mere half-guessed shadow-shape ahead of them. No watcher on the city wall would ever spot them as they drew near.

Elinor crouched in the wet grass, trying to get her bearings. 'It's this way, I think,' she said.

Ziftkin nodded – she could barely make out the gesture – but he said nothing.

Elinor started off again. Cold rain-water dribbled down her back. She blinked it out of her eyes. She was bone-tired and shivery, and her legs ached. Her truncated finger sent little stabbing pains shooting up her forearm. Her shoulder, where she had been cut by the dragon-spat projectile, was stiff and throbby. Her scarred leg ached. She yearned for the sword's strength. There was no sense, though, in drawing it yet. Its radiance would be a fatal liability here, where stealth was the only ally they had.

They were come to the wall now, the great dark mass of it rearing up over their heads. Rain-water came chorusing down the ivy, draining away in myriad rivulets through the turf.

'It all looks so alike,' Elinor said uncertainly. 'And in this rainy dark . . .' Somewhere ahead was the little door she had accidentally discovered under the growth of ivy. But where?

'Find me that door,' the songster had said, 'and I can open it.'

Elinor shivered, trying to make sure of the songster's position in the rain-dimmed shadow of the Sofala wall. The world was *tipping* her here along this path tonight; she could

437

feel it clear. But standing here, one hand pressed against the wet-cold stone of the wall, she felt a shudder of paralysing uncertainty go through her.

They had talked, the songster and she: about their respective lives, about humanimals and Sofala and Iryn Jagga, about the hidden Powers and the Fey and all. There might still be uncertainties, and much they did not know about each other, and she did not think he altogether believed her talk of Powers and slopes in the world. But things seemed to be aligned between them, nonetheless.

Seemed.

For Elinor knew nothing about him, really, save what he had told her himself. It was such an unexpected and unlikely partnership they made. And here she was, about to walk blindly into Sofala with him. What if he *were* somehow still in league with Iryn Jagga? What if this were all, somehow, an elaborate ploy to decoy her into the city?

No. Impossible. He had been too cruelly misused by Iryn Jagga.

Unless . . .

Ziftkin tapped her on the shoulder, lightly. 'Which way?'

Elinor started, blinked, wiped the cold rainwater out of her eyes. 'Along here,' she said. 'At least, I think so.' She tried to thrust suspicion from her and led off, one hand lightly trailing the ivy on her left, following the chill, wet intricacy of it.

They crept along, feet skidding now and then on the rain-slicked grass, skirting the wall's base until, to Elinor's great relief, it was there suddenly before them: a little darker shadow, a falling-water rush as she pulled the mass of ivy aside, the reassuring, hollow *thwunk* of her knuckles against the wet wood. 'Here!'

The songster crowded in beside her under the trailing ivy curtain.

Elinor drew the blade, and by its soft radiance they were able to see the door itself. She put her shoulder to it and shoved. The door gave not a fraction.

'Let me,' the songster said. Bent close to the door, he set the flute to his lips and blew a long note, but so soft as to be hardly audible. Then that single note broke apart into a quick, jumping tune. Even with the Fey-bone at her breast, Elinor felt the pull of that tune, felt her feet wanting to move. She shivered, faced so squarely with such an uncanny thing.

Ziftkin stopped. The only sound now was the falling tumble of the rain. Gently, he pushed against the door. It opened with a protesting *kreek* of rusty hinges.

'What did you *do*?' Elinor asked in a whisper.

'I . . . played up the locking bar on the other side so that it opened,' he replied.

Elinor pushed the door wider open, gripped her blade. There was no light of any sort from the inside, no sound, no indication of any guards.

Ziftkin swallowed. 'Shall we?' he said, gesturing to the city dark beyond the door.

'Are you certain sure?' Elinor said. 'You don't have to do this, you know.'

By the blade's soft light, she could see his face was clenched. 'I *owe* Iryn Jagga,' he said. 'And I owe it to others . . . for what I have done. The humanimals . . . now that I better understand what they are . . . I cannot just . . . turn my back and walk away.'

Elinor hesitated. She felt, once again, a stab of dark, unreasonable suspicion. There could be a score of armed Brothers on the other side of this doorway, crouched and waiting silently. He could be lying to her, leading her into a trap. The door had opened for him so easily . . .

She felt a sudden urge to run her blade through him. It would ensure things, prevent any possibility of future treachery on his part. She saw it in her own mind: the quick thrust, him collapsing onto the wet sod, dark blood spilling into the rainwater.

Her arm tightened instinctively, her balance shifted for the stroke.

But she held back.

She did not know where the violent reflex of that urge came from. From something that seeped into the air out of Sofala, perhaps. Or from the sword itself. But she would not let herself be swayed by it. Ziftkin was no enemy of hers. That, surely, was the truth of things here. She took a breath, let it out. Straightened herself determinedly. 'Come then,' she said.

Together, they entered into Sofala.

They were met by no stealthy movement of hidden guards, no sudden attack. Beyond the rain, there was only blind, black-night silence.

Elinor took a breath, swallowed, coughed. The place stank; of mould, of old decays, of things she could not – and did not want to – identify. She peered about, trying to find something to orient herself.

From Ziftkin's recounting of his experiences in Sofala, Elinor had recognized the building he had described as the place where the captives – both human and humanimal – were kept. She too, she reckoned, had once been captive in the cellar dungeon of that very same building.

So their task here was set: find the building where Gyver and the humanimals and the Settlement folk were imprisoned, free them all, and get safely out of Sofala.

Elinor shivered in the cold rain. The night-shrouded city seemed like some great, many-formed beast, crouched menacingly before them. She and this strange songster alone against Iryn Jagga and the Ancient Brotherhood and the whole of dark Sofala.

For a moment, she felt overwhelmed at the mere notion of it. It was madness. They would only come to grief . . .

But she could feel the way the sword fit perfectly in her grip, feel the uncanny strength of it *thrum* though her limbs. Her aches and pains were gone; her maimed hand barely throbbed; in her hurt shoulder, there was only a very faint stiffness now.

Elinor felt her pulse quicken. She had stood before the invaders of Gyver's homeland and vanquished them. She had triumphed against Iryn Jagga once before in this very city. She could feel the world *tipping* her along this path, as if she were in some great Power's employ. The Fey-bone hung warm against her breast under her tunic.

She felt a fierce exaltation fill her. The white blade of the sword seemed to blaze softly in the wet, dark air of the night, haloed by myriad diamond-bright rain droplets. What other path was there for her? She was become what she was become. She must walk where she must. She laughed softly. Let Iryn Jagga beware.

The songster was looking at her, uncertain.

'Which way?' she said.

He shrugged. 'Iryn Jagga never let me see much of the city. And in the rainy dark like this . . .'

Elinor squinted against the rain, but all she could make out was a dank maze of puddly, litter-filled alleyways and crumbling buildings. 'If we keep the city wall at our backs,' she suggested, 'at least while we can keep track of it. That ought to guide us towards the centre of the city.'

Ziftkin nodded.

They headed off, marking the position of the wall when they could see it between the mouldering buildings.

This part of the city seemed entirely deserted, and long abandoned. With Elinor in the lead, they picked a slow way through the rubble for what seemed like an endless, dark time, sloshing through filthy puddles, using the soft radiance of the white blade as a light, soaked through and shivering in the rain. The only sign of life they saw was two skinny rats who sat upon the crumbling sill of a second-storey window and chittered angrily at them in what sounded suspiciously like badly slurred words.

When Elinor raised the blade to see them better, they were gone.

Onwards she and the songster trudged. After a while the rain slackened, then stopped. The city was filled with the sound of dripping water.

'We're lucky,' Elinor said softly, wiping residual rainwater out of her eyes. 'No guards. No people. We must have come in through an old gateway nobody uses any more.'

Ziftkin nodded. 'Iryn Jagga told me only part of the city is inhabited now. He said he was going to improve things, to rebuild, to . . .'

'Shush!' Elinor said abruptly. They had turned a corner. Ahead, she caught the flicker of light. From a distance, interwoven through the *kwip kwip kwip* of the dripping rainwater, they heard the sound of human voices.

They were on a long, rubble-edged street that provided relatively easy walking, and that seemed to be leading exactly the way they needed to go. 'I don't fancy leaving this to detour through some mazy network of dark alleyways,'

Elinor said softly. She wiped her sword hand, re-gripped the sword. 'We go straight on, I reckon. But most carefully, all right?'

Ziftkin nodded.

They went on.

As they drew closer, they saw that the light was coming from inside the shell of a broken-down building. They heard the soft *wiffle-waff* of flames, the murmur of voices. Through the remains of the building's doorway, they made out a huddle of shadowy shapes about a fire.

The songster stopped and stared.

'Come on,' Elinor hissed, 'before they . . .'

But a soft shout went up suddenly from behind them.

Elinor whirled, her blade coming up, her feet automatically setting themselves as she fell into the Little-tree defensive posture.

Three ragged men were coming towards them. They carried twisted sticks as clubs.

'What have we here, lads?' one of them said. He pointed at Ziftkin. 'Look at that one's clothing.'

'Some young rich bastard an' his girlie come slummin' it,' said one of his companions.

'Never seen a torch like what she's carryin',' the third put in. 'Be nice to have a pretty little light like that, wouldn' it now?'

The three men sidled forwards like so many dogs, stiff-legged, wary-eager, teeth showing in feral grins. But as they drew near, they stopped.

'That's no *light* she's carryin',' one of the men said uncertainly. 'It's a . . . a blade!'

They stood, staring.

'It's . . . *her*!'

By now, the folk gathered about the fire had begun to shuffle out of the building, a filthy, skin-and-bones lot, men and women and children, all dressed in rags. They stared silently at Elinor and the songster with bleak, hungry eyes.

'Come on,' Elinor said softly to Ziftkin. She could smell the stink of those gathering about them, like a melding of over-ripe cheese and dank mould. She and the songster backed

442

away carefully. The ragged people stared and muttered amongst themselves, but made no move.

Once round the next corner, Elinor and Ziftkin fled, running, till they had put enough distance behind them.

'I never knew,' Ziftkin panted when they paused to take a breather. 'I never *knew*!'

'Knew what?' Elinor said.

He gestured about them. 'About *this*. All of this. And them back there! I never knew it was this bad. I only ever knew the . . . the other side, the bright side of Sofala. I never properly realized . . .'

Elinor reached a hand to him in instinctive sympathy, but he shrugged it off, shook himself, and walked away from her a few paces.

She looked at him, opened her mouth, closed it.

Looking ahead, she saw that there seemed to be an opening in the buildings, a larger street. 'This way,' she suggested after a little.

Onwards they went.

It was well beyond the dark middle of the night by now.

The buildings past which they crept were in better repair than those they had passed previously, but they saw nobody on the streets, and the place was grimly silent. Only the occasional flickering light high in a window overhead showed the presence of living human beings.

Once or twice, Elinor thought she had heard the sound of stealthy footsteps behind them. But each time she stopped to look, there was nothing. Her imagination, no doubt. Sofala was a spooky place.

'It's like a city of the dead and dying,' Ziftkin said with a shudder.

Elinor nodded.

They kept onwards.

The city wall had disappeared from their view, obscured by the height of the buildings set close all about, and they were without clear direction. They pushed on regardless; there was nothing else to do.

And then, unexpectedly, the street they were on gave onto

a large, cobblestoned square. Both of them stopped at once and said, each echoing the other, 'I know this place.'

They slunk out into the open, feeling painfully exposed.

From behind, Elinor thought she heard again a soft, stealthy noise. But when she turned, the buildings behind them seemed utterly silent and deserted, as did the square itself. They started carefully across the rain-slicked, puddled cobblestones. Ahead stood a complicated stone structure, the height of three tall men, composed of a central column and a series of platforms.

'What is it?' Ziftkin asked, pointing at the stone structure. 'Do you know? I saw it my first day, coming into Sofala.'

Elinor shuddered. 'It is . . . it is where the humanimals are murdered. A "Cleansing", the Brothers call it. They bring the humanimals here and . . . and murder them in a great public ceremony so that their blood floods the stone platforms you see there. All in the name of their male power. What's he called? I've forgotten . . .'

'Jara,' Ziftkin said quietly.

Elinor nodded. 'That's it. All that blood and death in the name of Jara. So the Brothers can *cleanse* the world and have it all to themselves.'

Ziftkin stared at the stone altar, his face stricken.

'Come,' Elinor said, turning her back on the square. 'I have my bearings clear now. The building we seek is along this way.'

Ziftkin nodded his agreement, and they continued on, quietly.

Elinor shivered, following the road out of the square. She had too many bad memories of this place. She gripped the sword tighter. The first time she had come into this square, a bound prisoner on horseback, the eaves of the buildings lining the street down which she had ridden had been hung with the rotting heads of the dead – some of whom had been dear friends of hers. The altar in the middle of the square had held dead and dying humanimals. And she herself had nearly died, a bloody sacrifice to black Jara, on that very same altar back there.

She shuddered. The palm of her left hand tingled uncomfortably – a sensation she had not felt in a long, long while. The world seemed to twist suddenly and she felt dizzy.

444

Ziftkin put a hand on her arm in concern. 'Are you all right?'

Elinor nodded. But she felt like a great, invisible current were swirling all about her, and through her. She laboured to get a clear breath. She wished irritably that it would just let her alone! She knew what she must do.

Ahead, she could see the tall rise of the building they wanted, a great black shadow-shape rearing up into the night.

'Come on,' she said. 'There it is ahead.'

XXXXI

They were inside the building.

Ziftkin stood propped against the wall, panting. There had been guards at the entrance, but Elinor had dealt with them – in a flurry of lightning-sharp sword-strokes that left only bleeding dead behind, too quick for the guards to cry out even. It had made Ziftkin's belly heave to see it. He had never imagined such quick, such controlled and utterly deadly ferocity.

'Which way?' Elinor demanded of him. There was an unnerving, almost inhuman fierceness to her face. Her eyes seemed to burn. The shining blade was webbed with blood now. It dripped, wetly, on the flagstone floor. Ziftkin faltered away, staring.

'Which *way*?' Elinor insisted.

Ziftkin shook himself, looked about. 'Along here, I think.'

He headed off down a dim, torchlit hallway, but slowly, for he was far from sure of his bearings; it was such a huge building, this, and they had come in from a side entrance he was not familiar with. Behind him, he could hear Elinor's soft footfalls. The two of them left a betraying trail of wet footprints behind them – hers commingled with blood.

What manner of creature was she, Ziftkin wondered uneasily, that she could do the bloody things she had and not seem to notice? What if . . . what if she had deceived him entirely? She could plunge that deadly, uncannily shining blade of hers right through him from behind. His back crawled at the thought.

All her strange talk of hidden Powers and slopes . . . What if, despite all she had told him, she was no more than the fell and bloody murderess Iryn Jagga claimed her to be, merely using him to gain entry into the city so that she could wreak

446

bloody havoc on all and sundry – and he no more than a stupid dupe?

But no. It was Iryn Jagga who had made a dupe of him, playing him for a fool country boy who would believe anything. *Ziftkin Salvator* . . .

Ziftkin burned, thinking on it.

He may not know what manner of person this Elinor of the white blade might or might not be, but what did that matter? All that counted at this point was that, indisputably, she was Iryn Jagga's enemy. He had brought her here into Iryn Jagga's stronghold. He would bring her closer, and loose her at Iryn Jagga himself.

The thought of it made his blood sing.

Iryn Jagga had danced him like a silly puppet, twisting and shading things, flattering him, lying, committing foul murder – no humanimals had killed that poor family; he was bitterly convinced of that now. And in the end, after all he had done for the man, Iryn Jagga would have murdered him. Ziftkin could not shake from his mind the disdainful look on Iryn Jagga's face, the utter unconcern as he turned and gave the order to light the death-spouting dragon-thing – while he, Ziftkin, was crying out for aid, on his knees and helpless before Elinor's blade.

Ziftkin gripped the warm shaft of the bone flute. How could he have been such a purblind fool? The humiliation of it ate at him like a needle-toothed beast alive in his guts. He was the cause of so very much harm, witless dupe that he was . . .

'How much further?' Elinor said from behind him.

Ziftkin blinked, looked about. 'Not too far,' he said, trying to sound more confident than he felt. He had expected to be able to lead Elinor along without much difficulty. But now all the corridors and passageways looked alike. He ran a hand over his face, winced at the sore, scabbed bit near his hairline where the dragon-spat projectile had nicked him. What with one thing and another, he had all but forgotten about it. He probed at it delicately with a fingertip. It hurt.

He looked ahead. The corridor before them was empty and silent. But there would be guard patrols about, Ziftkin knew, even at this late time of the night. They had been lucky so far not to encounter any. His and Elinor's feet had dried by now, and the sword's blade was clean of dripping blood, so they left behind no betraying spoor by which they could be tracked from the slain door-guards they had left behind them. But it would only be a matter of time before the alarm was sounded throughout the whole of the building.

This was a mad enterprise they were attempting, slinking into the city like this, breaking into this, of all buildings. He did not give much for their chances. But a fierce, bleak vengefulness had been riding him since he had found himself betrayed and abandoned outside the Sofala wall. Let him and Elinor die here, if they must, so long as they took Iryn Jagga with them.

He led on, and soon a set of steps appeared before them. For a long, uncomfortable moment, Ziftkin thought he was indeed truly lost – and envisioned the two of them wandering about ineptly until the alarm was sounded and the hallways filled with troops of guards.

But no. This was the staircase he had once taken to reach the below-ground halls – he was almost certain. Once down those stairs, surely, he ought to be able to recognize something. It was the way to Iryn Jagga's halls that he wanted, which he knew were somewhere near to the opulent room he had been given. He kept imagining the stricken look on the man's face as he, Ziftkin, flung open the door and Elinor and her deadly white blade swept through . . .

But the building was too huge, and he had no sure way of navigating to where he wished to be until he had found some recognizable landmark first; and down towards the familiar seemed a better chance at the moment than up into the unknown. So down he went, searching.

'Which way?' Elinor asked as they stood at the bottom. 'Where is Gyver being held? And the rest? Are they near here?'

'I'm not sure . . .' Ziftkin peered about at the torch-lit corridor uncertainly. It was Iryn Jagga he wanted to get to first, not Elinor's fur-man. Perhaps he ought not to have come this downwards way at all. There was still nothing familiar about his surroundings. He felt his heart sink. All he had done so far was to lead the two of them further away from where he wished to be.

448

'Come *on*,' Elinor hissed. 'Time is wasting.'

'You think I don't *know* that?' he snapped at her. 'Give me a moment to think!'

There seemed nothing to do save go on. This looked to have been the wrong staircase after all. They would just have to strike onwards in hopes of finding another, more familiar, set of stairs.

So onwards he led, his heart thumping anxiously.

'Where does it go, this corridor?' Elinor demanded from behind him in a whisper. 'Is this where Gyver's being held?'

Ziftkin kept onwards.

'Answer me!' Elinor snapped. 'Where are you taking me?'

'You'll see,' Ziftkin said vaguely. 'Come on, we . . .'

'Not until you tell me where you're leading,' she returned, reaching a restraining hand to his shoulder.

Ziftkin twisted away from her and strode hurriedly onwards, forcing her to follow. Rounding a bend in the passageway ahead, he went down a stretch of straight corridor, past a spluttering wall-torch, round a sharp corner . . .

And stopped dead. Elinor, trying to catch him up, bumped awkwardly into him from behind.

A barred door lay ahead, with a double brace of guards in front of it – who stared open-mouthed, seeing what was come suddenly upon them in the night.

Elinor took them in an eyeblink, leaping at them in deadly silence, her blade moving so quickly it was little more than a blur to the eye.

Ziftkin shuddered, watching. The four of them stood no chance at all.

He followed after, when she was done, stepping carefully round the gruesome mess that was all she had left of the guards. Even so, he skidded in a little slimy puddle of blood and smacked his elbow hard against the wall before he could properly regain his balance.

'Is Gyver in here?' Elinor asked excitedly. Her face had that fierceness about it again. Her eyes were like a falcon's, sharp and glittering.

Ziftkin shook his head. 'No. Your fur-man is not here.' He felt a sharp pang of bitter resentment. So much for his cherished plan of swooping upon Iryn Jagga. He and Elinor

449

were committed to another path, now. He knew where they were, now, recognized where this door led.

He lifted the door's locking bar and opened it. 'It's the . . . the farmer folk in here. Your . . . followers.'

Elinor's face lit up and she pushed past him.

Inside, there was a single torch burning. The raised wooden platform from which Iryn Jagga had harangued the crowded people was a looming shadow-shape. The darkened hall was filled with the soft sounds of people sleeping.

Elinor lifted the torch from its bracket. 'Heya!' she cried, stepping forwards past the platform and waving her torch high. '*Heya!* Wake up, you lot!'

There was a confused, sleepy muttering.

Somebody came forwards, took a quick look at Elinor, all bloodied blade and fierceness under the stuttering light of her flaming torch, and shrieked.

The hall came alive then. Folk cried out, pushing and shoving in sleep-blind panic.

But the word went round. Ziftkin heard it.

'Elinor!'

'It's Elinor Whiteblade.'

'She's come for us. She's back!'

They crowded close about her, shivering and shouting and laughing and crying, lighting new torches, calling a dozen questions at once, reaching hands to her.

'Quick!' she told them. 'We're getting out of here.'

There was a surge of people, voices chattering in excitement.

But one man came forwards, short, thick in the shoulders, with a round barrel of a belly. He raised his hands high. '*I'm* not going anywhere!' he cried. 'Not with *her*!'

They fell silent at that.

Ziftkin recognized the man who had spoken: he it was whom Iryn Jagga had singled out, whom he had brought out of here to answer questions about Elinor's fur-man.

'What are you saying, Olundar?' one of the crowd demanded. 'With Elinor here, we can *escape*!'

'Escape to *what*?' the man called Olundar returned. 'To scratching a meagre existence out in the forsaken wilderness? To be constantly worrying if the Brotherhood is going to find us and exact vengeance? What sort of a life is that?'

450

'Better than we'd have here at any rate!' somebody replied.

'No!' Olundar cried. 'We've our farms back again. We can live in peace here, as we used to.'

'As land-slaves!'

'No! Olundar's right!' a man with greying hair and chin whiskers agreed, coming to stand next to Olundar. Ziftkin recognized him as one of the the Committee members Iryn Jagga had called up.

'We have a chance for a new life here,' the grey-haired man insisted. 'A proper, ordered, prosperous life, like Olundar here says. We'd be *crazy* to throw that away.'

'That's right!' another man said.

Ziftkin saw that the three members of the Committee had joined together at Olundar's side now.

Elinor was staring about her in confusion. 'Where's Collart?' she asked. 'And Getta? And Passaly and Smitt and . . .'

'Dead,' a woman called out, 'Collart's dead.'

'Getta too,' added somebody else. '*He* killed them. That Iryn Jagga.'

Elinor faltered, looking about her in shock.

Two men pushed their way through the crowd then. One was older, lanky and bald, the other young with a thick black beard. 'Elinor!' the bald one said, and flung his arms about her in an impulsive hug.

Elinor hugged him back, but one-handed, keeping her blade free and one eye on the close-drawn crowd. 'What's *happened*, Passaly?' she said.

Bald Passaly shrugged unhappily. 'It'd be long to tell.'

The young black-bearded man came up and he and Elinor embraced. '*Good* to see you again,' he said.

There was silence then, for long moments.

Elinor broke it by saying, 'Well, come *on*, then! Let's be *away* from here!'

'I'm not going anywhere,' Olundar repeated. 'I've a chance here at a good life for me and my family. A better life than any we had out there in the wild lands. I'm staying!'

'Me too!' somebody called out from the back.

'And I,' added a third.

'Well *I'm* going,' a woman announced.

451

'And I!' shouted a voice.

The crowd erupted into a confusion of shouting.

'Quiet!' Elinor cried. '*Quiet!*'

Which settled them.

'We've got to leave, and that quickly!' she said. 'There's the humanimals still to be freed, and Gyver . . .'

'See?' Olundar interrupted. '*See?* She's more concerned with those *animals* than she is for us!'

'She's *trouble*!' put in the grey-whiskered Committee man. 'Nothing but trouble. I say we ought to . . .'

But he was shouted down in a general hubbub that shook the hall.

Elinor stared at them.

Ziftkin saw a little girl come squirming through the crowd. She called something out, but in the noisy confusion nobody paid any attention to her, as they had paid no attention to Ziftkin in all of this arguing, their focus being entirely on Elinor.

The little girl, however, spotted Ziftkin standing a little apart. She came scrambling up to him, pale-haired, skinny, dressed in dirt-stained, baggy farmer's coveralls. She looked up at him with big blue eyes set wide apart in a thin, triangular face. 'Where's Grub?' she demanded.

'What?' Ziftkin said.

'Where *is* he?'

Ziftkin only stared at her, perplexed.

'Where's Grub?' she repeated, tugging at his trousers now in desperation. 'He'll be with the other humanimals. Oh, where *is* he? Please tell me. *Please!*'

'Humanimals?' Ziftkin said.

'Yes!' she cried. 'He's one of them.' She shook him, her small hands gripping him with surprising strength. 'Take me to him. Oh, please, please take me to him.' There were glistening tears in her eyes, and the face she turned to him was desperate and imploring. '*Please!*'

He did not understand what it was that made this particular humanimal so important to her. He did not yet truly understand this humanimal business and how they were related to human people. But he understood – and recognized – the desperate longing, clear to be seen in the girl's face. He had longed for so much in his own childhood . . .

There was for him, suddenly, in all the shouting and confusion of the room, no denying this one, desperate, weeping little girl.

'Come on, then,' he said to her impulsively. 'I'll take you to the humanimals.'

But then a woman's voice cried out, 'Anstil!'

Barrel-bellied Olundar turned from shouting at his neighbour, and shouted at the child instead: 'Come *back* here, girl! What do you think you're playing at?' He took a step towards her, his hands out graspingly.

The little girl turned from him and ran.

Ziftkin followed.

'Which way?' she said, out in the corridor beyond the chamber, hopping agitatedly from one foot to the other. Her coveralls were spotted with the dead door-guards' blood. She had hardly given them a glance. 'Which *way*?'

Ziftkin hesitated uncertainly. There was pandemonium now from the other side of the door. He could see people struggling with each other, bottlenecked in the doorway.

'You!' somebody shouted at him. A man broke free of the press at the door, popping out like a cork from a bottle. 'You bring that girl *back* or . . .' He skidded on the blood-slick stone floor and went down heavily, head first, arms akimbo, smacking into the inert form of one of the dead guards, his face filled with horror as he realized what it was he had collided with.

The little girl tugged at Ziftkin desperately. Her face was white. 'Please! We have to go find Grub! Oh, *please*!'

Ziftkin hesitated for a last instant, then turned and ran, taking the girl up in his arms, the bone flute tucked awkwardly against his chest.

Behind him, people were spilling out the doorway in a struggling mass, slipping and sliding on the blood-wet floor, shrieking and shouting. Then they began to stream after him in a mob, bloody and furious.

He ran for all he was worth.

XXXXII

Elinor stood staring. She could not believe any of this was happening. The hall was emptying fast, folk whirling past her in a hysteria that had lost all order. She had seen several other young children hare off after those who had gone in pursuit of the songster and the girl he had run off with, followed by hysterical mothers, irate fathers, and the general, shouting mob.

What had the songster been thinking? What were these wailing folk thinking? It would rouse the guard, rouse the whole of the building, all this noise and wild confusion.

'Be quiet!' she cried to those still left in the room. But aside from a handful who had stuck close to her throughout, nobody was paying her any attention. The last stragglers fled the room without a backward glance.

'Good riddance to them, I say,' snapped black-bearded Smitt.

But it was not to be so easy as all that, Elinor knew. She had to go after them. 'Come on,' she said, and started for the door.

The mob was not hard to follow. The racket they made echoed down the stone corridor, and a red trail of bloodied footprints led away from the sprawled forms of the dead door-guards.

Elinor ran after, her little group at her heels, hoping she would be in time to avert any disaster that might erupt.

That *would* erupt.

She saw the stragglers ahead of her now, and ran in earnest, drawing on the sword's strength, leaving those that followed her to fall behind.

She heard sudden wails and wild shrieks. Rounding a corridor bend, she made out sombre-clad armed guards in the distance, saw blood spilled in a long splash across one wall. But even as she watched, the mob swarmed over the guards – there was only a handful of them – and dragged them down, screaming.

By the time she got there, the guards were only still, trampled forms, and the mob had moved on.

Elinor paused. It was madness, this. Almost, she was tempted to abandon them all then and there – let them rush headlong stupidly into disaster if they insisted. Save that they had become her responsibility. And there was Gyver still to be found somewhere in this place. And it was the songster who knew where he was – who was ahead of her, pursued by this mad mob.

Those that followed her came panting up, looking askance at the downed guards.

'Come on,' she said, before they could have a chance to ask any questions, and ran on.

Even with the sword's strength, she could feel herself tiring. Her breath came in laboured pants. The stub of her finger throbbed with pain, her hurt shoulder too. It had been too long since she had last had a proper night's sleep, or food . . . Damn these folk for a pack of idiots! Why could they not behave sensibly?

The corridor was empty ahead of her now, lit dimly by flickering torches. The sound of the mob dropped. She bent her head and ran, making the best pace she could, feet slapping on the stone floor, those behind struggling after.

And then more wild screeching came echoing back along the corridor ahead.

Thinking it was more guards – a larger force of them this time – she re-doubled her efforts, leaping forwards, skidding round the next corner with such speed she carommed against the far wall with bruising force before she could stop herself and carry on. Down the next length of stone corridor she went, round the next corner . . .

And smacked face to face into somebody fleeing the other way. She and the person went down heavily together. She felt a knee drive into her belly, and then the person was up and gone.

Gasping, Elinor got to her knees. The sword had been spilled from her hand, and she felt such a wash of exhaustion that she nearly fainted with it. She heard more frantic footsteps coming at her and made an awkward, falling grab at the sword's dragon-hilt, only just getting it as three people came charging past in a hysterical group.

She stood up, shaking, grateful for the familiar thrill of strength the sword gave. More folk streamed past her. She went forwards round the corner and stood, staring.

There was a short stairwell ahead, leading down to a now-open door. Out of this door spewed a squirming mass of humanimals, furred and feathered, filthy and emaciated and furious, grunting and shouting and wailing.

The scene was one of complete, nightmare chaos, with human folk screaming and pushing at each other and the humanimals struggling and scrapping and scrambling about in wild confusion. She saw a man cut at one of the pale, hairless hyphons with a sword he must have taken from a downed guard. The hyphon screamed, his side opened up by the sharp blade. A humanimal dog went for the man's throat, dragging him down in a frantic scrabble.

It was madness. All utter, bloody *madness* . . .

Over against the far wall, Elinor spotted the songster, white-faced and staring. The little girl was with him. She seemed to be holding a squirming puppy in her arms.

From behind her, Elinor heard more shouting. The small group that had stuck with her came pelting up. 'Guards!' bald Passaly gasped.

Those who had fled the chaos of the loosed humanimals came stumbling back again. Behind them, Elinor saw a solid mass of dark guards filling the corridor.

The shout went up. All eyes turned to the advancing guards. The mob swayed this way and that in desperate confusion, then streamed away. Caught up helplessly in it, Elinor ran with the rest, losing track of her companions, losing track of anything sensible, knowing only the frantic beating of her heart, her paining lungs, the violent thrust and shove of the mob as they scrambled over each other in panicky flight, with her trying to keep the razor-edged white blade up above her head and away from innocent bodies.

Suddenly, they were storming up a wide, spiralling staircase, up and up . . . And there was a high-ceilinged room before them, and a set of doors at the far end through which they burst like a tide, stumbling down a series of flat marble steps . . . and found themselves in a large, high-walled, dirt-floored courtyard, outdoors, the air stingingly chill, with the sky just lightening into dawn overhead.

Elinor stopped weakly against a wall, her sword trailing, gasping. Her heart felt like it was about to burst up through her throat.

The crowd – human and humanimal – swirled about in frantic confusion, for there was, it seemed, no way in or out from this place save that they had come by. For all their desperate running, they had merely trapped themselves within the confines of this outdoor courtyard.

The sombre-clad armed guards were forming up around them now in a dark, weapon-bristly hedge. Somebody was shouting. The mob screamed like so many lost souls.

'Quiet!' a voice cried. '*Quiet! QUIET!*'

The mob began to settle a little.

'*QUIET!*' the voice commanded.

Elinor slipped away behind a press of people against the wall, holding the sword low behind her to hide its betraying brightness, peering out from behind the backs of the crowd.

'*Quiet*, you rabble!' the voice cried. 'I will have *order* here!'

Iryn Jagga.

She saw the man standing on the crest of the steps down which they had come into the courtyard.

'Quiet!' he shouted again. '*QUI-ET!*'

To Elinor's surprise, the crowd was settling, both human folk and not.

'That's better,' Iryn Jagga said, loud enough for all to hear. He shook his head, regarding them. 'Stupid, *stupid* . . . What *do* you think you're doing? I ought to have you all killed out of hand.'

Behind him, Elinor now saw, stood a double-rank of crossbowmen, their weapons cocked and loaded and aimed at the mass in the courtyard.

A nervous shiver went through the crowd like a ripple through unquiet water.

'Elinor Whiteblade!' Iryn Jagga suddenly called.

Elinor froze.

'I know you are here somewhere,' Iryn Jagga went on. 'You sneaked into Sofala somehow. I *know* you did. And look at the chaos you have caused. I have guards – good men and brave – dead this morning on account of your violent madness!'

He stared at the milling crowd, trying to spot her. 'Step forwards, I say. Let me see you. I have a proposition to make.'

But Elinor stayed where she was, safe enough for the moment. Those near her seemed to have eyes only for Iryn Jagga.

'Very well, then,' Iryn Jagga said. He made a motion with his hand. Through the ranks of the crossbowmen, a little procession came.

Elinor gasped.

It was Gyver they brought forth, a pair of guards dragging him by the armpits. His head lolled and his eyes showed white. She could see the broken stub of the crossbow bolt still in his thigh, the fur about it spiky with caked-on, dried blood.

'Come forth, woman!' Iryn Jagga cried. 'If you value the safety of your . . . paramour here, show yourself to me. *Now!*'

Elinor hesitated, desperately trying to think of some ploy or other. She felt sick. Everything had gone terribly, completely wrong. There was no way out for her from this trap she had fallen into. She stood up, feeling her heart lurch, took a step forwards.

From the courtyard wall, suddenly, a ragged shout went up. Elinor swivelled about.

Heads were showing there, popping up all around, a horde of raggedy, filthy folk. They were screaming something she could not make out, vaulting over the wall into the courtyard, sticks and poles in their hands.

It was the wretched street people they had passed in the night – though more, many more than they had seen. What they were doing here, or how they had come to this place, Elinor had no notion.

'Shoot them!' Iryn Jagga screamed. 'Cut them down!'

The crossbowmen let loose a volley, *kar-kara-kwackk!* Ragged folk went down, shrieking in agony. But more replaced them, coming over the wall in a great, shouting flood.

Elinor turned and elbowed her way frantically through the crowd towards Gyver.

Standing at the head of the marble stairs, Iryn Jagga stared unbelievingly at the chaos before him, his face white and furious. He spotted Elinor as she came struggling out of the crowd towards the steps. 'You!' he cried. And then, seeing how close she had got already, he cursed and gave a quick, sharp hand signal to one of the guards holding Gyver.

The man whipped out a long-bladed knife and thrust it between Gyver's ribs, once, twice, three times, then shoved the fur-man bodily down the steps and fled away.

The crowd had surged forwards now, boiling past Elinor up the steps. Iryn Jagga took a last, unbelieving look at the violent confusion filling the courtyard and then fled into the safety of the building at his back.

Elinor paid none of this any mind, having eyes only for the poor, twisted form of Gyver.

She knelt next to him, put a hand out to him tentatively. Blood was spilling from the three puncture wounds in his ribs. She let the sword go and pressed both of her palms against him, ignoring the rush of exhaustion that shook her, trying desperately to stop the flow of his lifeblood. But it was no use. Might as well try to dam a river with one's hands. His warm blood pulsed up past her desperate fingers like a spring out of the ground.

'Gyver!' she said. '*Gyver!* It's me. Speak to me.'

His eyes opened, but they were blind to her. He thrashed about, groaning.

'Hold *still*!' she cried in despair. His moving about so was merely making him bleed more, and making it all the harder for her to keep her hands over the wounds.

But he would not hold still. His face had a terrible, fey wildness to it. It was hardly the face she knew at all. His eyes were wide and blind, his dark lips pulled back in a kind of snarling grin that had nothing human left in it at all. His head went back with a sudden *krump* against the ground and he cried out, an uncertain wail.

Under her hands, she felt a sudden hot gush of new blood. Gyver shuddered and cried out again.

'Hold still,' Elinor panted. 'Just let me . . .'

But it was too late. His body jerked. A stiff spasm went through it. Another. She heard his teeth grinding in his jaw.

'Elinor . . .' he said, softly but quite distinctly. Then he went limp.

His face was before her as she crouched over him, still clutching at the gushing wounds. His eyes stared upwards, looking right through her, dark and glistening and so poignantly human in his furred face. She could see herself reflected in them – or thought she could.

And then, as she watched, helpless, the life went entirely out of him and his eyes changed. One instant they were still alive and shining, still Gyver's eyes, however blind to her. The next instant, the glistening sheen of them was gone and they were clouded over with a dustiness that had nothing of life in it and he lay limp in her hold as an old, clotted rag.

'No,' Elinor moaned. 'No. Gyver, don't go.'

She shook him.

'Gyver?' His head lolled bonelessly. 'Come back, Gyver. Come back to me!'

But he was gone.

She did not think she could bear it. Looking down upon him, her eyes filled with tears; she felt her heart break. He seemed so thin, so frail. None of the sinewy strength she knew him to possess – to have possessed – was evident now. Only his sad mortality lay revealed. One of his legs was tucked under him at an awkward angle, the crossbow bolt sticking up out of it. His arm lay flung out, as if he had been reaching for something. His blind, dusty eyes stared into the empty morning sky.

She felt a hundred things at once, looking at him: remembering how he had used to move inside her; how his lips had curled back in that half-smile he sometimes had; seeing him slip through the forest silent as any ghost; recalling the play of his muscles under his sleek fur pelt; the smell of him; the way his eyes – oh, his glistening dark eyes! – had used to light up at the sight of something interesting.

She felt as if some part of her had been torn away, and that it was she who lay here with her insides leaking out onto the earth.

Never to hear his voice again. Never to feel his strong, gentle touch. Never to run her hands along the soft fur of his chest.

Never.

It was such a terrible word.

Never to have him with her again. All the things she had looked to do. All the places, the experiences, all the never-voiced hopes. Never again.

Gone. Finished. *Dead*.

'Oh, Gyver,' she whispered. She put her arms about his dead body, but it was like hugging so many sticks wrapped in wet sacking. She rolled away, sobbing, and buried her face in the ground of the courtyard.

It was wet with his blood. She felt the taste of it on her lips, earth and iron. She scooped up a little of the blood-clotted dirt, muddy-red, faintly warm. Putting her hand to her mouth impulsively, she nibbled the dirt from her fingers, swallowed, taking him into her. For long moments she lay staring at her muddy-bloody hands.

Then she rose and snatched up the sword, feeling its strength fill her again, feeling a great, burning rage fill her. Where was Iryn Jagga? She was going to cut him into small pieces!

About her, for all that she had been momentarily oblivious to it, there was still a frantic, violent swirl and clash – Settlement folk, humanimals, Sofala guards, the ragged street people. It was like a great storm, whirling blindly.

And then the music started.

Or perhaps it had been sounding all along and she only then, at that instant, became aware of it.

It was a violent, skirling melody. The very world itself seemed gone full of fury. Her limbs throbbed with the angry rhythm of it. The sword resonated, vibrating in her hand, shining like a torch.

A man came at her. Who it was, or why he leaped at her, she did not know. She felt a fury so great fill her that it was agony. She cut the man down, the sword singing, spilling his life's blood in a long arc across the dirt of the courtyard. There was a confusion of bitter fighting all around her. She took somebody else down, sliced a third man through the guts, not knowing who or what he was, spilling his insides out onto the dirt in a wet, squirming cascade.

The violent music beat at her, beat inside her.

It was like some terrible, frantic, mad dance, the white blade thrusting and slashing, those about her leaping at each other, dark guards and ragged street folk and Settlement people, all gone raging mad with it, the vaulting forms of the humanimals, wailing and shrieking and growling . . . and everywhere the violent, penetrating, insistent beat of the music, throbbing in her guts, in the very air, shivering the length of her flashing, blood-laced blade, furious and fast and terrible . . .

XXXXIII

And then, abruptly, the music died.

One instant it was there, in her blood, in everybody's blood, pulsing through them.

And then it was gone.

Leaving them gasping and empty.

The courtyard looked like a mad tableau. People stood transfixed, bent over, gasping, twisted in odd directions, caught in the middle of the sprawling, mindless fighting.

Slowly, they collapsed, white-faced and shaken, emptied of what had been driving them.

Elinor stared about her. She felt as if she were coming out of a fever-dream. Her hands shook weakly, and she nearly fumbled the sword – which was still vibrating in faint echo to the disappeared music. There were dead all about her, in a messy, bloody tangle. She felt sick in her belly, looking at what she had done. She did not even know who they were. The sword *thrummed* softly and wanted to dance in her hold.

She backed away. All about her, folk were stumbling, blinking their vision into focus, mumbling and whimpering. She saw two of the dazed Settlement folk help a dark-clad guard to his feet – too shaken to realize who it was they were aiding. Humanimals wove through everything.

There was a gap opened up through the crowd on her left, and, as Elinor gazed that way, she suddenly saw the songster, sprawled out on the ground near the courtyard wall like one dead. Beside him, in the dirt, lay the Fey-bone flute – shattered by the terrible force of his playing.

Elinor shivered, looking at it. What had possessed him to do as he had? The music that had filled this courtyard had driven them all mad with its violent skirling. She looked round at the bloody chaos all about.

His, the making of all this.

And then she thought: No. Not his. He had been merely a . . . a sort of channel. Long hatreds lived in this city, old pains and anger, so very much anger. She could see a growing mass of the ragged street people gathering on the other side of the courtyard. They were armed with sticks and hammers and blades snatched from dead guards. Now they began to pour up the steps and into the building, a shouting, furious mob.

Things were not over yet.

Elinor let go a long, sighing breath. She felt bone-achingly weary and utterly . . . *empty*. But hoarse shouts and the clash of blades could be heard from within the building now. And Iryn Jagga was in there somewhere.

She headed up the steps.

Inside, the building was a ruinous mess. Furniture had been torn apart, walls slashed. Anything breakable had been shattered. The ground floor was silent, inhabited only by the dead who lay at awkward angles across the floor and up against the walls. She saw one of the dark-clad Brothers, an officer of some sort by the look of him, hanging half off the stairwell balustrade, blood dripping from his torn throat.

There was noise coming up the stairwell. Elinor went downwards, taking the stairs carefully, for they were blood-slippery. In the room below, a group of the raggedy street people clustered over several dead guards, stripping them of possessions.

Seeing Elinor, the looters stopped. One of them made a deep bow of obeisance, lifted shaking hands out to her. 'Oh Demoness of the white blade,' he said in a quavering voice. His face was lit by a strange, mad exaltation. 'We follow where you lead us! We followed you through the night and into this new day of blood and brilliance.'

Elinor stared at him.

'Whiteblade Demoness . . .' said another of them. 'You who walk through our night and turn it into day. We serve you!'

Elinor faltered back, but they flocked after her. 'We are yours, Demoness. *Yours!*'

She turned and fled, leaving them behind.

Were they all gone insane? What were they saying? She

464

was no demoness. They were none of hers, these crazy, ragged folk.

But then she recalled the stealthy footfalls she had heard – or thought she had heard – behind her the night past as she and the songster had crept through the city. She shivered, imagining how it must have been . . . word going from mouth to mouth, a horde of silent, desperate, blighted folk gathering, slinking along behind her, thinking . . . She knew not what they had been thinking. But, somehow, they had incorporated her presence in Sofala into their own pains and hates and fears . . . and hopes.

And so brought events to *this*.

There was no semblance of organization here. These raggedy street folk had no leaders she could see. They darted here and about, shouting and laughing, weeping some of them. When they saw her treading past, they made bowing motions, or tried to kiss her feet, or covered their eyes from the brightness of the white blade in her hand and fled, moaning.

She kicked the grovelling ones away impatiently, embarrassed, and continued on. Despite them, though, she could not help but feel a kind of mad exaltation thrill through her. The building seemed to quiver with it. She began to feel like a very demoness, striding through bloody chaos, her worshippers bowing a way before her.

The white blade shone. She felt its strength, like hot liquid filling up her limbs. Her aches and weariness fell away. *'Demoness! Demoness Whiteblade!'* came the cry wherever she went.

She was an avenging spirit.

Where was Iryn Jagga? A great, cold fury gripped her. The sword shivered eagerly in her hold, and she could almost feel the meaty slicing of the blade as it passed through his flesh. She would not let him escape what he had done this day. He was *hers*.

But when she finally found him, it was too late.

Iryn Jagga lay sprawled near the foot of a set of steps in the building's lower levels. All was quiet down here, deserted and still. A lone torch flickered and smoked in a sconce on the wall. The leader of the Ancient Brotherhood of the Light lay half on his side, one hand caught in the stair's balustrade, staring sightlessly upwards. Somebody had thrust a pike through his back; he was rolled back against the haft of it, which half-way propped him up, the sharp blade-tip poking out through his front ribs. His mouth was open in a frozen cry of outrage. His eyes were gone dusty-dull – like Gyver's.

Elinor put the tip of her blade against his throat, felt the meaty resilience of his flesh. One quick thrust and the razor edge of the blade would open him to the spine. But it was pointless. She felt such a thrust of impotent rage go through her it made her sickly dizzy. He had escaped her after all. She slashed the air in balked fury, the white blade making bright arcs. That he should be killed like this, skewered from behind by some nameless rioter . . .

She could hardly get breath.

The looters had taken everything from him but the golden medallion with the image of Jara upon it. *That* they had left still hanging from his neck by its gilded chain.

Looking at the medallion, Elinor shuddered. Something prompted her to stoop down and lift it away from his stiffening body. It was her left hand she used, the sword being in her right. As she gripped the medallion, she felt a sickening surge go through her body. Her left hand blazed with sudden, white-hot agony. She tried to fling the medallion away, but it seemed stuck fast to her.

And then the medallion disintegrated.

One instant, it was heavy and metal, hard and solid: the next, so much faded dust falling between her fingers.

A faltering sigh seemed to go through the building.

Her left palm flamed, itched intolerably. She looked at it. The image of a face had appeared there, part human and part animal, long and slender of chin, with pointy ears and overlarge eyes. A recognizably female face, despite all its strangeness.

Elinor shuddered. The humanimals' Lady. She had not seen that face like this, clear as clear, since . . .

Her whole body was shivering, as if a freezing wind blew through her. She remembered the last time she had been here in Sofala, how she had been a . . . a channel through which opposing forces met in conflict. She saw in her mind the great black statue of Jara, the wailing priest, the crowd gathered for the brutal cleansing ceremony, red blood flowing on the altar in the square . . . and recalled how the Jara statue had been riven all to pieces in the final moment of conflict.

All of it coming to pass through her, through what this image on her palm represented. Some . . . Power beyond her knowing.

'Leave me alone, can't you!' she cried, sick to her bones at being so *used*.

She had done what had been required of her, walked down the slope of the world . . . And what was the result? She felt bitterness flood through her like acid. Gyver dead. Iryn Jagga slain by some anonymous hand. And who knew what violent calamities had overtaken the Settlement folk or the humanimals? She had saved no one. She had failed in everything.

The image on her palm flared into brilliance, the eyes seeming almost to come alive, looking at her. She glared back at it. This was all so appallingly unfair. What was the point of driving her here if she were to accomplish nothing? If she were to have all that mattered in her life torn away? There were . . . rules, weren't there? One gave service, and, in return, one received reward. She had given of herself, had allowed some Power or Powers to channel through her. And had received only grief.

She felt cruelly betrayed.

'Leave me alone,' she repeated bitterly. 'I want nothing of you!'

The female face scribed on her palm merely gazed at her – or seemed to. It was a quiet face, a wise face, a face in which suffering and knowledge mingled, in which animal and human did.

'You will tear me apart,' Elinor said to it, hoarse-voiced. 'I will not serve you.'

The image-face did not change. Elinor scrunched her hand, flexed it open again. The animal-human features were the same, the eyes still seeming to gaze at her. Her palm tingled.

Then, as she watched, it faded, leaving no trace save the little faint tingling in her flesh.

467

Was it gone from her for good now? Had her denial been heard? Was she freed from the compulsions that had ridden her for so long? She did not know.

There were deep Powers, and that female, animal-human face clearly reflected *something* that moved in some manner through the world . . . but what that *something* might be, and whether there was, in fact, anything truly individual she could appeal to behind the image-face, anything that could hear her . . . she did not know. She did not know how to know.

She stood, shivering, her heart beating hard, trying to get enough breath. The sword dangled in her slack grip. Dead Iryn Jagga lay sprawled before her like an abandoned straw doll. In the near distance, she could hear shouting and raucous laughter as the destruction and looting went on. The city was coming apart all around her.

There was nothing left for her here now. Nothing at all. She turned and stumbled away, heading up and out.

Out in the courtyard, Elinor struggled down the marble steps, dazed and dizzy.

She paused over poor Gyver's bloodied remains. He looked thin and small. His once-sleek fur was gone dusty-dull. His dead eyes stared into the sky, blind to her. She could not look at him for more than a few heartbeats, and turned away, her vision flooded with tears.

The sword felt heavy in her hand. Looking down at it, she remembered how, once, she had been Kess – all her former Elinor-memories knocked from her head; only Kess, without a past, pure, living in the moment, living for the blade . . .

She ached for that memoriless purity now. To be just Kess again, not to have to live with all she had done, and not done, all that had happened.

She took a breath, another. It was all she could do just to stand there. Breathe, breathe . . . She wiped at her eyes. The coolth of the morning air began to clear her bruised mind a little and settle her thumping heart.

Things were quiet here . . . Too quiet, she realized. She glanced about worriedly. Where were the Settlement folk? The humanimals?

It was hard to tell anything. She felt a bitter surge of hopelessness, for there were bodies everywhere. Were they all dead, then? Or fled away? Was she the only survivor left here?

But, as she looked more closely, she realized that many here were simply exhausted, lying listlessly – but alive. She began to search about, and in a corner, saw something that brought her up short.

They were still as still, huddled against the wall. Elinor took them for dead at first. But they were not.

Children, a full score or more, humanimals woven in amongst them, huddled all in a mass – a boy with a blue-winged, human-faced bird in his lap; two others with arms wrapped tight about each other, a small-eared humanimal rabbit pressed to them; a girlchild in torn coveralls, hugging a humanimal dog-puppy against her thin chest. And in their midst . . . little Sky-Flower, who had followed her dreaming here. Elinor shivered, thinking on the strange weave of things that had led to this moment.

The fur-girl was very still, her eyes staring sightlessly. About her, the rest sat completely unmoving – human and humanimal alike – their eyes wide and staring and sightless as Sky-Flower's own. They seemed, the group of them, like a single, complex statue.

'Sky-Flower,' Elinor said softly, walking over. 'Sky-Flower?'
No response.

Elinor put her hand gently on the fur-girl's shoulder. 'Sky-Flower!'

Sky-Flower blinked, shivered. She was bone-skinny thin, her fur matted and filthy. 'Death and horror . . .' she moaned. 'The poor little oness . . .' She looked up at Elinor. 'Oh . . . the poor little oness! I tried to ssave them, me. I tried to call them in. I tried. Oh, I *tried* . . .'

'But you *did* save them, Sky-Flower. Look about you. *Look!*'
Sky-Flower looked. Her eyes went very wide, seeing.

Those about her were beginning to stir now. One of the humanimals started to whimper.

'It's over,' Elinor said. 'It's *over*.'

*

469

But it was not over.

The Settlement folk – what was left of them – were beginning to gather, returning from inside the building, picking themselves up off the ground. There was talk and grumbling and anger.

A woman began to wail. 'Dead!' she cried. 'He's *dead*!'

'You!' somebody shouted. '*You* killed him!'

Elinor turned, dazed.

A man came stomping towards her, tall and skinny, with a beaky nose. 'I saw you do it. *You* cut him down. He went to you for protection. *Protection!*'

The wailing woman had come up now. She shrieked at Elinor: 'Murderer! *Murderer!*'

Elinor only stared at them.

'Look!' the man shouted in her face, pointing to a bloody tangle of dead near the marble steps. Her dead: the ones she had cut down during the madness of the songster's skirling, uncanny music.

'Look!' the man before her cried. 'Do you see him? You opened his belly with that cursed shining blade of yours. I saw you do it! He came to you for help, poor Olundar, and you *murdered* him!'

'My husband!' the woman wailed. 'You murdered my husband!' She flung herself bodily at Elinor, hands out like claws.

The white blade seemed to come up of its own accord, going through the woman's breast – like a hot wire into a slab of hard butter – almost before Elinor knew it had happened.

The woman shrieked.

Elinor tore the blade out, backed frantically away, numbed and shaken and sick. It was horribly familiar, this. Mad Lord Mattingly – he who had originally gifted her with the white-bladed sword – had flung himself upon her just as this poor woman had . . . with the same result.

There was a group facing her now, faces clenched in righteous fury.

'One of her *own* . . .' somebody said bitterly.

A man flung a bit of sharp stone at her. She batted it away with the sword. They moved in on her, muttering and growling. It was the mob coming to life all over again. Elinor backed away, not wanting – desperately not wanting – to spill any more blood here.

She bit her lip, feeling sick in her belly. She did not know what to do. Everything was gone fatally *wrong* . . .

And then a voice called, 'Sstop! *Sstop thiss!*'

XXXXIV

Ziftkin came back to the world uncertainly, feeling dizzy and sick. There was a dark something hovering over him. He squinted, trying to make it out.

It was a massive animal, with a broad muzzle and great ivory fangs. He jerked away.

'I will not harm you, Man,' the animal said. 'Do not be afraid. The time for harm is past.'

Ziftkin found himself with his back pressed against a wall. He half sat, staring at the being before him. It was a large bear, bony-thin, its brown fur spiky and scabbed with filth and dried blood. It regarded him with eyes that were altogether human and knowing.

The bear, it was. The one he had encountered twice already.

'Man . . .' the bear began.

Ziftkin tried to sit up properly, felt about him for the flute.

And saw it, lying in the dirt.

Shattered.

And everything came back to him in a rush . . . the blood and the fighting, the mad, confused swirl of it, him playing, playing, feeling some raging force pouring through him, as if *he* were the instrument rather than the flute in his hands, feeling himself over-filled, feeling himself . . .

What had he *done*?

There were dead everywhere. He stared, stricken. Blood soaked the ground. It was like a butcher's yard. His fault. *His* . . .

'Man,' the bear said, 'you were only a channel. The world has been leading to this.'

'To . . . to bloody *death* and *destruction*?' Ziftkin said, appalled.

472

The bear sighed. 'The world is as the world is. Does the bird question the wind it rides?'

Ziftkin shook his head. 'I am no . . . *bird*.' He stared in sick despair at the bodies strewn about the courtyard. Inside himself, he could still feel the faint after-echo of the terrible, violent music he had been playing. 'Folk are dead here because of *me*!'

'Folk are dead,' the bear agreed. 'Furred and otherwise. It was a great storm. Storms destroy.'

Ziftkin felt deathly sick. 'A storm *I* created.'

The bear looked at him for a long moment, its human eyes sad and knowing. 'The world is a cruel, sorrowful place, at times, Man. What happened here was long in the making. You did not create this. You merely . . . channelled it. The world *needed* this.'

Ziftkin swallowed. 'How can you know such a thing?'

'I *feel* it, Man.'

Ziftkin did not know what to reply. He stared at the bear. Utterly human eyes in a broad, furred face . . . He shivered, face to face with such a creature. 'What . . . *are* you?' he asked impulsively.

The bear blinked. 'What are *you*? You are not like any man I have ever met.'

Ziftkin swallowed. He reached for the splintered flute. It was split open along its entire length – irreparably. He gathered it up; it felt cold to the touch, as if, somehow, something in it had died.

'What am I?' he said, echoing the bear's question. He stared at the flute's sad, broken remains and shuddered. 'I am nothing, now.'

A great surge of bitter despair swept through him. He had done terrible things, been the cause of bloody death and grief and black destruction . . . but with the flute intact there had at least been a chance, a *chance* to set things aright, or, if nothing else, to avenge the wrongs done. Now there was . . . nothing.

He was like a bird whose wings had been hacked from it in a single, brutal blow.

He did not know how to live any more.

'Man . . .' the bear said softly.

Ziftkin turned, collapsing in upon himself, burying his head

473

in his arms. The shattered flute spilled to the ground. He did not care.

'Man,' the bear said, 'the world *needed* what happened here this day.'

Ziftkin said nothing.

'The world needed *you*.'

'Nobody needs me,' Ziftkin snapped. Even in saying it, he knew he sounded like some spoiled and petulant child. But it was a true sentiment for all that. There was no place for him in the world, no need for him. He had had only the one thing, and it was taken from him and destroyed.

'The world has killed me,' he said bleakly.

'The world *needs* you.'

'No!'

'Yes,' the bear returned.

Ziftkin lifted his head and glared at it. 'How can you know such a thing? How can anybody claim to know what the world needs or does not need? Leave me alone.'

But the bear did not. 'I can *feel* the insides of the world, Man. And so too can you, I think, if you try.'

'Me? What are you talking about?'

'Try, Man. *Feel* the world.'

'I cannot,' Ziftkin said with bleak certainty. He might have been able to do such a thing with the flute in his hands, warm and live. He *had* done something of the sort. But without the flute? No . . . Truly, he was a wingless bird, crippled and useless. There was no life left him, now.

'Try, Man. Try!'

'It's pointless. I am nothing.'

It seemed to Ziftkin at that moment that he had always been nothing. All his life, he had belonged nowhere, had been neither one thing nor another, lame, useless, pitiful. His foster brothers had been right to plague him: he was like the crippled little chicks, those born wrong, that the farm hens pecked to death.

Only with the flute in his hand had he ever been anything like whole.

'Man . . .' the bear said softly.

'Leave me be,' Ziftkin replied. 'There is nothing for me. I belong nowhere. Leave me be!'

The bear let out a long, snuffling breath. 'I know the feeling of . . . unbelonging, Man.'

Ziftkin looked up sharply.

'We are alike, you and I.'

Ziftkin shook his head. 'No.'

'Yes,' the bear insisted. 'We live in the painful *between*.'

'I don't . . .' Ziftkin swallowed, uncertain.

'There have been times I could not endure it,' the bear said softly.

Ziftkin stared at him. 'Why are you doing this? Why can't you just leave me alone?'

The bear said, 'I know you, Man. The world has been riven by a great storm, and at such times one's senses grow keen. I can scent the *betweenness* in you clear as clear. You are not like the dark Brothers, nor like others of your kind. You are a . . . a mixed breed. As am I. You have a man's tight-woven mind, but there is more to you. You are not blind to the world's hidden ways as most of human kind are.'

Ziftkin shivered. He thought of how he had experienced the hidden flows of the world through the medium of the flute. He remembered how, all through his younger years, he had been mesmerized by the world, which seemed to call to him with a soft, mysterious voice. And he recalled the way he had perceived the humanimals: mixed creatures in uneasy balance . . . and the immediate, instinctive sympathy he had felt for them despite all Iryn Jagga's dire warnings and connivings.

All this filled him, with recollection, wonderment, uncertainty . . .

'Open yourself, Man,' the bear was urging. 'The world is like a great river. You can *feel* the moving current that runs deep through it.'

Ziftkin shivered. He remembered the deep-hidden movement of the world he had *felt* while playing the flute . . . like a great, flowing, complex melody. He felt his heart jump. For a moment, under the compelling intensity of the bear's gaze, he thought he might indeed be able to do it . . .

But no. He could not. He knew he could not. The bear was wrong. He was naught but a crippled misfit, unbelonging and clumsy-dangerous, like any crippled thing. He felt the bitterness of it like a hard cord pulled through his guts. He had brought only death and destruction and despair into the world. He . . .

'*Man!*' the bear said into his face.

Ziftkin blinked, shivered.

'That way lies only death.'

Ziftkin said nothing.

The bear regarded him sadly. 'It is *not* necessary, Man.'

'How would you know?' Ziftkin snapped. 'What can *you* know of my life?'

The bear shrugged. 'I know my own, Man. I see the darkness of mine in the darkness of yours.'

Ziftkin opened his mouth, closed it.

'Try to feel the world, Man,' the bear persisted. The startlingly human eyes in that broad, brown-furred face were compelling. '*Feel* the world!'

Something in Ziftkin there was that rose to the bear's patient insistence – in spite of all.

Haltingly, he tried again to . . . open himself, remembering the experience of the flute, trying to *feel* beneath or above or beyond his senses . . . he did not know which.

He kept his eyes open wide, staring at nothing, at everything, his vision prickling, trying to look *through* the world. Was the bear right? Did one grow . . . *keen* at moments like this, when the fabric of the world had been riven by some great eruption? He stared and stared until a sick dizziness began to come over him and he was gasping for breath. The world seem to dance and shiver. He hung on, trying doggedly to fall away through his senses, staring, staring . . .

His belly surged, as if he had flipped suddenly over, or the world had, and for a timeless moment . . .

He felt the world like a great, multifold river beneath the surface solidity of things, many currents interwoven through the long years, merging and separating like lines of melody in a long, complex music.

And it came to him that here, in this land, the currents had been somehow twisted, dammed, bottled up. But such currents could not be constrained. They . . . *flowed*. It was their nature. And in their flowing they balanced each other in a dynamic of complex movement.

Here, such dynamic movement had been balked, the

tension building over long years, tighter and tighter, until . . . it had burst completely asunder.

Sofala was finished. Sofala had torn itself apart in a great spasm of blind, deep-fed violence. The world . . . *flowed* again after this.

Elinor, he realized, had been a part of it all, had been a part for some time. And he, too . . . *he* had been a channel through which this storm could break.

And then the clarity of it all snapped. He felt his belly heave again. The world danced in his vision. He took a long, shuddering breath, coming back, and looked dazedly about him. It was the same world he had left, the same charnel courtyard – and yet not. He wanted to grab hold of something for support. He felt like a man who had looked to see solid ground under his feet and had found, instead, only a shifting morass.

Such complex *depths* . . .

A shiver of unexpected joy went through him.

Perhaps it was his experiences with the flute that had led to this. Perhaps it had always been in him, dormant – his father's heritage. Perhaps it was – Ziftkin shivered – a part of the very flowing of the world. But he felt himself changed irrevocably. The world would never again appear the same for him.

He had been a channel, an instrument upon which some great Power or Powers had played.

He had been . . . He was . . . He did not know what he was any more.

He stared at the bear in mute astonishment.

The bear nodded.

Somehow, it was enough.

Ziftkin looked around again, taking in the high sky, the shimmer of the courtyard wall.

A little ways off from him, he saw a huddled group, children and humanimals pressed against the wall, perhaps a score or more, so close each to each it was hard to distinguish them one from the other. They were silent, shivering, hugging each other for comfort, staring with wide eyes at something in the courtyard. In their midst, he now saw, there sat a small fur-person. The same that had been one of Iryn Jagga's captives.

They seemed like so many rabbits, frozen before some

threatening predator. Ziftkin could sense something emanating from this little group, from the fur-person: a sense of . . . protection. He was astonished to see a faint radiance in a kind of screen about them. He blinked, rubbed his eyes.

'Something new is born in the world,' the bear said, regarding the little humanimal-human group. 'The storm was not only destruction, Man.'

Ziftkin blinked, looked at the bear, at the little mixed group huddled together against the wall . . . He had the strangest feeling that there was a . . . momentum to them. They sat there perfectly still, and yet were somehow moving onwards.

They were all still staring at something.

Ziftkin shook himself, trying to assimilate all the newness that was upon him, turned to the bear . . .

And, quite suddenly, became aware of what else was happening in the courtyard.

It was as if he and the bear had been cocooned away in some sort of insulating shell, so caught up in their own interaction as to be entirely oblivious of all else. Now, the air seemed suddenly to fill with shouting and anger, and Ziftkin became aware of what it was that so held the attention of the little group of frozen children and humanimals.

Elinor, blood-laced, shining blade in hand, backing away from an angry mob of her own folk.

Ziftkin stared, astonished.

'One of her *own* . . .' he heard somebody say bitterly. Somebody else was wailing like a lost soul.

A woman lay sprawled, quivering on the ground, bleeding her life away into the dirt. A mob of folk was pressing Elinor back menacingly.

And then a voice called, 'Sstop! *Sstop thiss!*'

It was the fur-person – a girl she was, or seemed to be. She had stepped out of the little humanimal-human group.

'Stay out of this, *animal*!' one of the mob shouted at her.

But she stumbled onwards, none too steady on her feet, till she had come to stand by Elinor's side. She was just a little thing, but there was something about her that made folk stop.

'The sstorm, it iss passt!' she cried. 'The great world flowss on. You musst flow with it, too, you. Or . . .'

To Ziftkin, having had the experience he just had, what she

478

said made perfect sense: the crowded folk here were still themselves part of the bursting madness, feeding it, keeping it alive past its time.

But none of what the little fur-girl said touched any of the mob. They jeered at her, telling her to shut up and get out of the way. They pressed closer to Elinor.

And then another voice called out to them. 'Stop! *Stop!*'

A child's voice, this, a human girl in baggy coveralls who came out, a humanimal dog-puppy trailing her, and stood next to the fur-girl. 'You're always shouting and fighting,' the little human girl said accusingly to the angry crowd. 'Why can't you just be *nice*? Why can't you just *like* each other? What's *wrong* with you all?'

She stood before them, small and defenceless, angry and hurt and vulnerable, her face bruised. The humanimal pup came scampering over and she took it up in her arms, holding it under the armpits the awkward way children sometimes do.

'Why can't you,' the small humanimal said to the mob in a child's high voice, 'just be *nice*?'

The mob shivered. A man came forwards, fists clenched. But he slumped, faced with something he could not combat. Faces fell. Folk folded, sitting down heavily in the dirt.

'She killed my friend with that cursed white blade of hers,' one man insisted grimly.

'Leave it go,' Ziftkin called out, surprising himself, the words came out so quick.

Eyes turned towards him.

Self-consciously, he walked over.

'Who are *you*?' somebody demanded.

'He was with that Iryn Jagga,' another answered. 'Up on the stage.'

'Listen to me,' Ziftkin began quickly, before they could begin to generate more anger. 'It's over. The time for fighting is . . .'

'It's *far* from over,' a voice interrupted. 'My Dennie's *dead*!'

'It's *over*!' Ziftkin insisted. He took a breath. He felt his insides shaking. 'It's over, here, in this place.'

'Folk are *dead* here!' somebody cried bitterly.

'Too many!' another added.

Ziftkin nodded. 'Too many indeed. But it's over, now. This is a . . . bad place, this Sofala. It has an old, evil history to it. Look around you. Listen! It is tearing itself apart in blind, bloody violence.'

Sure enough, they could all hear the shouts and cries of the looting mob of street people – from inside the building at their backs, from over beyond the courtyard wall, from all around.

'Get away from here!' Ziftkin cried. 'Before it infects you with its madness further.'

He had not intended to say any such thing, but now that the words were out of his mouth, he knew them for truth. Sofala was like a great, stagnant lake that had been bottled up behind a dam. Now the dam had been torn asunder and the lake was emptying itself in a great rush of filth and decay and violence.

'Get out of this place!' he repeated. 'Or it will be your destruction . . . And Iryn Jagga's final revenge upon you all.'

Folk looked at each other uncertainly.

'Now!' Ziftkin urged. 'Or it will be too late.'

'But what about *her*?' somebody demanded.

They all turned to where Elinor had been.

But Elinor was gone.

An angry cry went up. People began to surge forwards.

'Stop!' Ziftkin shouted. 'Don't do this! Leave her be. Get away from here!'

'He's right,' a woman cried. 'He's right! Let's away from here, fast as we can, out into the open where there's air to breathe!'

A general murmur went through the crowd.

They began to move, slowly at first, confusedly, then faster, catching up children and each other, the humanimals with them, all streaming away.

But Ziftkin stood where he was, too shaken by all that had happened to be able to move. It was all he could do, for the moment, just to breathe.

'Come, Man,' the bear said at his side.

Ziftkin turned, startled. He had heard no sound of its approach.

The bear gestured with its large head. 'As you say, Man, it is over. The world moves on.'

Ziftkin blinked, looked around. The courtyard was empty now, save for the sad dead. He took a shaky breath, put a hand

480

to the bear's shoulder for support, lacing his fingers into the thick fur.

They looked into each other's eyes, the bear and he, quietly. Ziftkin shivered. The sight of those knowing, human eyes in the furred animal face left him feeling . . . he did not know quite what.

But whatever the being before him might be, it was not, he now knew, the demented creature Iryn Jagga had insisted. He remembered the inexplicable sense of *kinship* he had felt with this bear when they had first locked gazes, him on the Sofala wall, flute in hand, piping the humanimals in. He felt it again now – a strange, unexplainable sense of connection. 'We are much alike,' the bear had said to him.

In his guts, somehow, he knew it was so.

'Come,' the bear urged softly, 'let us leave this place.'

Ziftkin nodded.

Together, they turned and walked slowly away.

XXXXV

Scrunch the bear sat dog-like, staring at the distant, tumbled shapes of the wild hills.

'We should never have let her go,' bald Passaly said.

'What, then?' black-bearded Smitt demanded of him. 'Tear apart the whole of what we have left of a community? Drag her back here and rub her face in her grief day after day? And how should we find her, anyway?'

'This isn't the way it's supposed to be,' Passaly insisted.

'The world is what it is, Man,' Scrunch said.

'So you keep saying,' Passaly replied tartly.

Ziftkin, standing by Scrunch's side, gazed at the wild lands. They stood, he and the bear and the two men, atop a grassy knoll, Sofala at their backs, the grey-green tapestry of the wild lands stretching ahead, rolling grassy country lifting into tumbled hills, beyond which loomed far-away blue peaks. Out there, somewhere, was Elinor. Gone from them. Headed the Powers alone knew where.

'We never even had a chance to thank her, to say . . . *anything*!' Passaly complained.

'Good thing she left like she did,' Smitt said. 'Half the folk here wanted to lynch her.'

Passaly clenched his fists. 'Ingrates! After all she's done for us.'

'It was for the best.' Smitt said.

Scrunch let out a long, snuffly, sighing breath. 'Something has been born into the world. And many things have died.'

The men grunted sober agreement.

'But the world flows on,' Scrunch finished.

'And Elinor?' Passaly demanded.

'Elinor is what she is,' Scrunch answered.

Passaly snorted.

'The world *flows*, Man,' Scrunch insisted. 'And living folk flow with it, Elinor as much as we. The currents of the world move us.'

Passaly shook his head and looked to Ziftkin, as if hoping to enlist his aid in disputing Scrunch's pronouncements.

But Ziftkin was with Scrunch on this. It was all still new to him, but he *felt* the flow of the world, the slow, deep current of it, in his own life, in events past, in this place where human and humanimal were gathered. They were all leaves upon a river. The world moved, and folk moved with it.

Turning, he gazed at the little crowd gathered at the base of the slope upon which he and the others stood. Preparations were nearly completed, he saw; supplies of food were packed, and packs cinched tight for the journey that lay ahead.

After much dispute, after shouting and anger and tears, after long days of talk, what had been one folk was now two: those who chose to return to what was left of their farms in the Valley – freed of the Brothers' cruel yoke, for all that had once been Sofala was utterly broken – and those who chose the high wild, the humanimals, the new life offered; a life unlike any that had been before in this land, humanimal and human intermixed so closely together.

Down amongst those preparing to leave, Ziftkin saw the little girl who had talked down the mob in the courtyard, Anstil her name was, and Grub, her small humanimal companion. Anstil waved to him, and he waved back.

'Come,' black-bearded Smitt said. 'It's time to leave.'

For a last, lingering moment they hesitated, staring at the empty wild in which, somewhere, Elinor travelled. 'May she fare well,' Passaly said softly.

The others murmured agreement. Then, slowly, the four of them turned and walked back down the slope.

There was cursing and laughter as folk made their last-moment preparations, both grim faces and bright. The air seemed to shimmer with anticipation. Ziftkin felt a little shiver go through him. He was one of this group, though how that had come about he was still not entirely sure: the thought of it still filled him with astonishment. He put a hand to Scrunch's furred shoulder as he walked, feeling the warmth under the thick fur.

'It's time! It's *time*!' little Anstil shrilled as they came near. She was pale-faced and pinched still, with little blue smudges under her child's big eyes. But those eyes flashed. 'Oh, Scrunch, my tummy's all full of butterflies.'

From behind her, the humanimal dog-youngster that was her constant companion came bouncing up. Behind him came an older humanimal dog, long-legged, limping. There were half-healed scabs all along her front legs and across her ribs, and her ribs showed all too clearly through her brown, fawn-mottled fur.

'Rigga,' Scrunch greeted her. 'You are well?'

The humanimal dog nodded. Though she looked weary and worn, her eyes were bright and green as wet moss. 'I am well enough to keep up with this lot at any rate.' She indicated the busy gathering about them with one stubby-thumbed fore-hand. 'They will not be travelling overfast.'

Human folk were buckling up big packs, slinging them on their shoulders, sorting themselves out. Humanimals flitted about everywhere.

Ziftkin felt his own belly all fluttery, seeing these final preparations nearly done.

'Come along,' he heard Rigga say to Grub and Anstil. 'The others are waiting.' A little distance ahead, he could see a group of children and humanimal dog-youngsters clustered together.

'And mind you don't wander off too far and get lost, either, hear?' Rigga added.

'I can *feel* the way,' Anstil announced. She lifted one of her bare feet to show Ziftkin. 'With these. Can you?'

Ziftkin nodded, smiling at her. 'A little. Scrunch is teaching me.'

There was a shout. Folk were ready. Anstil ran ahead excitedly, Grub at her heels, Rigga limping after.

A little ways off, a silent band of folk watched the departure – those that were returning to work their farms in the Valley. Goodbyes had all been said, or nearly so, more than a few of them teary-eyed.

'You'd better come back to see us again, young Tally!' somebody called from the silent group of onlookers.

'Promise,' came the reply, but it was breathless and

distracted, for the young man who had voiced it was struggling to swing a heavy pack over his shoulders. At his side sat a large humanimal cat, tail curled neatly around its hindquarters, a long walking stick held in its stubby, human-like forehands. As the young man finished balancing the pack, the humanimal handed the stick to him. With a quick wave toward the silent group of watchers, he started off, swinging the stick, the humanimal cat trotting at his side.

Smitt and Passaly had gone off to get their own packs. Scrunch had none. Ziftkin had no more than a shoulder bag.

He turned and took a last look at Sofala. Even now, long days after the violence, black smoke still hung over the place, and carrion birds flocked about. It looked decrepit and filthy. He was glad to put it behind him.

Folk were beginning to move off now. Ziftkin saw Smitt and Passaly up amongst the leaders, along with the little fur-girl, Sky-Flower, whose knowledge of the wild they were all relying on to make this trip easier than it otherwise might be.

Such a strange mixture of folk, this, Ziftkin thought. His life had turned out so strange. Who would have thought it? Only a few short months back, he had seen Seshevrell Farm as all the world. And now . . .

Now he felt like another person altogether.

'It begins,' Scrunch said. 'The current takes us.'

Ziftkin nodded. He felt like a man walking upon a river, the water surging under his feet. Human folk and humanimal were moving together all around them. He felt his heart beating fast.

Scrunch stood still for a moment, his nose up, snuffling the air. He gazed at the wild hills that lay all ahead of them, snorted, then said, softly, solemnly, 'May you fare well, Elinor Whiteblade,' echoing Passaly's benediction. 'May the world take you to some good thing.'

Ziftkin nodded. He, too, gazed at the wild hills in the distance. The world's current had swept him here, to this land, and left him stranded upon this strange shore. But for all its strangeness, it was a good shore, one he was glad to be upon.

And Elinor? The world's current had swept her onwards and away.

He wished her well with all his heart.

'Come, Man,' Scrunch said.

Slowly, along with all the rest, they started onwards.

XXXXVI

On a high slope, Elinor sat propped against the mossy surface of a rock hill-face. She could see the smoking ruins of Sofala below her in the distance, like a great ugly smudge pot tossed into the rolling green plain. On a grassy slope some ways before it, she made out little figures moving.

There seemed to be two groups: one heading slowly back past Sofala to follow the roadway to the settled farm-country; the other marching her way, across the rolling turfland, towards the wild.

So they had decided.

She did not know for certain, but what else could it mean? Humanimals and human folk together. Must be. Though the distance was far, she was sure she could make out the two intermingled in the group coming towards her.

They would march through the hills into the Settlement and re-inhabit it. Only, this time, there would be no threat of the Brothers looming on the horizon.

A new beginning.

She was tempted, *so* tempted.

In her mind's eye, she saw how it would be: she could trail them easily enough, overtake them and stand waiting as they filtered through the trees, call out to them. She felt her heart flutter at the thought of it. The excitement, the familiar faces lighting in smiles . . .

But there would be too many missing faces, too many memories, too much hard feeling.

And, temptation or not, there was something in her that would not let her go.

She looked down at the sword that lay crosswise on her lap. Wretched, wonderful thing that it was. She had felt such grief these past days that, some moments, she had not thought she could bear it. Half a hundred times she had been on the verge of pitching the sword from her.

But it was still with her.

Carrying it had brought her grief and confusion and terror. It was a kind of bane. But it was all she had now. It was all she *was*. It had broken her and made her, left her empty and yet filled her. A terrible, wonderful thing, to be possessed of such a blade . . .

She wished well those who were returning to the Settlement. She ached to join them. But it was too late. She and the blade would only foment difficulties amongst them. They did not need her any more, those folk.

Like it or not, her time here was over. She had done what had needed to be done, had brought about what had needed bringing about. There was a wind, now, blowing her away.

With a sigh, she stood up and slung the sword from her belt. It was hard not to feel a little bitter, not to envy the songster who, she was sure, had been taken up. She had lurked nearby in the courtyard for a little, on that last day when Sofala fell, and had seen the way Scrunch and he walked away, shoulder to companionable shoulder, when it was all over.

There was nobody to walk with her.

'Oh, Gyver . . .' she murmured once, softly, and refused to cry.

'I go,' she said then, to the sky, the hills, the wide world. 'But I will not serve you any longer.'

There was no response. She had expected none. It was an empty boast in any case – like a floating ant boasting it would not serve the river.

Slowly, one hand on the sword's hilt at her belt for the balance of it, she turned and walked away into the wild lands, towards whatever might await her, alone.

THE END